THE VAULTS

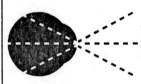

This Large Print Book carries the
Seal of Approval of N.A.V.H.

THE VAULTS

TOBY BALL

THORNDIKE PRESS
A part of Gale, Cengage Learning

GALE
CENGAGE Learning·

Detroit • New York • San Francisco • New Haven, Conn • Waterville, Maine • London

GALE
CENGAGE Learning·

LIBRARY OF CONGRESS CATALOGING-IN-PUBLICATION DATA

Ball, Toby.
   The vaults / by Toby Ball.
     p. cm. — (Thorndike Press large print reviewers' choice)
   ISBN-13: 978-1-4104-3624-5 (hardcover)
   ISBN-10: 1-4104-3624-1 (hardcover)
   1. Political corruption—Fiction. 2. Municipal archives—Fiction. 3. Archivists—Fiction. 4. Journalists—Fiction.
   I. Title.
   PS3602.A598V38 2011
   813'.6—dc22   2010052853

Published in 2011 by arrangement with St. Martin's Press, LLC.

Printed in Mexico
2 3 4 5 6 7 15 14 13 12 11

For Deborah, Jacob, and Sadie

ACKNOWLEDGMENTS

I owe a debt of gratitude to many people for their help and support.

Faith Ball and Susan Moger both read many drafts and their suggestions and critiques helped shape this book from the beginning. Jonathan Ball, Susanna Kahn, and Jacqueline Ball Smith also read early versions and provided feedback and support.

My life as a writer changed dramatically when I began working with my agent, Rob McQuilkin. He has taught me a tremendous amount and he, along with his colleague Rachel Vogel, provided crucial guidance in making this book much stronger and getting it into the right hands. I look forward to a long partnership.

I am lucky to be working with my editor, Michael Homler, and the people at St. Martin's Press. Michael guided this process with a steady hand and good humor, and was always available to explain, encourage, and offer insight.

There are more people than I could possibly name here who have helped me with their support, interest, and friendship, but I do want to single out a few people: Susanna, Pete, Jackson and Julia Kahn; Dorothy and Richard Saunders; Doris and Bob Ball; Terrence and Martin Sweeney; Paul Nyhan; Pete and Connie Walden; Chris Hodgson; my manager, Jacob Ball; the women at the Newmarket Public Library; and the people at Clean Air-Cool Planet, the Family Research Laboratory and the Crimes against Children Research Center who do the really important work. Also, thank you to the Newmarket/Durham mob: Vaso, Christopher, A-Train, Doug, Emma, T-Bone, Denise, Val, Tim, Blake, Britta, John, Lisa, Ian, Stephanie, Heidi, Cliff, Ben, Alex, Tim, Elly, Ollie, Tillie, Charlie, Morgan, Ted, Lauren, Dudley, Tom, Phyllis, Ray, Hunter, and Littlefoot.

Thank you to my parents, Faith and Jonathan Ball, for their lifelong love and support.

And finally, thank you to my wife, Deborah Walden, who has been by my side through it all, and to Jacob and Sadie, who give me joy every day. I love you very much.

CHAPTER ONE

The Vaults took up nearly half a city block. Files arranged in shelves arranged in rows; files from every case handled in the City for nearly the past century; files arranged, cross-referenced, and indexed. So complicated and arcane was the system that at any given time only one living person understood it. At this time, that person was Arthur Puskis, Archivist. He was the fourth Archivist, inheriting the position from Gilad Abramowitz, who had gone mad in his final years and died soon after taking his leave of the Vaults. Abramowitz had mentored Puskis for the better part of ten years, explaining, as best as his addled mind allowed, the logic behind the system. Even so, it had taken Puskis most of the following decade to truly understand. He was now in his twenty-seventh year in the Vaults.

As happened every day, several times a day, O'Shea, the messenger from Headquarters, had brought a list of files to be pulled. Several items on the list were preceded by an asterisk, which meant that Puskis was to pull all cross-referenced files as well. Puskis had a file cart that he wheeled down the long aisles, searching for the appropriate shelves. The cart had a loose wheel that squeaked rhythmically with each rotation.

Puskis completed his rounds and returned to his desk with the requested files. He opened the files that had been asterisked and took down the numbers of the cross-referenced files. He then took the file cart and went to retrieve those files. Each aisle was illuminated at thirty-foot intervals by a bare electric lightbulb. Every journey consisted of walking from an illuminated area into a more twilit space and then back into illumination. None of the bulbs ever seemed to burn out, and Puskis was vaguely aware that the City sent someone around to check them periodically. Their collective hum was like some primal sound, one that could have emanated from the earth itself.

He was at the shelf for the C4583R series, in a dimly lit stretch, when he found the two files. He was searching for C4583R series, subseries A132, file 18. It was in the correct location, just after C4583R series, subseries A132, file 17. He put the file in

10

the file cart and, out of habit, checked the next file to make sure that it was C4583R series, subseries A132, file 19. Abramowitz had suggested the method; an episodic way to check on filing accuracy in place of doing periodic audits as Abramowitz's predecessors had done. The files were too voluminous now to make that feasible.

Initially, when he saw the adjacent file, C4583R series, subseries A132, file 18, he assumed he had made a mistake and retrieved the wrong file to begin with. He checked the file cart and found that he had in fact taken the correct file. This meant that there were actually two C4583R series, subseries A132, file 18s. Puskis removed the spectacles from the end of his long, thin nose, rolled his head around to loosen his neck, replaced the spectacles, and looked at the files again. Nothing had changed. The two files bore the same label.

He opened the one that had been left on the shelf. It was the file for a Reif De-Graffenreid, FACT identification number such and such, with this particular address and so on. He opened the one in the file cart. Again, the name was Reif DeGraffenreid, same FACT number, address, etc. Duplicate files? Puskis could not imagine himself capable of such sloppiness. A puzzle.

Puskis put the second file in the file cart and returned to his desk to address this vexing problem.

Puskis took the two folders and, with his skeletal fingers, laid them on opposite sides of his barren desk. He removed the contents one by one, first from the file folder on his left and then from the one on his right. Puskis had, from years of experience, acquired an especially keen sense of paper of various ages. He would have told an inquisitive soul — if he ever actually interacted with one — that it was an instinct. The truth was that it was an acute understanding of the paper stocks of different decades and the effect that aging had on them, making them dry, crisp, and discolored — but each stock in a minutely unique way.

He noticed that the papers from the two files were not of identical age. The paper from the file to his right was not eight years old — too moist, it bent limply from his fingers, without the rigidity that crept into older paper. Taking a greater interest now, Puskis estimated the paper on the right to be three or four years old. He held the more recent paper up to the light to confirm this estimate. The Department's paper supplier for years had been Ribisi & Porfiro. They had imprinted their paper with a distinctive sea-horse watermark. Five years ago, however, they had been acquired by Capitol Industries, and to cut costs the corporation had done away with the watermark. The more recent sample, then, bearing no watermark, must have been created in the last five years. Puskis checked the paper from the older file, and as he suspected, it carried the watermark. Somebody had typed the more recent pages at least two or three years after the original file had been created. It was curious.

Also curious were the pages: same cover sheet, same personal information, same testimony — DeGraffenreid had been on trial for the murder of someone named Ellis Prosnicki — same verdict: guilty. The sentence had been "Life-PN," which was not the approved abbreviation for "penitentiary" — just another vexing detail of the unthinkable duplication that Puskis had discovered. Yet here, too, was an interesting difference. In the margin of page 8 of the testimony was a handwritten notation. It read "Do not contact — Dersch." An arrow pointed to the name Feral Basu, who was mentioned by DeGraffenreid as the man who had introduced him to Prosnicki. In the file to the right, it was written in green ink. In the

13

file to the left, the ink was blue.

He looked closer. The writing was nearly identical, but not quite. Where the *n*'s tailed off in the blue ink, they ended suddenly in the green. The angles at which the arrows were drawn, too, were slightly different. It was, he decided, as if someone had deliberately copied the notation from one file to the other as exactly as he could. Or not quite as exactly. He studied the two notations, trying to discern the forger's intention, before eventually conceding that, from the scant available evidence, this was unknowable.

Finally, he came to the photographs. The photo from the left-hand side (the older file) was a head-and-shoulders shot of a man with sunken eyes, a blunt, crooked nose, and receding hair. His mouth was slightly open, providing a glimpse of crooked and broken teeth. It might have been cropped from a mug shot. The photo from the file on the right was of a completely different person. This man had long, thin features, hollow cheeks that he had tried to conceal with extensive sideburns, and sparse hair parted in the middle. Most striking to Puskis was the man's stare, as though unaware of the camera, which could not have been more than ten feet away. It was,

Puskis thought, haunting.

This was a troubling development. Puskis picked up his phone and, for the first time in over a decade, dialed out.

Puskis felt more uncomfortable than usual in the Chief's office. He rarely deviated from his three destinations: his apartment, seven blocks from the Vaults; the grocer's around the corner; and, of course, the Vaults themselves. Anywhere else and he realized how eccentric — even grotesque — his nearly three decades in the Vaults had left him. He was alarmingly thin and stooped, the latter a consequence of years leaning to read files in the too dim light. His face was pale, and he sweated more than he liked when he was in the open air. He wore thick, wire-framed glasses, as the reading had left him nearsighted. Inside the Vaults he did not need to see beyond four or five feet.

The Chief was looking at Puskis with mild bewilderment. During his first years as Archivist, Puskis had occasionally come with some kind of request — a different kind of paper, a newfangled sprinkler system, a lockable door between the elevator and the Vaults, a bathroom — that the Chief could not possibly fund. In time, the consistent fruitlessness of these requests put an end to Puskis's visits. Now, after a decade, he was back. This was something quite different.

"Two identical files?" The Chief's jowls quivered when he spoke.

"Yes, sir. Two files in the C4583R series. An individual by the name of Reif De-Graffenreid."

"And the problem?" The Chief was polishing a badge of some sort with his tie.

"Well, sir, you see, there were two different photographs. The files were for the same person, but the photographs were of two different people."

"I'm not sure that I understand the problem, Mr. Puskis."

"It's just that, sir, well, it's just that there can't really be two Reif DeGraffenreids in the city with the same FACT number and address and everything else. It's just, well, not possible." At some level, Puskis himself did not necessarily believe this statement. But such was his faith in the unerring accuracy of the files in the Vaults that there seemed no other explanation.

The Chief sighed. "Mr. Puskis, it seems quite evident to me that somebody made an error in filing one of those photographs."

"But why the two files, sir? In my twenty-seven years in the Vaults I have never seen a duplicate file, and now, when I do, there are different photographs in each."

The Chief shook his head. "I don't know what to tell you, Mr. Puskis."

"That's exactly my point, sir," Puskis said somewhat desperately. "That is just the point I'm trying to get across to you. I don't know what to make of it either. I am bringing it to your attention so that an inquiry can be initiated."

"Into who misfiled the photograph?"

"No. Please, do not take this lightly. There are two Reif DeGraffenreids in this city, sir. They are different, but they are the same person."

"I'm not sure I understand what you mean."

"Neither do I, sir. That is the point that I am continuing to try to get across to you. I don't know what I mean either. It makes no sense, yet there it is. Sir."

"Maybe it's the files that are wrong," the Chief suggested in a softer voice.

"No. I'm afraid not. The files would not be wrong." Puskis did not mention the different-colored inks or the age difference in the papers. The former was a detail whose significance would escape the Chief. He would not understand the system by which the transcribers who assembled and notated the files worked. He would not understand the dramatic importance of the same comment appearing twice, but in different ink. What Puskis found most alarming was that he, Puskis, understood this detail to be of vital importance, but could not glean its meaning.

The Chief opened a file on his desk and leafed through its pages. Puskis watched the Chief's inexpert handling of the papers, his fat fingers occasionally pulling two sheets instead of the desired one.

"Mr. Puskis, when did you last take a vacation?"

The question caught Puskis off guard and he stammered before answering, "I'm not absolutely certain, sir. Not for a long while, but I fail to see —"

"Mr. Puskis," the Chief interrupted, his fleshy lips in a benign and sympathetic smile, "it was 1917. Eighteen years, almost to the day."

Puskis conceded this point in silence.

"I am ordering you to take this next week off. Go back to the Vaults, pick up your things, and don't come back until a week from Monday."

"But, sir."

"No, Mr. Puskis. The Vaults will be fine for a week. Take some time. Relax. The

Vaults can get to you. Eighteen years. My God."

Puskis, as he always did on his rare trips to Headquarters, received a ride back to the Vaults in a police cruiser. Outside the rear window a dismal rain lent a sheen to the road and sidewalks. People hurried, heads down under umbrellas.

"Nasty weather we've been having," said the officer driving. Puskis had not bothered to listen when the man first introduced himself and did not listen now.

"Doesn't matter down in the Vaults, I guess," the officer offered. Again, Puskis did not reply. The officer, who had heard all the rumors, sighed and pursued it no further.

In the back, Puskis fingered the hat that rested in his lap. He had not bothered to wipe the raindrops from his spectacles. He thought about being away from the Vaults for an entire week. Eighteen years, the Chief had said, since his last day off. That seemed about right, though he could clearly remember that last aberration in the regular rhythm of his life. He had begun doing crossword puzzles, quickly realizing that he could identify ten key words, then fill in the rest of the puzzle without using the clues. It was just a matter of knowing the letter

19

combinations. When this ceased to interest him, he had begun simply filling his own words into the puzzles, seeing if he could fill every square without revising. He had mastered this as well, then started putting letters at random spots in the crossword and filling in words. That had been Monday and Tuesday. Wednesday he had reported back to the Vaults and had reported every day since, including weekends.

The squad car pulled to the curb in front of City Hall. The Vaults were in the hall's subbasement. Puskis put on his hat and got out of the car without a word to the driver. He walked up the broad granite steps, the rain soaking his coat and pants. Inside he touched the brim of his hat to acknowledge the four guards posted at the front doors and walked to the bank of elevators. One of the elevator operators, a squirrel of a man named Dawlish, called out to Puskis, who passed through the opened gate and into the velvet-lined elevator.

"To the Vaults, then, sir?" Dawlish asked, as always.

"Mmm," Puskis said. As the elevator descended, he removed and wiped his spectacles.

"Here we are, then," Dawlish said, opening first the elevator door and then the brass gate.

"Yes. Yes, indeed." Puskis stepped out of the elevator, then hesitated.

"Anything I can do for you, Mr. Puskis?" Dawlish's English accent could still be picked up in certain words, such as *anything.*

"Mmm. Actually, yes. Yes, there is something you could do for me. I'm, well, I'm going to be away for a week or so."

Dawlish's eyebrows rose. "Never known you to miss a day, sir."

"Indeed. Indeed, that is quite true. But the fact is, well, the fact is that I am not going to be here for a week, and I was hoping . . ." Puskis hesitated.

"You were hoping, Mr. Puskis?"

"Yes, I was hoping that maybe you could keep track of if anyone goes down to the Vaults while I'm gone. I mean except for the courier from Headquarters, of course. And, I suppose, the usual cleaners."

"I would be pleased to do that for you, Mr. Puskis. I will keep a list, sir. Though, as you know, sir, there's no one goes down there except you and that courier you just mentioned. And, of course, the cleaners."

"Are you sure? Are you absolutely certain no one else ever goes down?"

Dawlish, sensing Puskis's urgency, narrowed his eyes in thought. "Mr. Puskis," he finally said, "I can not think of a one."

Chapter Two

Ethan Poole stood at the window of the Fox and Thistle Pub, nursing a scotch on the rocks. He watched the building across the street. The mark generally left at noon for his midday meal. Poole had been there nearly an hour. The mark must be taking a late lunch. A hood whom Poole didn't know came up to him.

"You Ethan Poole?"

Poole nodded and took a sip of his drink, mostly ice now.

"Jimmy McIntyre, pleased to meet you." The guy put out his hand. He was little, but Poole could tell that he was tough. Scar tissue above his eyebrows and a bent nose. He was a gangster. Poole shook the offered hand, engulfing it with his own.

"I want to thank you. You made me a mint when you were at State."

It was this again. His notoriety in some circles. Throwing games on the gridiron and making the mobsters some scratch. All for walking-around money. Every reminder of it was like an abscessed tooth.

McIntyre was still talking in that weird, high-pitched voice some tough guys had. "You had moxie, chum. All those other fellas, they did what they were asked to do, but you had goddamn moxie."

Poole smiled out of politeness. He hadn't enjoyed throwing games. He'd even resisted the idea at first. But with half a dozen others already on the take, why shouldn't the star running back cash in on a lost cause? It made sense at the time.

McIntyre droned on about games that Poole had tried to forget. Finally, Poole saw the mark emerge through the glass double doors. He was talking to another man, who, at that distance and through the rain-streaked window, was nearly his double — tall, fat, slightly hunched with age. They both wore dark suits. The mark made a gesture with his hands, then put on his hat and trotted over to a waiting cab. The other man put on his own hat, opened an umbrella, and walked down the block. Poole blurted a thanks to McIntyre, handing him his nearly empty glass, then ran to his car, parked at the curb.

Poole had the Ford running as the cab

pulled away. Traffic was sparse. He followed the cab across town, through block after block of brick row houses in Capitol Heights, then the claustrophobic streets of Chinatown — where he momentarily lost them behind an electric trolley, and finally down to the Hollows. As always, the Hollows made Poole uneasy. Blocks of warehouses were occasionally interrupted by a bleak brick-and-cement apartment building, inevitably with broken windows and bars on doors. Most eerily, and Poole found this to be true even when the weather was more agreeable, no life was to be seen. No one on the sidewalks. No grass lawns. No trees planted in boxes on the sidewalk. Just asphalt, brick, and cement.

Few cars were on the streets, which made tailing the cab more difficult. Poole hung a few blocks back and kept his fingers crossed that the hack would not lose him with a quick succession of turns. He didn't. Eventually, the cab stopped at a nondescript, eight-story apartment building. The mark got out of the cab and paid his fare, not waiting for change. The cab drove off. The mark walked briskly toward the building, shoulders hunched against the drizzle. Poole parked his car a block away, waited until the mark had disappeared inside, then jogged — the collar of his trench coat pulled high around his neck, his hat pulled low — to the building's entrance.

The glass in the front door was a web of cracks from where someone must have smashed it with a brick or a rock. Food scraps, old newspapers, and broken glass were strewn across the lobby's threadbare brown rug. Cockroaches scuttled along the walls. The two elevators wore OUT OF ORDER signs pasted on their doors. The paint was old and cracked. Poole located the door marked STAIRS and headed up.

A rhythmic thumping came from above. Poole took the stairs by twos. On the landing for the third floor he found a kid, maybe early teens, sitting with his back to a wall, tossing a rubber ball at the opposite wall and catching it on the rebound.

"Fat gink come up these stairs?"

The kid gave Poole an assessing look and nodded. Poole was big — six foot five inches, a few pounds over 220 — but the kid did not seem intimidated.

"Know where he went?"

The kid shrugged and returned to his game with the ball. Poole reached into his inside jacket pocket and took a dollar bill from his wallet. He folded it lengthwise and tossed it into the kid's lap.

"Miss Baker's." Poole got a look at the kid's mouthful of rotten teeth.

"Number?"

The kid hesitated.

"You're not getting any more money." Poole moved slightly closer to him, casting his shadow on the kid's body.

"Six oh two."

Poole nodded and continued up the stairs.

"Hey," the kid called after him, "what you got in that bag?"

Poole put his bag down outside apartment 602. He fished out a bandana, which he tied around his nose and mouth. He pulled out the camera and attached a large flash. Then he extracted a flat strip of tin half the width of a dollar bill that he slid around in the crack of the door until he found the lock. He jiggled the tin with a practiced hand and the door opened. Silently he bent down and brought his bag across the threshold, then took the camera and closed the door behind him.

He stood in the hallway, listening to the muffled voices until the talking ceased. He listened now to groans and sighs and heavy breathing. Then came the squeaking of the bedsprings, and he moved quickly and quietly through the apartment to the bedroom. He stepped through the open doorway and had taken the first shot before they knew he was there. The woman — Miss Baker, presumably — made a funny kind of braying noise and felt around for sheets that were inconveniently wadded up at the foot of the bed, while the mark, absurdly, covered his genitals with his hands and stared at Poole. Poole efficiently wound the film and took another shot. He wound again and got another shot before the woman finally found the sheets and crawled beneath them. He took a last shot of the mark.

"You'll hear from me," he said in his deepest voice, then left the room, picking up his bag midstride, and exited the apartment.

"He doesn't have much to hide, that one," Carla Hallestrom said, looking at the prints that Poole had just brought from the darkroom.

"It disappeared pretty quick."

Carla was wearing one of Poole's undershirts, and it hung to her knees. She was a slender woman, with walnut skin, courtesy of her Greek mother, and blue eyes from her Swedish father. Striking rather than beautiful, she wore her raven hair shorter than was the fashion. This allowed her to wear wigs when she wished to avoid notice.

"His life is beginning to get complicated," she said, looking at the man's face, frozen in panic. The man, Roderigo Bernal, owned a company called Capitol Industries and was, if not the richest man in the City, then one of them.

"And you're about to make it worse," Poole said, watching her as she framed the woman's face with her fingers.

"Do you know who she is?"

Poole shook his head. "Her last name is Baker. That's about it. Does it matter?"

"No. I just hope that he doesn't think she was involved. That she helped set him up."

Poole shrugged. "I'll mention that to him when we talk."

"Which is when?"

"When's the strike?"

"Tomorrow. You know that."

"Tomorrow night, then."

Carla smiled.

CHAPTER THREE

Puskis had never been to the Hollows. He had never, until now, even considered going. He watched without much interest as the lifeless neighborhood drifted past the back window of his taxi.

The cabbie brought the taxi to a stop at a block of row houses. No lights were on. No one sat on a stoop, though it was the first day that it hadn't rained in nearly a week.

Puskis handed the driver a five-dollar bill. "Could you wait a couple of minutes?"

His eyes on the bill, the cabbie nodded, and Puskis unfolded out of the backseat. He approached the steps leading up to number 4731 E. Van Buren Street. Hearing a noise behind him, he turned to see the taxi pull away from the curb and head down the street. This brought disappointment rather than irritation, and Puskis labored up the twelve steps with his shoulders stooped. To the right of the door were three buttons, labeled 1, 2, and 3. The address in the files had no apartment number, and Puskis wondered if the house might not have been turned into apartments since the file's creation. He pushed the button labeled 1, on the theory that if DeGraffenreid had split the house into apartments, he would probably have made his own apartment number one. Puskis heard the bell ring faintly from inside. He waited a minute, then pushed the button a second time, again without response. He progressed to number two. This time Puskis heard a window open above him. He looked up to see a woman with an enormous head looking down at him.

"My name is Puskis," he called up to her. "I'm looking for Reif DeGraffenreid."

"You're looking for Mr. DeGraffenreid?" Her voice was somehow both deep and shrill.

"That's correct. Reif DeGraffenreid."

"Well, you're about seven years too late."

"What's that?"

"You're too *late*," she repeated, louder. "He left about seven years ago. Haven't seen him since."

"I was wondering if, perhaps, I could speak to you for a minute."

There was silence for a moment and

Puskis's neck was beginning to get sore from looking up.

"What did you say your name was again?"

"Puskis. Arthur Puskis. Listen. I won't take more than ten minutes of your time."

"Okay. You look harmless enough." Her head disappeared from the window, and Puskis watched the front door expectantly, waiting for the woman to open it. Instead, he heard her voice from above him.

"Catch." She dropped a key from the window. Puskis was not able to react in time, and it fell to the stoop by his feet. He bent and picked it up.

"It's for the front door," she called down unnecessarily. Puskis tried the key, found it was upside-down, then managed to get it to work. He climbed the stairs, his footsteps muted by a drab, worn carpet. The door at the second-floor landing was ajar. Puskis stepped up to the threshold.

"Madam?"

"In here."

He walked through a filthy kitchen that smelled of rotting vegetables, then a dimly lit hall and into the dusk of a sitting room. The curtains were pulled shut, and only a golden light emanated from lamps whose bulbs were covered by heavy amber shades. Puskis found it distressingly hot.

"So you're looking for Mr. DeGraffen-reid." The woman was easily the most obese human being Puskis had ever encountered, the particulars of her body obscured by a huge, formless garment that was nonetheless pushed to its limits by her startling girth. Her head was big and round with hair pulled back away from her face. She did not so much sit as lean backward in her chair.

"Yes. Yes, I am. I was hoping that maybe you might be able to give me some information that would aid me in, well, locating his current whereabouts."

The woman looked at him as though he were an amusing insect. "His current whereabouts," she mused.

"Mmmh, yes." The air was stagnant. Puskis could see dust motes floating in the amber light.

"I can't tell you too much about that I'm afraid. Like I said, haven't seen hide nor hair of him for — what? — seven years."

"Oh. Oh, that's unfortunate. Hmmm, yes." This was torture for Puskis, and his desperation to leave this immense woman's apartment was preventing him from thinking clearly. "Well, maybe you could, in another tack, you could tell me what Mr. DeGraffenreid did for a business."

The woman gave a quick sputtering sound

that sent a wave of flesh down her chin and below the folds of her dress. "Mr. Puskis, in the Hollows you don't ask people about their business, and if you find out by accident, you sure as hell don't go talking about it to strangers."

Puskis coughed once, then found himself consumed by a coughing fit. The woman watched inscrutably as he fought to recover. "How about acquaintances?" he said finally. "People who came by?"

She frowned and turned her head slightly away from him. He understood.

"Well, I thank you for your time, madam. I truly do." He turned to go, flustered but also relieved to be leaving the apartment. The heat was beginning to make him lightheaded. He noticed for the first time — or had it just now formed? — a sheen of perspiration across the woman's forehead and wondered if her apparent placidity masked an effort made to control great pain. This thought changed her greatly in his mind; not eliciting sympathy, exactly, but a mild relief, at least, of his unease. He remembered the last thing he needed to ask.

"I was wondering, could you take a look at two photographs I have with me?"

She didn't answer, but inclined her chin, which Puskis took as an assent. He produced photos from the two DeGraffenreid files. First he showed her the one from the earlier file.

"That's Mr. DeGraffenreid," she said immediately.

"Are you sure?"

She gave him a stare, so he moved on to the next photo — the one with the unnatural look.

"Never seen him before."

"Could it be someone who visited De-Graffenreid?" Puskis tried. "An associate or an acquaintance?"

"Could be, but like I said, never seen him."

Puskis had to walk eight blocks before a cab passed by. The effort was exhausting. He sat in the backseat of the cab with his eyes closed, concentrating. A critical mass of information was needed to perceive order. He had not yet acquired that critical mass. But now, at least, he had a face to place with the name Reif DeGraffenreid. Who was the man in the other photograph who so unsettled Puskis? The name Dersch, referred to in the margin notes in the two files, was almost certainly a detective who had retired several years previously. A margin note strongly suggested that Dersch had not actually been involved in the case, but simply offered that piece of information to one of the transcribers, who had dutifully recorded it. But who was Feral Basu? And why was his name worthy of comment when his role in the affair was peripheral at best?

Puskis knew that attempting to force order on random pieces of information would be fruitless. The pattern would come to him only when the necessary information had been gathered. Until then he was left with questions.

Two blocks from his apartment building in the wealthy Capitol district, Puskis's cab encountered a police roadblock.

"Christ," the cabbie said through locked teeth. He took a left to circumvent the cordoned-off area and attempted to circle around to Puskis's block. A right turn, however, brought them to another police cordon.

"You can drop me here," Puskis said.

Behind the police line was a crowd, five people deep, straining to see what was happening a couple of blocks down. Puskis excused and pardoned his way to the front, where two imposing officers manned the barricade, night-sticks out and postures aggressive.

"Excuse me," he said to them, "my name

is Arthur Puskis. I'm trying to get to my apartment building, which is around the corner at the end of this block."

"Yeah, well, nobody's get—" the officer on the left began, his round, red face a mask of ill-humor.

"Shut up," the other said. "What's your name again?" he asked Puskis.

"Ahh, Arthur Puskis."

"Jesus Christ, Danny, this is Mr. *Puskis*." Then to Puskis: "Sir, you say you live on Sinclair?"

Puskis nodded. Sinclair ran perpendicular to the avenue that they'd cordoned off.

"We'd be happy to let you through."

"Of course," Puskis said. "What's happening here?"

"Bomb, sir. Somebody threw a bomb through a window two blocks down. Blew the front off the building."

"Oh dear. Do you know whose place it was?"

"Yes, sir. Individual by the name of Ian Block."

Block. The name was familiar. An industrialist, one of the mayor's inner circle. "Was anyone hurt?"

"Trying to ascertain that at this very moment, sir. Haven't heard yet. Keep you apprised, though, if you like, sir."

"No. No, that won't be necessary." The two officers moved the barricade to let Puskis through. As he approached his street, he could see a brownstone a block farther down, with a hole like a shotgun wound hemorrhaging blue and black smoke that, to Puskis's eye, seemed also to contain wisps of red. He stopped at the corner, noticing the ash that had fallen to the sidewalk and the papers that fanned out from the damaged building into the street.

Puskis watched the firemen saturate the smoldering building with thousands of gallons of water while policemen stood around watching or acting menacingly toward members of the public whom they deemed too curious.

He walked down his street, leaving the chaos of the bomb scene behind. *Ian Block.* Puskis reflected on the consequences of someone bombing Block's house. The mayor would doubtless take this as a personal affront. The force was going to be under intense pressure from both the mayor's office and the press. If Puskis clung to one precept that informed his sense of how the world worked, it was that the past was a sentient guide to the present and future if one knew how to evaluate it. That was the crucial importance of the Vaults and the files contained within. The consequences of the bombing did not require the close examination that Puskis prided himself on. Before this affair ended, blood would be spilled.

Chapter Four

Frank Frings strode quickly through the crowded newsroom of the *Gazette,* trailed by an assistant named Ed something.

"There was a bomb in the Capitol district," Ed said, struggling to keep up.

"Shit, you're kidding." Frings did not break stride.

"No, a bomb exploded in the district. Details are coming in, but Panos wants you out there pronto."

"What was bombed? A store, a house, what?"

"Well, we haven't got anything confirmed . . ."

"Of course not, but what the hell *do* you know?" Frings spoke quickly, without pauses between words, his sentences pouring forth as single, extended words with a disconcerting number of syllables.

"Reports are that it was Ian Block."

"Ian Block?" Frings stopped and fixed on

Ed, who took an extra step before stopping to face him. "Holy shit. Do you have any idea what that would mean?" Frings was of average height and lanky; still, he could intimidate with the intensity of his gray eyes, the aggressive jut of his jaw.

"Well," Ed stammered, "I think I —"

"Jesus H., Ed. I don't believe this." Frings was back moving again, as if he had springs in his joints, weaving through desks on his way to the editor's office. Ed was still trying to say something, two strides behind, but Frings made no attempt to isolate his voice from the general din of the newsroom.

Frings pushed through Panos's office door to find the fat, slovenly Panos smoking a cigar and humming a painfully off-key aria.

"What the hell's going on?" Frings asked, closing the door before Ed made it to the threshold. Adrenaline was flowing.

"Didn't that twerp tell you?" Panos growled. He stuck his cigar back into his mouth, under an unruly, overgrown mustache.

"He told me. But, Ian Block's place? How certain are we?"

"How certain are we ever until we see for our own eyes?"

Frings was used to the warmed-over philosophizing. "Okay. I'll get down there right away and call it in once I figure it out. You going to hold the presses until you hear from me?"

Panos grunted. The sweat stains blossoming from his underarms would soon overwhelm the dry areas of his shirt. "Don't screw around Frankie."

Frings winked at Panos. "Stay by that phone."

The mayor had a small circle of wealthy businessmen friends. In his columns, Frings called them the Oligarchy. If the membership of this group was somewhat fluid, the core people at least — Ian Block, Tino Altabelli, and Roderigo Bernal — were a constant. They bankrolled Red Henry's mayoral campaigns and received what to Frings's eye was a scandalous return on their investment.

So strong was the association of Block, Altabelli, and Bernal with Henry that an affront to one of them could only be seen as an affront to the mayor himself. That was what made labor action against any of their companies a dicey proposition. Effectively, the Oligarchs had the use of the City's police force if and when they felt they needed it. More important, they could use the Anti-Subversion Unit, which entailed a whole other layer of coordination and firepower. Certainly, the mayor would be using the ASU to track down whoever planted the bomb.

Order was beginning to emerge from the chaos at the bombsite. Rivers of water, gray from the ash, flowed through gutters on either side of the street. Smoke billowed from the hole that had been blown out of the brownstone. Most of the building façade was gone, too, so there was no street number. Frings figured the number from the two adjacent houses, however, and compared it to the address he had for Ian Block. It checked out.

He found an officer named Losman, whom he had met on a couple of previous assignments and did not seem particularly busy at the moment.

"Frank Frings with the *Gazette*," Frings said, offering the cop a Lucky. "Anybody inside when it went off?"

"No one that we know of. We located Mr. Block at his club, and he said that there might have been a cleaning woman today, but that he didn't think so. He didn't have his calendar with him. But we haven't found a body."

"What was Mr. Block's reaction to the news?"

Losman gave Frings a funny look. "*I* wasn't there. Why? How'd you take it if someone tossed a bomb through your window?"

"What type of bomb?"

"Sticks of dynamite, wrapped with rope. Found fibers on some of the wrapping down the street. Probably used a long fuse, lit it, tossed the bundle through the first-floor window, and had about a minute to get out of there."

Frings nodded, taking it in. "Any idea who?"

"Usual suspects, I guess. Don't print this, of course. Anarchists. Communists. Always the 'ists' though, right?"

"No one specific, though."

"Not yet. You can print that. But we'll find them soon enough. No doubt there."

You'd better, Frings thought, or there's going to be hell to pay with the Mayor. Which, from any remove, was hardly a pleasant thought.

Frings walked back outside the perimeter and talked to a few bystanders, trying to find an eyewitness or anyone with something interesting to say. Failing in this, he thought of Panos growing more annoyed and began searching for a phone booth.

Frings dictated the story to one of the secretaries back at the paper and thought about trying to get a quote from the Chief or maybe even the mayor himself. But then Frings began to feel its onset: daggers of pain behind his eyes, the feeling of a cold spatula slowly separating his brain from his skull. Soon his vision would begin to go on him, and maybe his balance, too. He scanned the street for a cab, but they were avoiding the area because of the barricade. So he trotted downtown, each stride intensifying the pain in his skull by a small increment. Finally he got to the trolley line at Grand Avenue. He had to sprint to catch one as it pulled away, timing his jump so that his momentum took him through the rear door and into the car. He collapsed into a seat and shut his eyes to the light of the world that was causing him this agony.

CHAPTER FIVE

Red Henry sat at the head of a heavy oak table. To his left sat a cohort of city officials, the people supposedly necessary for this kind of affair. To the mayor's right was the congregation of Polish businessmen who wanted to open a factory in the Hollows, because this was not a great time to be in Poland, with Germany and Russia restless. At the far end of the table was a translator.

Henry was torn between bemusement and annoyance at the pace of the proceedings. He wanted the Poles in the City with their factory, and they obviously wanted to be here. So shake hands and get on with it, the details would work out. His counsel, though, insisted that the details be worked out first, and some established businesses in the City did not necessarily cotton to these Poles adding yet more options for the labor force. As if Red Henry were going to do any more than let these folks vent. The mayor wanted the Poles here, and rarely did he not get what he wanted.

The Poles, it had finally been decided, would bring their own workers with them on the boat from Poland. Henry glanced down at his huge, misshapen hands that were resting, palms down, on the table. The knuckles were swollen and out of alignment, the result of his driving his fists repeatedly into people's skulls during a long and successful boxing career. He was just over six and a half feet tall and weighed nearly 350 pounds. Even during his fighting days, when he weighed eighty pounds less, he had dwarfed his opponents in the ring.

The stories that were told might be exaggerated in detail, but they were true in the essentials: how he had been told to throw a fight at the Garden by some made men and had knocked Monty Kreski unconscious with savage blows in under a minute before then crawling through the ropes and thrashing the two thugs where they sat in the second row of the stands. How he had once knocked out both Kid Cuevas and the referee with one ferocious left hook.

By now, the flaming mane that had earned him his nickname was gone, his cranium bald and slightly coned at the back. His face showed all the evidence of his craft: flattened nose, ears so deformed they looked like giant pink raisins, scar tissue around the eyes. But Henry's mental acuity was uncompromised. And he could still punch. They say that's always the last thing to go — the force of a punch. Well into his fifties he could still use his massive physical presence to intimidate when he needed to. Now he just sat and stared at his hands, listening without actually hearing as first one side of the table said something, then the translator repeated it in either Polish or English, then the other side responded.

A movement in the far corner of the room distracted him and he saw Peja, his secretary, a squat young man with slicked-back hair and slightly crossed eyes, slip into the room. An intrusion like this was unusual and did not auger well. Peja strode over, avoiding eye contact with anyone but his boss. The conversation stopped.

"Keep going," Red Henry said, and the conversation resumed awkwardly. Peja was at his side now and whispered in his ear for several seconds, before straightening. Red Henry stared straight ahead, impassive to all eyes. He had learned that skill in his years of boxing, completely relaxing in his corner no matter the amount of adrenaline pumping through his veins or the terrific stress of a close bout (of which there had been few). He kept his body still and his face slack even as his mind dissected the information he had just heard, probing it for cause and impact and consequence.

A bomb at Ian Block's. While the Poles were here. He could think of a number of reasons why this should be seen as a calculated personal insult to him. Somebody was going to realize that he had just made the biggest mistake that he would ever live to make. Red Henry would make sure of that.

Putting this issue aside for now, Henry refocused on the conversation around the table. After a while the translator said to the Americans, "They are asking if there is some civic need or effort that they could contribute towards." Red Henry had been waiting for this.

"I have to leave for another meeting," he said, rising from the chair to his full height. "Dan," he said to his counsel, "I believe you know how to handle things from here?" Then to the rest of the Americans he said, "Thank you for your time, you may go." Finally, he addressed the Poles. "We look forward to a lasting and prosperous relationship with our friends from Poland. Please excuse my early exit, but I have a prior commitment to attend to. My counsel will speak for me as the negotiations go forward. Thank you."

He smiled with empty warmth at the Polish congregation as the translator spoke his words in Polish. The Poles nodded and smiled back to him, then stood as he shook hands with each of them in succession, their hands like so many children's in the grip of his gigantic paw.

He left the room to find Peja waiting for him in the hallway. "Get the Chief for me. My office in an hour. And call Feral. I'll meet him tonight by the bridge. Ten thirty."

CHAPTER SIX

"Who is this?"

"You know who it is."

"What do you want?"

"We need to meet."

"Okay."

"You know that phone booth across the street from your office?"

"Yes."

"Be there in three minutes. I'll call you."

Poole left the phone booth and strode two blocks to a different one. He was not worried about being watched. Yet. The danger would come later. Just now he was worried about people listening in on the other end of the line, specifically the cops. Or tracing the call, which he'd heard that the police could now do with the help of an operator.

The streets were alive with people rushing about on this weekday morning. The sky was obscured by low, gray clouds and the City seemed to reflect its narrow range of hues. People walked with their shoulders hunched and heads down against a cold wind that swept through the canyon of buildings like a glacial river. Leaves and litter danced crazily in the street and around the legs of seemingly oblivious pedestrians.

He arrived at the second phone booth and entered, pulling his gray fedora down to hide his face, then dialed the number for the phone booth outside Bernal's building.

"Yes?" Bernal was breathing hard. Poole guessed that he had taken the stairs down.

"Listen carefully because I am not going to stay on the line long. We need to meet face-to-face. Do you know Greer Park?"

"Yes."

"The pond in Greer Park. On the west side there's a gazebo."

"I know it."

"Tomorrow night at eleven p.m. You will bring five thousand dollars in small bills. We'll talk for five, maybe ten minutes. Then I'll blindfold you and leave you with a timer set for five minutes. When the timer goes off, you will take off your blindfold and go home. I have people who will be watching the area, so if you're not alone, they'll know and the pictures will be sent to every newspaper in the City and to your wife. If you leave before the timer goes off, the same thing will happen. Do you understand everything that I have told you?"

"Yes."

Poole hung up.

Carla was not home when he returned to the apartment. She was at Bernal's factory helping organize the strike that had begun that day. As always when she was out on these endeavors, he worried about the City's leading capitalists' capacity for violence and, perhaps more to the point, that of the mayor and the police. It gnawed at him.

Carla had found him at the end of their time at State, a time when everyone was either vilifying Poole or indebted to him for actions that he himself found repugnant. Carla was oblivious to all of this, however. She didn't follow football. She was a Red, spending her free time selling ads to keep the City's underground Communist paper in production or trying to organize workers who did not even share a common language.

Poole liked her because she had a clear vision of right and wrong. She could assess a situation and make the kind of confident judgments that he found he could not. And there was something else. A moral fierceness. A commitment to making things change married to a sense of how they should be. It was a daunting example.

Why had she chosen him in the first place? he sometimes wondered. Some women liked to have the initiative, maybe. Certainly, Carla drove their relationship. That was the way she wanted it and that was the way he wanted it, too. Then there was the physical attraction . . .

Poole walked through their living room, sidestepping the books and newspapers stacked around the worn leather couch and chair that sat facing each other across a coffee table made from an old door. The kitchen was small but had an alcove at the end with a wooden table and two chairs. The window looked out on an alley that, over the past few years, had become the nocturnal domain of a clique of young prostitutes. Poole felt as though he had watched these girls grow up.

Today's paper lay open on the table with an article circled in red pencil. He sat down. The headline read "Bomb Blasts Block's Building." Next to the headline was a picture of the building, with a ragged hole with smoke billowing out from it. The press had not set the ink accurately, and the picture was a double image.

The article itself was short, nothing much to report. The reporter, Francis Frings, wrote that the investigation would be a priority for the police department. Poole knew what that meant and knew, too, that the danger to Carla had just dramatically increased. Whenever the City's capitalists were victimized, the suspects were always the same; at the top of the list were the Socialist union organizers.

He considered calling Frings, whom he knew to be sympathetic to the City's Socialists, but was interrupted by a knock at the door.

CHAPTER SEVEN

Frings woke at nine, his head cleaved into two hemispheres of pain. Squinting his eyes, he took mincing steps to his bureau and opened a small drawer on the top left side, where a small tin held several hand-rolled marijuana cigarettes. He took one, along with a butane lighter, and moved to the window, which he cracked open an inch. He sat with his back against the wall under the window and lit the reefer. He filled his lungs, held the pungent smoke, then exhaled through the side of his mouth, directing the majority of the smoke out the window. It took him five minutes to smoke the entire cigarette in this fashion, and by the time he was done the headache had receded to a level of mild annoyance.

From his seat on the floor he watched Nora Aspen as she slept. Nothing was more demystifying, he thought, as watching this normally glamorous creature with her mouth ajar, her face pale and swollen with sleep. The crimson silk sheets that she favored lay draped over her famous curves, and the idea that hundreds, if not thousands, of men would envy his situation right that second seemed somehow absurd. He, Frank Frings, the paramour of this jazz-singer pinup. It seemed so odd that he almost laughed. Almost.

He stood up and wandered into Nora's expansive kitchen, where he found a loaf of bread and some Brie. He ate quickly, as though she might wake at any moment and take it from him. His tongue explored the contrast between the firm, creamy cheese and the coarser, crumbly bread, and he eventually becoming consumed with fascination.

He was brought back to the present by the sound of movement from the bedroom, and a moment later Nora appeared in a silk robe over what there was of a nightgown. Her shoulder-length blond hair was muddled, and she looked alluring without arousing in Frings a need to do anything about it.

"Migraine still bothering you?"

"It was."

"I wish you wouldn't smoke in the bedroom. I don't know how many times —"

"I know, I'm sorry." He smiled in spite of himself, knowing that it was just going to piss her off. "You know that when I wake up like that I just need relief as quickly as possible."

She glared at his grinning face and returned to her bedroom. "Make some goddamn coffee."

Nora was in the shower when the phone rang. Frings didn't answer her phone normally, but somehow found himself with the receiver in his hand without consciously deciding to pick it up.

"Frings?"

"Yeah?"

"It's Merrick at the paper."

"Oh. What's the rumble?"

"Well, we just got a call from a guy. Wouldn't identify himself. Says he needs to talk to you and no one else will do. Says he's at this number for the next ten minutes. I ran it by Panos, but wasn't sure if it was worth rousting you. Anyway, he said to go ahead, so I tried to reach you at your place and then Ed said to try you here. So, I guess you've got maybe two or three minutes to ring him." Merrick read the number.

"Francis Frings?" It was more of a rasp than

a proper speaking voice — an effective mask.

"That's right."

"Listen, I need to meet with you. Soon. I know things you might find very interesting."

"Who am I talking to?"

"No. Not now. Listen. I have information about corruption in the mayor's office. I have information about murders and disappearances."

"Any evidence to back up all this information?"

"When you hear what I have to say, you'll be able to find your own evidence. The day after tomorrow. You know the Harrison Bridge? Under the City side. Eleven at night. I'll watch you arrive and then show myself. We can talk there."

"I'll see you then." Frings sighed. He'd heard this kind of thing many times before. It never panned out, but neither could he simply ignore it. Should even one of these shadowy tips turn out to have legs . . .

Frings hung up as Nora came into the living room wearing a white terry-cloth robe with her hair up in a towel wrapped like a turban. Drops of water still clung to the skin around her collarbone. Her lips were swollen from the hot shower.

"Who called?"

"Nobody. It was for me."

Nora swirled the coffee in her cup and tapped her toast around the plate with her middle fingers. She wasn't eating, and it bothered Frings.

"Not hungry?"

She gave him a long look.

"What's wrong?"

She shook her head. Light from the kitchen window illuminated half of her face, and Frings saw the concern there and thought it made her look only more . . . desirable. Something about the angle of her mouth, maybe, pursed slightly with anxiety.

"Come on. Spill." He wondered if she was still angry with him for smoking the reefer.

"I don't know. It's nothing."

Frings waited her out, watching the coffee do circuits inside her cup.

"It's . . . It's a feeling I have. Nothing in particular. You know I'm working with Dick Riordan's band right now, and he's such a creep. The way he looks at me, and I can *hear* the things he says to the boys."

Frings nodded sympathetically. Riordan considered himself a rake, he knew, but was harmless. That wasn't what Nora wanted to hear from him, however, so he kept his mouth shut.

"And I've been getting more hate mail. Marty won't let me see them, but he told me all about it. I get a lot of mail, Frank. Most of it is really nice, but some of it is so vile . . ."

There wasn't much to say to that, but he tried. "Look, there are unpleasant people in the world. They see someone like you and they want to take you down a peg. Only they don't have the guts to do anything, so they send you a letter blaming you for all their problems."

He knew she needed more from him, though she gave him a sad smile for his effort.

After too long a pause he tried again. "I —"

She cut him off. "It's okay, Frank. It's nothing. I'm tired is all. I just have tonight and then I'm off for a few days, so I can get some rest. My voice needs a break. Things always seem worse when I'm tired."

Nora returned to staring into her coffee. Frings wondered who the man on the phone was.

CHAPTER EIGHT

Puskis had not used his home phone in years. It had been even longer than that since he had actually received a call. Which made it all the more unusual that he would receive three phone calls in a single morning.

Puskis lived in an efficiency above a bakery seven blocks from the Vaults. His furnishings were sparse, a single bed in the corner, a small dinner table with one chair, and the easy chair that he now sat in. The floor was bare, but the walls were hung with rugs that his mother had brought from the old country, their colors muted by age. Puskis appreciated the fine logic and order of the symmetrical patterns. He often stared at them from his bed at night, the half-light washing away the color so that only the designs remained.

Puskis was reading the newspaper when the first call came.

"Yes?" he inquired tentatively.

"Mr. Puskis?"

"Yes?"

"Mr. Puskis, this is Lieutenant Draffin. I hate to have to tell you this, sir, but the Chief needs you back in the Vaults. Everyone's being pulled in."

"I expect this is about the bombing."

"I expect it is, sir. Anyway, the Chief says not to come in today. Take this one more day off, sir, but be at the Vaults tomorrow morning. Can you do that, sir?"

"Yes. Yes, that should not be a problem."

Puskis hung up with a sense of relief and the first feeling of surprised happiness that he had had in a long time. For without the stimulus of his work in the Vaults, he was, frankly, at a loss. With nothing to occupy his mind, he spent his time going over past issues — the difficulty he had faced, for instance, when classifying a recent string of rape/murders on the East Side. Crimes of sexual deviance or murder? In reality, both of course, but which of the two, for the purposes of the Vaults, should be the primary classification? Eventually he had decided on a primary classification of sexual deviance, due to Abramowitz's treatment of a similar string of crimes forty years earlier.

In any case, the phone call left him feeling

reenergized, and he went to his kitchen to make a pot of tea.

The second call came as he finished his last cup. This, if anything, surprised Puskis more than the first. A call could conceivably come anytime, he reasoned, and since Puskis was hardly likely to go the rest of his life without receiving an incoming call, it could as easily come one time as the next. Two calls in one morning, however — that was a true anomaly.

"Puskis," the voice on the other end of the line said.

"Yes?"

"You'll find Reif DeGraffenreid at this address." The caller read an address in a country town called Freeman's Gap, which was a couple dozen miles from the City's limits. His voice was slow and honey-tinged with an accent that, to Puskis's considerable frustration, he was unable to place.

"Who is this please?" Puskis asked, but the line was dead.

Puskis hung up the phone with trembling hands. He sat back in his chair and closed his eyes. He tried to see the logic behind the call. What was the caller hoping to accomplish? Was he, Puskis, supposed to journey out to Freeman's Gap to find De-Graffenreid? Who had called and why did he want him to take this course of action? What would the caller gain?

Puskis was contemplating these questions when the third call came. By this point, he was beyond surprise. He had pulled out the photograph of the man who was not Reif DeGraffenreid and it sat, faceup, on the pocked dinner table before him. He was staring at it, trying to make sense of the visceral reaction he had to the face; or the expression; or whatever information was being subliminally conveyed to him from that image.

He picked up the receiver to find that it was Lieutenant Draffin again, sounding apologetic. "The Chief asked me to call you back and tell you that there is a meeting he needs you to attend this Friday."

"A meeting?" Puskis asked. Never, in his nearly three decades in the Vaults, had he been asked to attend a meeting. One-on-one chats with the Chief were not unheard of, but never a full-fledged meeting. And scheduled two days ahead, no less.

"Did he happen to mention, ah, mention what it was about?"

"No, sir, he didn't. He just told me to tell you to be at that meeting."

"Hmmm. Yes," Puskis said, thinking. "Lieutenant Draffin, I was wondering if I

might be able to, well, let me put it this way:
I was wondering if the force had a pool of
autos, you know, for use by officers . . ."

"You mean unmarked?"

"Yes. Yes, I suppose that would be prefer-
able."

"Yes, sir, we do."

"Do you think that you could arrange for
me to borrow one?"

"I don't see how that would be a problem,
sir. When would you like it?"

"Today, actually. Today would be fine."

CHAPTER NINE

Back when Frings was starting out as a reporter, the *Gazette* had an aging, alcoholic reporter on staff by the name of Tomasson, who was something of a legend among the younger journalists; his seediness seemed to hold a kind of glamour. To Frings it had seemed that Tomasson had seen everything, his insight informed not merely by conjecture or personal bias but by previous *experiences.* Frings had often gone drinking with him at the old Palomino Tavern, before it was torn down, along with half that block, to put up the Havana Hotel. Frings could never match Tomasson and always left him at the bar, ranting to whoever would listen — and people did generally listen. Frings had kept careful track of the wisdom that Tomasson imparted on those nights and still remembered most of it clearly, though as Frings grew in experience, he found that he disagreed to a greater or lesser degree with much of what Tomasson had once said.

Like most reporters of the time, Tomasson was deeply cynical about the City's government. There seemed no end to the stream of corrupt mayors who took the City's helm. Darwin, Tomasson had claimed, explained it all. The most able of the "criminal class," as he called it, rose to the top and were able to defeat any honest challenge through vote-rigging, bribery, intimidation, and downright theft. The strongest criminal, he said, always prospered.

Frings agreed that Darwin explained it, but he understood Darwin a little differently. To Frings, it was a matter of innovation: Innovation was required to gain and hold power; thus, old methods of corruption and graft became obsolete quickly, and success depended on being able to quickly and constantly formulate new methods and forms of acquiring wealth and maintaining power. Maybe, in the end, Tomasson's argument was essentially the same. But to Frings, the nimble mind trumped all other attributes.

Frings's desk sat in a corner of the newsroom, part of a maze of desks, topped by black Smith-Coronas and Bell telephones.

At the best of times the room buzzed with noise. Inexperienced reporters struggled to concentrate amid the tumult. Today, just a day after the Block bombing, the newsroom had all the intensity of a squadron scrambling for battle. The assistants scuttled around purposefully, answering to the frequent shouts from reporters at their desks. Everyone seemed to be smoking a cigarette or a cigar, obscuring the ceiling in a haze of tobacco smoke.

Frings, though, was in a marijuana-induced zone, undistracted by the maelstrom around him as he typed a column that would run in the next day's newspaper.

A Man of Action
By Francis Frings

Provocation will bring out the true nature of the provoked. A man who is by nature contemplative will consider his options and select one that seems to best respond to the provocateur. This is the modus operandi of the chess master, the debater, the general. In short, this is the method observed by men for whom an improper response is irrevocably disastrous. The contemplative man's opposite number is the man of action. Like a drunken lawyer caught with an ace up his sleeve, the man of action's response to provocation is to flail out with frenzied violence at the first unfortunate to cross his path. His violence is used as a salve to his own wounds, rather than to punish the offending party.

I bring forth these two types of men because I fear for the political Left in the City in the substantial wake of the recent bombing directed at the mayor's cohort Ian Block. Why do I fear? The mayor is, I feel indisputably, a man of action. He is a retired professional pugilist who, by training and nature, responded to insult to his person with immediate, furious, and overwhelming violence. Does anyone doubt that his instincts in the mayor's office have been the same as his instincts between the ropes? Ask the thugs of the White Gang, who were eradicated like so many culled rabbits in the wake of the Birthday Party Massacre. Draw your own conclusions as to the justice of that remarkable period, but understand that other, less obviously culpable targets may be the next to feel the mayor's considerable wrath.

Why do I fear for the political Left? Because when the mayor begins his flailings, the easiest and most obvious target will be the anarchists and communists. Who else would you expect to bear the burden of blame? The Bristol Gang? They are now part and parcel of the mayor's regime, as much a part of the king's court as the industrialists who are the public faces of the mayor's cabal. Who else? I cannot think of one to supplant the anarchists and communists from the top of the mayor's accounting of conspirators and subversives. And, in this, the mayor may very well be borne out. My point is that the mayor must wait for the uncovering of actual evidence before acting in what will surely be a direct and devastating manner. The mayor is in no danger of losing his opportunity for personal vengeance against those who have dared to cause injury to the property, if not the persons, of his cadre. He must take the course of the contemplative man and identify the transgressors and punish them accordingly.

Frings pulled the paper from his typewriter and placed it in his empty out-box. Barking out for a newsboy, he then headed for the diner on the ground floor of the *Gazette* building.

The coffee was thick and strong, and stray grounds found his tongue as he sipped. He sat alone in a booth, thinking about his column. What was the point in writing it? Partly, he supposed, to provide cover for the people he knew would be scapegoats. Though not a Red or anarchist himself, Frings was outraged by the mayor's easy demonization of the Left as a means of advancing his business friends' interests. Workers had legitimate beefs, and tainting them with labels, such as *unionist* — generally perceived as a euphemism for *Communist* — was a disservice to the City. If Frings could boldly predict their bearing the brunt of the mayor's retaliation, then maybe there would be pressure not to target them automatically and, instead, to conduct a proper investigation.

This was, of course, the nobler of his two reasons. The other was his distaste for the mayor. Red Henry was arrogant, corrupt — a bully. This, in itself, was hardly notable in a mayor. But Henry had entered with so much promise, had been such a strong presence, that Frings and others had dared to hope that he might be incorruptible. Frings himself had risen in prominence during Henry's campaign and in the early months of that first mayoral term. He had been supportive of Henry in his columns. Briefly, it had seemed as if that faith had, indeed, been well-placed. But then, less than a year into the term, the Birthday Party Massacre and Henry's subsequent response had felt like a betrayal. The incorruptible Red Henry had, it seemed, chosen to be corrupted. And now he was driving the corruption.

Frings gored Henry in his columns with the rage of an apostate. Any chance Frings had to antagonize him was taken. None of this was lost on the mayor, who was not, despite everything else, stupid.

Just then, as if the workings of the universe were somehow tailored to his thoughts, a man slid into the seat across from Frings. Tall and handsome, his blond hair greased and combed straight back, he wore an expensive suit with bold pinstripes and wide shoulders. He settled in, placing his black fedora on the seat next to him. His expression was benign, but his eyes were intent. "How are you, Mr. Frings?"

Frings had run into this man before. His name was Smith and his job seemed to be keeping people in line for the mayor. In Frings's experience this meant trying to intimidate reporters into giving the mayor positive coverage. Or at least to discourage the negative.

Frings shrugged. His pulse raced.

"You don't look so swell from this side of

the table."

Frings snuck a look to see who else was in the diner, both to establish whether the man had brought backup and also in the hope that he could rely on someone for help if things went south.

"The mayor's been keeping me busy."

"I'm sure you mean the bombing has been keeping you busy."

"I imagine it's keeping both me *and* the mayor busy."

Done with the small talk, Smith leaned over the table. "The mayor was wondering whether you would be commenting on the bombing in tomorrow's paper."

Frings looked at Smith dully, his high rapidly fading and his headache beginning to reassert itself at the front of his skull. "Sorry. No sneak previews."

"Don't be a wiseass with me, Frings."

"No wiseass. You'll have to buy a paper, read it tomorrow."

"Don't make things difficult for yourself, Frings. This one is personal for the mayor. He's not going to put up with your bullshit on this. One of his closest friends was nearly murdered."

"I'm not criticizing the mayor, if that's what he's worried about, okay? I just want to make sure they get the right guys and not just the most convenient ones."

"Yeah, well, you'd better watch your words very carefully." Smith grabbed the salt shaker between his thumb and index finger and shook it into Frings's coffee. Amateur tough-guy stuff. Holding Smith's eye, Frings picked up the mug and took a long sip of the coffee. More stupid tough-guy stuff, he knew, but when you were dealing with stupid tough guys . . .

Smith winked and stood up. Putting down the mug, Frings watched him saunter out the door and into a black Ford idling at the curb. One of these days, Frings thought, I'm going to push him too far.

Chapter Ten

Stenciled on the outside of Poole's door in black-edged gold paint were the words ETHAN POOLE, INVESTIGATIONS AND INQUIRIES. This work was not exactly a steady source of income, but it did augment the money he got from his less legal endeavors. Mostly it consisted of tailing husbands or wives or business partners and either confirming or allaying his clients' fears. Sometimes he falsely reported good news while blackmailing the disloyal spouse or scheming partner, depending on who the client was. He looked to Carla for guidance in those situations, trusting her to determine where his clients were positioned in the chain of production. This visitor, though, was not his typical client.

The woman was in the twilight of middle age. Her hair was chopped short, haphazardly. Her face and body were puffy and pale in a way that didn't seem to make sense. Clearly, her features had once been attractive, and Poole saw a dignity even now trying to assert itself on the drooping shoulders and heavy gait. Her eyes, however, were lost and, half-covered by their lids, moved slowly in their sockets.

Poole's living room served as his office. He gestured for the woman to sit in the chair opposite his couch as he placed a pad on the inner thigh of his crossed leg and pulled a pen from his breast pocket. She sat with her hands in her lap, her gaze directed at his black brogue, which he wagged restlessly.

"I want you to find my son," she said, her words slurred around the edges.

"Okay. When did he go missing?"

"Seven years ago."

"Seven *years* ago?" he asked, confused.

She nodded.

"Have the police been looking for him during this time?"

She shrugged. "I guess so."

"Wait. You mean to say, you haven't been in contact with the police?"

She shook her head.

Poole closed his eyes hard to refocus his thoughts. Her son missing for seven years and she doesn't know if the police are looking for him? And she waits this long before contacting a detective? There was more to it, too. Her manner . . .

"Okay, what were the circumstances of his disappearance?"

"We were separated."

"How do you mean?"

She shrugged.

"By who?"

She shrugged again, seeming neither impatient nor frustrated by these questions she could not answer.

"How about your son's father? Your husband?"

"He was killed."

"When was this? The same time you and your son were separated?"

She nodded. "Around then."

"Do you have any thoughts about where your son could be?"

She did not. Nor did she have a picture of her son or her husband or any other type of starting point for Poole.

"What's your son's name?" Surely she knew this, at least.

"Casper."

"Okay. Last name?"

"Prosnicki. His father was Ellis Prosnicki."

When Lena Prosnicki left, Poole uncorked a bottle of red wine and poured a fair amount into a pint glass. He looked at his notebook, open to a page of mostly unanswered questions. She had left saying that there was no way of contacting her, but that her son, Casper, would know how to find her once Poole found him. This made no sense, of course, but then little about her had. Poole would normally have run from such a situation without a second thought, but Mrs. Prosnicki had handed him five hundred dollars in cash and said to do whatever amount of work for her that might cover — and if he had still not found Casper, then he would at least have done his best. She was so odd and defeated and — what? — that he did not expect she would be able to find anyone else to make inquiries for her. So he had accepted and she had nodded in that vague way of hers, seeming neither particularly happy nor satisfied.

The other point that left him uneasy was her sheer lack of understanding or concern about what had happened to her son. They had been "separated." Her husband had been killed. But she was unable to supply even a hint of the circumstances of these events. Nor did she mention them with any attendant emotion.

The one thing she had supplied him with was the address where they had lived at the time. It was, at least, a starting point.

These thoughts were interrupted by Carla's return from the picket line at Roderigo Bernal's plant. Poole was, as always, relieved that she had come back safe.

"How was it?"

She gave him a thin smile. "It was fine."

"Fine?" The wine had relaxed him.

"We shut down the plant. The cops came and watched."

"But?"

"Too quiet. The cops, management, everybody. Nothing happened. It worries me."

"You think they have something in the works?"

"Wouldn't surprise me."

"Spill."

Carla shrugged, her eyes narrowing with worry. "I have no idea."

"You've faced these things before. I'm sure it's nothing that you haven't seen or that you can't handle."

"That's true if they're planning some kind of action against the union. What I'm worried about is whether Bernal is holding off until he can do something about *you.*"

Poole sat back, pondering this. "I've done this before, Carla."

"Just listen for a second. I was thinking about this on the line today. On the same day that Block gets his building blown up, Bernal gets burned. I'm concerned that maybe the mayor sees two of his little pals get pressured —"

"And figures maybe it's coordinated," Poole finished for her.

"So, if Bernal tells Henry, and Henry thinks it's some kind of plot against his inner circle, he'll be very anxious to get his mitts on the blackmailer."

Poole nodded slowly. "Maybe. But would Bernal go to Henry with this? Normally, I would say not a chance. He doesn't want to show that kind of weakness. But with the bombing, I don't know, like you said . . ."

Carla shrugged. "I have no idea if he would tell Henry or not, but you need to be very careful tonight, okay?"

Poole had the feeling he had stepped off a precipice with no idea of the distance to the bottom.

CHAPTER ELEVEN

He's a scary little bastard, Red Henry thought, which was as high a compliment as anyone was likely to receive from him. Henry leaned against a concrete stanchion, sucking on an unlit Cuban, casting an enormous shadow in the empty warehouse deep in the Hollows. Facing him, standing relaxed, with his feet shoulders' width apart, his knees and shoulders loose, was Feral Basu. Feral was fully a foot and a half shorter than Red Henry and a third of his weight, but if the mayor didn't fear anyone, he also didn't relish the thought of Feral coming after him.

"Know who Arthur Puskis is?" Red Henry asked.

Feral shook his head. His skin was dark and smooth, and even in the dim light of the warehouse, his eyes were somehow arresting.

"Everyone on the force does," Henry

explained. "He's the police Archivist. Works under City Hall. Something of a legend, in truth."

Feral waited.

"He's trying to find Reif DeGraffenreid."

Again Feral said nothing, though Henry noticed a subtle tensing in his slender frame.

Henry said, "So, we tipped him as to where DeGraffenreid is."

"You did?"

Henry was always perplexed by Feral's accent. He thought he detected a trace of the Carpathians or maybe the Muslim south of Russia, which might have explained his coloration. He looked as if he might be from India.

"Yes. We need to discourage him from *continuing* this line of inquiry."

"What do you mean, exactly?"

"I mean that you need to make him understand that looking for Reif DeGraffenreid, or any other actions he plans to take regarding DeGraffenreid and/or Prosnicki, is folly."

"Don't kill him?"

Red Henry had considerably more patience with Feral than with anyone else. "No. Don't kill him. Two things are important. The first is that he understands that his pursuit of this inquiry will have consequences for him. The second is that he does not talk to DeGraffenreid. That something you can take care of?"

"Yes."

With that, Henry knew that it would be taken care of, that he did not need to think about it further.

CHAPTER TWELVE

Puskis turned the unmarked Nash borrowed from the police pool off the pitted road that ran through what there was of Freeman's Gap and pulled into a petrol station. Three men sat on folding chairs around a card table playing rummy. Their clothes and skin were the color of the dust that blew through the street. They were war vets, Puskis thought.

He got out of his car and approached them. A perimeter around the table was discolored with tobacco spit. Two of the men projected streams of the brown juice and looked up from their cards.

"Excuse me. I was wondering if you could tell me how I could get to this address." He read them the address the caller had given him. The men exchanged brief glances with each other, then looked back at him.

Puskis tried again. "Do you know where this address is?"

The man closest to him, whose hair had come out in patches and whose hands could have belonged to a man forty years his senior, tore a piece from the pad they were using to keep score. He drew a map with a grease pencil, his filthy hands staining the paper where they occasionally touched it. When he was done, he handed it to Puskis and let out a wheezing cough, his lungs ravaged by gas. The map was precise and easy to read.

"Thank you. Thank you so much," Puskis said, and retreated to his car, never quite turning his back fully on the three men. As he drove off, he noticed that they were once again engrossed in their game.

Toward dusk Puskis rumbled down the dirt road where he would find Reif DeGraffenreid. The low sun shone red, turning the tops of the seemingly endless fields of corn an orange, and the wind moved the plants in waves so that it looked like acres of inferno. It was, Puskis thought uneasily, like traveling through a maze of fire. The withered corn was too high to see over, and he had been traveling for several miles with the plants encroaching on the road from both sides, only occasionally broken by a clearing in front of a decrepit farmhouse.

The Nash rattled ominously as the wheels found potholes. Even as he approached the farmhouse that was DeGraffenreid's, Puskis was becoming nervous about driving back to the City at night. He pulled into De-Graffenreid's dirt driveway and parked behind a rusting pickup truck. The wind through the corn sounded like a light but persistent rain. The sun was no longer visible beyond the close horizon. A rhythmic knocking came from the small, two-story house before him. Probably a shutter out back. Puskis hesitated before walking toward the front door. Each footstep made a complex sound as rocks and gravel were rubbed together under the soles of his shoes. It was a country sound, one he could not recall ever having heard.

The steps to the porch were bowed in the middle and groaned under his weight. Behind a much patched screen door, the inner door stood open. The interior was too dark to peer into.

He hesitated for a moment. "Mr. De-Graffenreid," he ventured. He waited for several seconds, then tried again, a little bit louder. "Mr. DeGraffenreid." When this again drew no answer, he eased the screen door open and crossed the threshold. Coming from the twilit outdoors, he had to wait for his pupils to dilate in the dark interior. He called out again, "Mr. DeGraffenreid," but knew now that he would get no response. As his eyes began to adjust to the darkness, he became aware that he was in a large, rather bare room, and that a pile of something lay in the center. There was a strange, sweet smell, too, that he knew right off, even if his mind at first refused to acknowledge it. In an act more of denial than courage, he approached the pile.

When he was close enough, he saw what, in fact, he had understood was there all along. The knees were tucked under the body, which was bent over so that the shoulders touched the ground and the arms were splayed, as if frozen during some Islamic prayer. But the head was missing, and what might have been a misshapen prayer rug was, in fact, scarlet blood pooling out from the open neck.

The head, Puskis now saw, was propped on the windowsill, its hair almost completely gone and its eyes bulging. But there was no mistaking that crooked nose from the picture in the file. Puskis had not felt fear in so long that he did not recognize it now in his accelerated heartbeat and the sweat on his upper lip and brow and his shallow breathing. He knelt next to the headless body and felt one of the hands. It was still warm. De-Graffenreid had recently been alive. Maybe as recently as thirty minutes before.

Then Puskis heard a sound from outside. A shuffling on the dirt along with a clicking noise. He looked up from the body, concentrating on the noise, and saw that something had been written on the wall. It was too dark to make out from where he was, so he straightened up and walked across the room. The message contained only two words, written in DeGraffenreid's blood: PUSKIS DESIST.

He stared at it, thoughts racing, for once, incoherently. He reached out to touch the letters, then stopped himself before actually making contact. He shook his head slowly and let out an involuntary moan.

The noise from outside again penetrated his consciousness, as the strange shuffling and tapping sounds were now close, then replaced by the creak of the front steps and a new tapping sound of wood against wood. Puskis turned to face the door. The only other points of egress were the windows and a door to his left. He didn't go for them though, and a silhouette appeared in the door.

"Mr. Reif . . . Mr. Reif, you there?" The man waited for an answer. Puskis worried the man could hear his breathing.

"Mr. Reif, you there?" The man opened the door and Puskis saw an old black man in overalls and a straw hat. A farmer. He was blind, with blackout glasses and a cane. Puskis stood still, trying to control his breathing.

The blind man walked forward, tapping ahead of him with the cane. "Mr. Reif?" He took two more steps and his cane hit De-Graffenreid's body. He stopped and probed the body with his cane. Then he bent down and touched the body. "Mr. Reif," he whispered as his fingers came away wet. He stiffened and craned his neck, searching with his ears rather than his eyes.

"Who's there?" he said sharply. Puskis stood transfixed. "I know there's someone there," the blind man said again, his voice edging toward hysteria. "Something terrible's happened here. Who's there?"

The blind man rose and began advancing toward Puskis, his cane tapping in semicircular sweeps. Puskis retreated to the back wall, and the sound of his footsteps stopped the blind man short. Puskis started to edge his way toward the door to his left, but the blind man, hearing him, made a move to intercept him. Puskis stopped and began to circle the room the other way, but the blind man followed his footsteps, cutting off the room the way a boxer cuts off the ring.

"Who is that?" the old man rasped.

Puskis circled faster to his right and the blind man made a move to beat him to the front door, only to trip over DeGraffenreid's prone body, his cane skidding across the floor toward Puskis as he fell. Puskis seized his moment, moving as quickly as he could out the front door. He took the three steps down to the ground, then trotted, clumsy and out of breath, to the car. To his relief it started on the first try.

He turned to the house and saw the blind man on the porch without his cane. "What has happened here?" the man yelled out. Puskis reversed out of the driveway onto the road and sped away into the maze of cornfields, now turning purple with the onset of night.

CHAPTER THIRTEEN

Frings watched Nora smoke a Chesterfield through a holder. She had long, elegant fingers for a woman so generously proportioned. Her eyes on the jazz band up on the stage, she showed no indication of enjoyment or boredom. She was simply there. Not that this was unusual. Nora's pleasure in music came from performing, from the exchange of energy between herself and the audience. It was, Frings supposed, a sensual feeling for her to be onstage; her ability to translate this feeling through her voice, along with her physical beauty, made her the sex symbol she was. The upshot, however, was that she did not especially enjoy being in the audience for a jazz show. Given a choice, she would probably have rather been at the symphony.

They were at the Palace on the City's East Side — its black side. The place was nearly full, with Frings and Nora two of only a handful of Caucasians. It was their favorite place; for Nora, because here she could relax somewhat, away from the usual attention. On the East Side, the black musicians were the celebrities, while she was just one of the vanguard of fashionable whites who ventured here to enjoy the scene and — if less so in her case — the music. As for Frings, he liked the music, but it was also where he could score his reefer.

"You enjoying the band?" he asked her as the musicians paused between songs to retune their instruments and take a quick sip of whatever they were drinking.

She shrugged and frowned slightly, watching something across the room. She was distracted, in her own world, which tonight had Frings alternating between an anxious sadness and complete indifference. The bond between them had always been unclear. She was the chanteuse of the City's vibrant white jazz scene. For now at least. He was a "name" reporter, stirring up trouble among the wealthy and powerful. As a couple they seemed to epitomize the glamour of the City that was at once elegant — her — and seedy — him. But while this played well as a symbol, their relationship had, from the start, been based on a mutual sense of excitement that had eroded with time. Leaving what? More and more nights like this in which they seemed only to be living lives side by side.

A tall, elegant man in a tuxedo walked over to their table. He wore his hair slicked back, and a thin mustache was barely visible against his dark, dark skin. He leaned over Nora and they exchanged kisses to each cheek. Then he shook hands with Frings.

"How are things, Frank?" said Floyd Christian, the floor manager at the Palace. Frings had known him for years. "What do you think of the band?"

"They're hitting on all sixes," Frings said. Floyd looked to Nora. "Nora's not talking," Frings explained.

She had returned to staring vacantly at the stage, blowing smoke through parted lips with practiced sensuality that by now seemed unconscious.

"Floyd, if you've got any reefer . . ."

Floyd gave a low laugh. "These days, I'm *always* holding. My cup runneth over, I think is what they say. Those headaches bothering you again?"

Frings smiled. "Not so funny when you have them."

Floyd nodded in sympathy. "Hey, there's something I need to tell you. Some hood was poking his nose around in here asking about you. He didn't know from nothing but he was fishing."

"Big guy, yellow hair, pole up his ass?"

"That'd be him."

Smith. "Anybody say anything?"

"Shit."

"Yeah, sorry. Of course not."

"He official?"

"Afraid so."

"You got yourself into one?"

Frings nodded.

"Now I see why you need that mezz. I'll be back."

The band took a break and Nora turned to Frings with a look that made him realize her distance that night had been less the product of indifference than anxiety. She put her hand over his, holding it. He let her, but did not move to take hers in return.

"There was someone watching me at the club last night."

"You're onstage — *everyone's* watching you."

"No, they're watching the show. This man was watching *me*."

"You're thinking too much."

"Am I?"

"How can you possibly tell, a roomful of

people like that, that one particular person is watching you like . . . differently from just watching the show?"

"How many shows do you think I've done, Frank? I can read people in the audience. I can tell when men are thinking what it would be like to sleep with me, or to hurt me. I can see the women who are jealous or who think I'm a tramp."

"Or who also want to sleep with you," Frings suggested with a smile.

"Don't be an ass. I'm serious. This was different. This wasn't . . . I don't know. He seemed to be there with a purpose, and it wasn't seeing the band. He was watching me. For a reason."

"Guy with a crush?"

Her temper flared, though Frings knew that it was triggered by fear, not anger. "People look at me every goddamn day, Frank. I have a pretty good sense of the difference between being ogled by a guy with a crush and being *watched.*"

Frings thought about this for a second. A woman with Nora's beauty and fame was bound to be an object of obsession for any number of men, and she ran into that problem frequently. Frings had seen it for himself on more than one occasion. It didn't rattle her. So if this one did, Frings figured, maybe there was something to it.

"Okay. Listen. Describe him for me." For some reason he assumed this might be Smith. The guy was showing up everywhere lately.

"He was little and had dark skin. Like an Indian. From India."

"Did he say anything to you?"

"No. Just hung around at the bar and watched."

"Was he with anyone?"

"I don't think so. Didn't see him talk to anyone."

She pulled her hand away from his. Cross-examination was not what she had wanted from him, Frings knew, but he did not know what else to say.

"I don't know, Frank," she said into her drink. "I'm off for a week, so maybe he'll get bored and screw."

The conversation seemed to be over, as Nora turned from him to watch the comings and goings of the people close to the stage. These were the City's Negro elite, and Nora was fascinated by them; perhaps because she had no entrée into their world. Few doors were closed to her. Frings leaned back in his chair and smoked a Lucky, trying to force himself to care more about Nora than he did. It was a depressing exercise, and he was relieved to see Floyd approaching.

"You got a call on the office phone, Frank."

Frings excused himself to Nora's back and followed Floyd to the club office, red velvet on the walls and black leather furniture. A telephone perched on an ebony desk, the earpiece off its hook. Frings brought it up to his ear and spoke into mouthpiece at the base.

"Frings."

"Frank, it's Panos."

Christ, what was he doing calling him at this time of night? "What's the rumble, chief?"

"There's been another bomb."

CHAPTER FOURTEEN

Two years back, Poole had been doing blackmail and private dick work long enough to be self-assured, but not yet long enough to be scared. The scars from State still burned, and he was often overwhelmed with self-disgust. He drank more then and was more than willing to use his size as an instrument of intimidation and fear.

One night the excuse was a young pro named Alice. She was leaning against a wall, smoking — couldn't have been more than fifteen — and Poole saw that both her eyes were black, swollen down to slits. He asked her what happened. She said to screw. He persisted and she finally gave in, as much to get rid of him as anything else, it seemed. A john had gotten rough — hit her, kicked her in the ribs, left without paying. Her pimp had taken care of her other eye.

Poole took Alice on a walk. Eventually they found the john shooting craps in the alley next to Lambert's Tavern. Poole grabbed him, dragging him deeper into the alley as the other gamblers watched. The energy from their collective adrenaline fueled Poole's anger. He braced the john. The man went down on all fours, then Poole broke his ribs with a kick. He gave the wallet to Alice, who took the money she was owed and tossed the rest on the man, now groaning in a fetal tuck.

Next they found the pimp, who surprised Poole by being no older than Alice. No matter. Similar story. When the pimp had finally had enough, Poole held him at eye level and told him, if there was ever any other trouble with Alice, to come to him. If the pimp ever touched her again, he would be back. The pimp nodded and Poole dropped him in a pile.

Alice had only one way to thank Poole, and he wasn't interested. Someday, he said, you might be able to do me a favor. Now he was calling in that chit.

Poole walked through the intermittently lit paths in Greer Park with Alice on his arm. She was blond and thin and her face was painted with ghoulish makeup. She wore a cheap cocktail dress under an overcoat she had for the cold.

The gazebo stood in a clearing a few yards from Greer Pond. Surrounding the clearing was a well-groomed stand of trees without any undergrowth, an improved version of nature that offered no effective cover. If police were waiting, Poole would spot them without trouble. As they approached the gazebo, Poole scanned the perimeter of trees for any human shape or movement. Finding nothing, he and Alice continued on.

Low clouds were illuminated a gray yellow by the City lights, and wisps extended downward like the tentacles of jellyfish. The noise of the City was muffled here, and it was easy enough to picture this as some bucolic country scene.

Poole had Alice sit on the floor of the gazebo. This spot was often used by prostitutes, and tonight Alice was Poole's cover.

"If someone comes other than the mark," he said to her, "I'm taking it out of my pants. You just stand up like you're surprised."

"I can make this more realistic, if you'd like."

Poole laughed. "I don't think Carla would appreciate that so much." This was not the first time she had been direct with him, and he was used to her enticements.

She slouched back against the interior wall

of the gazebo while Poole kept watch on the path for Bernal. Right on time came his footsteps on the pine-needled dirt path, sounding like someone punching a bag of rice. His silhouette came into view; hat, overcoat, and briefcase. Poole reached into his bag and pulled out a pillowcase with two eyeholes. He tossed it to Alice. "Put it on."

She looked at him inquiringly and he repeated his command. He didn't want her to be the target of any reprisals. She pulled the case over her head and adjusted it so she could see out the eyeholes. He took a stocking from the bag, removed his hat, pulled the stocking over own his face, then replaced the hat. They looked absurd, he knew, but it was essential to keep their identities a secret. He had also found that under such circumstances, absurdity could be quite unnerving to the mark.

Bernal hesitated twenty feet from the gazebo, and Poole beckoned him forward with an expansive arm gesture. Bernal resumed walking. Poole noticed that he did not look over his shoulder. At the foot of the three steps leading up to the gazebo, Bernal paused again.

"Move," Poole said.

Bernal ascended slowly and stepped to the

center of the gazebo. He gave the hooded Alice a look but did not seem perturbed.

"Set the case on the floor."

Bernal did as he was told.

"Did you bring the police?"

Bernal shook his head.

"Because if you did, now is the time to tell them to screw. I have an associate with the photos. I don't return, they get sent to all the rags."

"I didn't bring the police."

"Okay." Poole showed Bernal his Luger. "I have one, just so you know." He replaced it in the shoulder holster. "You wearing?"

"No gun." The man's face was expressionless. He did not seem scared, though he was certainly tense.

"Mind if I check?"

Bernal spread his arms and legs, keeping silent. Poole, patting up his sides and legs and finally his back, found nothing.

"Okay, open the case."

Bernal got down on one knee and sprang the two latches. Then he slowly lifted the lid to reveal the stacks of twenty-dollar bills.

"Pick one out from the bottom and show me."

Bernal dug his hand into the case and removed a packet of bills. He flipped through them, showing Poole that they were all twenties. The wind gusted now, and the trees made a soft noise like fire on wet wood. It would be harder now to hear an approach.

"You know that if you're short —"

"It's all there."

"Okay. The other thing you are going to do for me is, you're going to meet the union's demands and end the strike."

Again, Bernal remained silent, but now his face betrayed him.

"Savvy?" Poole prompted.

"I don't think you understand," Bernal began, then thought better of it and tried again. "It's not something I can just do."

"I don't believe you."

"You can believe me or not. I can't do it."

The wind was constant, the scent of phosphorus overwhelming the Christmas smell of the pines. The ripples on the water below began gathering into tiny waves.

"You have two days to make it work. I don't care what you have to do. I don't care what excuses you have. Two days. Forty-eight hours. Then the photos go to press."

Bernal shut his eyes, and picking up the great tension in the man's body, Poole realized that Bernal would hunt him dead were he ever to suss out his identity. Poole felt a sudden chill and with it the first stirrings of panic at all the sounds that would not be audible beneath the wind.

"Close the case." His words sounded shrill.

Bernal opened his eyes, his gaze locking on Poole's. Poole wondered just how effectively the stocking was managing to disguise his features.

"Close the *goddamn case,*" Poole shouted, his nerves rioting.

Bernal dropped to one knee again, closed and latched the case, and then stood up.

"Turn around and walk to the wall."

Bernal turned his back to Poole and took two steps until he was leaning against a wall overlooking the stirring pond.

"The girl in the apartment," Poole said, "she wasn't in on this, got it?"

Bernal shrugged.

"If she's hurt, it will make things more difficult for you."

Again Bernal shrugged. Poole grabbed the case with one hand and with the other grabbed Alice's arm, jerking her up with more force than he intended.

"What time do you have?"

Bernal checked his watch. "Five after eleven."

"Wait until ten past."

Bernal nodded.

They half-walked, half-trotted down the path, the wind blowing pine needles and dead leaves around their ankles. Poole pulled the pillowcase off Alice and the stocking from his face and stuffed them in a coat pocket. He had left the bag at the gazebo, but it would not be of any use to the police.

He parted with Alice, giving her one hundred dollars for the night and telling her to go home and keep her head down for a day or two. Then he walked home, every passerby sending his adrenaline spiking. Some actions you can't backtrack on, and he was now committed to chiseling one of the most powerful men in the City. Poole was about to find out if Bernal's ruthlessness in business translated to other facets of his life.

He saw a tower of blue smoke rising into the blue and yellow neon of the Theater District across town, but it did not register in his preoccupied mind as anything of significance.

CHAPTER FIFTEEN

Red Henry sat in his favorite leather chair, feet on the matching ottoman, reading the *Gazette.* Occasionally, when he read something particularly annoying, he snorted in disgust or took quick, deep breaths to calm himself. It was not that the *Gazette* actually ran anything untrue — they were a respectable paper. It was not even their seemingly insatiable need for sniffing around City Hall trying to catch the scent of corruption. Scandal sells papers, and he certainly understood the profit motive. No, what left him particularly aggrieved was that they did not seem to see that when the City did well, the *Gazette* did well. And the City did best when Henry was given some goddamn latitude to make things work.

"That shit-ant Frings," he mumbled half-audibly.

"What's that?" His mistress, Siobhan, was stretched across his couch reading Nietzsche or some such crap. She was wearing a green silk sleeping gown that a previous mistress had left. It was alluringly snug and accentuated her long red hair.

Henry looked at her; then decided it was worth answering. "Frings. He wrote a column, thinks he's going to tie my hands."

Siobhan returned to her book. "Nobody ties your hands, sugar," she said evenly.

Henry gave her a heavy-lidded look, then put the paper down, and rose out of the chair, wearing only his slacks from the day, his suspenders hanging loose around his knees. His bare upper body was massive without being particularly fat or muscular. There was simply a lot of him. He stood at the window, taking in his fourteenth-floor penthouse view of the City. Actually, it was the thirteenth floor, but the elevator skipped straight from the twelfth to fourteenth floor. It disgusted him, indulging people's ridiculous superstitions. Still, one must pick one's battles and he had plenty.

Henry pressed his palms against the window, slightly farther apart than his shoulders. It looked as though he were holding the City between his hands.

The phone rang, and Henry turned slowly to watch Siobhan's body moving beneath the silk as she went to the set. She answered, listened, then held out the phone as if she were offering him a martini. He walked slowly across the room.

"Yeah," he grunted, taking the phone.

"Sir, there's been another bomb."

Henry didn't answer.

"Sir?"

Henry remained silent.

"It was Altabelli's apartment." Altabelli ran a meat-processing factory. Along with Block and Bernal and a few others, he was part of Henry's inner circle.

"Was he there?"

"Sir, yes, he was. But he's okay. He was in the john, I guess, and now he's at the hospital, but they said it was only a precaution."

Henry's skin prickled with heat. "Call the Chief. Tell him my office in an hour." He hung up the phone.

"What was that?" Siobhan asked, without looking up from her book. Henry ignored her and walked into his bedroom, where he had a better view of Altabelli's neighborhood. Sure enough, a spire of smoke was rising up over the Theater District. He watched the smoke for several minutes, its undulations focusing his thoughts somehow, as he considered just how furious his response would need to be to maintain order in the City.

CHAPTER SIXTEEN

At this very hour of the night, in an airless sitting room illuminated by the flickering light of an oil lamp, Joos Van Vossen flipped through page after page of his tight, meticulous script. Something he had come across needed attention; a detail that had eaten at him throughout the afternoon and evening, its implication unclear. Only as he prepared to retire for the night did the context finally come to him, and now he found the pertinent passage, several hundred pages back.

Typical of a certain type of criminal known colloquially as a "block boss" is Reif De-Graffenreid, who held sway over four blocks on Delft Avenue between Trafalgar and Wellington streets. As with others of his particular type, he collected protection money, kept book, and served as an intermediary for residents who had some concern to take before the gang bosses.

The block boss would pay the gangs, either the Bristol Gang or the White Gang or sometimes both, a percentage of his takings and would make himself scarce when they sent their hard men in to do some of the heavy business.

DeGraffenreid's career was unspectacular when compared to those of his fellow block bosses, though the standard they set was, of course, high. He was purportedly the lover of Janey May Overstreet — known as Queenie — who owned the Bull Ring Saloon, a favorite among hoodlums and roustabouts. This claim is subject to some suspicion as the sum total of her reported assignations and the jealousies they would have inspired surely would have raised the City's homicide rate noticeably. Nevertheless, this rumor puts in perspective his reputation as a peer of such notables as Jimmy McQuaid in lower Capitol Heights, Hamish Berry (who, in fact, was himself briefly married to Queenie Overstreet), and Johnny Acton, and, in deed, though not style, of Trevor "Vampire" Reid.

As was the case with all block bosses, DeGraffenreid was compelled to tread a careful line during the escalating violence between the Bristol Gang and the White

Gang. Initially, as was the case with so many others, he endeavored to ingratiate himself to both sides by performing small tasks unlikely to upset either one too much, such as his alleged arson of the restaurant owned by the Hungarian named Praeger — who had endeavored to run a book without paying either gang its "vig."

In the end, he fell in with the Bristols, ended the flow of cash from his blocks to the Whites, and performed menial services. His call to greater action, and the eventual end of his criminal career, came when he was ordered to murder the husband of a cousin, Ellis Prosnicki, who was suspected of being a police informant.

DeGraffenreid shot Prosnicki in an alley off Delft Avenue and was arrested within forty-eight hours on the evidence of several eyewitnesses after they were assured by Bristol thugs that they would not be subject to retribution. DeGraffenreid was convicted and thus ends his story for our purposes.

Dipping his pen into a well of green ink, Van Vossen took out a fresh sheet of paper. *The case of Ross Carmargue,* he wrote, *who was running prostitutes on DeGraffenreid's blocks, confirmed that Prosnicki had received money from the police in exchange for information. However, Prosnicki's informing did not, ironically, extend to the books being run out of several Bristol-associated restaurants, the transgression of which he actually stood accused.*

Finishing this, Van Vossen marked the appropriate sentence with a footnote and put away his work for the night.

CHAPTER SEVENTEEN

Puskis returned to work to find three full pages of file requests. In a deviation from his normal routine, he spent several minutes reordering the slips so that he could make a single, efficient trip to fulfill the requests; he wanted some time between completing this round and the next that would surely come in the midmorning. The second bombing would increase the force's work exponentially.

As he began his circuit, pushing the squeaking cart before him, he thought about the sensation of fear that he had experienced the previous night. Fear. In his twenty-seven years at the Vaults, he had not once felt fear. Anxiety, pressure, fatigue — all disagreeable states, to be sure — had visited him at one time or another. But never fear. Even now, with the experience so recent, he found he could not summon up the actual feeling, could not remember precisely what it had

115

felt like. This may have been why the blood-etched warning to desist had little effect on him. If anything, it only served to drive him forward.

Having collected the files, Puskis returned to his desk to reorder them in the sequence in which they had been requested. This done, he placed the lot in a box labeled OUTGOING and returned to the shelf holding C4583R series, subseries A132, where he had earlier that morning returned the two DeGraffenreid files. Removing the De-Graffenreid file that contained the picture of the real DeGraffenreid, he placed it into the wire cart and headed to the southeast corner of the Vaults, where institutional records were kept.

Unlike the files — which were full of loose sheets of paper and were constantly added to — the institutional records were hard-bound tomes that served as official records of criminal-justice activity in the City. Puskis pulled a heavy, black-leather-bound edition from its shelf. The spine read, in gold inlay, *Criminal Court Verdicts — 1927.*

The janitors treated the leather bindings of these books on a rotating basis to ward off any cracking or deterioration, so that the entire southeast corner smelled of leather and protective oils. Abramowitz had called this area the Stable. Puskis himself had never been in a stable, but assumed that Abramowitz had been correct in his association.

The first half of *Criminal Court Verdicts — 1927* was composed of indexes that organized the verdicts by last name of the defendant, last name of the judge, charge against the defendant, City district in which the crime took place, and so forth. The second half of the book was a chronological list of the verdicts, including the charge(s), names of prosecutors, defense lawyers, defendant, judge, courtroom, and any additional minutiae that could be of possible interest. The only pieces of information missing from the listings were the names of jurors, who were kept anonymous for their own protection.

Puskis quickly located DeGraffenreid's case in the defendants' index. The entry was unremarkable. An assistant DA had prosecuted, while DeGraffenreid's attorney was a familiar name in trials involving criminals of this ilk. A senior judge, now deceased, had presided. The verdict was guilty of murder in the first degree. The courtroom notation, however, was unfamiliar: *NC*. He turned to the rear of the book, where the abbreviations were listed, but found no *NC* under the courtroom list. There was a *BC* (Banneker Wing, Room C), and Puskis considered the possibility that this was nothing more than a typographical error, *B* and *N* being adjacent on the typewriter keyboard. He decided he was willing to accept this explanation if his next inquiry produced unremarkable results.

Replacing *Criminal Court Verdicts — 1927,* he then walked two rows down and found *Incarcerated Persons, City and State Correctional Facilities — 1927.* A slimmer volume than the *Verdicts* records, *Incarcerated Persons* contained lists of all prisoners in jails and prisons, their institution, the terms of sentence, as well as their confinement and release dates, if they occurred during 1927. The search did not take long. He scanned the alphabetical list of prisoners, then the list of prisoners in each of the twenty-three facilities listed. DeGraffenreid's name did not appear. Puskis placed the volume into his cart, then returned and collected *Criminal Court Verdicts — 1927.*

Returning to his desk, he found that the courier had come and gone, taking the stack of files that Puskis had left for him and leaving a long list of new file requests. Puskis took the list and, before beginning his rounds, returned to the Stable to replace the two volumes. He had never been disturbed by anyone during his years in the Vaults, but understanding that these were becoming exceptional times, he did not want to be in possession of those books any longer than necessary.

Chapter Eighteen

"How you doing, Frankie?"

Frings shrugged. Reynolds, the cop in charge of the crime scene at Altabelli's place, was an acquaintance of Frings's. They used to drink at the same neighborhood bar uptown before Frings had become a celebrity and Reynolds had gone on the wagon.

"You still with Nora Aspen?"

Frings smiled, ready to shoot the shit. "Still am. Not sure why she keeps me around."

Reynolds gave him a knowing look. The Theater District, usually so alive at night, was quiet this morning. The lights that attracted people to this or that theater were off, and where the usual throngs of tuxedos and furs milled around, waiting for the act 2 curtain, there were now merely a scattering of service people running errands, sweeping streets, stocking the bars with liquor. The streets here, impassable in the evening for all the theatergoers, were now impassable for the delivery trucks that stopped in the street, holding up traffic until their drop-offs were complete.

"You want to look around?" Reynolds asked.

Frings nodded.

"I'm going to have to walk with you. Word from the Chief says no one in the site without an escort."

"Sure. We can talk."

Some of the debris had already been cleared by the uniformed officers, about ten of whom were still sifting through fragments. Something was different about this site, Frings thought. Where Block's building had been blown out into the street, this one seemed to be blown back into itself.

"This one," Frings said. "The bomb was on the *outside?*" He was high. That was another problem with the migraines. He'd smoke a reefer to ease the headache, but then, when the headache was gone, he'd smoke because he liked being high. He had done that this morning, sitting on the fire escape outside Nora's apartment with a juju as she showered. He'd tried to act straight when she emerged and even thought he'd succeeded, though he couldn't completely trust his perceptions. Which was part of the point. But it also undermined his confidence in his own reasoning, so he used Reynolds to validate his observations.

"That's right. We think whoever it was put a bundle, maybe five sticks of dynamite in a bag, on the sidewalk and then lit a long fuse."

"That square with the bomb at Block's?"

Reynolds shrugged. "Well, that was dynamite, too. And, of course, there's who they are, you know." He looked to Frings, who nodded that, yes, he knew.

"Off the record, I think we're pretty sure they're connected. *On* the record, we're exploring a connection. Got it?"

"Makes perfect sense."

"At Block's," Reynolds went on, "the bundle was thrown through a window, already lit. Again, a long fuse."

"So why not toss through Altabelli's window, like Block's?"

"Altabelli says he had bars across the windows. Says the Theater District can get a little dicey late at night."

They walked to a jagged hole in the pavement where a flag was stuck into the rubble.

"The detonation point," Reynolds said.

"What're those?" Frings pointed to two chalked circles drawn just outside the detonation crater.

"Shit. Yeah. Two kids. Found what was left of them across the street, but they were literally blown out of their shoes. They must have been curious, you know, come to have a look, and then . . ." Reynolds left the obvious unsaid, a rueful look on his face.

"Jesus." Frings repressed a shudder. He bent down and picked up a scorched brick. "What about Altabelli?"

"He's fine. Working late, or so he says. One of the lads heard that they had to track him down at a cathouse on the edge of the Heights."

Frings tossed the brick to the side. There was a smell of burned chemicals and scorched brick. His eyes had begun to water from it, and his throat burned with each breath of air. Reynolds seemed impervious.

Two kids dead. Two innocent kids dead, while Altabelli, off whoring, gets away scot-free. Except for the house, of course. But still . . .

Frings asked Reynolds, still looking at the hole in Altabelli's apartment building, "Off the record, do you have any idea who this might be?"

Reynolds laughed. "I thought *you* knew. You wrote a goddamn column about it, didn't you? The brass were steaming about *that,* I can tell you. They won't like me beating my gums with you, neither, but they know we go way back. Anyone else, I don't think you're going to get too far. So, the unions? The anarchists? But who exactly, we don't know. And the *why,* well, they don't really need a why, do they?"

Frings frowned slightly, not willing to affirm the statement. They usually had their reasons, he thought, though these were never acknowledged by the police, or the City, or the newspapers, for that matter. Whether it was a true lack of understanding or willful ignorance, Frings could not say — though he had his suspicions.

Back at the barricades, a uniformed officer was shouting for Reynolds. After admonishing Frings not to poke around while he was gone, Reynolds hurried over to the wooden barriers. Frings watched them talk calmly enough, the urgency nonetheless plainly evident in their postures. Reynolds turned to him and beckoned with a wave of his arm. Frings hurried over, holding his hat on his head with one hand.

"Problem?"

Up close, Frings could see the stress lines between Reynolds's thick eyebrows.

"Yeah, you could say that. Seems to be some trouble across town at the strike. It sounds like the ASU moved in, and there's some street fighting. We're being called in."

The ASU was the Anti-Subversion Unit of the police department. While it technically reported to the Chief, it was a badly kept secret that it took orders directly from Red Henry, which was a constant source of tension within the force. Frings thought Reynolds didn't seem enthusiastic about going to the ASU's rescue. Then again, it might be the reefer.

"I'm coming with you," Frings said.

"Suit yourself."

CHAPTER NINETEEN

It was an hour before Puskis returned to his desk with the two books. The procedure was simple. He opened the two books to the alphabetical index; the one on the left listed defendants convicted in court, and the one on the right listed inmates in correctional facilities. Having found that DeGraffenreid, who should by rights have been in prison, wasn't, Puskis now wanted to see if anyone else shared this apparent good fortune. There were several.

He wrote their names down, eight in all — all convicted of murder, and none with records of incarceration. The names seemed familiar, but that was not surprising since everyone's file would have passed through his hands at least once. It was unusual for Puskis to come across names that did *not* trigger some sort of recognition, however vague.

He carried the books back to the Stable

and replaced them, then took out their counterparts for the following year, 1928. Back at his desk he made the same comparison as before and found twelve names. The last one he found was that of Otto Samuelson, who, convicted on July 18, had apparently never been incarcerated. He wrote down these twelve names, then returned to the Stable again, exchanging the 1928 volumes for the 1929 volumes.

The 1929 volumes, he discovered back at his desk, contained no cases of unincarcerated murderers. Still, to be sure that July 18, 1928, was the last of these incidences, he retrieved the 1930 volumes, but they too were in order. The next step would be to trace back to the first instance that he could find, but Puskis decided first to determine what it was, in reality, he was investigating. It was more than a clerical error, certainly, but that did not help him define the issue. In any case, he now had a list of twenty names, one of which — DeGraffenreid — he had already cross-referenced. Puskis took his cart and began to collect the other nineteen files.

The organizing principles for the files stored in the Vaults had been decided more than a half century previous and were the source of tremendous debate. Two methods of organizing information were common at the time. The first was chronological — simply storing the information according to the order in which it was received. The second was by name — generally alphabetized by last name and then first name. Either of these was, in principle, perfectly efficient for the retrieval of any particular file. The controversy sprang from the desire on the part of certain key decision makers — primarily Thorpe and Krause — to make the organization of the files information in and of itself. To put it another way, *the way* the files were stored would provide information for the people using them.

This involved a classifying system. The most basic category, it was generally agreed, would be the offense. Murders, for instance, would be grouped together, as would rapes, assaults, kidnappings, and so forth. These groups were themselves categorized by the nature of the crime (violent crime, property crime, etc.). Then came issues of conviction and acquittal. It hardly made sense, for example, to group innocent men accused of murder with actual murderers. So categories were further divided.

What other information might be useful? Taking murder again as an example, how was that murder committed? Using a hand-gun, or knife, or baseball bat? What was the motivation behind the crime? Jealousy, or money, or revenge? In what part of the City did the crime take place? What time of day? Was it a solitary crime or one in a series of offenses? And, as later became crucial, was it a crime related to the activities of a broader criminal organization, and if so, which one?

By categorizing the files in this manner, it was reasoned, individuals with similar criminal habits would be filed with each other. This would allow for easy analysis of similar crimes and an even greater ability to create lists of possible suspects based purely on modus operandi: Describe the crime, find the proper file category, and you produced not only a list, but the actual files themselves. The system was almost magical in its precision and utility, so long as someone thoroughly understood all of its mechanisms, exceptions, and nuances. Given the number of crimes and individual criminals in the City over the past seventy years or so, the system had grown so complicated that even a man with an advanced aptitude, such as Puskis, took literally years to understand it fully. The product of constant revision and addition according to the individual whims of the successive Archivists, it required at once a mathematical and an intuitive sense, along with an empathic understanding of the specific psychology of the previous Archivists. One had to think as his predecessors had to determine what their decisions would have been.

All this time and care and bother, and it had been invested for just such a moment as this.

Before collecting the files, Puskis consulted the *Master Index,* an annually produced volume listing, by last name of the perpetrator, the numbers for all the files generated in a given year. As intended, by merely listing the classification numbers of the files, he would be collecting provided information. To begin with, they were all C4000 series, the *C* designating a violent crime and the 4 designating murder. Further, they were all designated in the 500 category of the C4000 series, meaning that they were offenses that had the additional factor of organized crime. From this commonality the files diverged, but this information alone served as a valuable beginning point. Organized-crime-related murders up until July of 1928. Puskis was too distracted by

his investigative process to notice the significance of that date.

In retrospect, Puskis determined that whoever was doctoring the files had started
slowly, removing and replacing the file
contents so that unless someone actually
examined more than one of them, there
would be no evidence that they had been
tampered with. Then, according to Puskis's
guess, this person must have realized that
time was running short or been put under
some other type of pressure, because things
became sloppier. And this person must have
been working off much the same list and
sequence as Puskis was, because the sloppiness increased as he progressed from file to
file.

The first indication of tampering was a
file that had been pushed in too far, so that
the label was no longer fully visible. He
could conceivably have made this mistake,
though it would have surprised him. But
then more evidence: Files a slot or two out
of place were most common. Another had
been put in backward. Whoever had done
this seemed to have feared the consequences
related to the time pressure more than the
discovery of his work.

Puskis brought the files back to his desk,

already knowing that the information in them would be useless. He opened them in the reverse order in which he had retrieved them. They were dummies — the papers they contained identical: a trial transcript from a recent, wholly unrelated case; a photograph of a rat-faced man with bruises under both eyes, who Puskis felt quite sure was of no relevance. The paper stock itself was new, produced within the last two years and possibly inserted into the files as recently as the days he was on vacation.

Puskis sat back in his small leather chair and considered the different probabilities. How long ago could these files have been switched without his coming across them? The switch must have been recent, though he acknowledged this assessment could simply be clouded by vanity. Indeed, what were the chances that these switches were not related to the two DeGraffenreid files and Puskis's subsequent discovery of his freshly murdered corpse? Extremely unlikely. Which meant that, in response to Puskis's inquiries into DeGraffenreid, someone had not only murdered the man, but also removed a number of files that Puskis had to assume in some way related to him.

For the second time in the past twenty-four hours, Puskis realized that the vaguely uncomfortable feeling he was experiencing was fear. His phone rang. An observer would have noticed Puskis's subtle tensing in response to the sudden peal of noise as a minor response. Had they managed to peer into his close-set eyes, however, they would have registered the true depths of his terror.

CHAPTER TWENTY

Poole was back in the Hollows. It was overcast, but the clouds were high. The wide streets were empty and he picked up the scent of garbage rotting somewhere nearby. He parked in front and walked up twelve steps to the front door of the brick apartment building. The buildings were low in this part of town, he noticed — mostly warehouses and small apartment buildings — nothing over four or five stories. Three buttons were to the right of the door, with only numbers on the labels. He pushed the top one and heard the buzzer sound inside. When there was no answer, he pushed the middle button. Again he heard the ring and then footsteps, practically above him. He looked up to see the window above the door slide open, and a woman's enormous head appeared, looking down at him.

"No one's here," she said, the folds of her neck rippling.

"I'm looking for Casper Prosnicki."

The woman responded with a whistle. "I haven't heard anyone say that name in a long time. Must be nostalgia week. Hold on."

What did she mean by "nostalgia week"? Poole waited as the woman's footsteps progressed around the apartment, then she reappeared at the window. She had a key in her hand that she dropped straight down toward him. He pulled his hat off and caught the key with it.

Her apartment door was open, so he walked in, his hat in his hand. The kitchen reeked of mold and spoiled food. Thankfully, the light was dim and Poole held his breath until he was in a corridor that was merely stale with must. He heard labored breathing coming from the room ahead of him. Only at the threshold of the room did he get a full look at her, this enormous woman wearing a tent of a flowered housedress, her swollen, pale ankles visible below the hemline.

"Come on in, let's have a look at you," the woman said from her chair. The room stank of years of her. Sweat, smoke, urine, spoiled food, and he did not want to think what else. Poole stepped into the room now

135

and looked around. The walls were lined with shelves jammed with books. "Well, well, well. Another visitor. Polly's lucky week, this one."

"Someone else has been here?"

"Why don't you introduce yourself first, fella? Come and sit down." She motioned to an upholstered chair. Poole sat down in it without enthusiasm.

"My name's Poole."

"Hmmm. Poole. You got a first name Poole?" When she spoke, her neck did a funny quivering thing, and Poole found he could not pull his eyes away.

"Ethan. Ethan Poole."

"Mine's Polly. Pleased to make your acquaintance. So tell me, what brings you to my abode today, Mr. Ethan Poole?"

"Like I said, I'm trying to find a person by the name of Casper Prosnicki. I understand that he used to live in one of the flats here."

"Used to's right. Left about seven years back. Same as DeGraffenreid, come to think of it. Right about the same time."

Poole shifted in his seat, uncomfortable under her steady, intense stare. "Who's De-Graffenreid?"

"Another former tenant. Gink came by the other day asking about him. Reif De-

Graffenreid and the Prosnickis — at least Casper and his mom. Oh, Lord, *what* was her name?" She squinted her pig eyes in concentration, as if determined to snatch the name from memory.

"Lena."

"That's right," she said, sounding both pleased and surprised. "Lena. But I guess you would know that; she must've hired you. Must be terrible not knowing where your kid is. I can't fathom."

"She was very upset. Very upset. But, Polly, why was this person, you know, this gink, why was he looking for what's his name . . ."

"DeGraffenreid."

"Yes. Why was this person looking for De-Graffenreid?"

"Didn't say. He had two pictures, though. Wasn't sure which one was Mr. DeGraffenreid. So I told him."

"Do you remember his name?"

"Of course, I do, dear. I don't get visitors here every day, you know."

She was making him work for it. "What was his name, Polly?"

"Arthur Puskis. Funny little gink. Looked like he had just crawled out from the grave. Nervous, too, but official. He might have even been police. He just might have."

The name Puskis meant nothing to Poole. He got up from his chair and walked to the bookshelves to Polly's right. She had a lot of books, and scanning the titles, he was surprised to find that a number of them were in foreign languages. He recognized German, Spanish, and Russian. Other titles were in languages he could not identify. Italian maybe, and Portuguese. Several tomes were in Latin. The colors of the book jackets were muted by a layer of dust. He found a section of books with English titles. The Bible. The Torah. The Bhagavad Gita. The Koran. Translations of Cervantes, Dumas, de Sade.

Polly was watching him. "Are you a spiritual man, Mr. Poole?"

He was absently tracing a line through the dust on one of the shelves with his finger. "Not particularly, I guess."

She made a noise that seemed some kind of judgment.

"Do you have any idea where I might find Casper Prosnicki?"

"I would say with his mother, but, then, I doubt you would have come to me if she had him."

"What did the Prosnickis do?"

"For a living?"

Poole nodded. The dust and the heat and

the smell of the place were starting to give him a headache.

"What does *anyone* do for a living down in the Hollows, Mr. Poole? They did what they needed to do. He was a butcher." She said it as if it were of but marginal relevance to the question.

"But I take it he did other things."

"Everyone in the Hollows did other things. Everyone had an angle. You didn't make your scratch unless you were in the game."

"So what was Mr. Prosnicki's part of the game?"

She began to cough, sending ripples down her body. Finally she stopped and leaned over her chair slightly, spitting into a brass spittoon. "Are you paying attention to what I'm saying or are you just dim, Mr. Poole? I don't know any specifics. Nobody knows anyone else's exact business around here. That's what can get you hurt. Especially in the old days. Which, as a matter of fact, pretty much ended after the Prosnickis and Reif left. Pretty soon after that. Even now, you wouldn't want to stick your nose into anything, mind you. But you're not likely to get a visit in the middle of the night anymore, neither. I'll give the mayor credit for putting an end to the gangs. Now it's just hoods, and they aren't half as crazy."

Poole was beginning to realize that she could talk all day, but was not going to say anything. "So you don't really have any ideas, then, where I could find Casper?"

She smiled, lips pressed together, hiding her teeth. "I'm sorry, Mr. Poole. I would certainly love to help you."

Polly watched Poole emerge from the front door and go to his car. He stood on the running board to rub at a scratch on the roof, then got in. The car executed a U-turn, then glided back toward the center of the City. When it was out of sight, she reached over to the telephone on the end table to her left. Taking the stem in one hand and the earpiece in the other, she gave the operator the number she wanted.

"Yes?" The answer was immediate.

"It's Polly. I've got a message for the mayor. Tell him I've had another visit."

CHAPTER TWENTY-ONE

Feral had learned from the bouncer at the Prado that the previous night's performance would be Nora's last for at least a week. He spent the morning at the diner across the street from her building, washing dry toast down with muddy coffee. Earlier, he had scouted the two alleys that ran along either side of her building and the small, grassy park just behind. He spent several minutes from each vantage point, noting the placement of windows and fire escapes. A service entrance out back was locked. Feral spent a moment there, too, noting that the lock needed a key from either side, and slipping a piece of wax into the keyhole. Holding the end of the wax between two fingers, he heated the lock with a lighter. Then he let the wax cool and harden before slowly pulling it out and storing it in a tin cigarette box.

Sitting in the diner, he sketched each

angle of the building. His proportions were careful and accurate, even if the drawing was not exactly of draftsman quality. He then sketched a map of the three-block radius. The trouble, he realized, was that she was recognizable. It was easy to walk an anonymous person wherever you wanted to. With Nora, chances were good that someone they passed would recognize her and recall the small, dark man who accompanied her. He would have to find another way.

Feral was in the alley that bordered the west side of the building. The fire escape was on this side, the bottom twelve feet from the ground. He dragged two tall garbage bins to a spot beneath the fire escape to provide some visual cover from the street.

Feral pulled a laundry bag from a pocket of his trench coat. From it he removed twenty feet of thin rope. He took off his trench coat and hat and placed them in the laundry bag, which he then tossed up to the landing at the bottom of the fire escape. It took him three tries to throw the rope through the railing of the landing. He played the rope down until he had both ends, which he then tied into a knot. This was the most dangerous moment. He looked down the alley and watched pedestrians cross the opening without looking toward him. Anyone looking in then would have been astonished to watch the little man pull his way up the rope with the practiced ease of a spider navigating its web. On the landing, Feral pulled the rope around until he had the knot, which he quickly untied, then coiled and stuffed the rope in the bag with his coat and hat.

Nora's apartment, he knew, was on the sixth floor. He moved up the stairs nimbly, his soft-soled shoes barely making a sound. He was in a vulnerable position, easily visible to anyone who bothered to look from the street. But no one did. Feral knew that most people did not look at the upper floors if they happened to glance down an alley. They were usually looking for a person who might be a threat. That person would be on the ground, not fifty feet up.

He left the laundry bag two steps down from the sixth-floor landing. The window to the fire escape looked in on the living room. Feral lay on his back and pulled a cosmetic mirror from his pocket. Holding it up at a shallow angle, he used it to survey the living room from his supine position. It was empty.

He rolled to his knees and peered in. The living room, he thought, looked like the interior of a pastry, the walls a pale pink with snow-white trim, the furniture luxurious and pristinely white. Elegant paintings hung on the wall, too. Feral recognized a painting of a woman sewing lace — a Vermeer — and wondered if it was real. Sensing, rather than hearing, Nora coming into the room, he dropped back to his earlier position on his back. Carefully angling the mirror again, Feral watched her.

Nora was looking for a book on the low bookshelves. She wore a thin, yellow dress that held her form as she moved. The movements, as she found the book and walked to the couch, were familiar to Feral from the club. The length of her stride, the rhythm of her steps, the roll of her hips with each stride. He had watched these, studied them intensely from his table in the shadows at the back of the Prada.

Feral flashed back to the previous night and the moment of near intimacy that they had shared. Nora looking at him from the stage, their eyes briefly holding each other's. She knowing that he was not just another patron and he sensing her knowledge. It was brief. That was one thing he felt they shared — a heightened awareness of the motives and instincts of others. From that quick look could she possibly have gleaned what lay in store?

Now that she was sitting and absorbed in her reading, Feral got to his knees and looked in. Although he was plainly visible, he knew that she would not look up. He watched her as she read — placid and beautiful. She moved her lips, he noticed, ever so slightly, and he wondered, if he put his ear right up to them, whether he could hear the words she was reading.

A subtle change in her posture sent Feral again to his back. He held the mirror up and saw her rise from the couch and walk to the next room. He stood up and walked to the edge of the fire-escape landing. He sat on the railing and swung his legs over so that they dangled fifty feet above the alley. A narrow concrete ledge, perhaps two or three inches wide, delineated each floor on the building. Twenty feet in front of him was the wider ledge beneath a window. He twisted so that his stomach pressed against the railing and lowered himself to the level of the ledge. He grabbed the ledge with the fingers of his right hand, then swung his body and grabbed the ledge with his left hand as well. Hanging from his fingertips, he edged his way along until he was at the window ledge, then he pulled himself up so that his chin was even with the bottom of the window. It was her bedroom, he saw, and it was empty. He pulled himself up so that he was kneeling on the ledge. He shook the window slightly and determined that it was locked. He pressed his ear to the window, trying to hear movement inside. There was nothing. He thought that she was probably back on the couch, reading. He fished a thin file from his pocket, slid it up between the top and bottom window frames, and jimmied the lock.

Putting equal pressure on both sides of the window frame, he slowly pushed the window open. It made the slightest grinding sound, but nothing that would be heard in another room. When he had it two-thirds of the way open, he slid through headfirst. Once he was all the way in, he lay still for several seconds listening. Again, there was no sound. He got back to his feet and pulled the window slowly closed.

The enormous bed had a white canopy and thick, white blankets lying disheveled. He walked silently past and held his mirror in the door's threshold to get a look into the next room. She was on the couch, facing away from him. He couldn't see a book from his vantage point but assumed that she was still reading. The living room opened into a foyer to his right. He stepped into the living room. Nora was sitting with her back against one of the arms of the couch. Her blond hair was pulled up and he saw the graceful lines of her neck, pink with tiny blond hairs. She had a mole on the back of her neck, and this imperfection thrilled him.

He walked slowly, taking a step, then stopping for a beat before taking the next. His heart rate was down to under forty beats a minute. His breaths were deep and infrequent. He was silent. His concern was not that she would hear him but that she would sense him. Feral controlled every aspect of his presence that he could, but his body was ninety-eight degrees and it did displace air, and his movements did alter the flow of air in a room. A person could sense these things and he knew he was vulnerable. Yet he did not allow this knowledge to escalate to apprehension. Such was his calm that he paused briefly to steal a glance at what he realized now was a copy of a Vermeer, executed by a mediocre painter. The painting was poor — lacking grace. For a horrible moment he wondered if maybe she had painted it herself. But he dismissed this. It was not possible.

He came to the foyer now and she had not moved except twice to turn the page. On a mahogany table with legs carved to be lion's paws sat a gray ceramic bowl with three sets of three keys. Each set was identical, held by identical rings. With his thumb and middle finger he pulled one of the sets slowly from the bowl. The keys converged at the lowest point of the ring with a slight sound, and Feral froze, waiting for Nora's scream. But there was nothing. Once the keys were clear of the bowl, he carefully cupped them in his left hand and turned back to the living room.

Nora put her book down, and Feral flattened himself against the far wall, out of her line of vision. She swung her legs off the couch, stood up, and stretched, her hands reaching for the ceiling. Feral watched, transfixed, at the intimacy of the moment. He became aware that he had prepared himself for the likelihood that up close she would not live up to the image of perfection that she projected onstage. This had turned out to be wholly wrong. The only thing imperfect about her was the mole on her neck; like the imperfection that the ancient Greeks would leave in their crafts so as not to offend the gods.

She walked around the couch and to her left, out of sight. The kitchen, he assumed. This time he moved quickly, but no less silently. He crossed the room in six long strides and was at the window. He unlocked it with his thumb. From the kitchen he heard the sound of ice dropping into a glass. He slowly pushed the window up. It moved smoothly, as if it was often opened. He stepped through and pulled it back down again, then flattened out on his back with the mirror in the air. Within seconds she had reentered the room carrying a tall glass of what looked to be whiskey on the rocks.

CHAPTER TWENTY-TWO

Red Henry did not need to know the language to sense that the Poles were coming around. There were smiles now, and an atmosphere of fraternity. Anticipating an agreement, he had arranged for a contract-signing celebration in three days' time. He hated the events that always seemed to go along with these deals, but the foreigners loved them. It seemed to fulfill some idea they had about America, and if it helped at all, Henry was willing to grit his teeth and indulge them.

They were touring one of Block's factories. This one made stoves. They walked up and down aisles of assembly-line laborers, the Poles chatting with the interpreter and Henry smiling when it seemed appropriate but otherwise keeping to himself. His secretary, Peja, trailed behind, talking in hushed tones to some bureaucrat whose name Henry could not remember but whose breath was rancid with garlic. Every once in a while, for reasons that Henry could not glean, the Poles would want to stop and inspect some aspect of the stove assembly. They would murmur among themselves, and Henry would look to the translator without interest, and the translator would shrug as if to indicate that the conversation was not one Henry should worry about.

What Henry did worry about was the strike at Bernal's plant. He had debated in his mind the wisdom of bringing the Poles over to watch his police break it. He assumed that businessmen would appreciate a government that enforced their interests when necessary. But you could never tell with these goddamn Europeans. They could share your values but not your methods, or your methods but not your values, or both or neither. And who knew how things came across in translation? There was something indefinable about the translator Henry disliked, which was possibly a good sign, because Henry was generally sure about what, exactly, he didn't like about a person. Still, there was just no way of knowing how good he was. How *tactful*.

So they were at Block's. About as far away from Bernal's as he could get without looking as if he was trying to shield them from the strike. A thought came to him about how to pitch the strike to the press, and he turned to tell Peja, only to find, to his intense annoyance, that Peja was no longer there.

It was remarkable, he thought, how clean the cavernous factory was, yet, how dirty the workers. How could that be? One of the Poles, a squat man with a mustache that hung below his jawline, was looking at Henry expectantly. Henry turned to the translator.

"He wants to know if Block stoves are the best you can get in America."

Henry smiled through the idiocy of the question and, looking at the Pole, told the translator, "Tell him that the quality of American stoves is such that people debate which is the best. For myself, I prefer Block."

Henry listened to the translator spew a rush of Polish and, hearing the one word he expected to understand — "Block" — returned to his thoughts.

"Mayor?" It was Peja.

"What? Is the strike broken?"

"The strike? It, uh, it may be. But this is something different. Polly called on the special line."

Henry felt his stomach clench.

"She left a message. She said another gink came by today, asking about the Prosnickis. Specifically Casper Prosnicki, she said."

"Jesus Christ. Who the hell was it?"

"She said his name was Poole."

"Christ, Christ, Christ. Did you get in touch with Feral?" Henry's volume was rising.

"We're looking for him."

"Get me Smith."

"Smith's with the Anti-Subversion Unit out at Bernal's."

Enunciating each syllable carefully and distinctly, Henry said, "Get me goddamn Smith now."

Peja scurried away, leaving Henry to face the Poles, who were watching him with interest. He tried to smile benignly, but clearly the Poles weren't buying it.

CHAPTER TWENTY-THREE

The wind rarely came out of the northeast, but when it did, it sometimes bore the ash spewed from the plants across the river. On days when the atmospheric conditions were right, the ash would fall on the northeast corner of the City like gray and black snow. As they drove in the squad car to the headquarters of Bernal's Capitol Industries, Frings noticed the soot, initially falling lightly, but increasing in intensity as they progressed farther into the Hollows. It looked like a photographic negative image of a snowstorm, the snow darker than the ground it fell on. Was this odd because he was high or was it actually as strange as it seemed? The policemen did not seem to take much notice.

They parked at the end of the block, and Frings saw the chaos that the strike had become. The police seemed to be outnumbered nearly two to one by the picketers. In some parts of the block, in open fighting, picketers were swinging sticks that had held their ragged signs as the ASU retaliated with billy clubs. The gray-suited ASU were getting the better of it, and a couple of dozen of the strikers lay or knelt, stunned and bleeding. In other spots, picketers were lined up with their hands against the wall and their backs to the cops, who were systematically cuffing them and making them sit. All the while, ash fell, covering the sidewalks, cars, and the people themselves. Blood revealed itself as darker patches of ash on people's faces and the sidewalks beneath them. Frings, who lacked firsthand knowledge, imagined it looked like some wretched battlefield on the Western Front. *Somme in the City.*

He glanced at Reynolds, who seemed hesitant to enter the mêlée. "This seems a little extreme," Frings said.

"The ASU is that way," Reynolds said, motioning two uniforms toward the line of strikers waiting to be cuffed. Frings stood and watched for what seemed like several minutes, getting the description for the paper clear in his head. The ash was making breathing difficult.

Capitol Industries' headquarters was a nondescript six stories of concrete and brick. Frings could see the silhouettes of onlookers in the windows of the top floors. Bernal would be among them. That was where his scoop would be found. Not out here where the *Gazette* doubtless had another reporter, not to mention the *News* and the *Herald.*

He moved toward the front door, holding his press pass in front of him like a white flag. Little pockets of order were carved into the chaos where the ASU had strikers in cuffs or lying facedown on the ground. It was, in his intoxication, slightly unreal to Frings, and even a stray elbow that caught him in the mouth was not enough to jar him from his sense of wonder — like a child's in a fun house.

The front door was manned by two men in ASU uniforms, standing stiffly, their hands resting on their holstered pistols.

"Frings. With the *Gazette.*" He held his pass in the taller guard's face. The guard looked across Frings to his partner, who shrugged.

"All right," he said, and stepped aside to let Frings in. Frings went through the doors, then down two steps to the lobby, which was appointed with chrome and mirrors and a green-tiled floor. Beyond the empty reception desk was a bank of elevators. Only one operator was at his post. Frings guessed that employees had been removed from the lobby so they were not a temptation for the picketers.

"I have a meeting with Mr. Bernal."

The operator gave him a fatigued look and pulled back the gate and then the elevator door. Bernal's office was on the top floor, and the operator did not make small talk during the brief ride.

Off the elevator now, Frings faced a floor of empty oak desks that showed signs of recent use — stacks of papers, coffee mugs, telephones. Then he heard voices and followed the sound to find the office's occupants at the windows watching the fracas below. He recognized Bernal from pictures — fat and dark, with a thin, meticulous mustache over a small, weak mouth. Bernal was talking to a graying woman in hushed, yet intense tones. Other people at the windows strained to listen while keeping their eyes focused on the activity outside.

Frings ambled over to Bernal, getting close enough that Bernal looked up. "Yes?" Malice wasn't in his voice as much as annoyance. Frings understood, given the circumstances.

"Mr. Bernal, my name is Frings. I'm with the *Gazette.*"

Bernal colored momentarily, his mouth gaping to reveal little, yellowed teeth. And as quickly, the expression was gone.

"Mr. Bernal, I won't take much of your time. I just wanted to get your comments about the strike and today's police action."

Bernal was wary. "Yes. Of course. Why don't you come to my office and we can talk."

The woman was now staring out the window with the others, and Bernal led Frings to a corner office, encased in glass. When they were safely inside and seated, Bernal said, still smiling, "What are you doing here?"

This caught Frings a little off guard since it seemed the answer was obvious. This brief pause seemed to unnerve Bernal for some reason, and he kept talking. "You're here about the strike today, correct? The strike?" His expression was relaxed, even pleasant, but Frings would see sweat beading on his brow and glistening in his mustache.

"Yes, Mr. Bernal, the strike." Frings wondered why Bernal needed to clarify Frings's intent. Was there another story here, somewhere? "This is big news. Every paper will be covering it. I came up here to see if you wanted to give a statement. Pretty standard practice."

Frings saw the tension leave Bernal's posture, and it sent up flares inside him. Bernal started in on a statement about his company's policies regarding the resolution of strikes. Frings dutifully took notes, his mind working on the puzzle of Bernal's strange behavior. It was almost as if Bernal had been expecting a different . . . And then it made sense.

He interrupted Bernal midsentence. "You rang me the other day. We have a meeting —"

"Good Christ," said Bernal, coloring again.

"This is balled up."

Bernal nodded, running the fingers of his right hand back through his hair. He was keeping his face calm, but his eyes were wild.

"Listen," Frings said, "we just go through with the interview. Then we forget the other part that just happened."

"We don't meet tomorrow."

"Of course we do. Jesus. I interview people all the time. No way they trace anything back to this meeting."

"But . . . ," Bernal sputtered. It was hard to keep a smile while panicking.

"But nothing. Look, in a strange way this might actually work in our favor. Nobody'd ever think that I would be such a sap as to visit you in public if you were grassing. Might actually be the perfect cover."

Bernal considered this unhappily. "Okay. I see there is a point to what you say."

CHAPTER TWENTY-FOUR

Poole and Carla stood in the shadows of an alley looking out on the chaos of the same street that Frings and Bernal watched from above. A layer of gray ash collected on Poole's hat and the shoulders of his coat. Carla wore a scarf around her head and another covering her nose and mouth to filter the air. Poole had come here after his interview with Polly, expecting to have a quick lunch with Carla. Instead he had found her staying out of sight, watching as the strike she had organized was crushed by the police. They were both aware that the police here were mostly from the ASU and that the ASU took their orders from the mayor rather than the Chief. This, however, made matters worse if anything. The mayor was taking a personal interest.

"I can't leave," Carla said.

Poole could see only her eyes, but that was enough to tell him that she wouldn't be convinced otherwise.

"You have to. They're going to round your people up and toss them in jail. Someone needs to be outside, to get them out."

She understood the logic, but Poole could tell that she was reluctant to abandon her people. They had talked about this before, about her willingness to put herself in harm's way for the unions. "You have to have something you are willing to go over the top of a trench for." She had that something. Poole wasn't sure that he did.

"Don't be stubborn. They need you to be smart."

Two officers appeared at the mouth of the alley.

Shit. "Go," Poole whispered, and gave her a gentle push toward the opposite end of the alley. She ran, nimble, a good athlete. Poole stepped out to detain the officers, but they were not interested in Carla.

"Ethan Poole?" The officers had their sticks out. Poole nodded slightly, his eyes on their hands.

"Come with us, Mr. Poole. They want to talk to you at the precinct."

Poole felt his pulse quicken with panic. How dim could he be coming right to Bernal's front door? He had no doubts about what would happen to him at the precinct.

He raised his hands to shoulder height, showing his palms in acquiescence. The smaller of the two officers looked down at his belt, reaching for his handcuffs. With a boxer's quickness, Poole snapped a punch, shattering the other cop's nose. As the bleeding cop fell to his knees, his partner flicked his wrist, bringing the nightstick hard into Poole's side, cracking a rib. Poole pulled his left arm close to his body to cover the point of pain and grabbed the front of the officer's shirt with his right, pulling him forward and down to the ground. He kicked hard at the cop's stomach and heard him groan. Then Poole felt a sharp pain in his spine as the cop with the broken nose cracked him in the back with his stick. He felt consciousness ebb momentarily. Turning, he moved closer to Broken Nose to cut off his swinging radius and caught a forearm in the mouth. Tasting blood, he leaned back, then brought his forehead hard into the officer's damaged nose. The cop crumpled to the ground, unconscious. Poole turned now to the other cop, who was on his hands and knees. Poole reached down and grabbed the back of his shirt, then felt a sharp pain at the back of his head.

CHAPTER TWENTY-FIVE

Leather chairs and desks were scattered at five points in the Vaults. Puskis always sat at the desk facing the elevators, using it as a barrier between the files and anyone entering the Vaults. Not that anyone ever came down except for the courier from Headquarters, and he — or they, since there had been several of them during Puskis's tenure — never proceeded beyond the desk, where the files were dropped off and picked up.

The other four desks were placed in locations in the Vaults that, presumably, someone had thought would be convenient for some reason. One was more or less in the middle of the C section, where files on most homicides were kept. Another was in the Stable. The third was in the A section, where files on open investigations were kept. The final desk was in Q section, that eclectic mix of financial crimes, arson, and election fraud. Q section was the farthest from the elevators, probably the reason for the desk's placement there.

None of these chairs had, as far as Puskis knew (and nobody would have a better sense than he), ever been sat in. He had never used one, and his predecessor, Abramowitz, had claimed to have never used one. That accounted for four decades or so of the chairs sitting empty. Yet the cleaning crew was just as diligent about keeping the chairs and virgin desks spotless as they were the files, so they looked as if they could have been purchased yesterday.

In some ways, the moment that Puskis fully comprehended that he was entering into an unfamiliar and potentially hazardous endeavor was when he took the files in the C4571 series to the desk in the C section and sat down in the green leather chair, which hissed with escaping air as, for the first time, it encountered human weight.

The earlier phone call had been from the Chief's secretary, reminding him of the next morning's scheduled meeting. He had wanted to ask several questions, but he had merely assured her that he would be there and hung up. Then, because he had been more content during the years when the phone never rang, he pulled the cord from the phone.

The mystery surrounding the subject of this meeting with the Chief worked at the edges of his mind as he leafed through the files, the contents of which he knew by heart. His looking was merely a way to allow the information contained within to form into something more tangible and profound than his memories of things read at some points in the past.

The pictures, as upsetting as any of the thousands that he had seen, commanded the most attention. These matter-of-fact black-and-white documents chronicled the depths of human behavior. The bodies of men and women and, mostly, children, scattered among the tables at a small restaurant, blood pooling by each corpse. There was no question about their sleeping, Puskis reflected, because their bodies were in poses that clearly indicated fatal trauma. Other photographs showed the restaurant with the furniture now removed but the bodies undisturbed so that they looked as if they had been dropped out of the sky and come to rest, shattered, like baby birds. Close-ups showed the bodies and then the faces, many with their eyes open, staring without sight at the camera.

Looking at the head shots jarred something in Puskis' memory, and he stood up from the desk and hurried down the aisles between the shelves toward his desk. Once there, he unlocked the center drawer of his desk and removed a folder that he brought back to the desk in C section. He opened the folder, and inside were the two photos that had been in the two DeGraffenreid files. He took the one that he knew to be DeGraffenreid and put it aside. This left the photo of the spectral man with sunken cheeks and the sideburns and the odd stare. He put it among the head shots of the victims he had before him. In this context it was so obvious that Puskis might have felt foolish if he were prone to assessing himself in such a way. This man clearly belonged in the company of the subjects of these other photos. It was the face of a corpse. Ellis Prosnicki, he thought. DeGraffenreid's victim.

This realization did not seem to provide any particular insight other than that, if it was indeed Prosnicki, the person who had doctored the files had an agenda that Puskis ought to be able to deduce. It was a matter of ordering his thoughts correctly.

That evening, when he was ready to return to his apartment for the night, Puskis summoned the elevator. It arrived quickly, and Dawlish opened the door and stood in the threshold, waiting for Puskis to enter.

"Through for the day, sir?" Dawlish asked, as always.

"Mmm, yes, I suppose I am. Listen. Mr. Dawlish, I was wondering if I might ask you, well, yes, how should I say this? Mr. Dawlish, has anyone come down to the Vaults while I have been absent? Except for the courier of course. But anyone else? Anyone who you might have dropped off and left here for a period of time, perhaps?"

Dawlish stared at him miserably but did not speak.

"If you did, well, if you did drop someone off, I certainly would not blame you or consider you neglectful in your duties."

These conciliatory words seemed to have no effect on Dawlish, who continued to stare at Puskis.

Puskis produced a pen and proffered it to Dawlish. "If you would, Mr. Dawlish, would you return this pen to my desk the next time someone comes down here while I am absent? Other than the courier, of course."

Dawlish took the pen from Puskis's hand and dropped it into the inside pocket of his uniform jacket. He was uncharacteristically silent during the short ride to the lobby.

CHAPTER TWENTY-SIX

Panos's office reeked of sardines and his mustache glistened with oil. Crumbs littered the front of his wrinkled blue shirt, collar open, tie loose down to the second button. From some quality to his expression, something in the clear brown eyes, Frings knew things were afoot.

"What in the heaven happened to you?" Panos said, looking with distaste and amusement at Frings's ash-covered clothes.

"I was at the strike."

"I heard about that particular thing. You find the story there, ah?"

Panos played the idiot sometimes, usually when he was sitting on something big.

"I talked to Bernal. I think that's got everyone beat. Everything else you could get by watching from the street."

Panos smiled. "You took notes?"

"Of course."

"Give them to Klima. He was down there,

too. Doing what, that is what I don't know. He can write the story from that and use your notes, too." Panos focused his eyes carefully on Frings's face. Frings knew that Panos thought he was going to throw a fit for losing a story that big. But he was high enough that it didn't really seem to matter, and thinking about Panos waiting for him to get mad gave him a goofy grin that he couldn't suppress. Panos's eyes narrowed and he yelled to his secretary, "Woman, get me Klima."

While they waited for Klima to arrive, Panos pulled two cigars out of his desk. Panos smoked a lot of cigars, but rarely offered one of his prized Cubans. It was a sign that he was in a particularly good mood. Frings watched as Panos sliced one end off each cigar, then made a thinner slice at the opposite end with a mock guillotine that sat on his desk. Frings had heard a story that Panos had used the guillotine on the pinkie of a guy named Cantor for reasons that were unclear. Frings had run into Cantor and had noticed a missing pinkie, but didn't get confirmation on how he had come to lose it.

Panos leaned back in his chair, sucking on his cigar, then letting the smoke rise out of his mouth as if he were some sort of overfed

170

dragon. Frings watched this, slightly dazed from the cigar on top of the reefer. Klima came in, looking frail and bald in a too big suit and food-stained tie. He had done his best to wipe off the ash from the strike, but he was still a mess.

"Qué pasa?" he asked Panos.

"While you were down watching the blues giving those strikers the what-for, Frings was actually doing some reporting."

Klima turned to Frings with his mangy eyebrows raised. The bottom of his jaw was red with irritation from shaving; dark, puffy bags drooped beneath his eyes. Frings wondered, as he handed his notebook over, if Klima had some kind of chronic disease.

"That is Frings's notebook with his notes from his interview with Bernal," Panos continued.

"From today?"

"Yes, from today. Listen, it is today your lucky day. You will use Frings's interview in your story on the strike. You think you can do that?"

Klima nodded, confused not by what he was being asked to do, but rather by why he was being asked to do it. He looked questioningly at Frings, then was assailed by Panos.

"What do you wait for? For the heaven's

sake, beat it and write your story. My God." Panos gestured with his cigar for Klima to leave, and he did with one last glance at Frings, who shrugged with exaggerated helplessness.

With Klima gone, Panos smiled a crooked smile, and a thread of smoke escaped from the corner of his mouth. "You wonder what it is that I have for you."

Frings nodded.

Panos opened the top drawer on his desk, removed an envelope, and tossed it across the desk to Frings. It took a chaotic turn in midair, and Frings missed it. He had to get out of his chair to pick it up from the floor. The envelope was addressed to Francis Frings — the name he used in his byline — with the *Gazette* as the address. No street address, city, or state. It had a canceled stamp, though, so it had come through the mail. It had been opened.

"You guys opening my mail now?" he asked half-seriously.

"Only when it's interesting." Frings couldn't tell what Panos meant by that or if he was kidding. "Read it."

Frings opened it. On a sheet of plain white paper a short message had been written in pencil.

FRANCIS FRINGS. WE ARE THE BOM-
BRS. WE WANT TALK TO YOU. BE ON
THE TRAKS BETWEEN KOPERNIK &
STANISLAUS, 11 AT NITE, FRIDAY. YOU
NO IT IS US CAUS WE BOMBD BLOCK'S
HOUSE.

Frings looked at Panos and shrugged. "It
could be anyone."

Panos shook his head.

"It's a crank."

"Postmark, Frank."

Frings examined the envelope. It was
postmarked two days ago, before the bomb
at Block's house. Frings took in a breath.
Panos smiled. "You see now why I am in
such a mood that I give you one of my fin-
est cigars?"

Frings nodded, running through the implications of this letter. For instance, why him?

"Hey," Panos said sharply. "You smoking
that reefer again?"

Frings shrugged. "I get these headaches."

"I tell you that I don't want you to smoke
that reefer anymore."

Frings laughed. "If you want to fire me,
Panos, go ahead. I'm sure the *Trib* would be
interested in the letter."

Panos laughed, coughing plumes of

smoke. "You are a funny man, Frank. You got a funny sense of humor."

CHAPTER TWENTY-SEVEN

Poole sat on a bunk in the cell, crowded with a sweating, ashen mob of union men. He had his elbows on his knees and his hands supported the weight of his head. His cellmates gave him some room because they knew that he was with Carla and that he was in pain. He rubbed the back of his head and felt a knot the size of a lime. His hair was prickly with dried blood. He focused to fight back nausea from the heat and the stink of the cell. Two men next to him were talking in a language he could not identify. He heard the sound of metal scraping on metal and a low squeak as the door to the cellblock was opened, causing a momentary wane in the noise. A sudden increase followed as the jailed men began yelling at the guards in their native languages.

Poole listened to the footsteps advance down the hall, then stop at the door of his cell. He kept his head down.

"Everyone away from the door."

From the corner of his eye Poole saw the dozen or so other men in his cell retreat from the door and stand with menacing postures at the cell's perimeter. He heard the sound of the key being fitted to the lock and then the slip of the bolt.

"Poole."

Poole's pulse quickened and blood ran to his face. He did not look up.

"Poole." This time it was more insistent. Poole looked up to see three men, dressed in the distinctive gray uniforms of the Anti-Subversion Unit, their batons out. The one in front was shorter, older, built like a razorback. The two behind him were bookend Atlases.

"Time to answer some questions. Get up."

Poole rose from the bed, and the effort cost him his sense of balance for a moment and he hesitated before shuffling slowly toward the door. His cellmates had been watching with barely controlled agitation. When one yelled out something in Portuguese, it sparked the rest of them. The cellmates shouted and pointed and shook fists, but stayed at the perimeter of the cell. The two bigger men stepped forward with their batons drawn, their expressions set, their body language showing fear.

Poole walked past the two officers. The older ASU agent stepped aside to let Poole out the door. The other officers backed out of the cell, and the older man shut the cell door and locked it. Poole was cuffed while the other two men watched with nightsticks at the ready in case Poole made a false move. Poole was slightly bigger than the officers and guessed that he could take any one of them in a fair fight. But not all of them and not now.

They left him to wait in an interrogation room. He sat in a steel chair that was bolted to the floor at a steel table that was also bolted. A single, naked lightbulb burned behind a mesh cage. The floors were gray concrete and the walls painted industrial white. Poole thought he could make out faint stains on the walls and had visions of janitors, on their knees, scrubbing off spattered blood with cleaning solution.

Head pounding, he leaned forward and rested it awkwardly on the tabletop. It was not comfortable, but he nevertheless managed to fall asleep — or was it lose consciousness? — in this position. He knew this because he awoke to someone pulling his head up a couple of inches by the hair and then, without too much force, pushing his face down onto the steel table. His eyes watered and his nose went numb. A hand jerked his head back and then planted itself in his chest to keep him upright. Poole felt warm liquid flowing across his mouth and down his chin. He tasted blood.

"Mr. Poole," said a man who now came into focus, leaning against the wall on the opposite side of the table. Tall and thin, he had the smooth face of a matinee idol and short blond hair. Poole couldn't figure why he wasn't wearing a uniform. He had a charcoal suit with dark blue pinstripes. His hat sat on a chair by the door. He held a cigarette carelessly between his ring and middle fingers.

The man sighed, then repeated, "Mr. Poole," as if to make sure that he was, indeed, talking to the right man. Poole started to nod, felt a wave of pain, winced, then grunted something affirmative.

"Mr. Poole, you are getting yourself into a world of shit. You sent two officers of the law to the hospital. Do you follow?"

Poole looked at the man without expression, trying to keep his eyes focused. How could they have found out about Bernal so quickly? Had Bernal really been able to identify him through the stocking? He felt a dull yet excruciating pain in his side as the man behind him jabbed his baton just below

Poole's ribs. He coughed meekly, then nodded.

"Two in the hospital," the man repeated slowly as if only now realizing the significance of this fact. "That is a world of shit to be in, Mr. Poole. Usually, police don't treat ginks who have assaulted police — put them in the hospital — with the delicate care that you have received. You with me?"

Poole choked out a "Yes" to avoid another shot from the nightstick.

The man smiled. "I'm sure you are. Yes, you're probably aware of that." If the man gave a signal, Poole didn't see it. The nightstick was not jabbed this time, but swung so that it hit the third vertebra down from his skull. He felt consciousness slip away and then, to his intense frustration, return.

"But, you see, this thing with assaulting the police, that's not even remotely the beginning of the shit you are in. *Do* you understand what the problem is, Mr. Poole?"

Poole stayed silent and braced himself for another blow.

The man took a deep drag on his cigarette, held it for a beat, then exhaled through his nose, sending twin jets of smoke past his mouth. "Why are you looking for Casper

Prosnicki?"

Poole just stared at him, stunned. Was that what this was about? How could this man know? Only one possibility came to him, and he wondered if he was thinking clearly through the pain.

"Can you hear me?" the man asked, stepping away from the wall and squatting down to look at Poole from across the table. "Why are you looking for Casper Prosnicki?"

"Someone asked me to. They hired me." His lips felt swollen and clumsy as he talked.

"Who hired you?"

"A twist. Didn't give a name."

The man straightened up and walked around the table behind Poole. Poole tried to crane his neck around to see what the man was doing, but the man with the nightstick held his head firmly in place. Poole felt his sleeve being pulled up and then a searing pain on the inside of his biceps as it was burned with a cigarette tip. Cold sweat beaded on his face as Poole bit through his lower lip and blood flowed into his mouth. The pain was relieved only somewhat by the removal of the butt.

The man walked slowly back to his previous spot across the table and squatted down again. "Who hired you?"

"Her name was Lena Prosnicki."

The man's eyes narrowed. "That's not possible."

"She said her name was Lena Prosnicki," Poole said, weary with fear and pain.

The man closed his eyes and made a subtle motion with his head. Poole felt his hair being pulled taut.

CHAPTER TWENTY-EIGHT

Puskis poured his tea slowly, careful to prevent any leaves from flowing into the cup. The air in his apartment smelled of tea, mint, and orange rind. He walked carefully from the kitchen into his sitting room, holding the cup by the handle with one hand and the saucer beneath with the other.

He sat, surrounded by hanging rugs. Their colors — reds, oranges, yellows, browns — though muted, retained some of their former brilliance. Their geometric patterns were framed by lighter borders with abstracted scenes from the Serbian past: the Battle of Kosovo, the overthrow of the Ottoman Turks. They were as much a history text as any of the tomes on his bookshelf.

Tonight he was not going to read. Nor was he going to contemplate the rugs, an activity that he often spent hours doing, reflecting on this abstract method of marking the past — a stark contrast to his rational practice. Even the geometric patterns, he felt, contained historical information. He had at times agonized over them, trying to divine their meaning, without progress. But he had his eyes closed tonight, turning his thoughts to 1929 and the Birthday Party Massacre and the furor that had followed.

Puskis was usually isolated from the occasional bustle of police activity following a high-profile crime. But even in the Vaults the repercussions of the Birthday Party Massacre were felt, the first sign being a stack of file requests, all with the notation *EU* for "extremely urgent." EU requests were not made lightly, and eighty-six at once was, in Puskis's considerable experience, unprecedented.

The second sign had been the phone call from Mavrides — the Chief's assistant at the time — who had never called the Vaults before. The strain in his voice evident, he'd checked to see how the file requests were coming. They were coming along fine. They always came along fine. The only thing preventing Puskis from continuing to fulfill requests was the phone call. Puskis hadn't said this, of course. He had said that they were coming along well and that he was moving with the greatest haste. Mavrides had said, "Good, good," without actually seeming mollified.

If there had been any doubt — written requests and a voice on the phone were not fully reliable indicators — the appearance of the pale, exhausted courier (Puskis could not now recall the name, though he felt sure it was Polish) confirmed his suspicions that something big was happening. Puskis found his condition surprising, as couriers did not generally encounter much stress. If the courier was in this state, the rest of the department must be under siege.

"What has happened?" Puskis asked. He had discerned certain things from the files that were requested. Organized crime. Crimes at restaurants. Shotgun murders. Child murders. The sum of these factors was not pleasant, but enough to cause this type of commotion?

"A, uh, mass homicide. At a restaurant." The courier's voice had been faint. He had seemed an apparition. Puskis felt that if he closed his eyes, the courier would be gone when he opened them again.

"There were children killed?"

"A lot of children. Gunmen walked in on a birthday party and killed everyone. Children, women, and the men, of course. The mayor wants this taken care of immediately. No one on the force is getting a break until this one's solved."

"Who were the victims?"

"Members of the Bristol Gang. Gunmen and their families."

This made the problem clear. Puskis and the courier stared at each other briefly, knowing that there would be no peace until the culprits were found. The courier left and Puskis busied himself gathering the next stack of file requests.

The obvious suspects were members of the rival gang, the Whites. The Whites and the Bristols had, for many years, engaged in a brutal struggle to control certain parts of the City, but especially the Hollows, where the warehouses offered myriad entrepreneurial, if not quite legal, opportunities. The death toll, Puskis remembered, had been alarmingly high in the decade or so leading up to the Birthday Party Massacre. High enough that Puskis at times wondered who could be left in these gangs when you subtracted both those who were killed and those in jail for the killings. But they continued on — until June 11, 1929.

That incident was so barbaric and so unnecessary that the newly elected Red Henry felt compelled to do what previous mayors had not — end the gang war once and for all. If the Whites had thought that this show of brutality would intimidate, they had sorely miscalculated. Photographs of the corpses of young children ran above the fold of the two major dailies for days. Socially minded reporters and editors called for drastic action from City Hall. Puskis remembered a reporter named Frings being particularly vehement in his demand for steps to be taken. This same Frings would later be the loudest voice in condemning the mayor when he put an end to the Whites for good through the efforts of a previously dormant division of the police force known as the Anti-Subversion Unit.

As with everything that happened in the City, Puskis had learned about the crackdown partially from the newspapers but mostly from the stream of files that came in and went out of the Vaults. This was the first time, too, that files began to return with material removed rather than added. At least it was the first time that he noticed this happening, and he felt sure that no previous doctoring of the files would have escaped his attention.

The first time he noticed one of these files was less than a week after the massacre. The file for a White-family lieutenant named Trevor "Vampire" Reid came back light. He had been dubbed Vampire because he was sucking the lifeblood from businesses on the south end of the Hollows. Reid had liked the name so much that he had filed his front four upper teeth into points. He displayed these teeth proudly in the mug shot in his file. The photo was still in the file, but most of the appendix to the trial transcript had been removed. Only the first page of the appendix, which included the end of the actual trial transcript, remained. The appendix text on the bottom half of the sheet had been blacked out with ink. Angered by this breach of protocol, Puskis took a blank sheet of paper, placed it over the blacked-out text, and rubbed lightly with a soft-lead pencil that picked up the depressions made by the typewriter keys. The result was what appeared to be the beginning of a list of names. Puskis recognized them as other hoods in the White family and disposed of the paper so as not to arouse suspicion.

While thinking of the men whose names he had coaxed from the paper — Teddy "the Leper" Smithson, Otto Samuelson, Fat Johnny Acton, and Sam "Blood Whiskers" McAdam, among others — Puskis fell into a deep sleep in his chair, head back and mouth open to the ceiling.

CHAPTER TWENTY-NINE

As instructed, Frings arrived at the river-bank first. It was cold, the breeze blowing from the north. Frings decided that smoking the hand-rolled juju he had in the breast pocket of his coat would help. So he leaned against a thick timber that had at one time served as a post for a jetty and with his collar up and hat down inhaled the sweet, moist smoke and felt the cold become a more-interesting-than-uncomfortable sensation on his skin. In the darkness, he closed his eyes and listened to the lap of the water against the river bank.

As he waited for Bernal, he thought about Nora and what it would be like without her. It was useless trying to think of specifics while high, but it was interesting to think about what it would feel like if he did not have her to go back to that night — or any night. It was a strange exercise and he was thinking about the difference between not having somebody in general and not having her in particular when he heard footsteps on the hill above him. Frings strained to hear other sets of footsteps above the low noise of the breeze, but without result. Bernal, as promised, seemed to be alone.

Frings watched Bernal's cumbersome figure, silhouetted by the City's lights, make its way down the slope. At one point Bernal put a hand down for balance and then righted himself. When he finally reached the bottom, his breathing was heavy.

"Frings?" Bernal's voice was strained; maybe from exertion, maybe from nerves.

"That's right."

"Christ, it's cold tonight."

Frings didn't know what to say to this. Bernal fumbled in his coat pocket for something and produced a silver cigarette case at the moment Frings realized he could very well be pulling a gun. Bernal held the case open to Frings, who took a cigarette, then Bernal lit both. The flame illuminated Bernal's face, and even in the orange glow it was pale and perspiring. The authority that he had emanated that afternoon was gone, his hunched body enough for Frings to know he was terrified.

A minute passed in silence, then another. Bernal did not seem ready to begin the

189

conversation, and Frings knew enough not to force the issue. Finally, Bernal coughed into a gloved fist and Frings took that as a cue.

"What are we here to talk about?"

"Corruption in the mayor's office."

Frings barked a laugh despite himself. "Thanks for the tip."

"You don't understand," Bernal said wearily, "this is different."

Everybody always thought that his information was different, and Frings's experience was that it rarely was. Still, Bernal was taking a big risk being here. "I'm listening."

Bernal sighed. "Not tonight."

If he had not been high, Frings would have been angry. But in his current state it merely seemed odd that Bernal would take this risk in order to tell him nothing. "Why are we here then?"

"I do want to tell you things. If all goes well, I'll tell you more later. But I need to know that I can talk to you. That you're safe. For me to be sure, you're going to have to find the information on your own. I'll point you in the right direction, but you've got to find it for yourself. I can help you understand it once you've found it. This way, there is no trail back to me."

"Okay."

"First, so I know I can trust you and you're as capable as I believe you are, I'll point you towards a story. You find it, come back to me, and then we move forward."

"Why should I take the time?" Frings asked, surveying the silhouette of the hill above them, but finding no observers.

"Because this is worse than you think. You don't know what has happened — what is happening. The Birthday Party Massacre, the move on the Whites, the Navajo Project, hospitals that are really prisons, the disappearance of whole families. These are all of a whole." Bernal spoke quietly but with an intensity that startled Frings.

"I don't know what —"

"You're right. You're right. You don't know. Nobody knows. That's why I've come to you. You can expose the truth."

It was all melodramatic, but Frings could see that this was Bernal's personality. "Okay. What do you want me to do?"

"Otto Samuelson. Does that name mean anything to you?"

"No."

"This I'll tell you. He murdered someone in 1928. Find him, talk to him, and then come back to me. I'll be expecting a piece of information. You have it for me, we'll begin to dig further."

"Okay. I find Otto Samuelson, get his story, then what, I contact you?"

"In your column, I'll look for the words *golden age.* When I see those words, I'll meet you here the next night at this same time."

Frings nodded. He'd received this request — a code phrase in his column — from others in the past. It seemed overly complicated. He did not want to scare Bernal off, however, so he acquiesced. With the meeting over, he extended his hand. Bernal looked at it, then at Frings. Frings thought he saw a sad smile on Bernal's face.

"Why are you doing this?" Frings asked.

"Because there will be trouble when the mayor's arrangements fall apart, and I want to know when that will happen, as it must. I don't want to die, Mr. Frings, and people will die before this ends."

CHAPTER THIRTY

A uniformed officer met Puskis just inside the front door of Headquarters and escorted him down a flight of stairs into the basement. Puskis was aware of officers glancing at him as he walked by. He had not experienced this before, though he attributed it to his heightened awareness rather than any increased interest in him. He was noticing things that he had not previously. That night he had been disturbed by footsteps on the stairs outside his door. Again he had felt fear. He was becoming accustomed to it. The footsteps had continued up to the next floor, and a door had opened as the man who lived directly above him received a guest. Puskis had awoken in the night to the sound of footsteps, trying desperately in the haze of half-sleep to identify the location of the steps. As before, they came from the apartment directly above him. Footsteps in the hall, his upstairs neighbor walking in his apartment — events that had surely occurred in the past, but which he had not noticed.

Puskis followed the officer down a long, well-lit hallway and through a set of double doors into an auditorium. A wooden stage ran along the far wall, and before it several men in suits congregated, talking to the Chief. A curtain was drawn across the stage, and Puskis detected the odors of steel and oil — the smell of machinery.

His entrance broke up whatever conversation the men were having and the Chief strode over, grinning.

"Welcome, Mr. Puskis," he said, extending his hand.

"I trust that I am not too late."

"Not at all, not at all. Very punctual."

Puskis was relieved to hear this as he was truly concerned that he might be late, what with the men waiting on him. Tardiness was an affront to order.

The Chief walked him over to the group of men and introduced each. Puskis, dazed by the blur of activity, shook hands solemnly with each man and in doing so missed their names. The last man introduced seemed the key member of the group, and Puskis did remember his name — Ricks. Ricks, like the others, was dressed in a dark, expensive suit. He was short and slight, almost like a child. His face was pinched, left eye pointed sightlessly up and to the left.

"Mr. Ricks has come up with something that is going to make your life much, much easier," the Chief said with a bit too much enthusiasm. "We know how you love the new technologies." He was looking sharp, Puskis noted, his normally disheveled uniform nicely pressed and his shoes recently polished.

"We are very excited about the potential." Ricks spoke quickly in a high-pitched lisp. "We are, and the mayor is as well. Very excited."

Puskis looked at Ricks in confusion. "I'm sorry, Mr. Ricks, I'm afraid I don't know what you are, what you are speaking of."

"No. No, of course not. It's been kept under wraps you see. Until now. Now it is being unveiled, so to speak, to you, Mr. Puskis — the inspiration and greatest beneficiary, if that is the word, of this new machine. I have admired your work, Mr. Puskis, from afar. Yes, I have admired it greatly."

Puskis simply stared at the little man, processing certain words that seemed to have greater importance — *unveiled, inspiration, machine, admired.* None of it made the slightest bit of sense, and Puskis became anxious to see what lay behind the curtain not out of curiosity, but out of a desire to bring to an end this sense of disorientation.

The Chief looked at Ricks, who gave a little nod. The Chief yelled, "Okay," over his shoulder, and the curtain parted with surprising speed. Now revealed was a large machine that Puskis had not previously seen. Two huge spools of what appeared to be paper had numbers printed at various intervals. Each spool contained roughly half the paper, and a portion spanned the six or so feet in between the two spools. By the spool on the right was a box with a grid of buttons, not unlike a typewriter, but with close to ten times as many keys. The spools were about six feet high and the paper about the height of four sheets of regular paper laid from end to end.

Puskis was aware that people were looking at him, gauging his reaction. He looked helplessly at the Chief, who in turn looked toward Ricks.

Ricks cleared his throat and said, "It's called a Retrievorator," as if that explained anything.

"I see," replied Puskis, who unaccountably felt his spirits sinking.

"Well, I don't think you do quite yet, actually. Not yet. Please, come on up to the stage with me and we'll take a closer look so you can see for yourself exactly what this thing can do. Up close."

Ricks walked to the side of the stage where there were stairs, and Puskis followed him with the Chief bringing up the rear. The other men stayed below the stage and talked in hushed voices while watching the action above.

Ricks led Puskis to the box by the right-hand spool. Up close, Puskis could see that what had at first appeared to be paper was actually something much stronger, something thin and, he thought, composed of some sort of metal. The numbers he had seen from below were actually somewhat raised from the rest of the surface. On the edge of each sheet was a collection of seemingly random holes. Puskis tried to determine a pattern, but only five sets of these holes were visible, which was not enough to allow analysis. Ricks waited for Puskis to get a good look before speaking.

"Come here to the codeboard. I want you to see how this machine works."

Puskis walked over to the codeboard box and saw that it was composed of vertical lines of keys marked as either letters or numbers. They were arranged so that the initial column was letters, followed by four columns of numbers, followed by two of letters, then five of numbers. It was, Puskis realized with alarm — though not surprise — the pattern used for the files in the Vaults.

Ricks was talking again. "We just put together a demonstration, so this clearly doesn't hold even one percent of the amount of information that the Vaults contains, but it does show you how it works. I think you'll find it quite intriguing. What I want you to do is put in a theoretical file number in the A1000 series. What you do is depress one key from each column so that you end up with a file number. So just make one up and you'll see what happens."

Puskis approached the codeboard tentatively.

"Start off by pushing the *A* in the first column and then the 1 and the 0 and so on," Ricks said.

Puskis depressed the *A* with his index finger; there was a click and the key remained depressed. He then pushed the 1 key in the next column, resulting in a similar click. He continued on until he had depressed the buttons A1000CR21027. When he was done, he looked up at Ricks, who was bouncing up and down on his toes. The

Chief stood behind him, smiling benevolently.

"Now pull the switch," Ricks said.

A switch, perhaps six inches long, was to the right of the columns of buttons. Puskis pulled it down, then jumped back as the machine began to hum and the spools began to spin, pulling the sheets too fast for Puskis to follow what was happening. It took less than a minute of the spools revolving and Ricks bouncing and the men below the stage watching in anticipation. Without warning, the spooling stopped, followed by a whining noise coming from a tall, rectangular box behind the right spool. Four sheets of paper dropped into a collection box just below the codeboard. Ricks picked up the pages and showed them to Puskis. On each was printed A1000CR21027, the code that he had punched into the codeboard.

Puskis looked at Ricks, then at the Chief.

"You're wondering how it works," Ricks said, though Puskis wasn't actually wondering about that at all. "Come over here and look at this. It's fairly simple, but it's what makes the whole system work." Puskis noticed that Ricks was profusely sweating from his forehead and temples. He wondered how important it was to the Chief for him to be impressed.

Ricks beckoned Puskis to the area between the spools where five sheets stretched across the gap. "Look here," Ricks said, and indicated an area with a pattern of small holes, barely bigger than pinpricks. "This is it. This holds the code and allows the machine to find the correct records."

Puskis brushed the tips of his fingers lightly over the holes.

"When you punch in the code, it pushes forward steel pins in a specific sequence. The spools spin until the pins all fit into the holes in a sheet. That will be the desired record. Each record has a unique pattern of holes that correspond to the filing system at the Vaults. Or, I should say, *will* have. But not too far in the future. Not as far as one might think."

"You are going to put the files in the Vaults on this machine?" Puskis asked, talking slowly and precisely.

"Yes, well, no. Actually, let me show you the other side. Actually, you can't really see it, so let me tell you how it works. See how the type on these sheets is raised? When the correct record is found, the sheets are heated and then pressed against paper that's treated to turn black where it's touched by the heated surface. It comes out looking like type on a page. Like the pages that you have in your hand."

"But how, let me see, how does it work with a normal sheet of paper?"

"It can't," said Ricks cheerily. "It needs to be on this special metal. All the information in the Vaults is going to be transferred onto these sheets."

Heart racing, Puskis looked over at the Chief. The Chief smiled.

"We have fifty machines for typing on these sheets. We'll have one hundred and fifty people working in three shifts around the clock. We think it will take two or three years to transcribe all the documents."

Puskis closed his eyes. My God, he thought, they're trying to destroy the evidence.

CHAPTER THIRTY-ONE

Nora's head rested on the flesh between Frings's shoulder and his sternum. He gazed down at her tangled blond hair and the smooth back beneath it, rising and falling with each breath. They had made love in semiconsciousness, and she had fallen asleep afterward, and now he was hopelessly awake and wondering how to get out of bed without disturbing her.

The previous night was a reminder of how things had been at the beginning for them. He had returned from his meeting with Bernal to find her asleep on the couch, an open book spine-up on her stomach. She had listened with great interest as he told her about the meeting with Bernal and the impending meeting with the bombers. He watched her face, more beautiful without the makeup, brightening with excitement from the stories. This was the essence of their relationship in its best sense. She, entranced by the intrigue of his work. He, entranced simply by her — her beauty, her aura, the confidence she had as a star.

This morning he lay still, breathing shallowly so as not to disturb her, and wondered what it all meant. Was this the end of a period of discontent in a continuing relationship, or a brief instant where everything was as good as it could possibly be as their attachment eroded? He thought about the reefer in his coat pocket and the appeal of banishing these thoughts with the pleasant haze. He inched slowly away from her, eventually cupping her head in his hand and letting it down gently onto the pillow. She muttered something without actually gaining consciousness, and her regular breathing resumed. Frings rolled out of bed and walked naked to the kitchen to boil water for coffee.

He had finished a full pot by the time Nora came out to the kitchen. She was wearing a lavender silk gown and came over to kiss him at the table with half-shut eyes.

"That was nice last night," she said, her lips close to his ear.

Frings nodded, and something in his manner made Nora straighten up. "Is something wrong?"

Frings looked up at her. "Don't you keep your bedroom window locked?"

She nodded, her lips pursed in uncertainty.

"Because it wasn't locked this morning."

"That's queer," she said. "I haven't opened it in ages."

"I crack it sometimes."

"To smoke."

"To smoke. But I am absolutely conscientious about relocking it."

"How can you —"

"I am conscientious about it because of who you are," he said with a seriousness that made her pause. "It's not locked now. Why isn't it?"

"I . . ."

"Someone unlocked that window, Nora. It wasn't me. It wasn't you. Has anyone else been in here?"

"Oh, shit, is this some jealousy thing? Because, you know, if that's an issue, then —"

"Of course not. Like you said, it's queer. You have to be inside to unlock it, and if neither of us unlocked it, that means somebody else has been in here."

"I think you're getting all balled up over nothing," she said. "Maybe it was Clarice." The cleaning woman.

Frings hadn't considered this possibility and it calmed him. The reefer was getting to him, he thought. He pulled her to him, his right hand bunched in her hair. They stood that way in silence, and Frings was overwhelmed with the feeling that this might be the last time.

CHAPTER THIRTY-TWO

Puskis was in the men's bathroom at Headquarters. He cupped his hands under the tap and doused his face with the cold, amber water. The drops that stuck to his lips tasted like rust. His hat rested on the sink next to him, and he ran his wet hands through his thin hair, plastering it back against his skull. His skin was stretched tightly over his cheekbones, nearly translucent except for the darkness under his clear, focused eyes. He locked gazes with his reflection in the mirror, staring himself down — finding that a focal point helped him slow the thoughts that were threatening to overwhelm him.

The final fifteen minutes of the Retrievorator demonstration were lost on him. He knew what was happening, and no further explanation was necessary. They were going to take the records in the Vaults and would, by transferring them to the sheets that were used by that odd machine, thoroughly cleanse whatever information they felt was so threatening. The actual sheets of paper would be lost, with the commentary in the different colors of ink, the telltale traces of files that had frequently been handled — the dog-ears, the coffee stains, the unintentional marks with pen or pencil — and the pristine condition of those that had been all but forgotten. These were pieces of information that at times were nearly as valuable as the actual contents of the files. They would be lost forever. Worse, Puskis could see nothing that would prevent files from being falsified without any possibility of detection. Puskis had asked Ricks what would happen with the files once they were typed onto the new sheets, and Ricks had looked at the Chief, who had shifted uncomfortably then mumbled that they would be burned. The Chief said there would be no need for them, knowing that this statement would crush Puskis. And it would have crushed him, had he not already known the answer.

Now he realized that there was greater urgency. Once the conversion began, nothing would prevent them from starting with the most threatening files. According to the vague timetable that Ricks had indicated, Puskis had maybe a week to get what he needed, if, in fact, those files had not already been altered. He needed to make headway, and the first step would be to talk to a person who might know what was going on. For the first time in nearly twenty years, Puskis did not feel that he could rely on the accuracy of the files, and this realization struck him with the force of excommunication.

For seventeen years Puskis had maintained an indirect relationship with the transcribers. *Transcriber* was not, actually, an accurate description anymore. The transcribers were initially — and this went back fifty years or more — the men who created the official records of trials from the shorthand taken by court clerks. As the technological advances in typewriting machines obviated the need for this step, the transcribers became commentators. They — as a rule, only four of them at any time — read over the transcripts of trials and the content of other sworn testimony and wrote comments on the events or people that they contained or referenced. They also produced the cross-referencing lists for each file that Puskis would then turn into an index with actual file codes to replace the names and cases indicated by the transcribers.

By tradition, each transcriber used a different color of ink, and that color was passed to a new transcriber in the instance of a retirement. The ink colors were black, red, blue, and green. In Puskis's seventeen years as Archivist, there had been only one black transcriber, but two reds and two greens, and three blues. Puskis felt he had come to know the transcribers to an extent through the mountain of notes that he'd read over the years. The current red transcriber, for instance, was suspicious of names. He apparently harbored a theory that a number of people changed the form of their name based on the ethnicity of the people with whom they were dealing. So, for instance, a man with the last name Brown might be Braun for the Germans and Bruni for the Italians, and Brunek for the Slavs, Bronski for the Poles, and so forth. A name fetishist, the current red transcriber, Puskis thought.

But though the constant analysis of the written commentary on the records and the selection of files requested had rendered each of the four transcribers (indeed, eight total during Puskis's tenure) distinct and tangible as individuals, Puskis had never met any of them. Staring at himself in the bathroom mirror, Puskis decided that he needed to introduce himself immediately.

The Transcribers' Room was tucked toward the back of the fourth floor at Headquarters, among evidence-storage rooms. Stepping inside, Puskis felt a rush of familiarity. It took him a moment to realize that it was because, like the Vaults, this room did not have the stink of cigarette smoke that was omnipresent in the rest of the building. The room was spare — bare white walls and a black-and-white-checkerboard tile floor. In the middle of the room stacks of files were piled on a square oak table. Fanning out from the table were four desks, and at each desk was a man, leaning over papers either reading intently or scrawling comments in one of the four colors of ink.

"Excuse me," said Puskis. All four men looked up, apparently startled by the unfamiliar voice. "I'm Arthur Puskis."

The man at the desk closest to Puskis stood up. He was the youngest and corpulent, his shirt untucked and his pants held up with suspenders. "Mr. Puskis?" he asked, the awe in his voice evident.

"Um, well, yes."

The other three men were up now. Between them they defined the states that a body takes when deprived of physical activity. One, seemingly the oldest, was skeletal and stooped — not unlike Puskis's own appearance. The second was not particularly fat, but even beneath his suit Puskis could tell that his body lacked muscular definition. He was like a sausage and his suit was the intestinal lining that held the meat together. The last had the frame of a large man but without any extra weight, so that it appeared that his suit was hanging from a rack rather than adorning a body. They all wore black suits and the dazed expressions of people for whom interaction is a rare and difficult endeavor.

The fat one shuffled past Puskis, leaned out into the hall, checked both ways, then closed the door. The other three had gathered around Puskis, a little too close for a man unused to physical contact. He gazed at them uneasily and for a few long moments there was silence.

The older, stooped man spoke. "What brings you here after all this time?"

Puskis had rehearsed his response, and for once the words flowed smoothly. "I am interested in speaking to the man who used green ink seven years ago."

The transcribers looked at each other significantly. The fat one spoke. "That was Van Vossen. He left, let's see, he left five years ago. He was my predecessor."

Puskis had known that he would not find the man here. The hand-writing in green ink had changed since the false DeGraffenreid file was created. Now he had a name. "Do you know where Mr. Van Vossen is now?"

This request led to another round of exchanged glances before the oldest again spoke. "Why do you want to speak to him?" His voice seemed somehow to come from a distance.

"There was a . . . discrepancy in the files. To be clear, it was just one file, but one with a discrepancy that may, well, hold some significance. The pages are marked in green ink. I am hopeful that the person who marked the pages can, um, lend some insight into the discrepancy."

"What file?" The men leaned in, eager for the answer.

"The file for the murder of Ellis Prosnicki. The trial of Reif DeGraffenreid."

The old man nodded and the others began to fidget, rubbing hands together or scratching ears. The old man turned to the fat one. "Write down the address for Mr. Puskis."

The fat man returned to his desk and wrote on a piece of white paper. The large man seemed to lose interest and drifted back to his desk and began rummaging through his drawer, half-looking for something. The man with the sausage body moved closer to Puskis. He smelled of gin. "Do you know what they plan to do with the files?" he whispered.

Puskis recoiled slightly from the smell of the man and the hiss of his voice. "Well, I suppose that I, I . . ."

"Don't worry," the sausage man continued, "we know. We know exactly what they are doing."

The fat man returned and offered the sheet of paper with Van Vossen's address. Puskis accepted it without turning his attention from the sausage man.

"What exactly are they doing?" Puskis asked.

"You know," he said, his voice intense now. "You know and we know, and nobody else except for them. They are destroying the past. They are erasing their deeds from history."

"What are they erasing? Why do they want to destroy the files?" Puskis asked with a pang of desperation. The sausage man stared at him, breathing hard, his eyes wide.

"Maybe," the old man said, "Mr. Van Vossen has the answer."

Footsteps were audible in the hall and the three other men scurried to their desks. The old man took Puskis's head between his spidery hands. "Be careful, Mr. Puskis. They are going to great lengths to destroy this information. I don't think they will allow anyone to get in their way."

Puskis stared back into the man's gray eyes. His head was hammering. "Who are they? Who are they?"

The man released Puskis's head and turned to the table. The door swung open to reveal the Chief and a uniformed officer.

"Mr. Puskis," the Chief said brightly, "we'd wondered where you'd gone. Why doesn't Riordon here give you a ride back to the Vaults. I understand the boys have sent quite a bit of work over for you." The Chief put a massive arm gently around Puskis's shoulders and guided him out of the Transcribers' Room and into the hall. The uniform pulled the door shut as they left.

CHAPTER THIRTY-THREE

Excerpt from Van Vossen, *A History of Recent Crime in the City* (draft):

While the details of the Birthday Party Massacre are no doubt familiar to anyone interested in crime in the City, it is important to elucidate the pivotal role that this episode played in the cessation of the mob war between the White Gang and the Bristol Gang. In fact, it can and has been said that without the Birthday Party Massacre, the conflict had no prospects for a terminus.

It was an accepted truth among the officers of the Force and the City's criminal underworld that the pursuit of justice for violence and homicide committed against criminals by criminals would not be pursued with the vigor that equivalent crimes against law-abiding citizens would. In this way, until the early to mid-1920s, there was a consistent and accepted attrition rate among members of the White and Bristol gangs and their associates. Around 1923, however, a marked increase in homicidal attacks between the gangs was observed. The period between 1923 and the Birthday Party Massacre in 1929 witnessed an increase in both the number of homicides and the lack of regard for public order on the part of the gangs. Thus, Eddie Peguese was murdered in front of a crowd of hundreds at the Independence Day parade in 1926, Piers Da-Court was ambushed by gunmen in front of the Opera House in 1926, and Justice Davies was pulled from his car during mid-day traffic in 1928, never to be seen again. These are but examples from the litany of outrages perpetrated by the White and Bristol gangs and their criminal cohorts.

But even against this ghoulish standard, the Birthday Party Massacre proved an act of such moral turpitude that the public, the Police, and Mayor Henry agreed that a new policy had to be pursued. The White Gang, as the perpetrators of the Birthday Party Massacre, were savagely eviscerated through the combined might of the Bristol Gang and the police force, especially the newly reconstituted Anti-

Subversion Unit. The degree to which the ASU and the Bristols coordinated their assaults upon the Whites was a matter of some dispute in the newspapers and pubs of the City. While no conclusive evidence has ever been provided, there was, at minimum, a tacit understanding that the Bristols would not be prosecuted for crimes against the Whites. . . .

CHAPTER THIRTY-FOUR

The *Gazette*'s library maintained a copy of each issue going back the thirty-odd years of its existence. Lonergan, the librarian, was small and slight, wore his hair unfashionably long, and sported a neat goatee. As far as Frings could tell, Lonergan's sole responsibility was to retrieve newspapers when so requested by *Gazette* reporters. It was hard to imagine an easier job. Panos had told Frings, with a laugh of disbelief, that he understood that Lonergan spent his free time in the library writing a philosophical treatise. Frings wanted to talk to Lonergan about this — his curiosity was part genuine interest and part amusement — but Lonergan was not approachable and Frings decided it wasn't worth the effort.

Lonergan's invaluable talent was his ability to recall with startling accuracy the date of even minor events. So when Frings asked him for the *Gazette*'s coverage of the murder committed by Otto Samuelson, Lonergan was instantly able to narrow the date down to within a week's span. He retrieved all the newspapers for that week and the following four weeks and turned them over to Frings, who carried them down a flight of stairs, stacked them on his desk, and began to learn about Otto Samuelson and the murder of a small-time hood named Leto.

Cy Leto had been a runner for the White Gang. He collected on gambling debts, picked up protection money, and, on occasion, braced someone who had transgressed in some way against the Whites or, occasionally, against Leto himself. He had been a small man, according to the newspaper reports, but quick to anger and apparently with few qualms about perpetrating violence upon his fellow man. The second article about his murder mentioned a prior conviction for pushing a woman down a flight of stairs in front of her young children. This, because her husband, who had run out on her, owed the Whites gambling money.

Leto was murdered by Otto Samuelson, a thug in the White Gang. Samuelson was, according to the detective quoted in that same second article, a "homicidal maniac" responsible for a number of murders of Bristol Gang members. He had been shot several times in the years leading up to the Leto murder, but escaped serious injury each time. "A veritable Rasputin," the cop said.

Leto's murder was the penultimate in a series of increasingly audacious killings that ended with the Birthday Party Massacre. Both the Whites and the Bristols had, by early 1929, lost any fear they might have had of the powers of the police and government. Red Henry had just been elected but had not yet taken office, and the outgoing mayor was fully consumed with consolidating and hiding his takings from the graft and corruption of the previous twelve years. Leto's murder was shockingly bold, but not unprecedented.

The newspaper described the murder as occurring around noon on a clear, warm day in Capitol Heights amid a teeming crowd on the sidewalks and in the streets. According to several eyewitness accounts, as Leto drove his Buick toward the intersection of Van Buren and Virginia, a man (Samuelson) stepped into the street, holding up his hand to stop traffic for another man who was carrying a large bucket. Leto's car stopped, halting traffic, and another car did the same in the opposite lane. When the man with the bucket was in front of Leto's car, he put his right hand under the bucket and tossed its contents — a viscous tar — onto Leto's windshield, completely obliterating his view out the front. Samuelson quickly but calmly walked over to the driver's-side window — which was rolled down because of the pleasant weather — and fired six shots into Leto, who was struggling to pull his own gun from under his seat. While nearby police raced to the scene, Samuelson and the man with the bucket disappeared into the panicking crowd.

Samuelson and the other man, named Kiehl, were identified that afternoon by witnesses eyeballing mug books. The *Gazette* ran their names and mug shots the next morning. The police apprehended Samuelson thirty-six hours later at a whorehouse down in the Hollows. The cops raided Kiehl's apartment and found him facedown on the living room rug, a garrote still around his neck.

Samuelson's trial was set for November, but his lawyer filed a guilty plea, and there the coverage ended. Frings went over the last week of newspapers a second time in case he had missed any mention of Samuelson's sentencing and/or place of detention. He found nothing.

Frings carried the stack of newspapers back up the stairs and found Lonergan in deep concentration, writing with a pen in a thick, leather-bound journal. Frings dropped the newspapers on the desk from a height that made enough noise to get Lonergan's attention. Lonergan was not startled, looking up slowly and without irritation.

"Found what you were looking for?"

"Almost. I noticed that we followed the events pretty closely until his sentencing, and then there's nothing. That strikes me as pretty queer, right?"

Lonergan thought about this. "Yes," he replied slowly, "in a case that received as much attention as the Samuelson case — yes, that seems a mite unusual."

"Could you check and see if there's any word of Samuelson after the batch of papers you gave me?"

"Already did. Samuelson isn't mentioned again, except peripherally in articles about other murders and the White Gang. That's it as far as the *Gazette* is concerned."

Frings felt his temper rise. It was irrational, he knew — Lonergan was not responsible for what news the paper did or didn't cover. "Look, I mostly want to know where I can find Samuelson now. I need to talk to him."

Lonergan leaned back in his chair and cast his eyes to the ceiling. He mumbled to himself, "Where to find him, where to find him?" He straightened up and looked at Frings. "You know, the best person to talk to is probably Arthur Puskis."

The name was vaguely familiar. Frings looked at Lonergan with eyebrows raised, waiting for further explanation.

"Arthur Puskis is the Archivist at the Vaults down at City Hall. He maintains all the records. If anyone can find where your buddy Samuelson is, it's him."

CHAPTER THIRTY-FIVE

Poole was aware of voices before he fully regained consciousness. One was familiar, and though his mind was unable to process a name or a relationship, he knew that this particular voice — Carla's — should be a comfort to him. The other voice, though unfamiliar, was calm, and he was aware on some level that the conversation was friendly, and Poole's last moments of semi-consciousness were content, almost blissful.

Full consciousness brought pain that seemed to envelop his body. He saw Carla in blurry outline and tried to speak to her, but only managed a faint croak. That alerted Carla and her friend, and in seconds they were leaning over him.

Carla smoothed the hair back from his forehead. "How are you doing?" His eyes better focused, Poole could see the patches of dark beneath her azure eyes and the slump that came to her shoulders when she was exhausted. He began to speak, but then, with an effort, just pointed toward his mouth.

"Water?"

Poole nodded.

"Enrique, could you get a glass of water?"

The dark, powerful man made an affirmative grunt and disappeared toward the kitchen. Carla took Poole's face between her hands and stared into his eyes. "Are you okay?" she asked, not actually expecting a verbal response but probing his eyes for signs of psychic damage.

Enrique returned with a glass of water, and Carla gently placed it to Poole's lips. The water brought some life back to Poole, and after finishing the glass, he pulled himself up to a half-sitting position, eyeing Enrique.

"He's okay," Carla said. "Enrique's an organizer at Bernal's plant. We're just meeting about our next step."

Poole's head throbbed. Carla had spoken of Enrique in the past, but Poole had never actually met him. A stalwart, Carla said. Poole's mind was starting to clear.

Carla anticipated his first question. "They dropped you at our doorstep. Just pulled a car to the curb, opened the door, and pushed you out."

"Who?"

"Don't you know?"

"ASU?"

"That's our guess," she said, indicating Enrique. "We don't know for sure."

"Do I look . . . ?" Poole began, then felt the room move beneath him, his eyes rolling in his head. His thoughts fractured into irrationality and he again lost consciousness.

Enrique was gone. He and Carla had finished their meeting as Poole slept. Now Poole and Carla sat at the kitchen table, the photographs of Bernal and his lover strewn messily about. Poole fought to focus through the pounding in his head. There were many things to figure out and not much time.

"Enrique and I talked," Carla said. "We need to get the photos to a newspaper."

Poole tensed the way he always did when he disagreed with Carla. He had black-mailed close to a dozen people over the years, but they had always come through with the money, and he'd never had to follow through on his threats. The photos were his only leverage. Once they were public, he could do nothing to threaten Bernal — or protect himself.

"I don't know," he said.

"We have to. Don't you see? Either way,

we lose our leverage. If we don't get the pictures into a paper, then he thinks we're bluffing and ignores us. If we do get them printed, well, that puts more pressure on him, doesn't it?"

Poole conceded the point. She was right, and anyway, arguing would get him nowhere. It bothered him, though, that Enrique was suddenly taking part in the decision making. Not the least because Carla was Enrique's ally in this, not his.

"We need to get back at him," Carla said, leaning across the table. "We can't let him and those goddamn ASU cops walk all over us. We need to respond. This is all we've got."

"Okay."

"Are you worried because you got picked up? Was Bernal behind it? Pulling in a favor from the mayor?"

"No, actually." Poole was still bewildered by this. "I thought they pinched me because of Bernal, but that wasn't what they were asking me about. They asked me about Casper Prosnicki."

"Well, what the hell could you tell them about him?"

"Nothing." He hesitated.

"What?"

Poole sighed with exasperation. "There

227

was one thing I did know. They asked who hired me."

"You didn't tell them."

"I did." Poole anticipated the coming judgment. "I wasn't able . . . They worked me over pretty good. I wasn't thinking . . ."

Carla shushed him and stared at the table. Poole tried again. "I —"

Carla held up a hand and Poole knew to let her think.

"You have to find her," she said finally. "She needs to know."

Poole knew this was coming. "Call your people. See if you can get an address for her. I'll go talk to her."

Carla closed her eyes and Poole saw the terrible strain in her sunken cheeks and downturned mouth. He made a motion to reach across the table and touch her hair, but the movement made his head swim, and by the time he recovered, she was gone. He heard her voice from the other room, inquiring over the phone as to the current address of Lena Prosnicki.

Carla made several phone calls in the next two hours before returning to the kitchen. Poole slept in his chair, using his forearms crossed on the table for a pillow. He awoke to her gently massaging his shoulders. At another time he would have found this arousing. He wondered if he had been kicked in the genitals, but they didn't hurt, so he decided that maybe his lack of response was from the stress and pain.

"Baby," she said, "I've got bad news."

His pulse quickened. "What?"

"No address for Lena Prosnicki in the City or any towns around here."

Poole nodded. "So she's either in from out of town — which I don't buy — she's homeless, or she lives somewhere without an address."

Carla saw where he was going. "Like a hospital."

"But people in hospitals usually have a home to go back to. An address. I'm thinking more of an institution, probably an asylum. I remember she was queer, like maybe she was doped. Maybe she's at an asylum and they've got her on something."

Carla nodded. It was a place to start.

CHAPTER THIRTY-SIX

Dawlish, the elevator operator, greeted Puskis with a serious look. Puskis, still shaken from the Retrievorator demonstration at Headquarters, assumed that Dawlish was reacting to some physical manifestation of that shock. He stepped into the awaiting elevator and was surprised to see Dawlish do a quick, surreptitious glance around the lobby before closing first the gate and then the elevator door. He hesitated before beginning the descent into the Vaults.

"Mr. Puskis, sir, I wanted you to know that I am through with your pen but not yet able to return it." He then pulled the lever, and with the distant whirr of metal gears, they descended.

Puskis squinted at Dawlish, realizing this cryptic statement was significant. Through great concentration he suppressed his worries about the future of the Vaults and thought about Dawlish's words. The signal had been to return the pen when someone went into the Vaults. What did it mean that he was finished with the pen but not ready to return it?

The elevator came to a stop, and Dawlish opened the door, then the gate. As Puskis exited, Dawlish touched his arm — perhaps the first time they had ever made physical contact — and stared at him with panicked eyes. Puskis stood staring at the elevator as Dawlish closed the door, then listened as it made its short ascent.

I'm through with your pen but not ready to return it. The implication was that the conditions for return had been met but the time was not proper. *Conditions and time.* The required condition was that someone go into the Vaults; and this, if he understood Dawlish correctly, had happened. The timing then — Puskis took a step back so that he was pressed against the wall — the timing had to mean that the person had not yet left. Someone else was in the Vaults *right now.*

The logic behind this deduction was not foolproof, yet Puskis knew he was right. He stood motionless, listening — hearing the ambient noise as if for the first time. The humming of lights. The hiss and clink of the heating system. Distantly, the noise of the street through the thick walls. He felt fatigued from the fear and from the unaccustomed physical activity. He eased over to his desk on stiff legs and sat, straining to hear a noise beyond the usual.

Seventeen years since another person had been back in those stacks. More accurately, it had been seventeen years since someone had been back in the stacks while he had been in the Vaults and known it. He had already established that someone — or some people — had been there while he was absent. And the cleaners came when Puskis was away. He had never actually seen them, but their work was apparent.

It came almost as a relief when the sound that he strained so hard to hear was finally audible. A step, like the click of a pen on a wooden desk; followed by another. Someone was walking back in the Vaults. Puskis struggled with a range of reactions: fear, anger, curiosity, dismay. He felt a quick surge of energy as adrenaline coursed through his system. Fight or flight. He had never before faced that choice. Even at Reif DeGraffenreid's there had been no one to fight. Fleeing from the old blind man was a result of his general panic, not because he felt physically endangered. He straightened up, knowing that this was the first step in any possible reaction. Without making a conscious decision to do so, he began to walk into the stacks.

He had forgotten, over time, just how hard it was to determine the direction of noise in the Vaults. Sound bounced around the shelves and ceiling, sometimes seeming to come from four or five distinct points at once, and other times sounding as though it came from a vast general source. It was the aural equivalent of a house of mirrors.

Puskis tried to search efficiently, walking down the wide center aisle, attempting to determine which side the footsteps were coming from. He would take four or five steps, then stop, listening. Hearing nothing, he would move on another four or five steps. Occasionally he heard a footstep while he walked and would instantly stop, but no more footsteps would come. As he progressed, the shadows cast by the intermittent lights seemed to move, an effect of his changing perspective.

Nearly halfway down the center aisle, he heard another sound, like a rug being pulled across the floor. As a result of some fortuitous arrangement of aisles and shelves, the direction of this sound was more easily determined. It came from his left and in front — farther into the depths of the Vaults.

He shuffled forward to where another wide aisle bisected the Vaults at a perpendicular angle. He repeated his earlier method, taking a few steps and then listening. He heard a footstep that sounded as if it came from behind him, and he questioned his initial impression of the source of the sound. But soon he heard a burst of four footsteps confirming that he was cornering the intruder in the far-left reaches of the Vaults, a backwater of fraud and number-running files.

To this point the challenge of trying to home in on the source of the footsteps had distracted Puskis from the danger that he might be facing. But now he detected an unfamiliar odor, a cologne of some sort, though not one that Puskis associated with anyone in particular. He took it as a sign he was closing in on the intruder and was confronted with the question of what, exactly, he would do if he was successful in his search. He stopped and pondered the wisdom of confrontation until the footsteps started again. This time they were rapid and no attempt was made to move quietly. Puskis could not determine their exact direction, but the increasing volume signaled that the intruder was headed toward him.

He froze momentarily, then, with short, hasty steps, fled into the stacks in a direction that would not intercept the intruder if he was trying to get to the elevators. When Puskis felt he was far enough to the left that the intruder would not happen upon him by accident, he stopped, gasping for breath. He stood behind the end of a row of shelves and looked back toward the main aisle. The intruder was taking the wider aisles back to the elevators. Puskis could follow the steps now and caught a quick glimpse of a man in a dark suit, his fedora pulled low as he flashed across Puskis's aisle. The moment passed too quickly for an identification, even if Puskis knew who the man was.

He waited where he stood until he heard, in the distance, the elevator door open and then close again. He thought he heard muffled voices, but in the end he was not sure. He stayed for several more minutes in the unlikely event that the intruder had used the elevator as a deception and was, in fact, waiting for him by the desk. Finally collecting his nerve, he made a cautious journey back to the front of the Vaults. He crept to a position in the stacks where he could get a good view of his desk. Seeing no one, he returned to his station and collapsed into his chair. On the top of the desk, next to a short stack of file requests, was the pen he had lent Dawlish.

CHAPTER THIRTY-SEVEN

The nun working reception at St. Agnes' Asylum on a forgotten street in Capitol Heights was as gray, peeling, and cracked as the building itself. She peered at Poole through dirty bifocals, a grimace of distaste on her face. Poole could imagine the picture he presented with his swollen face and limp.

"I'm here to see my aunt." He struggled with his swollen tongue, slurring his words. "Her name is Lena Prosnicki."

She continued to stare at him.

"Ma'am, I'm here to see Lena Prosnicki." He carefully enunciated the words this time in case his slurring had confused her.

She turned from him and walked through a wooden door behind her desk, leaving Poole to wonder whether she was reacting to his query and, indeed, if she had even heard him. He leaned over the counter that partitioned the room into the public and the official halves and scanned the reception desk for anything of interest. A filthy registry book was open among scattered sections of newspaper. A coffee mug contained only mold, and two plates had the crumbs of earlier meals.

Wincing with the pain in his knees and ankles, Poole pushed through the swinging gate and examined the registry. The most recent entry was from two weeks prior. The place did not get much traffic — at least officially. The names on the open page were not familiar, and he flipped back a page.

Poole had expected to hear the nun's footsteps returning, but either the door provided remarkable soundproofing or she moved quietly because the door swung open without warning and the woman reappeared with a younger, worn-looking nun trailing. Finding Poole on the wrong side of the divider, the woman scowled, walked to the desk, and slammed the registry shut.

"Sister Prudence will take you back to Dr. Vesterhue."

Sister Prudence kept her eyes down, acknowledging Poole by looking at his stomach. She turned and pushed open the wooden door through which she had arrived. With an uncomfortable look at the older nun, Poole followed.

They walked down a short, dim corridor

and through a double set of steel doors, each of which Sister Prudence had to unlock and then relock once they were past. Then another corridor, though instead of walls, this one had bars. On either side, elderly men, in various combinations of gray institutional uniforms and tattered personal clothing, sat or lay or walked aimlessly. Probably fifteen or so of them were on each side, and Poole was struck by their seeming obliviousness to his and his companion's presence. Indeed, they seemed unaware of each other's presence. An ambient moaning sound accompanied the stench of sweat, urine, feces, and stagnant water.

Sister Prudence walked with her head down, the spectacle long ago ceasing to affect her. They passed through a single steel door — repeating the ritual of unlocking and locking — at the opposite end of the corridor and were met with another sound entirely, a hymn as if sung by the angels themselves. They walked past an intersecting hall and then by an open door, the source of the singing. Poole looked in on a choir of girls, most not even in their teens, the older ones in habits, singing at the direction of a matronly nun. Poole stood transfixed in the doorway until one of the girls noticed him and then they all noticed him and the singing stopped.

Poole caught the stare of one of the girls — one of the older ones, dressed in a habit. Something about her was familiar. From her look, this recognition was clearly reciprocated. Poole realized that the context had thrown him; he saw her nearly every day — one of the prostitutes who habituated the alley below his apartment. Confused, he backed slowly out of the room to find Sister Prudence waiting for him at the end of the corridor.

"Who are they?"

She didn't look up. "Initiates."

Through another door and into yet another corridor; this one had solid-metal doors on both sides at four-yard intervals. Banging came from the inside of some, shattering the corridor's silence. Sister Prudence led Poole to its end, where a door stood open. He stepped into an office that had clearly once been a cell.

In the yellow light that filtered through a filthy window, a round man in a soiled white shirt sat behind a small desk. His small head was made smaller by thick sideburns that flowed down to his jawline. His face was gray and tired, but his eyes shone like those of a child who is awakened in the dead of night. He motioned for Poole to come in.

"I'll send the visitor down to your door when I'm done, Sister."

Sister Prudence gave a barely perceptible nod and drifted off.

"You're looking for Lena Prosnicki?" Dr. Vesterhue asked.

"That's right."

"And you are?"

Poole was prepared for this. "Laszlo Prosnicki. Lena is my aunt."

Dr. Vesterhue did not look perturbed. "You're lying. But that's all right. Please sit."

Poole sat in a spare wooden chair that barely fit between the desk and the wall, his knees crammed against the desk.

"Are you a detective?"

Poole hesitated.

That was enough for Vesterhue. "Of course you are. Someone has finally come looking for those poor women."

Women? "Is Lena Prosnicki here, Dr. Vesterhue?"

"Here?" Vesterhue shook his head with a spiteful laugh. "No. No, she's not *here*."

Poole sighed. It would have been too easy, finding Mrs. Prosnicki at the third sanitarium he visited. "Then why did you bring me back here?"

"Oh, she's not here. No. But I know where she is."

"You know where she is?"

"Yes, I'm afraid I do."

Something about Vesterhue's eyes spooked Poole. They were too sharp for the fatigued features of his face. Poole took a quick scan of a row of medicine bottles without making any of the labels.

"Where is she, Dr. Vesterhue?"

"Let me tell you. Let me tell you where I met Lena Prosnicki. It was six years past or so. Maybe seven. At that time I was working at a place called All Souls' Sanitarium. It was a place much like this, except that it was cleaner and the building was better kept.

"I was one of the specialists there. It was called All Souls', but it was run by the City. Back in the nineties the City bought it from the Church. It was a common place, no different than a dozen others in the City. Occasionally we would get a former city official in an advanced state of dementia and we'd give him special care. But for the most part, it was a typical institution.

"Something like six years ago, a man named Smith came to All Souls', and there was a meeting with the specialists and the administration. This man, Smith, told us that All Souls' was going to be used for a special group of women. They were all suffering, he said, from extreme trauma, the source of which he couldn't tell us. A consequence of this was that all of the current patients were going to have to be transferred to other institutions.

"Needless to say, this was most unusual. The City's sanitariums are, of course, overcrowded, and the prospect of essentially dispersing one institution's patients to the others . . . well, it was a radical suggestion. Scandalous. But it wasn't up for debate. We spent that month preparing and then transporting the patients throughout the City. I can tell you that the staffs at these receiving sanitariums were not happy with taking extra patients.

"Regardless, when the last patient was gone from All Souls', we were given two days off. When we returned, the women had arrived. Forty-two of them — a small number for an institution of that size, especially considering the numbers elsewhere. They were all heavily sedated. There were other new people, too. Police. There were a lot of police, or I guess I should say ASU. They mostly stayed at the entrance, but there were also guards posted at the stairway on each floor. They were armed.

"This Smith fellow — I got the feeling that this was not in the normal scope of his work — returned, and there was another meeting. Smith told us that our job from this point on would be to administer the drugs at pre-assigned dosages and to monitor their behavior. He emphasized that we were not to change the dosages or attempt any type of talking cure. Medicate and observe. Nothing else.

"It became apparent to me — and some of the others as well, though they had the good sense to keep their own counsel — that the women weren't exhibiting any symptoms beyond those caused by the medications. I mentioned this to my supervisor, and less than a week later I was transferred here."

After a pause, Poole said, "They transferred you here because you thought the women's only problems were from the medication they were taking?"

"I thought that they would quite likely be perfectly healthy if they were just given relief from the drugs. I wasn't alone in this belief, but I was alone in voicing it."

"What was the point? I mean, why were they drugged if there was nothing wrong with them?"

Vesterhue's bright eyes did not seem

focused on anything in particular, giving the peculiar impression that they were focused inside himself or, possibly, on the past.

"I really don't know. I have thought about it often. There was something odd and sad about all those women. Unable to function, and we were just giving them more and more drugs." He sighed. "I just have no idea. None at all."

"Have you been back to All Souls' or have you seen any of these women again?"

Vesterhue's eyes were back to focusing on Poole. "No. I have not left this building in three years. My quarters are in the basement. The City has given up on this place, on these people. No one comes here anymore. I have nowhere to go. So here I am. Me, the lunatics, and those lovely girls with their singing. Are you familiar with eschatology, Mr. Prosnicki?"

CHAPTER THIRTY-EIGHT

In the back room of Lentini's, a bar in Capitol Heights and a meeting place for Red Henry and his cronies, Ian Block was breathing hard, cigar smoke flaring his asthma. Henry himself sat across the round table from Block and blew plumes of smoke at him. Also around the table were Bernal, who was drinking from a tall glass of whiskey on the rocks, and Altabelli, who had a beer and a cigar. They were discussing the bombings and Bernal's good fortune, to date, in not being a victim.

"Curious, Roderigo, that you should be spared the bombs so far. Very curious. You must feel very fortunate." Altabelli had a thick Italian accent, and Bernal had difficulty figuring whether this comment was meant as a joke or not. He became defensive.

"They have only bombed twice. One of us would have to be left out. So it is me? So what? Now I must wait until my house is attacked. I moved my wife and children to the country until this thing is finished. Besides, there is me and there is the mayor. He has not yet been bombed."

Altabelli reacted with either false or sincere shock. "You would accuse our mayor, our good friend Mr. Red Henry, of turning on his good friends and putting them in, ah, mortal danger?"

Bernal had not meant this at all, and he looked nervously at Henry, who was relaxed and smiling. This came as some relief to Bernal, who did not want to upset the mayor during the best of times. Leaking to Frings had his paranoia spiking. Any undue attention, he knew, was an invitation for trouble.

"No, no," he protested. "You misunderstand the intentions of my comments. I mention the mayor only to show that because one has not been bombed does not necessarily make one the bomber."

The familiar pattern of two knocks, a pause, and then a third signaled that the visitor had official business with the mayor.

"Come in," Henry roared, the cigar still in the side of his mouth.

It was Peja, looking as if he had eaten something rotten. The three men at the table looked to Henry. The look on Peja's face turned Henry's mood ugly.

"What is it?"

Peja was used to speaking in front of these men. "It's the Poles, sir. They sent word. They are close to signing, but they caught wind of the strike and they're concerned. They're worried about having to deal with the unions."

Henry snarled at Bernal, who went pale. Then Henry, maintaining his calm, said, "Didn't they hear that the strike was taken care of? Order has been restored without any concessions."

Peja nodded. "They do know that. We made sure to tell them. But . . ."

"But what?"

"They think that might have been done for their benefit. They think that maybe you wouldn't normally come down so hard on the unions."

Henry's bald scalp was turning a peculiar red. "From your conversation with them, what do you think needs to be done?"

"I think that it would help for you to show them that the unions aren't a problem."

Henry nodded.

"In a clear and personal way," Peja continued.

"I understand what you mean." Henry

looked toward Bernal now. "Who's that little spic leading the strike?"

"Enrique Dotel. Him and that woman." Bernal was glad to be offering something positive.

"Dotel." Henry looked back at Peja, eyes blazing. "Get Dotel and get the Poles and have them at my office tomorrow morning at ten. They'll see what happens when people push me."

Peja nodded and hustled out the door. Henry leaned back in his chair and rediscovered the cigar protruding from the corner of his mouth. He sucked on it and held the smoke in his partially open mouth, wisps of smoke rising like steam from a cauldron. Then he blew out the smoke in a long, steady stream toward Block, who started coughing again.

CHAPTER THIRTY-NINE

Frings was exhausted and anticipated a long night ahead. Panos unlocked the night editor's empty office so he could take a nap on the couch. The office had the newsroom odor of stale coffee and cigarettes, and the couch was too short. But the familiar hum of talking, typewriters, and the general bustle of the newsroom soon had him hovering in that irrational zone between consciousness and sleep.

His thoughts were of Nora, but not of trying to understand her or their relationship. Instead it was like finding a collection of random photographs and from them taking away an impression of the thoughts, lives, and attitudes of the people in them.

There was Nora, in a red, strapless dress, her hair dyed black, being introduced in the crowd at the opera house, standing and waving and smiling shyly. In his proximity to her, he felt the charge that came from the focused attentions of so many adoring people. He felt extraordinarily lucky to be the recipient of affection from this woman who was idolized by so many.

There was the hollowness in his stomach when he paid an unexpected visit to her during rehearsals with a new orchestra to find her cozied up with the bandleader, David Winter, laughing as he whispered something into her ear. She had played it quite unself-consciously, breaking away from Winter and embracing Frings and kissing him provocatively. But as he stood around watching the rehearsal, he caught looks from Winter. Looks that seemed to say, "I've had something of yours." Frings had been too timid to bring it up again with Nora, but the queasy feeling was hard to shake.

There was Nora, sobbing irrationally to Frings during one of the few nights they had spent at his apartment. It was the first time he had seen her insecure side and experienced the privilege of being her protector. The cause of these episodes was never clear, and he eventually learned to provide general comfort, but on this first night he had desperately tried to find the source of her grief, only to find that it stemmed from her lack of certainty about anything. Nothing in life was certain, Frings knew, and he was comfortable with that — in fact, he felt it to be one of the encouraging aspects of life. But he didn't tell that to Nora that night. Eventually he just held her until she fell asleep on his tear-soaked chest.

Another memory: Nora at a gala banquet celebrating the fiftieth wedding anniversary of the famous conductor Eli Hodge. She was wearing an ivory cocktail dress and a tiara and was an absolute distraction to the men attending. She was also not talking to Frings, who knew no one else in attendance. It was a virtuoso piece of humiliation. Frings stood mute in her shadow as she flirted and gossiped and became the focus of the party's considerable energy. Afterward, her lovemaking with him had been saturated with desperation, and he found, to his disgust, that he could not harbor any anger toward her.

He and Nora out with a friend of hers, a movie actress named Greta Van Riepen, and her paramour, a dour, fey little man named Marco, who Greta claimed was some type of Italian royalty. It was a strange feeling to find refuge in conversation with Greta, whom he barely knew, as Nora and Marco chatted with troubling intimacy. It went as well as could be expected given the strained situation, until Greta glimpsed Marco rubbing Nora's forearm with the tips of his fingers and the evening ended with Greta's tearful departure, trailed, reluctantly, by Marco.

As Frings had instructed, the office boy woke him at half past four. Frings gathered his note pad and several pencils and stashed them in the pocket of his trench coat. An envelope had appeared on his desk during his nap. He yelled for Ed, who arrived with an aggrieved expression that Frings ignored.

"Where'd this come from?"

"Some skirt dropped it off for you."

"Did you catch her name?"

Ed shrugged. "No. She was easy on the eyes, though."

"Well, I'm glad to hear that," Frings said sarcastically, causing Ed to stalk off in a huff. Frings was anxious to leave the office, but this could be another communication from the bombers, so he slit the envelope open with an ivory-handled letter opener that Nora had bought for him.

"God damn it," Frings said aloud when he saw the contents of the envelope — four high-quality prints of Bernal naked and in bed with a woman who Frings was fairly sure was not Mrs. Bernal. He slid the photos back into the envelope, hidden from the gaze of reporters that had turned his way in response to the outburst. There was a note, too: *For your use. I'll be in touch.*

This was exactly what he did not need. Bernal was potentially a gold mine of information about Red Henry and his circle. Now it seemed someone else was sweating him, and Frings was experienced enough in these situations to see the danger. He took a breath to calm himself. Frings was adept at putting problems to the back of his mind until he had time to address them. He didn't have time for this now. He needed to get over to Puskis's apartment building. He had a juju in his pocket that he would smoke on the way. It would take the edge off his anxiety.

CHAPTER FORTY

All Souls' was on the edge of the Hollows, in a building that was once the main Catholic church before they built St. Mary's in the Theater District. The imposing structure of brick and granite had a façade distinguished by two tall spires, and an arching stained-glass window looming over the main entrance. A small square in front of All Souls' was concrete with a granite inlay in a geometric pattern that Poole had a notion was based on something in Italy (he had attended *some* classes while at State). Pigeons seemed to have taken over and the square was empty of people, save for four ASU officers smoking and chatting at the top of the stairs leading to All Souls' entrance. Poole imagined it was a pretty easy assignment.

He stood across the square from All Souls', out of sight with his back against an apartment building. His conversation with Dr. Vesterhue did not give him much hope of seeing Lena Prosnicki, and he had no stomach for dealing with the ASU again. He was here to confirm Vesterhue's claims about the security around All Souls'. Vesterhue had not exagerrated.

While this was a dead end, he had given some thought to Casper Prosnicki during the walk here. Where would you find a boy whose father was murdered and whose mother was in an institution? An orphanage.

Orphanages in the City, Poole knew, were neither uniform nor regulated. He was familiar with them from a case he had worked three years prior when a woman named Dagmar Rehmer had hired him to find her daughter, Ursula. He hadn't considered this point before, but Dagmar Rehmer was another woman who had told Poole not to contact her. While an unusual arrangement, it was not unique to Poole's experience. He was, by design, available to people who wished to avoid any undue attention. This was partly due to his relationship with Carla. Communists and anarchists, people who knew that the police would provide them with more problems than they would solve, were often Poole's clients. Word had got around, too, in the City's vast underground that Poole would provide honest services without asking sensitive questions of his clients. This was unusual, as other operatives available to these marginalized people would generally take advantage of their clients' desperation or lack of alternatives. Poole, though, was scrupulous with the most marginal of his clients. His targets were often a different story.

Ursula Rehmer, according to her mother, had been sent to an orphanage when Mr. Rehmer was killed in a car accident and Dagmar had suffered a breakdown. The case had been relatively simple — visit orphanages until he found the one that housed Ursula Rehmer. He was too late, though. She had died several months prior to his visit — a fact the beleaguered chaplain had read in her folder. *Death by misadventure* had been the cryptic notation as to cause. The chaplain had stared helplessly back at Poole in response to a query for more specifics.

Ursula Rehmer's orphanage had been St. Cecilia's in the Hollows. Poole knew from that investigation that St. Cecilia's was the sister orphanage of St. Mark's, also in the Hollows. St. Mark's seemed like a reasonable place to start.

■ ■ ■ ■

St. Mark's had once been a tenement building, condemned to be torn down. The City,
then under the previous mayor's regime,
bought the building and converted it to an
orphanage. The condemnation order was
rescinded. Seeing the building, Poole was
convinced it should have come down years
ago. It was amazing that people actually
lived here. The building no longer even
stood straight, instead listing slightly, but
noticeably, to the south. A number of
windows were broken. Poole counted seven
on the front of the building alone. There
were five floors.

Poole opened the front door and stepped
into a dim lobby. The odor inside — of sew-
age, rotting food, sweat, other things —
caused him to pause. As his eyes adjusted,
he found no one to speak to. He walked
ahead. The parquet floor was filthy and
uneven. Poole called out.

He waited, heard footsteps — many of
them — coming down stairs that he could
not see. He backed toward the door, un-
nerved by the apparent number of people
reacting to his arrival. A door in front and
to his left opened, and six young boys

careened into the room, coming to a stop at the sight of Poole. Poole guessed that they ranged in age from eight to about thirteen.

They approached him cautiously, the youngest obviously in awe of Poole's size. One of the boys, bare-chested and sinewy, took a step forward from the group. Ill-fitting pants were cinched with a rope and he was barefoot. The others also wore clothes seemingly chosen at random.

"Who're you?" the boy asked.

"My name's Poole."

While the boys stared at him, he took off his hat and lowered himself so that he was at the lead boy's eye level.

"Who's in charge here?"

The boy seemed confused by the question and looked back at Poole in silence.

"I need to speak to an adult," Poole said, speaking slowly and carefully. "Where is an adult?"

Again the boys seemed to confer without speaking. The oldest said, "Come," and turned back toward the stairs. Poole followed him, and the rest of the boys followed Poole. The stink of urine in the stairwell brought tears to Poole's eyes. The boys seemed unaffected as they continued to ascend. In the semidarkness of the landings, Poole thought he could make out cracked doors and eyes examining him. At the landing of the fourth floor they hesitated.

The oldest turned back to the other boys. "Stay." Then he grabbed Poole's hand. Poole was surprised by the heat in the boy's hand and wondered if it was fever. They walked into the fourth-floor hall, and the smell of decay told Poole all he needed to know.

The boy led him down the hall and stopped at a closed door. Poole opened it tentatively. The smell had been strong in the hallway, but it did not remotely prepare him for what was in the room. The stench had an almost physical presence. A decomposing corpse in a priest's frock lay supine on a cot. Poole shut the door and breathed into his sleeve with his elbow bent, trying to filter the odor before he was sick. He was not an expert, but his guess was that the priest must have died in the past month. Did nobody know about this?

Poole walked back to the stairwell with the boy following. The group was still on the landing and greeted Poole with searching eyes. He tried to smile kindly.

"Does anyone know about this?" Poole asked the oldest.

He shook his head.

"Is there another adult?"

Again the shake of the head.

Poole was reeling from the smells, the condition of the boys, the body in the room. *Focus on what you came here for.* Upstairs he heard light footsteps and imagined more boys looking over the railing at the scene below.

"Listen. I'm looking for a boy named Casper Prosnicki."

"Casper?" The oldest boy brightened at the name.

"You know him? Where is he? Is he here?"

"Gone," the boy said, then made a gesture with his hand like a bird flying away.

"Gone? Gone where?" Poole's adrenaline spiked.

"He's on the streets."

"He's gone to the streets? Where?" Poole grabbed the boy's shoulders, harder than he intended. "Where is Casper?"

The boy was frightened and his companions backed away from Poole, eyes wide.

"Where?"

The boy shook his head, tears beginning to flow down his cheeks.

CHAPTER FORTY-ONE

Smith sat by the phone at a bar two blocks down from the Puskis's flat. He was on his third scotch and his hands had finally stopped trembling. Now he was waiting for the phone to ring. It would be nice for it to happen this time. When he had finally managed to get out of the Vaults, he had called Riordon at Headquarters and asked him where the hell the phone call was telling him that Puskis was returning. Riordon said that he had called and the phone had rung but no one had answered. That was a lot of horse shit, Smith knew, because he could not have missed the phone down there. Riordon hadn't called, and there wasn't much to be done about it except remember and pay it back when the opportunity presented itself. In this case, however, if Dawlish, that fastidious elevator man, didn't call, Smith would take the frustration out on *his* hide.

Just thinking about it got him in a state

again, so he threw back the scotch and ordered another.

Two men in cheap suits sat just down the bar, talking. One was saying he thought that people could be divided into two groups: one that thought that their mood should affect everyone around them; and the other that thought that they should keep their moods to their own goddamn selves. The talker placed himself in the second group and his boss in the first. His companion nodded and started in about his wife.

Smith thought about this. He didn't feel as if he really had any moods. Or maybe it was that he had only one mood all the time — pissed off. Did he let it affect the people around him? Not if they kept their goddamn distance.

The mayor definitely had his fucking moods. He didn't have to say anything, though. People recognized his moods and acted accordingly. Even Smith steered clear when he sensed Red Henry's rage. It wasn't that he feared the mayor. Smith didn't fear anyone. But hard men understand the pecking order, and Henry was right at the top. Smith was right there after him, but Henry was still number one. Smith could live with that, and with the fact that he could always put a bullet in the mayor's head if he needed to. No one was safe from anyone. Not the mayor and not Smith. Exactly the way he liked it.

He had worked his way through his scotch when the phone rang. It was Dawlish, saving himself a beating. Puskis was on his way home.

Smith stood beneath the awning of the building across the street from Puskis's. The flow of afternoon pedestrian traffic rendered Smith essentially invisible. Puskis was hard to miss, looking like a praying mantis with his long, skinny frame and his odd, stooped lope. Smith watched him as he made his slow progress along the sidewalk, approached his front door, and paused to fish keys out of his pocket. Puskis stopped suddenly and turned his head as though someone had called out to him. He stood looking to his left, and even from across the street the tension in his body was evident. Smith took an unconscious step forward for a better look.

A man was now talking to Puskis. A hat obscured the man's face, but something about him was familiar. They talked some more and the man gestured and Puskis nodded. Puskis turned back and unlocked the door. The man held the door as Puskis entered, then followed him in. At the threshold, however, the man stopped and took a brief look back at the street.

Jesus Christ, Smith thought, it's goddamn Frankie Frings.

CHAPTER FORTY-TWO

Frings kept his eyes on his notebook. Avoiding eye contact calmed people who were nervous about talking to him. Puskis had been nervous from the start, down on the street. The way he froze when Frings called his name. The look on his face as Frings approached. He was scared of something, though not of Frings. Puskis was merely nervous about talking to him. Possibly, Frings thought, Puskis was nervous about talking to anyone. So he concentrated on his notebook and asked his questions gently.

"I know you aren't in the habit of talking to reporters."

"I'm . . . no, I actually am prohibited from giving information to reporters. A stipulation of my contract. I'm afraid I will not be of much, um, assistance to you."

"I understand. Let me just ask you what I want to ask, and you can decide whether you want to answer."

Puskis considered this. "Well, I suppose that is fine. Though, again, I'm afraid I will disappoint you."

"That's fine. I'm looking for information on a man by the name of Otto Samuelson." Frings stole a glance up at Puskis and saw the same look as when this odd man had first heard his name on the street; bewilderment and fear. "Do you know that name?"

Puskis was slow to speak. "Why do you . . . why do you want to know about this man?"

"Because someone I talked to told me Samuelson is the key to a big story I'm working on. Because it is important that I talk to him. Because when I did research into his story I learned that he was convicted of murder but couldn't find any information on his sentence or where he is being held. I was told you were the person to talk to."

Frings let Puskis think about this and stared at the rugs hanging on the walls. A smell was in the air. Something that Puskis had cooked in the last few days — spices and meat and maybe rice.

Finally Puskis spoke. "I don't have an answer for you, though that is information in itself."

Frings looked up, confused.

Puskis continued. "There are twenty men

who were convicted of murder during the years 1927 and 1928 and were not incarcerated."

"What happened to them?"

Puskis shook his head with a look of profound distress. "I don't know. Like you, I did research. I have access to the City's official records. There is no question that it is a complete accounting of the affairs of the City's legal system. Yet there is no record that any of these men are serving time."

Frings's breathing became shallow, his pulse fast. "Do you know the names of these men?"

Puskis recited the twenty names while Frings wrote them down in his pad. The man's recall was amazing.

When he had finished the list, Puskis said, "At least one of the men is now deceased."

Frings nodded for him to continue.

"Reif DeGraffenreid. I went to see him. He had been decapitated shortly before my arrival."

Jesus. "Where did you find this De-Graffenreid?"

Puskis related the story of his journey to DeGraffenreid's and his discovery of the corpse. His speech came in torrents, both hesitant and fast, like water under great pressure being forced through a small hole.

When the story was done, Frings asked, "How did you know where to find De-Graffenreid?"

"I received . . . it seems so obvious in hindsight . . . I received an anonymous phone call."

"Do you think it was from DeGraffen-reid?"

"No."

"It was a setup? Trying to scare you off?"

"That would appear to be the case. Yes."

Now it was Frings who paused. He was slightly high and had to assess what he had just learned. He had a number of questions and hoped that Puskis had already thought to look into them.

"When you did your research, was there anything about these men that seemed strange or that they had in common?"

Puskis scratched his temple. "Beyond what we just discussed?" He thought. "They were all gang murders. They were all part of the, uh, the gang war that was active at the time between the White Gang and the Bristols."

Frings nodded and wrote, as much to keep Puskis talking as for his memory. "What else? Was there anything else?"

"There was a small thing."

"Okay."

"When I first discovered the DeGraffen-reid file, it had a sentence notation of 'life,' followed by the acronym PN. PN is not an approved acronym and I was puzzled, but assumed that it was a typographical error because PB is an approved acronym and the B and N are adjacent on the typewriter. But as I continued to research these cases, I found that all of these men had received the same sentence notation: 'life,' followed by PN. It is clearly more than a coincidence, but I do not know what it means."

When he was finished taking notes, Frings looked up at Puskis, who was visibly energized by this unloading of information.

Frings asked, "What do you think happened to these men?"

"My first assumption, as you might expect, was that they were executed. Perhaps in an, an extrajudicial manner."

"But then you found DeGraffenreid alive. Or he had been alive."

"Correct. He was indeed alive up until the time of my visit. He was living in the country."

"So, your thoughts?" Frings prompted.

Puskis shrugged sadly. "I am not used to conjecture on the basis of such limited facts. Perhaps they were sent off to exile."

"But why these particular men, Mr.

Puskis? Why them?"

"I don't know."

They looked at each other for a minute, Frings sensing some kind of weird bond between them, wanting to give Puskis something in this exchange. Something that would cement this bond, make it possible for him to come back to Puskis later if he needed. Frings recognized a name from the list of twenty. He had information.

"One of the men on the list, Vampire Reid."

Puskis lifted his thin eyebrows in query.

"Well, you said one of the men on your list is deceased. It's actually two, at least. They found Reid a few years back out in the sticks somewhere. I remember it because they cut him up pretty good, like someone really had a thing for him."

Puskis took this in with a grim expression.

"Just thought you'd like to know," Frings said.

CHAPTER FORTY-THREE

Red Henry's driver pulled up to the curb across the street from Puskis's apartment building. Henry watched Smith as he stood at the corner, chin buried in his coat against the brutal wind now blowing. The driver gave a quick punch to his horn. Smith looked up and jogged over to the awaiting car. Henry took up most of the backseat, forcing Smith to lean hard against the door, and still there was an uncomfortable amount of physical contact. Henry was unperturbed. In fact, he liked other men to experience the power of his body. It was another way to intimidate.

Henry said, "Why am I here?"

It was only a seven-block drive from City Hall, but Smith had insisted that it needed to be a face-to-face and that it needed to be here, on the street. Henry was torn between annoyance at being dragged from his office and interest in what was so goddamn important that Smith would dare to insist that Henry take this trouble.

Smith came straight out with it. If he had screwed up by bringing Henry out here, delaying would only exacerbate the situation. "That's Arthur Puksis's building. I'm eyeing him, just like you told Peja to tell me. He comes walking up to his door, you see, and out of nowhere comes Frankie Frings. They chin for a second and then they go inside together."

Henry sat absolutely still, thinking. This might be a good sign or it might be a terrible one, Smith knew.

"Are they still in there?"

"Yeah, pretty sure. I was gone for maybe — what? — a couple minutes calling you. I don't think I'd have missed him in that time."

"You have any idea what they might be talking about?"

Smith shook his head.

"Okay. Good work. Stay here and keep an eye on Puskis. What building is this?" Henry indicated the building where Smith had been standing.

"The Bangkok Hotel."

"Get yourself a room where you can watch the street. No use in you catching goddamn pneumonia out here."

It was the most compassionate thing Smith had ever heard Henry say.

Feral was in Red Henry's office a half hour later, watching Henry smoke a cigar and pace. Feral could comfortably wait almost indefinitely — a skill that was valuable with Henry, who didn't like to be rushed.

"Sit down," Henry said, billowing smoke as he talked.

Feral sat. Out of habit, he placed most of his weight on his feet and on his forearms, which rested on the arms of the chair. He could do this without significant physical strain.

"For once, Smith actually did something useful. He was watching Puskis — that troll who runs the Vaults — and saw Frankie Frings talking to him. They went up to Puskis's apartment. Might still be there."

Feral nodded. This situation was fraught with possibility.

Henry continued, "As you no doubt realize, this is a very bad development. Mr. Puskis has been expressly forbidden to talk to the press, but things have been a little dicey for him recently and he may be moving in his own direction. The catch is that we can't deal with this situation in the usual ways. Puskis is too valuable in the Vaults.

There's no one who has any idea of what goes on down there. This new system that Ricks is putting together will be fine, but we have to have Puskis to shepherd the process. We need him, as strange as it seems. Frings, on the other hand, is a whole different problem. If anything happens to him, there will be an investigation, public pressure, all holy hell. So we come to our earlier plan."

"Nora Aspen."

"That's right. As soon as possible."

CHAPTER FORTY-FOUR

What passed for the intersection of Kopernik and Stanislaus streets was in a desolate part of town at the northernmost reaches of the Hollows. It was hard to believe that such a barren, empty place existed in the City. The tracks here had been abandoned nearly two decades ago when the railroad was rerouted south and east at the behest of some member of the City Council who stood to profit from the new route.

As the letter instructed, Frings stood on the tracks. He was exposed out there, with at least a two-hundred-yard sprint to the nearest cover. Kopernik and Stanislaus streets were themselves largely abandoned, unpaved and scarred with ruts and potholes. It was a strange place to meet, the one advantage being that the bombers could easily see if Frings had brought anyone.

Frings stood with his hands in his pockets and his back to the wind, which cut through his jacket as if it weren't there. He had made a call to the newsroom on the way here, instructing Panos to run the version of his column for tomorrow that contained the phrase *golden age,* the signal to Bernal that Frings was ready to meet. He wondered if what he had learned from Puskis would be enough to satisfy Bernal. He had a huge piece of the puzzle: that Samuelson was one of a couple dozen murderers who didn't go to prison after their convictions. He hoped that Bernal could tell him why they were never incarcerated.

The cold was uncomfortable and the wait indeterminate, so Frings pulled a reefer from his coat pocket. The sweet, green smoke felt good in his lungs, and his sensation of the cold went from its being consuming to an odd, vaguely irritating feeling on his skin. The purple light above the City was interesting. And those searchlights beaming from the top of City Hall . . .

Frings's muscles were stiff from the cold by the time a lone figure approached down the tracks. He was fifty feet away when he called out, "Frings?" The voice was high and tense.

Frings waved. The figure beckoned Frings with an arm motion and Frings followed, maintaining a constant fifty-foot distance, intuiting that this was his contact's safety zone. They walked the tracks, past abandoned warehouses with the smoke of squatters' fires filtering out through broken windows. Occasionally Frings saw a person lying at the bottom of the track-bed berm, either asleep or dead — it was impossible to tell in that light.

They arrived at a warehouse emitting smoke and even some light from its windows. Frings's escort came to a stop by the front door and waited for Frings to catch up. Up close, Frings was surprised by how small his companion was — maybe just five feet. His escort knocked an intricate beat, and with a scrape of metal on concrete the door opened from within.

Inside, seven fires burned at various spots throughout the vast warehouse, illuminating oases in what was otherwise an indigo void. A fire near the door backlit a group of five standing figures. Like his escort, they were small as well, and it dawned on Frings that they were children.

"You Frings?" one of the boys asked, stepping forward, apparently the leader.

"I'm Frings."

"We did them bombs."

Frings wondered if he heard correctly. "You did those bombs?"

The leader grunted in the affirmative.

"Okay. If you are the bombers, what's the point? What are you trying to prove?" Frings heard the doubt in his own voice.

"You don't believe me." From his position it was hard to get a sense of what these kids looked like — they were merely silhouettes.

"You weren't what I was expecting." Frings had never questioned children before and felt clumsy. In this situation, he thought, the reefer might actually help. Maybe.

The leader looked down at his hand and Frings could see the silhouette of the boy's pocket-watch chain hanging.

The boy said, "Wait. Wait."

Frings stayed quiet, not understanding.

"Wait. Listen." The leader pointed at his watch as he spoke.

"Wait for what? What's going on?" Frings's pulse accelerated. Something was not right.

"The bomb. Then you'll know."

Frings nodded, guessing that he at least had the basic idea. The group waited in silence. From other parts of the warehouse came hollow noises and echoes. The boys, Frings noticed, were alive with excitement and tension, shifting weight from foot to foot, sighing.

"Out," said the leader, motioning with his head. Frings followed him back out the door, the other boys in their wake, hunching their shoulders against the wind.

"Watch," the leader said, and pointed off down the tracks. Frings squinted and thought he could make out two figures and something else; maybe a barrel or drum. After a quick spark, the figures ran off into the darkness. Everyone was still. Frings strained to hear.

A flash was accompanied by the deep bark of exploding dynamite. The kids were jumping up and down and clapping and laughing as debris rained around them. Two grabbed forearms and danced in circles.

"Ummm," said the leader. "Now you know us."

"Okay. I know." Frings stared at the boys. What the hell was going on here?

This statement seemed to excite the boys anew and there was more clapping.

The leader's voice was ecstatic, nearly yelling. "Got Block. Got Altabelli. Bernal next. We'll get all of them."

The boys let out whoops to accentuate this statement. "*All* of them. *All* of them. *All* of them."

Some of the boys were uncontrollably shivering. Frings followed the group as it retreated back inside to their oil-drum fire. It was insane.

"Why? Why are you bombing them?"

"They owe us. You know? They owe us."

"They owe you? Block, Altabelli, and Bernal owe you?" What was he talking about?

The leader nodded vigorously. "They owe us. They owe us."

"They owe you what?"

"Scratch."

"Scratch?"

The leader made a hand motion as if he were dealing cards. Or handing out money, Frings realized.

"They owe you money?"

"Money." The leader nodded. "Money."

"For what?" This wasn't making sense.

"They stole it. They took our scratch, uhmm, money, took our money."

It didn't seem possible that these kids could have any money to take, much less that Block or Altabelli or Bernal would bother to take it if they did.

"Why would they take your money?"

"We're orphans. We're owed," he said, stretching out the o in *owed*. "They stole that scratch they owed."

Frings thought he understood what they were trying to tell him, but it didn't follow. The way these kids spoke. They were orphans. They had probably never seen the inside of a school.

"Why did you want to see me?"

"You're that writer. You're the writer we need to tell about the bombs and the scratch they owe."

Frings stared back at the child.

"You write what we said. You write it."

"You want me to write what you said?"

The kids clapped and nodded.

"You want me to write that you are orphans and they owe you money and that is why you bombed them?"

"Yes," the leader said, smiling. "Yes."

One of the boys snuck behind the group and put something on the fire and the flames suddenly leapt, reaching ten feet in the air. Frings felt the contrast of the heat on the front of his face and the cold on the back of his head. The higher flames illuminated the boys' pale faces, coloring them orange. They were gaunt, skeletal creatures, some smiling under dull eyes.

Frings broke away from the boys and the fire and looked back at the leader. They locked eyes. The boy's were feverish.

"What's your name?" Frings asked.

The boy pronounced his name with great care, as if he had practiced it often. "Casper Prosnicki."

CHAPTER FORTY-FIVE

Feral stood outside Nora's door, listening to the tinny music coming from her Victrola. Verdi. He tried the door cautiously and found it locked. He took the keys that he'd nicked on his previous visit and carefully unlocked the dead bolt. With intense concentration he turned the knob until he felt the tongue slip out of the hole, then he eased the door forward at a painfully slow pace, careful not to let it squeak. Once in, he closed the door with equal care until the tongue had eased back in place, then laid the keys back on the table in the foyer and found the spot where he had previously watched Nora.

She was reading on the couch again, her back to him, a martini glass within easy reach on an end table. Almost exactly the same as the first time, except this time he had work to do.

He stood silently, and after perhaps an

hour her head drifted slowly to the side and, with a start, straightened up again. Sleep was coming soon.

A man on the street, an off-duty ASU officer, was to honk if Frings returned. Feral knew that this particular night was not vital. If it did not work out, there would be other opportunities. Red Henry, though, liked his orders to be carried out quickly, and there was no reason to needlessly disappoint him.

Finally, her head lolled to the right and her shoulders rose and fell in a slow, regular rhythm. He reached into his jacket pocket and retrieved a vial. He removed the cork from the top, and holding the vial at arm's length so as not to get any of the fine powder around his face, he tapped some of it into his hand. Moving slowly, he crept to the couch, kneeling down next to Nora. He had known this moment would arrive, but the reality of being this close to her — this intimate — made him uncomfortable. He had thought of this moment often, the two of them meeting in the flesh. These were not romantic or sexual thoughts, though he knew that at some level he desired her. But that was not the focus of his thoughts of her. It was merely to touch this woman who had so enthralled him from a distance under the blue spotlight.

He held the palm with the powder in front of his mouth and gently blew the contents into the air. She inhaled the powder, had a slight convulsion, as if she were about to cough, then settled back into a deeper sleep. Feral grabbed her under her arms and pulled her to a standing position so that she leaned against him, reached down, put his left arm underneath her knees, and picked her up, his right arm cradling her back. This was the only dangerous time — the only time that Frings could return and he, Feral, would not have control of the circumstances.

He carried her to the door — opening it with his left hand — and then out, closing, but not locking the door behind them. He carried her down the emergency stairwell, beginning to perspire into his suit, his arms straining to hold her. As he descended, he began, dangerously and out of character, to think to the immediate future. Of her waking up and their actually talking. He felt that, in some sense, he knew what she would be like. Her personality seemed so apparent onstage, in the way she moved, the things she said between numbers, her posture as she interacted with others. She embodied certain traits, he thought: grace, humor, a kind of traditional decency that Americans liked to think they had, but which she truly did.

They came to the back utility door, which Feral had unlocked with the key made from his wax impression. His car was waiting a hundred feet away, across the tiny green. This was the other dangerous moment, though the danger did not come from Frings. Feral had a story — he always did — if he was stopped by someone. But while the story would work for most women, it was unlikely to work when the unconscious woman he was carrying was Nora Aspen.

He moved quickly across the green. His arms burned with her weight and he needed to get her to the car before anyone saw them. He held her upright briefly as he opened the rear door to the car. Then he was at the wheel, with Nora sleeping deeply in the backseat. His pulse raced, as it often did, once the danger had passed.

CHAPTER FORTY-SIX

While Feral drove through the streets of Capitol Heights with Nora unconscious in his backseat, Frings was on the East Side at the Palace, sitting in Floyd Christian's crimson office, drinking beer from a bottle while Floyd drank scotch. The air was thick with marijuana smoke. Frings could feel his body sag in exhaustion, the reefer giving him a comfortable feeling. He would happily have spent the night there on the leather couch.

"You all right, Frank?" Floyd asked, concern on his face. That bothered Frings because Floyd was not one to let much worry him.

"I'm tired."

Floyd laughed and pushed Frings a little. "All right. All right. I know it's more than that, but if you don't want to say . . ."

Frings sighed. He was high and fatigued and was having a hard time thinking through consequences. It was dangerous to talk about his pact with Bernal, but he knew that telling someone would provide an almost physical release of tension. Floyd was trustworthy, and furthermore, Floyd lived in a different world. The East Side was segregated from the rest of the City, almost a completely separate, self-contained municipality. Floyd would never have any reason to come into contact with anyone who would be interested in the information, much less be able to use it. The bombing, on the other hand, was definitely off-limits.

"I'm working on a story. It's a little fuzzy right now. Ever hear about somebody getting convicted of murder and then not being put away?"

Floyd gave him a funny look. "All the time, Frank. The hell do you think happens to your fellow ofay when he happens to murder my fellow Negro for looking at a white woman? Happens all the time. No white man has ever been sent to prison for murdering a black man."

Frings thought that was probably a debatable point, but not what he was talking about in any event. "I'm talking about something different, Floyd. Gang murders. The White Gang and the Bristol Gang." Frings hesitated for a moment, realizing that as a club owner, Floyd had inevitably dealt with one or both of the gangs at some point. Floyd's face, though, showed only interest. "I'm talking about gang hits, sometimes on the street with all kinds of witnesses, and then they go to trial and get convicted, and then, nothing. Don't go to prison. Just kind of disappear."

Floyd was quiet, concentrating on his interlaced fingers resting on his knees.

"What're you thinking, Floyd?"

"This scenario you're telling me about. It reminds me of a story I heard here from one of the rummies. A fella who does some work for me sometimes and I give him free drinks. Anyway, John — that's the rummy — comes back one day from doing some work out in the sticks. He does that, picks up with construction gangs, and they bring them to this place or that. So he says he's out in the country — some town, I don't think he even said what town it was — working on a crew that's putting up this church in a lot right next to this garage. He says they take a break around noon for lunch, and they're all sitting under this old oak tree for the shade 'cause it's so damn hot. And this oak tree is actually on the garage's property. So he's eating his lunch when this truck pulls up to get gas, and he tells me that he wouldn't believe it if he hadn't seen it, but out steps 'Blood Whiskers' McAdam. Still has those big red whiskers, though he says they're going a little gray, and those little peepers he's got. Anyway, John knows Whiskers because I used to send him downtown to pay my subscription fee to ol' Whiskers so that my bottles show up when they're supposed to. So he says that Whiskers sees him and knows that John knows who he is, and John says he gets all red in that scary way that Whiskers has, and John gets ready to take a beating. Then, he says, Whiskers just gets back in his car and drives away. And that's that."

Frings recognized Blood Whiskers from the list that Puskis had given him. "And Whiskers had been convicted for murder."

"Correct. I remember it, too, because there were a lot of happy people thinking he was going away for good or maybe even taking the juice. And then no one sees him for a few years, until John sees him out in the sticks, driving some old farmer's truck."

"You're sure that your buddy wasn't mistaken? Maybe it was someone else?"

"You ever meet Whiskers?"

"No."

"Well, he's not the kind of guy you get

confused with anybody else. He is a uniquely scary individual. A bad gee if I've ever seen one."

"I think I need to get together with your friend John."

"Sorry, Frankie, you're going to have to wait to meet him in heaven."

"He's dead?"

"Died of pneumonia a couple of years back."

CHAPTER FORTY-SEVEN

Excerpt from Van Vossen, *A History of Recent Crime in the City* (draft):

We will take a brief diversion to examine a personage who has been mentioned in either a central or peripheral role frequently in this narrative to date — Sam "Blood Whiskers" McAdam, known as Whiskers. A more violent predator this City has never seen, nor likely, God willing, ever will.

McAdam disavows any knowledge of his parents, and, indeed, many of his victims have questioned whether such a man as McAdam could actually spring from human loins. The speculation of experts on matters such as these suggests that he was the child of a prostitute named Ada Toddle. The father could have been nearly any of the men who worked the river wharfs and visited the professional ladies who plied their trade there. Limited time spent in an attempt to identify anyone named McAdam working on the wharfs during the appropriate period — approx. 1885–87 — has been unsuccessful.

Regardless, Whiskers McAdam was one of the legion of street urchins who haunted the Hollows and upper Capitol Heights before the Turn of the Century. His first City incarceration occurred at the age of eleven, though the file from this incident — the robbery and beating of a man by a gang of six young boys — indicates that he was well-known to the police even at this tender age. His first murder is thought to be the stabbing death of a procurer named St. Jean when McAdam was thirteen. There began an unmatched campaign of violence that led to McAdam's control, personally and without thugs, of twenty square blocks in Little Lisbon and the western Capitol Heights. We have previously attended to the deaths of many of the figures that McAdam removed on his way up the ranks: Cerone, Coehlo, Kaladze, Bauer, and others. A greater number were maimed or simply intimidated by McAdam's violent and unpredictable nature.

The nickname Blood Whiskers is commonly thought to refer to his pronounced, red whiskers. This may account for the duration of this moniker, but the truth behind the story is more sinister and appalling than commonly believed. It stems from an incident in which Gheorge Kaladze's brother and three other hoods from deep in the Hollows had ambushed McAdam in an alley behind the pub run by Sally Bannard. The four had at him with chains and pool sticks, eager to exact revenge for Gheorge's murder. Witness accounts varied, due to the astonishment and horror that common citizens feel when observing such a spectacle, but it is clear that McAdam brutally dispatched all four men with the use only of his hands, feet, and mouth. The blood from his savage bites, according to witnesses, poured from his mouth and dripped from his saturated sideburns. Hence the name Blood Whiskers.

CHAPTER FORTY-EIGHT

Morning light filtered through the blinds, illuminating strips of Poole's naked body as Carla applied salves to his lacerations and ice to the bruising around his ribs and groin. As she worked, he told her about the previous day's work and the impossibility of getting into All Soul's and the abandoned boys at the orphanage. She listened patiently, reacting occasionally when he flinched from some sudden pain.

"You think you're going to find Casper Prosnicki?"

Poole took in a sudden breath as the ointment stung a raw spot on his shoulder. "I guess I am. But I'll tell you, I'm worried about his mother."

"Why is that?" Carla was kneeling above his head, rotating his shoulder, probing for a catch in its motion.

"That place. All Souls'. She got out of there somehow. But I have no idea how she could get back in. That place is locked tight. It's crawling with ASU bulls."

"I wonder," Carla said, stopping her work. "Do you think they always have all those cops there? Because if they do, you have to wonder why. At a women's asylum? It doesn't make sense. And if those cops aren't always there, it means that they're putting up extra security because she escaped. Why do they care so much?"

"Maybe the boy knows something."

"Or maybe the idea of people escaping from that asylum scares them. But it can't be because they are dangerous. Lena Prosnicki could barely tie her shoes, much less hurt anybody. There must be something else."

"Maybe she knows something," Poole said.

"Maybe they *all* know something, Ethan. The point is, what could it be?"

Poole grunted as she got back to work. To change the topic, he asked, "Did you drop the photos off at the *Gazette*?"

"Of course."

"Maybe I should give him a call."

"Maybe." She jerked his head, eliciting a crack in his neck that sounded like a substantial tree limb breaking.

In some ways, Poole reflected, this was

worse than his time at Headquarters.

For some reason, this kind of doctoring made Carla affectionate, and Poole rolled over on his stomach and refused to move because the pain was too intense for him to enjoy any physical pleasure. She tickled under his ribs, finding the few spots on his torso that weren't bruised. He gritted his teeth but was about to give in to her when the phone rang. Her voice told him that something was wrong.

"Say it again, Angelina, I can't understand when you talk that fast." Poole could hear the buzzing of a voice through the earpiece.

"Taken by who? Taken by the police?" Carla talked slowly and deliberately, as if to a child. "Listen, Angelina. Could those police have been ASU? Did they wear gray shirts? . . . Gray? . . . Yes. . . . Yes. . . . They said the mayor wanted to see him? . . . Okay. All right. Listen, Angelina, you stay exactly where you are. I'll take care of this. He'll be okay."

Carla hung up, staring blankly at the table.

Poole saw her chest heaving, breathing hard as she approached panic. "What is it?"

"They've taken Enrique to the mayor."

Poole didn't understand. "What does that mean?"

She turned to him, "Jesus, Ethan, think

for a second. What do you *think* it means?"

Taken aback, Poole said, "The strike?"

Carla shook her head impatiently, as if trying to come to terms with some deficiency
of Poole's. "Of course it's about the strike."
She was moving around the apartment now,
gathering a sweater and shoes, all the while
talking. "There's a group of businessmen —
Poles — looking to open a factory here. It's
a big deal for Henry. We thought maybe if
we timed the strike right, when the Poles
were here, it'd put some extra pressure on
Bernal and Henry. Get things settled
quickly."

"But that's not what's happening," Poole
said, searching the living room for his wallet.

Carla stopped and looked at him. "No.
No, it's not. They're taking a different ap-
proach. I just wonder what that bastard
Henry is thinking."

She was at the door. "Jesus, Ethan, come
on. We need to go."

Chapter Forty-Nine

Puskis could have followed a route to the brownstone of the transcriber Van Vossen that avoided City Hall. But Puskis, a man for whom visceral pleasure was a feeling as foreign as, until recently, fear, thought he might find some odd satisfaction in walking his normal route to work, then continuing on instead of ascending the granite steps.

He thought about the information that Frings had passed on. Vampire Reid was dead. The system in the Vaults had few flaws, but one was that when a person left the City, he was lost to the Vaults's files. Information such as Frings had was interesting, but beyond the scope of the files as they were currently understood. Puskis thought about this: people leaving the City and being lost from the files and Reif DeGraffenreid with his head ten feet from his body.

Passing City Hall, Puskis saw a commotion. An ASU car pulled up to the curb and four officers escorted a single man — powerful, swarthy complexion — up the steps. He walked with dignity, but Puskis got a good look at his eyes, and the fear was impossible to miss.

Puskis continued past City Hall, wondering if the frightened man's file had ever crossed his desk. Why was he arriving at City Hall with that kind of escort? If he were a criminal, surely they would take him to the precinct or even to Stansbury Prison on the border between Capitol Heights and the East Side.

Puskis wove his way along the sidewalk of Government Boulevard, then went right, back into one of the bourgeois neighborhoods composed of block after block of brownstones. Few people were on the street back here, and Puskis took his time, finding an unexpected pleasure in peace without solitude. He noticed things that were common to the point of invisibility to most residents of these neighborhoods: trees in their planting boxes; pigeons neurotically probing for food; and so many squirrels, darting up and down trees and from stoops across the sidewalk. He observed all of this with the hyperclarity of a dream. In this state he arrived at the foot of the eight stone steps that led up to the front door of Van

Vossen's stately brownstone.

Van Vossen himself answered the door. He was Puskis's height, but heavy and soft. Long, unruly gray hair ringed his bald dome, and his basset-hound face was framed by thick sideburns that descended to his jaw and then arched above his mouth to form a thick mustache. He stood in the doorway, assessing Puskis.

"Who are you?" he asked with an air of surprise, as if unaccustomed to visitors.

"I am Arthur Puskis, Mr. Van Vossen. I must speak to you about something very urgent."

Van Vossen held Puskis's gaze. "Puskis," he said, his eyes wide.

"Mr. Van Vossen —"

"Come in Mr. Puskis. Please, come in. All these years and we have never met, and now, at last, you show up on my doorstep." Van Vossen's voice seemed to hold genuine relief at this turn of events. He led Puskis down an ill-lit hall with pedestals at close intervals displaying vases and urns and busts. The hall opened into a library. At one end was a table stacked with books and reams of paper. A spot was clear and Van Vossen had apparently been working there when Puskis rang the door chime.

"Please, have a seat." Van Vossen indicated two wingback chairs that faced each other across an ancient Persian rug. Puskis took one and noticed his host retrieving a small tin from where he had been working.

"You are writing a book?"

Van Vossen lowered himself into the seat opposite. "Mmmh, yes. It is both a record and a reflection on the topic of crime. A distillation of my experience as a transcriber. A recounting of criminal activity during my twenty-odd years and an analysis on the causes and patterns of the same."

"This, um, recounting. You do it from memory?" This work of Van Vossen's intrigued Puskis. He imagined taking all the information that he had from the files in the Vaults and putting it into prose. Subconsciously, his mind was already organizing this information into trends, categories, chronologies.

"Some from memory. Much more from journals. I wrote about the day's cases every night. It was, in fact, my reason for taking that job, to create this work. I didn't need employment, I chose it." Van Vossen rubbed his hands together in front of his face, and Puskis noticed that the nails of his pinkies protruded about a quarter of an inch past the tip of the finger.

"Chose it?"

"Yes. My father was Wim Van Vossen. Perhaps you've heard of him. He was in shipping. Very wealthy. I was bred to be in the business. But my fascination was crime, and the work of a transcriber offered the best window on this world. Except, perhaps, for your position."

"Perhaps."

"My God, Arthur Puskis," Van Vossen said with a sudden burst of energy, as if just now recognizing the esteem in which his visitor should be held. "I'm sorry, Mr. Puskis, I have been waiting for this visit for such a period of time. I am quite overwhelmed and, as you can see, rambling like a fool."

"No. No, Mr. Van Vossen, you are hardly rambling. But the reason I came, well, I came to ask you about the DeGraffenreid file."

Van Vossen turned serious. "So, you found the DeGraffenreid file?"

"Well, actually, I found two. One original file and, I believe, one that you, uh, you copied."

"Yes. Yes, of course." In a motion so effortless that it went almost unnoticed, Van Vossen dipped a pinkie nail into the tin that sat on his lap, brought his finger to his nose, and inhaled. "I did copy that file and send it back to the Vaults."

"Why?"

Van Vossen sniffed. "I needed to get a message out to somebody, but I had to be sure that it could not be traced back to me."

"I don't understand. There was no message."

"You're here aren't you? Listen. It was too dangerous to put an actual message in the file. Suppose the file was requested and sent out with the message still inside. Or, God forbid, another transcriber got his hands on it. I couldn't risk it being traced back to me. I knew that two files would hold great significance for you, but would be dismissed by others as the inevitable consequence of the sheer volume of files in the Vaults. This way you could find me and I would not have to worry about anyone else doing the same." Van Vossen smiled at the memory of his plan.

"But you did this years ago."

"Four years. Give or take, of course."

"Again. Why? What message were you trying to get out?"

"It was a frightening time. Listen. In late 1927 we started to get these cases of gang hits. These maniacs were going through the judicial process and being convicted, but they were never sent to prison, as far as we could tell. We got the first couple and we thought that perhaps it was some sort of oversight, so we made a note and shipped the files to you. But corrections never came. We got a few more and we called the others back from you. They all had this same notation that we hadn't seen before."

"PN," Puskis said.

"That's right," Van Vossen said without surprise. "Do you know what it means? Neither did we. So I queried our liaison with the Department of Prisons — a gentleman named Kraal. I met with Kraal over lunch and I asked him what the hell was going on with this notation PN. What does this mean? He gets very serious and he says, didn't they tell us about the Navajo Project? I had never heard of this."

Van Vossen looked at Puskis to see if this registered, and seeing that it did not, continued, "So I ask him what the hell this Navajo Project is that we haven't been told about. He lowers his voice — we were at a pub — and says that it is a new method of punishment that they are experimenting with. He says it is very controversial and it is very hush-hush in the department. He says they send these convicts out of the City and their cases aren't handled by Prisons but by the office of the mayor. Then he began to get nervous and says that that is all he knows about it. It was obvious there was more, but he changed the subject and ignored my other questions. About a week or so later, he comes up to me on the street as I am walking home. He says that he was mistaken about the Navajo Project and that it was a plan that had been considered but never adopted. I asked him how that could be, and he said he didn't know, but that there was no Navajo Project. He was scared, you see. It was clear to me that he was terrified."

Van Vossen stopped for a moment and repeated the procedure with the tin in his lap. Puskis looked again at the stacks of paper that must have been the book that Van Vossen was writing. There were thousands of pages.

"And that was it for him," Van Vossen continued, as if recounting a dream dreamt long ago. "I never saw him again. Not that it means anything happened. It is perfectly understandable that our paths would never cross again, particularly if he were trying to avoid me. And I would have most likely taken his disavowal at face value if it wasn't for what happened afterwards."

"What was that?"

"Nothing overt. Nothing obvious. I actually didn't notice it at all. But a transcriber named Talley crabbed it by chance. I don't need to tell you that each file has date stamps for when it is taken from the Vaults and when it is returned. What Talley realized was that it took some files longer to reach the Vaults from us than others. We might send ten files to you, and eight would get to you that day, and two would get to you the next. Do you understand?"

Puskis nodded.

"At first we weren't sure. We thought that maybe we weren't remembering the exact day or the exact run, you know — morning or evening — that we had sent them back. So we started keeping track and requesting the same files again to see what date you had checked them in. And it turned out that we were right. Some were taking longer than others."

"And you assumed that someone was looking at the files after you sent them," Puskis said.

"That's right. Listen. We first noticed this — what? — two months or so after I had talked to Kraal. So this started to make me nervous, you see."

"Did you notice if there were particular kinds of files that were being delayed."

"We experimented with that, too. Talley

and me. We requested certain types of files
— homicides or gang-related crimes, for
instance — to see if there was any pattern.
If there was, they held back other types of
files as camouflage. We couldn't figure it
out."

Puskis rubbed the sides of his nose with
his fingertips. "Who do you think was looking at the files?"

Van Vossen shrugged. "Does it matter? It
was either the police or someone from the
mayor's office. Either way, you can understand that it had a chilling effect on us. But
it seemed vitally important to get the message out about these criminals who were
apparently part of the Navajo Project,
whatever that was. I didn't feel safe about
openly contacting anyone, and there was no
way to safely conceal anything in a file. It
was a risk even to involve Talley. It's no
secret that the mayor had an ear in the
Transcribers' Room.

"So I came up with the idea of getting a
duplicate file into the Vaults. It seemed like
a good solution. I would plant the duplicate
file, request it, and then when you noticed
that there were two files, you would look
into it. The genius of the approach was that
if you approached the Chief or anyone else
about the duplicate files, they would assume

that it was just an inevitable mistake or that you were beginning to lose it just like Abramowitz had."

"Why didn't you request the file again?"

"They retired me. Almost immediately after I had the second file planted. Maybe they knew, or maybe they were suspicious that we were playing games with the system and decided to make me the example. Maybe Talley was the mayor's man. I never knew. They sent me off and I didn't have the nerve to ask any of the others to make the request. Who was I to trust? So it sat until a legitimate request was made, I suppose."

Puskis was overwhelmed by this story. "How did you get the duplicate file into the Vaults?"

Van Vossen laughed without much pleasure. "That was simple. One of the women who cleans on our floor was married to one of the cleaners for the Vaults. I gave her twenty dollars to have her husband stick the file in the right spot. Apparently he did."

Puskis searched the street as he walked back toward City Hall from Van Vossen's house. Van Vossen had told Puskis that the police, or more specifically, the ASU, kept a watch on his house, but that he thought the surveillance had more or less been abandoned at this point. Reacting to a stricken look from Puskis, Van Vossen smiled.

"You don't have to worry. You may be the most important person in the City for them. In the Vaults they have a tremendous amount of important information. The information that could harm them is most important of all, you see. But all this information is absolutely worthless if there is no way to retrieve it. Nobody understands how it is organized but you."

"To be honest, that seems like a reason to get rid of me."

"No. Quite the opposite, in fact. Listen. It is like a cancer. How can you treat a cancer if you don't know where the tumor is? It is the same. They need you because you can find the dangerous files. They may try to manipulate you into finding them. If they get scared or think you may have figured it out, they'll force you to do it. But either way, you are indispensable."

That argument had logic but not enough to quiet the thundering of Puskis's pulse. As he walked, he noticed a man on the opposite sidewalk keeping pace with him.

Chapter Fifty

The Poles were assembled in Red Henry's office. Extra chairs had been brought in, and the senior Poles sat while the others stood at attention behind them. Peja sat opposite the Poles, and the translator stood in the middle of the room, turning this way and that to follow the conversation.

Henry said, "We realize that the recent strike at one of our factories has caused some concern." He waited for the translation and watched the head of the contingent, a walrus-looking guy named Rinus, nod gravely and then respond. The translator turned back to Henry.

"He says that there is some concern. He suggests that the police are not an . . . efficient means for dealing with that type of problem."

Henry forced a smile, though the audacity of the criticism brought blood to his face. "Tell him that I am going to show him a method he may find more efficient."

Henry watched as Rinus nodded judiciously, looking at Henry rather than the translator.

Henry beckoned the translator to his desk. "I'm going to bring in somebody and have a chat with him. I want you next to Rinus, and I want you to keep a running translation of what goes on. Don't water it down."

The translator nodded with annoying earnestness and pivoted to go to his new post.

"Another thing," Henry said, before the translator had taken a step away. "This might get rough. Nothing that happens here leaves this room. You will probably understand why you shouldn't be on my bad side after this morning."

The translator turned a shade paler and hurried to Rinus's side. Peja had taken up a post by the door, and Henry nodded to him. The door opened to admit two burly ASU officers, one on each of Enrique's arms. They marched him into the middle of the room and then left him there, retreating to positions by the door.

"Enrique Dotel?" Henry asked.

Enrique nodded. Henry made sure the translator was in place.

"You were the organizer of the strike this

week at Capitol Industries?"

Enrique again nodded. His composure, a subtle show of defiance, irked Henry.

"The strike is now over. Do you understand? You are personally responsible for making sure that the shifts are back to full capacity beginning tomorrow morning."

Enrique kept his chin up and met Henry's eyes. "The strike is not over. I do not control the workers. They make decisions for themselves. I am only an organizer. The strike will not end because I am in prison or anyone else is in prison."

Henry looked over to Rinus, whose head was cocked to hear the frantic translation.

"I don't want this to be a problem," Henry said quietly. "I want to be clear, and I want you to understand and guarantee me that you can do as I ask."

"Again, I am not in a position to fulfill your request. If I was in such a position, I would not grant it."

Henry rose from his chair and walked around his desk so that he stood over Enrique. He might have been half again the weight of the smaller man.

"I'm afraid that I'm not making myself as clear as I might."

Enrique did not back down. "You are clear. I hope that I am clear as well."

Henry grabbed Enrique by the front of his shirt and lifted him off the ground so that they were face-to-face.

"You are making a big mistake, friend."

For the first time, Enrique showed fear. He was a big man and not used to being physically dominated.

Henry looked at Peja and nodded toward the window behind the mayor's desk. "Open it."

Peja looked at him, confused.

"Open the goddamn window."

Peja scurried across the room to open the window. The translator kept translating, but fear was in his eyes. Rinus squinted, concentrating on what was happening while he listened. The other Poles watched with anticipation.

When Peja had the window open, Henry carried Enrique over and shoved his upper body through to the outside. They were on the fifth floor, sixty feet to the sidewalk below. Henry grabbed Enrique's ankles, then extended his arms out the window so that Enrique dangled upside down with Henry taking his entire weight. Henry held him there for several seconds until an odd whimpering sound drifted up to him.

Rinus and several of the more senior Poles were crowding around the window to get a better view.

"Again," Henry said with exaggerated calm, "I need you to have the workers back at the factory tomorrow morning. Is that something you can guarantee me?"

CHAPTER FIFTY-ONE

Poole held Carla's hand as they walked. It was rare for them to be out together like this. At one time this had been common-place, but their work now made it nearly impossible, and they had settled into a hid-den relationship, seeing each other almost exclusively within the confines of their flat. While something about that was both excit-ing and cozy, it was also nice to be together away from that confined space every once in a while. The mood was, of course, spoiled by Carla's anxiety.

"Why are you smiling?" Carla asked.

Poole shrugged. "I like walking with you. It's a break from what I've been doing."

"Good God," she said, exasperated. "En-rique is being dragged into the mayor's of-fice and you're enjoying the walk?"

Poole shrugged, still smiling. "I guess so." He didn't know Enrique and was, to be honest, not sure that he wasn't jealous of the time that Carla spent with him. But there was more than that. Poole knew that he could not fulfill something in Carla. He was not able to match her ideological certainty or zeal, and he wondered if Enrique could. He was concerned about what could happen to Enrique, but it had more to do with Carla's happiness than Enrique's well-being.

She gave him a hard look but squeezed his hand, the kind of mixed message that she often gave and that Poole had long ago decided not to try to figure out. They were a block south of City Hall.

"What's your plan?"

Poole knew that her instinct was to go straight up to the fifth floor and have a go at getting into the office. He also knew that she understood that this plan was not likely to work, that if they did somehow manage to get past all the security and into the mayor's office, it would probably do more harm than good.

"I think we wait and watch and make sure he comes out sometime soon. What time is it?"

Ten thirty.

They waited five minutes. Poole tried a couple of amiable tracks of conversation, but Carla was having none of it.

She gasped. Poole followed her eyes and saw Enrique dangling from a top-floor window. It was nearly surreal. Enrique hung motionless from two arms that protruded from the window.

"Oh my God. Oh my God. Oh my God."

Poole worried that Carla was going to hyperventilate. He slid behind her and cupped her shoulders gently in his large hands.

"He's going to drop him! He's going to kill him!"

CHAPTER FIFTY-TWO

Five stories above, Red Henry was enjoying himself.

"Is that something you can guarantee?" he repeated, looking past Enrique's dangling body to the street below. It was a hell of a drop.

Enrique gasped something unintelligible. Henry jerked his hands a little and Enrique screamed, "Yes. Yes. I guarantee. Yes."

Henry looked over his shoulder and winked at Rinus, who was smiling with one side of his mouth. Henry stepped back and pulled Enrique roughly back into the room. He was weeping and shaking, and when he got to his feet, a large wet stain showed he had lost control of his bladder.

"You may leave now," Henry said. "Thank you for your assistance in this matter."

Enrique staggered toward the door. The two ASU officers took his arms, showing no sympathy for the man's state. The door was ajar and Enrique was halfway through when Henry called out to him, "I know your sister who works at the bakery on Vasco da Gama Street. If I need to find you again, I will go to her first."

The guards released Enrique's arms. He couldn't find the energy even to give Henry a hostile look. He just turned and walked out.

"Well, translate," Henry roared, feeling good.

The translator spoke quickly in Polish as Peja closed the office door. Most of the Poles laughed and the others smiled. A couple even clapped.

Henry smiled, too, not with them, but because his assessment of the Poles and what they would respond to had been so accurate. His intuition was one tool — and physical intimidation was the other — that he knew he could count on.

Rinus came over to him, his hand out-stretched. "That dotted line that you talk about. We are ready to sign on it."

Henry, a man who did not like surprises, actually laughed. He looked over at the translator, who shrugged in ignorance. Those goddamn Poles were cagey, Henry thought, shaking Rinus's hand.

CHAPTER FIFTY-THREE

Poole knew that Red Henry — no one else had arms like that — was not going to drop Enrique in front of all these witnesses. He also knew that telling Carla that would not alleviate her anxiety in the least. After a few excruciating moments, the arms pulled Enrique back into the building. Poole realized he was breathing hard. Carla was fighting back tears.

"It's okay. It's over." Poole brushed her hair with his hand in an attempt at comfort he knew was wholly inadequate.

She turned around into him and wrapped her arms tightly around his waist. He stroked her hair gently.

She pulled away. "We stay here until he comes out."

Poole nodded. He was in no hurry to begin searching the Hollows for Casper Prosnicki. He expected a long wait and was surprised when, only a few minutes later, he saw Enrique walking unsteadily down the front steps. Carla started to move toward Enrique, but Poole saw the urine stain on Enrique's trousers and grabbed her arm.

"What are you doing?" she asked, trying to pull free.

"Let him go home on his own. Call him in a half hour. Don't tell him you saw him here."

She looked up at Poole, puzzled. She hadn't noticed Enrique's pants.

"Just trust me on this. It's for his sake."

Carla nodded. Poole knew that when he made an unequivocal stand, she would trust his judgment. He leaned down and kissed her on the mouth. She wrapped her arms around his neck, and he straightened up so that her feet dangled and her body pressed against his.

"Are you scared?" he asked.

"No."

He could tell by the feel of her body that this was the truth. He grabbed her around the waist and eased her back to the ground. Then, with regret, he turned east toward the Hollows.

CHAPTER FIFTY-FOUR

Nora awoke in a haze, as though coming out of the deepest phase of sleep. Without opening her eyes she knew that something was not right. It was the smell of the place — potpourri in the air, but not the type she used. The mattress was too soft. She opened her eyes and her disorientation took on a visual dimension. She was in her room. But at second glance, she was not. She was in a room very much like her own. The walls were the same pink with white molding. The bed was the same four-poster. The bookcases were like hers, filled with books. But the room was roughly half the size of hers. And there were no windows.

She sat up. She was wearing the nightgown she had fallen asleep in. A pink robe hung from a hook on the only door in the room. She eased out of bed and put on the robe. It wasn't hers, but it fit. She tried the door handle — locked. She sat back down on the bed and rubbed her eyes with the palms of her hands. She wasn't scared, just bewildered.

Fear came five minutes later with the sound of footsteps beyond the door. Until then she had clung to the illusion that this was some bizarre dream or some fault with her perception. Was she going mad? If so, it was not nearly as unpleasant as she would have guessed. But the footsteps forced her to acknowledge that this was real. Someone had taken her from her apartment and brought her to this room, which had been made to look as exactly like her bedroom as this space would permit.

She brought her knees up under her chin and laced fingers over her shins, like an armadillo rolling into a protective ball. She had come to terms long ago that her being a sex symbol meant she was the object of lust for hundreds or even thousands of men. Among these men, inevitably, were the sadists and the unbalanced and the deranged. For them, she knew, she was the object of rape fantasies or perhaps even worse. The similarity of this room to her own had initially been comforting, but now, facing the reality that someone had obviously spent time making this likeness and had therefore seen — or perhaps even been in — her bedroom, it was terrifying.

She sat like that, listening to footsteps, her mind wildly running through worst-case and best-case scenarios of what was happening. She heard the footsteps approaching, finally reaching the door. The bolt pulled back and the door opened. She tried to push farther back on the bed. A small, lean man with dark skin — like an Indian, Nora thought — entered carrying a tray with breakfast on it. He wore tweed pants and a sleeveless undershirt. He placed the tray on a table next to the door.

"Who're you?" she asked, recognizing him as the man who had watched her at the club. She surprised herself with the composure of her voice.

He gave an apologetic smile. "I'm sorry." His voice was soft and carried an accent that she couldn't place.

"Why am I here?"

He smiled again. "Don't worry. Nothing will happen to you. I will keep you as comfortable as possible. This is not about you."

"I don't guess you would tell me what it is about?"

"Sadly, no, other than to assure you that it does not involve harming you. We merely need you here for a short while. Please enjoy your food. Knock on the door if you desire anything."

He turned away from her and she saw how his undershirt bridged the depression between the muscles on either side of his spine. He turned back again.

"Miss Aspen. You are lovelier by far here, in person, than you are on the stage. Please do not worry about your safety. I would not allow anyone to harm you."

He left. His words, uttered by someone else, might have been creepy or threatening. But something about this man made her feel safe and comfortable, and she ate her meal in serenity.

CHAPTER FIFTY-FIVE

Puskis was two blocks from City Hall when an ASU officer intercepted him.

"Mr. Puskis?"

"Yes?"

"I'm glad we've found you, sir."

"Found me?"

The officer was young and earnest. "Yes, sir. When you didn't show up for work, they sent us out searching."

Odd, Puskis thought. Then again, he hadn't been late for work in nearly two decades. They must be wondering why now. Why does he go missing as soon as we unveil the new Retrievorator? And, as Van Vossen had said, he was more important to them now than he had ever been.

He allowed the young officer to lead him back to City Hall, noticing how the other pedestrians gave them considerable room to pass. The officer seemed oblivious of this effect, though, as an ASU officer, he most likely took it for granted.

At City Hall, a contingent of ASU officers along with two men who Puskis recognized from the mayor's staff met them.

"Mr. Puskis," said one of the mayor's men, "where have you been?" He was a huge man in a pin-striped suit that might have been cut for a bear.

Puskis hesitated. Had he been watched? Did they already know where he was or would they be able to find out later? What were the consequences of lying? He was not used to making quick decisions. Nothing was ever split-second in the Vaults. "I, uh, I went for a walk." It was slow coming out and everyone knew it was a lie.

The big man looked at him menacingly. "A walk? You've never been late for work as far as anyone can remember. Why did you go for a walk today, Mr. Puskis?"

Today of all days.

The big man's words had given him time to think. "I received some news yesterday that required contemplation. News that affects my work in the Vaults. On the way to work I decided to take a walk to, well, to clear my head. I assumed that my record of punctuality would allow me one transgression."

The big man was not satisfied but apparently decided not to pursue it further. "You see, Mr. Puskis, we were particularly concerned because we believe that you may be under threat."

"Under threat?"

"I'm afraid so. I'm sure that you've heard about the bombings around the City recently."

"Yes."

"We have reason to believe that you may be a target of these madmen."

Puskis was astonished. "Why would you think that?"

One of the ASU officers stepped forward. "We have reasons, sir, but they're confidential at this time."

Confidential? Puskis saw every file generated by the City's justice system. Nothing was confidential from him. But this was not about an actual threat. This was an excuse. He shrugged. "I apologize for any . . . anxiety that I've caused."

"You're safe and sound now, Mr. Puskis. That's what matters," said the Bear. "Two guards are being assigned to you at all times for the foreseeable future. They'll be with you down in the Vaults and will stay outside your door when you are at home. Six officers rotating in eight-hour shifts."

"Is this necessary? Even in the Vaults?"

"The order came directly from the mayor himself, sir."

That's that, Puskis thought. No way around it.

"There are two officers already stationed in the Vaults. Pretend they're not there, go about your business as usual. I imagine there's quite a bit of work for you, what with the bombings and whatnot."

Puskis nodded and went to the elevators. Dawlish wasn't there. Instead, a much younger man was at the one elevator that descended to the Vaults.

"Good morning, sir," he said pleasantly.

"Mmmh, yes. Where's . . . where's Mr. Dawlish?"

"Mr. Dawlish, sir?"

"Ummm." Puskis then seemed to break out of a trance. "Oh, yes. Mr. Dawlish. The man who normally works this elevator."

"Sorry. I don't know anything about the previous chap. Just told me to take my post at this elevator. This is going to be my elevator, they told me. I'm new, see?"

Yes. Puskis did see. Puskis saw that he was now under house arrest and that his inquiries into the Navajo Project had come to an end.

CHAPTER FIFTY-SIX

Nora decided that her glimpse of her captor's forearms had put her at ease. A strange thought, but there it was. His forearms were thin, but looked as though they were made from intertwined cables, reminding her of the arms of a former lover, Tino Juarez, a boxer whom the Americans called the Magician and the Mexicans called el Matador. He had been small, like this man, and hard. He had been a sophisticate. Nora had been out at the Palms with him when he was approached by a fan who said that he thought Tino was a great fighter.

"I am not a fighter, I am a boxer," Tino had replied. "Fighters are barbaric, unskilled, sadistic. I am a scientist, an artist, a philosopher."

And to an extent, she thought, he was. He earned his nickname because he was nearly impossible to corner or hit to any effect. He rarely knocked an opponent down but so thoroughly confused and eluded him that the judging was a foregone conclusion. Tino's skill worked against everyone but the champion, a brawler named Phil Lawson, who was as quick as Tino and more brutal. Tino had twice fought for the title and twice been knocked out by Lawson.

The trauma of the second fight (she had not known him at the time of the first) ended their brief relationship. She remembered him, though, as a gentleman and as her kindest lover. It was irrational to draw a parallel with her captor based merely on the similarity of their forearms. But once this connection was made, she noticed other similarities. The way he carried himself. The way he looked at her. Something in his eyes was the same as in Tino's, and it made her think of kindness, though the expression on his face betrayed nothing. What had Tino's eyes revealed? Kindness? Or had they been the window on the part of his soul that caused pain to other men? Because, his style and philosophizing notwithstanding, his career as a boxer was rooted in his past as a storied street brawler.

Nora shuddered and rolled over onto her side, staring at the wall. She began to think about how to escape.

CHAPTER FIFTY-SEVEN

That morning Frings came across a headline reading, "Woman Pulled from River Identified," buried on page 11, with other minor news items printed below the obits. The woman had been found lying on the rocks at the river's edge by indigents who were there to fish. The body had been identified, the article said, as that of Lena Prosnicki. No other information was given about her, not even an address, which was standard in these types of articles. The last name he recognized, to his concern, was the same as that of the boy he had talked to the previous night. He would have to look into it when he arrived at work.

Frings had been a little surprised not to find Nora, or at least a note, that morning. She might be at a number of places, at girlfriends of hers from her life before stardom. She might also be with a man. He had never known her to be unfaithful to him, but with their current unease with each other and the reality that she could have nearly any man at her whim, it seemed within the realm of possibility. Frings was not a jealous man, though, and his only anxiety in this regard was for losing her as a part of his life. And he wasn't even sure how he felt about that.

She would be back, he knew, when he returned late that night from his meeting with Bernal.

Eddie, the assistant, was waiting for him at the door to the newsroom, more highly strung than usual. His hair was wildly askew.

"There are some people here from the mayor's office to talk to you. They're in Panos's office waiting."

Frings wasn't surprised by the visit, given his column in that morning's paper. But he began to sweat from his back and under his arms.

"Panos there?"

"Yep. They wanted to talk to you alone, but Panos wouldn't have it."

"Look. Do me a favor while I'm in there. Go down to the library and ask Lonergan to dig out any article we have on Vampire Reid getting murdered a few years back. Can you do that for me?"

Ed nodded, and Frings headed for Panos and his visitors.

Panos's office was silent when Frings walked in. Panos was leaning back in his chair with his feet up on his desk, eating an orange, the juice flowing down his chin. Two men in suits watched this spectacle with disgust. One was Smith. The other was a smaller man with a face like a terrier's.

Panos pulled his feet from the desk and sat up. "Frankie," he said with exaggerated cheer. "We have some people here to talk to us. Your names are what again? Smith and Rider?"

"Rivers," said the Terrier sourly.

Nobody offered hands to shake.

Frings took a seat while Panos took another huge bite of orange.

"What can I help you fellas with?" Frings asked, all innocence.

Smith held up that morning's *Gazette.* "In this article, you claim you spoke with the bombers." Frings had filed the story just under the deadline for the final edition.

"That's right. Last night, in fact."

Smith leaned forward in his chair, his face red with rage. "I'm not playing, Frings. Who the hell are they? Where did you meet them? This is a matter vital to the safety of the citizens of this City."

"It's a matter of safety for your boss and his rich chums. If you'd read the story, you'd have that figured."

"I'm trying to be patient. Who are they, Frings?"

"You know I'm not going to tell you that. I rat out my sources every time you came knocking, no one's ever going to talk to me. I won't be able to work. The chief'll back me up on that one, too. Right, chief?"

Panos, who had started on a second orange and had his mouth full, muttered something unintelligible and nodded.

"This is not the time to be cute, Frings. You and that fat shit boss of yours think this is some kind of goddamn joke. You tell me who they are now, or you're going to get hurt."

Frings laughed. "Take a walk. You know you're not going to get anything here."

The Terrier was up and out of his chair and had a knife at the side of Frings's face. The blade depressed, but did not cut, the skin. Their eyes met. Frings saw the man's eagerness to inflict pain.

Panos stood.

"You want to try again?" Smith asked.

Frings said, "What, you're going to have this maniac cut me right here in this office?" He moved his lips as little as possible as he spoke, not wanting to cut his face on the knife.

Smith nodded, and with his knife, the Terrier lifted the inside of Frings's top lip, and with a subtle flick he sliced through it. Warm blood poured from the wound into Frings's mouth and down his chin.

"Goddamn it," Frings said, clutching his mouth and falling from his chair onto his knees, blood flowing through the gaps in his fingers at an alarming rate.

"Get the goddamn hell out of here," Panos roared, rounding the desk to get to Frings.

"We'll see you again," Smith said, and the Terrier kicked Frings hard in the ribs. "Maybe then you'll spill."

Panos insisted on accompanying Frings to the hospital. A surgeon saw them almost immediately and put four stitches into Frings's lip to stanch the bleeding, then left to track down some painkillers.

"It hurts?" Panos asked. Sympathy was an unusual side of Panos, and Frings found it a little unnerving.

"I'm not going to lie to you, Panos. But I appreciate your coming here with me."

Panos made a dismissive wave of his hand.

"Panos, I saw something in the early edition today. It was a story on the skirt they pulled from the river. It had her name, but no address or anything else. Just a name."

Panos scrunched up his face with suspicion. "What's this about?"

"I'll tell you after you answer the question."

"You're talking about that Parsnippy woman?"

"Prosnicki."

"Right. There was no address. Nothing in the police report and we couldn't track anything down. She wasn't a bum."

"What do you mean?"

"She lived somewhere. She wasn't living in the streets."

"How do you know?"

"I saw photos of her body. She was soft. She didn't have the hardness they get when they are in the streets. She ate well, Frank. Or at least she ate enough. And another weird thing, she was wearing a strange dress. Like a sack."

"A sack?"

The doctor returned with a bottle of pills that Frings was to take for pain. Frings popped two, and the surgeon, horrified, admonished him to take them one at a time.

"Will it leave a scar on that pretty face he has?" Panos asked.

The surgeon looked startled and said that there would be a mark, but it wouldn't be very noticeable if the healing went well. Panos looked relieved.

As they walked down the hospital corridor, Panos pointed to a woman in a hospital gown making her way down the hall on crutches. "Like that. That Parsnippy woman's dress looked like that."

By the time Frings was back at his desk, the painkillers had taken effect, his lip didn't hurt, and he was in a pleasant daze. He found the envelope containing the pictures of Bernal. No message on his desk. The person who had taken the photos had not called.

Ed came by with a newspaper that he tossed onto Frings's desk without a word. It took Frings a second to remember what this was about, and when he muttered, "Thanks," the stitches pulling at his lip when he spoke, Ed had moved on into the newsroom's labyrinth of desks.

Frings flipped through the paper until he found the article he was looking for under the headline "Madman Found Murdered." The story was short and much as he remembered. Police in a rural hamlet called Centerville turned up the body of Trevor "Vampire" Reid in a shack on the edge of town after the neighbors complained of wild dogs howling and scratching at the door. The article made dark reference to "mutilations" and to his long criminal record in the City. It fit into the popular newspaper genre of "come-uppance," and no question was raised as to why Reid was not in prison at the time. Not illuminating, but nice to have his memory confirmed.

Frings dug in his desk for a fresh sheet of paper that he fed into his Smith-Corona. He pulled out his notebook and typed out the list of twenty names that Puskis had dictated earlier. Ed was making the rounds again, and to his evident dismay, Frings waved him over.

"Go back down to Lonergan and take him this list," Frings said. "I want anything from, say, the last five years on any of these ginks. Anything. Got it?"

CHAPTER FIFTY-EIGHT

Walking toward the Hollows, Poole realized that in the commotion over Enrique's coerced visit to City Hall, he hadn't called Frings about the photos. He found a phone box on an uncrowded corner, connected with the *Gazette,* and asked for Frings.

"Frings." The voice was slurred, as if someone were holding his lips.

"You get my package?"

"Sure."

"You've seen what's inside?"

"Yes."

"I guarantee they are the real McCoy. You need to see the negatives?"

"No. No, it's fine. I just need to talk to you about them. Not over the phone."

This triggered alarm bells. "There's nothing to talk about. You print them or I send copies to the *News* or the *Trib.*"

"It's not that simple."

Poole frowned. This was bullshit. "Why not?"

"Listen, we need to meet. You name the place and time. I'll come first, whatever."

Poole thought about this.

Frings spoke again. "Look, I want to burn this guy as bad as you do, right? Just hear me out. I think this could work better for both of us."

"Okay," Poole relented. "You know the Hound and Fox?"

"Sure."

"Six this evening. I'll show up sometime afterwards."

"I'll buy."

"Save your cash." Poole hung up.

Finding a kid on the streets was an almost hopeless task. Poole needed to narrow the range of possibilities. He found himself walking toward the block where his prostitute friend Alice and four other young pros lived in a run-down squat. Once the homes of laborers, these town houses had gone from modesty to squalor in the past decade.

A thin girl with a delicate face and skin the color of tea answered the door.

"I'm here to see Alice."

"Alice is off duty," she said, appraising him. "How about me?"

"That's not it. I'm a friend of hers."

"Sure you are. Like I told you. Shop closed."

"How about this. Go tell Alice that Ethan Poole is here and that he just needs to ask her a couple of quick questions. If she doesn't want to come out and talk to me, I'll screw. Okay?"

The girl weighed this, then shut the door. Poole waited on the stoop, unsure if she was fetching Alice or simply ignoring him. Eventually the door opened again and it was Alice, looking as if she'd just rolled out of bed.

They sat together on a couch in the living room with the other girl, Mem, in a chair opposite them.

"I'm looking for a kid named Casper Prosnicki."

"Don't know him," Alice said, and looked at Mem, who shrugged.

"I need to find him. He used to be at a place called St. Mark's. The boys there say he's on the streets somewhere."

"St. Mark's is a bad place," Mem said with a tone that spoke of experience. "He's better off anywhere than there."

"If he left St. Mark's, is there anywhere in particular that you think he might go?"

Mem shrugged. "Don't know."

Alice asked, "How old is he?"

"Fourteen or so, I think."

"Because sometimes kids that age, they like to stay together in groups. Makes them feel a little safer from the adults. When I was on the streets, there were a few places that you knew you could go to find other kids your age. You figured if you were around them, there was less chance that some adult was going to get his hands on you."

"That's true," Mem agreed. "There were places. Let's see. If you were at St. Mark's, you would probably go somewhere pretty close."

"Maybe the warehouses," Alice said. Mem nodded.

"The warehouses?" Poole asked.

Mem was excited now. "That's right. Back where the old tracks are. There's blocks of these warehouses. There's nothing in them now but people. Groups of people. There's a lot of those warehouses, but he might just be in one of them."

As he was getting up to leave, Alice said, "We were just about to smoke our last reefer. Want in?"

Poole shook his head. He'd never smoked

reefer and didn't plan to.

"Okay." Alice shrugged.

"You know," said Mem, "hold on to that. I'm going to take a ride and roust some more, so we don't run out."

Alice seemed satisfied with this, and Mem followed Poole out the door.

"You need a cab?" Poole asked.

Mem smiled and nodded. Poole stood at the curb and eventually flagged one down. Mem hopped in the back and Poole leaned through the shotgun window to talk to the hack, dropping a five on the passenger seat.

"Where you going?" Poole asked Mem.

"Pierce and Richmond."

Poole addressed the hack. "Take her there and wait out front for her. Then bring her back here. Don't drop her off. Savvy?"

The hack nodded and gave Poole a half smile. The cab sped away. Poole began his walk to the warehouses wondering why Mem had to travel all the way to the East Side to buy her Mary Jane.

An approaching front divided the sky into crystal blue and a dull gray that had consumed the sun. The air here was stagnant and the warehouses were silent. Poole walked along the old train tracks, looking at the dilapidated buildings and listening to his feet grind the gravel underfoot. People were silhouetted in some of the broken warehouse windows. Some ducked when he looked in their direction, others stayed. He expected, even desired, someone to yell down at him — even abuse. But it was silent.

If Carla were here, he thought, she would talk about the cruelty of capitalism and the consequences to people such as these, who were unable to find a place in the system. Right now, that seemed beside the point.

He didn't enter any of the buildings, instead walking along the row, looking at them as if he could somehow divine Casper Prosnicki's presence. Occasionally he would yell for Casper, or for anyone who had seen Casper, but his own voice was the only break in the silence. He loathed himself for not having the courage to enter. He did not fear bodily harm, but rather the chaos he would encounter. His imagination conjured images of disorder and human degradation that he did not have the stomach to witness. So he continued his in effective reconnaissance.

He kept this up for over an hour. By then the thick cloud covering and the evening's advance brought a virtual twilight and Poole became uneasy. His retreat from the warehouses was taken at a trot, and now he heard voices echoing from inside the warehouses as if the inhabitants had suddenly awoken. The words were indistinct, muffled, and reverberating upon themselves. As he passed one of the warehouses, he thought he heard the name "Casper," and it brought him to a stop, staring at the building. Figures silhouetted in the windows stared, motionless, back at him. His unease spiked. The noise from inside increased, the echoes making it exponentially louder. Poole wavered, then continued his retreat. It must have been his imagination anyway. He hated the goddamn Hollows.

CHAPTER FIFTY-NINE

Nora was no longer surprised by any of the details that the little man seemed to know about her. He brought her chicken Florentine with rice and cooked carrots and served it with a glass of red wine that clearly was of a good vintage. She had told *Radio World* magazine this meal was her favorite. Her response to the meal was complicated. She was grateful, certainly, but also exhausted. These continuing attempts to make her captivity seem "normal" were, in their own way, disconcerting. She could see in his face that he had perceived her distress and this made him uncomfortable.

She said it without thinking. "Who are you?" She wasn't sure what she was trying to find out. A name would not reveal much to her.

The little man stared at her, his eyes betraying confusion. She watched him as he thought, wondering what he was struggling with.

He looked at her. "There is nothing."

Something about this was heartbreaking, and Nora felt tears come. The man saw this and backed slowly out of the room, unable to hide his distress.

CHAPTER SIXTY

Frings was hopped up on painkillers by the time he arrived at the Hound and Fox. He was popping them compulsively every hour or so, enjoying the buzz. Nora was still absent when he stopped by the apartment, and he had found that discovery disconcerting, but in a rather abstract way. He tried to force himself to examine the facts of her disappearance and make a rational decision about whether to be concerned, but it took more effort than he could muster, so he smoked some marijuana to see how it would mix with the painkillers.

He was aware of two separate sensations on his walk from Nora's apartment to the Hound and Fox. The first was that his head was somehow not attached to his body and was, instead, floating just above it as his body navigated the streets on its own. The other, wholly separate, sensation was of a hyperawareness of the crowd of pedestrians around him. He felt able to quickly scan the crowd on the street and memorize each face. He continued his walk and did another scan and thought he was able to pick out the people who were still walking with him. He took a meandering, roundabout route to the Hound and Fox, hoping to make any tails. By the time he reached the pub, no face from his original scan of the crowd remained.

He ordered a coffee and waited for Poole to arrive, wondering if he felt so certain that he wasn't followed because of his chemically enhanced sensitivity, or whether he was just too intoxicated to make good assessments of anything — crowds, his perceptions, whatever. He hoped that he would sober up by the time he had to meet Bernal.

Poole arrived on time and slipped in across from Frings. Assessing the bruises on Poole's face, Frings thought that they must look like a couple of gladiators taking dinner together. Frings's lip didn't hurt, but a tightness around the stitches felt odd when he spoke.

"I saw you play a couple times at State. I enjoyed it."

"The games were fixed," Poole replied.

"Even so . . ."

Poole just stared at him.

"I got your photos," Frings said after an awkward silence.

"What'd you think?" Poole was clearly glad to be on to business.

"Well, I don't doubt they're authentic. The thing is that I can't print them. Not right now."

Poole sighed in frustration. "Don't give me that bunk. You don't want to print them, that's the problem. You can print any damn thing you want."

It took a moment for Frings to process the hostile reaction. He smiled, despite himself. "No. No, you don't get it. Listen."

"Okay." The waitress returned with coffee for Poole, giving Frings some time to compose his blurred thoughts.

"The man in those pictures . . ."

"Bernal."

"That's right, Bernal. I shouldn't tell you this and I certainly don't need to tell you this, but since you're here and you have the pictures, what the hell, right? You see, Bernal is peaching to me. He's giving me some very important information that is forming the basis of an investigation into City government." It was amazing how he could slip into this kind of official talk. "I am extremely reluctant to jeopardize my investigation by printing these photographs."

"What investigation?"

"That's really all I can tell you. I can't talk any more about it."

Poole leaned forward so that his shoulders were over the table. "I will send those photos to the goddamn *Trib* and the goddamn *News* if you don't print them. Don't tell me you can't talk. If this really is going to put the kibosh on your plans, then you need to give me the full story."

Frings blinked a couple times. "Why are you so hot to get at Bernal?"

"Why the hell do you think?"

Frings nodded and remembered now the other things he knew about Poole: He was the private dick with the Red girlfriend. It was about the strike. He had no illusions that Poole was bluffing, so he spilled, hoping that Poole would see the larger picture and the greater advantage to him and to labor if he went along with Frings.

"Bernal's turned on the mayor. He's feeding me information about corruption in the mayor's office."

"I need more."

"I don't know much more. He's taking it slow. But from what I know already, it'll be big."

The waitress came to refill their coffee

cups. Frings waited for Poole to speak. When he did, it was not with any evident satisfaction or dissatisfaction with Frings's explanation.

"What happened to your face?"

Frings touched the stitches. "Shaving."

Poole stood up.

"Hold on. I got cut by one of the mayor's ginks. You?"

Poole sat back down. "Here's a story for you." He lowered his voice and leaned across the table. "I was pinched at the strike, along with a lot of other people."

"I was there. I saw it. Not you, but I saw what went on."

"Well, after I was brought in, they took me from my cell and brought me to an interrogation room. This guy, I don't think he was police, he asked me questions while some cop braced me whenever I didn't give the right answers. But the point of it, I guess, was that they wanted me to stop an investigation that *I'm* in the middle of."

This had Frings's attention. "What investigation is that?"

"Missing person."

"Who's missing?"

"I don't know if —"

"Why would you even bring this up if you don't want to tell me who's missing?"

This seemed to make sense to Poole. "It's a kid. A kid named Casper Prosnicki."

CHAPTER SIXTY-ONE

The mention of Casper Prosnicki brought life to the reporter's eyes. Poole wasn't sure what to expect from Francis Frings, big-time reporter and Nora Aspen's lover. Until that moment, he had not been impressed. But the name Casper Prosnicki had sparked something, and Poole felt for the first time that he was seeing the Francis Frings who was something of a legend in the City.

"You know that name?" Poole asked.

Frings paused. "You've been honest with me. I met him last night."

Poole leaned back in his chair, his leg vibrating with excitement. "Where?"

"The warehouses down by the old tracks in the Hollows."

It was confirmation of what Alice had told him. He had been close to Casper. All signs had pointed to it, and he had not had the courage to take the steps necessary to actually find him.

"What were you doing in the Hollows?"

Frings shrugged. "I can't tell you that. But he's down there. Or at least he was."

"Jesus Christ. Okay, thanks. I appreciate that piece of information."

"Well, I've got another piece of dirt that might interest you."

"How's that?"

"Lena Prosnicki, his mother, is dead."

Poole rubbed his eyes with the heels of his palms, feeling that the further along this went, the less he liked it. "How did she die?"

"They pulled her out of the river."

Poole nodded. "So they put me through the ringer and then they kill his mother. They don't want this kid found. Why?"

Frings shrugged, playing it cagey. "Could be any number of reasons."

Thanks, Poole thought. He said, "The guy that cut you. Did it have to do with Casper Prosnicki, your meeting with him?"

Frings's hesitation was his answer.

Poole continued, "Big guy. Blond hair. Scar on his lip?"

Frings nodded.

This was spiraling out of control.

"I'm going to find that kid," Poole said. "You think he'll be down in the warehouses tomorrow?"

"Could be." Frings's eyes were dead

again, though this time Poole guessed it was a ploy. Frings seemed to have reached his limit. He wasn't going to divulge any more.

"I'll hold on to those photos for a while," Poole said.

"Appreciated."

"You played straight with me. I'll do that for you. For a while."

Frings frowned and nodded his head. "I don't need long."

Poole got up from the table and did not shake Frings's hand. "What if I need to get in touch?"

"Call me at the paper. We can set up a meet. I'm not going to give you up. I start giving up sources and I'm through."

So Poole was a source now. "All right."

He found the night considerably colder than when he had arrived. The sidewalks were empty. The streetlights illuminated bright circles in the hard pavement and asphalt. A lorry rattled by and a hack slowed to see if Poole was a fare. He shook his head and the cab crept on. He pulled his collar up against the wind and started the long walk home.

CHAPTER SIXTY-TWO

Frings sat alone at the table contemplating and trying to sip his coffee with the good side of his mouth. Why didn't they want Casper Prosnicki found? It didn't make any sense. Did they know that he was the bomber? Wouldn't it make more sense, if they did know, to catch him and show that they had the City under control? And if they didn't know he was the bomber, why did they care if anyone found him? Frings was missing something, some deduction or some information.

Was the key in Casper's bizarre claim that the mayor's cohorts owed him money? Did this destitute boy had some leverage on the most powerful men in the City? If Casper Prosnicki had such knowledge, why didn't he spill it last night? Frings wondered if Casper could communicate well enough to tell *anyone* his secrets.

Frings finished his coffee and ordered a

bourbon on the rocks. Prosnicki. Bernal. Samuelson. Twenty murderers free. What did it mean? Prosnicki and Bernal. Bernal and Samuelson. Prosnicki and Samuelson? Was that the key? Wasn't Casper Prosnicki's father murdered by someone on that list of men who weren't in prison? Was this all of one piece or was Bernal a common factor in two otherwise unrelated issues?

It was frustrating and Frings's buzz was waning. He popped another painkiller as the hint of a burning sensation licked at his lip.

Chapter Sixty-Three

Part of the new regime, Puskis was learning, was to eat meals out, which was fine. He sat with his two minders at Kostas' Diner, eating pasta with tomato sauce and garlic bread. The two men ate sausage sandwiches and drank coffee.

Puskis asked, "How can I afford to eat like this every day?"

The smaller of the two men, sporting a trim mustache, seemed to be in charge. "You get a per diem."

"Do you have it?"

"What do you mean?"

"Do you have it? Do you have my per diem?"

"Of course. Lead man on each shift will have it."

"Can I have it?"

"Your per diem?"

"Yes. Can I have the money? I would prefer to be responsible for my own finances, if that is acceptable."

The mustache shrugged. "I don't see any harm." He pulled a clip of bills from the breast pocket of his jacket and handed two fives over to Puskis.

"Thank you."

The junior of the two men was uncomfortable in silence. "You must have seen it all, Mr. Puskis."

This seemed an odd thing to say. "I haven't actually seen anything," he replied. This, he reflected, was true and not true. He had not witnessed anything beyond the incoming and outgoing paperwork that made up his life. But the sheer volume of knowledge that he possessed did probably add up to "seeing it all," or experiencing the big picture of crime and justice in the City.

"Come on," said the younger man. "You've been at the Vaults forever." He then asked a succession of questions about mobsters and psychopaths who had enjoyed brief flings with notoriety in the recent past. Puskis indulged these questions as a way of passing the time and on the theory that there could be no harm in ingratiating himself with his minders.

The checks arrived, creating an uncomfortable moment. The Mustache gathered them up, but Puskis insisted on paying for his himself.

"I'll take care of it, Mr. Puskis."

"I'm sorry to be a bother, but I have my money. You gave it to me. I would much prefer to handle my own affairs as much as possible. Surely that can't be a problem for you?"

The Mustache puckered his face in annoyance and gave a dismissive wave of the hand. It wasn't worth an argument.

Puskis handed his bill to the man at the register, a Hungarian named Ferenc.

"Could I keep the slip?" Puskis whispered.

Ferenc leaned in. "What's that again?" Mimicking Puskis's hushed tone.

Puskis looked over at the two ASU men at his table. They were looking at him but not really watching.

"I need the slip."

Ferenc followed Puskis's glance to the two officers, then looked back at Puskis. "Of course." He slid the slip across the counter. They exchanged payment and change, and Puskis scooped up the slip along with the bills.

"Thank you," Puskis said. "Will you be here tomorrow morning?"

Ferenc nodded.

"Then I will have something for you."

CHAPTER SIXTY-FOUR

Red Henry and Ian Block sat next to each other in an otherwise empty sauna at the Capitol Club. Henry sat with his hands on his knees and his elbows pointed outward. The heat had caused red blotches to emerge on his massive back. Block, not even half of Henry's size and darker complected, leaned back into the raised bench.

"So the Poles are going to come around," Block said.

Henry nodded.

"Peja said it was you scaring that little rat-fuck union commie goatfucker. What's his name?"

"Enrique Dotel."

"Yeah, Dotel. Peja told me he pissed his goddamn pants. Said you hung him out the window by his ankles and he pissed his pants. Said the Poles loved it."

Henry nodded.

"What's wrong, Your Honor?" Block said,

gently mocking.

Henry turned to Block. "Where are the others?"

"What? You mean Altabelli and Bernal?"

Henry nodded.

"Altabelli, it's his anniversary. He's been married to that Jane for twenty-five years, if you can believe it."

"I know it's his goddamn anniversary," Henry snapped. Block was a misogynist, and while it could be amusing at times, it generally pissed Henry off.

"Bernal said he had a meeting."

"Who with?"

Block shrugged, but Henry wasn't looking at him now and missed it.

"Who with?" he repeated louder.

"I don't know," Block replied quickly. "He didn't say, I didn't ask. What's eating you?"

Henry turned again to face Block. "Who would be the first to betray us?"

"Betray us?"

"Yes. The four of us: you, me, Altabelli, and Bernal. Who would be the first to betray us?"

Block looked surprised, but then warmed to the question. "Well, I figure it wouldn't be you, and I know it wouldn't be me."

Henry nodded, eyes on his steepled fingers.

"So Altabelli and Bernal. I don't know. You think someone turned?"

"Just answer the question," Henry said with a seriousness that had Block concentrating on the question again.

"I don't know. It's a hard one. I had to say one, I guess I would finger Bernal. He's so goddamn nervous sometimes. Why?"

Henry rubbed his face with his giant hands. "I don't know. I've got a feeling. Things are getting dicey. I told you that this clerk from the department went looking for Reif DeGraffenreid?"

Block nodded and leaned forward.

Henry continued, "So I put Smith on him, follow him around a little. Guy never leaves his office. But the other day, who pays him a visit? Frank Frings. And then goddamn Frings writes a column that says he's met with these guys that've been planting the bombs."

"So you think this clerk is the bomber?" Block asked, puzzled.

Jesus Christ. "Of course not. We've got a couple of guys chaperoning him, but not for that reason. He's harmless except that he went looking for goddamn DeGraffenreid. So I've got two problems. One, these bombers Frings says he's met with. Two, this clerk found out about DeGraffenreid and then talked to Frings. So on the one hand I need Frings to tell me who the bombers are, and on the other hand I need him to not look into the DeGraffenreid case, or any of the other Navajo cases."

Block shrugged as if it were no big deal. "So? Make him talk. Put the fear of a vengeful fucking God into him. You know how to do that shit. Look what you did to that poor commie bastard this morning."

"Don't be a goddamn moron. Frings is untouchable. He'd write about it in a second, and no matter how goddamn charming and innocent I act, half the people will believe it. So I did a couple of other things. You know Frings's girl? Nora Aspen?"

"She's a nice piece."

"Feral's got her."

"No shit." Block seemed to enjoy this news.

Henry nodded. "He pinched her from her apartment. Left a note for Frings to drop the case."

"Has he?"

"Not yet. He may need her to suffer a little first. Let him know the gloves are off. I also sent Smith to have a chat."

"I'm guessing that didn't go over."

"No. But he cut Frings a little. Gave him

something to think about."

"Well, don't hurt that Aspen piece too much. Wouldn't do too much good for the American male's morale."

Henry shook his head. "Another thing. Lena Prosnicki got out."

"Christ almighty. How'd she do that?"

Henry frowned. "We're looking into it. We've got no idea what she did once she escaped. One of the nurses noticed she was gone during bed check. Feral was busy, so I sent Smith after her and he took care of it."

"Jesus, Red, there's a lot of shit happening."

Henry nodded, staring at the far wall.

"So what does Bernal have to do with any of this?"

"I don't like that this is all happening right now. Doesn't make sense to me that, like you said, it all happens at once like this. There's always something, but in drips. This is a goddamn flood."

"So what're you going to do?"

Henry didn't answer. He had a funny look about him. Block was about to ask again, then thought better of it.

CHAPTER SIXTY-FIVE

It was late, but she said she wanted a bath. Of course, without windows, she had no way to know the time. The drug-induced sleep would have contributed to her disorientation, as well. Feral had not foreseen this request — stupidly, he told himself — but it seemed reasonable enough. Still, it posed some logistical problems. He went through his bathroom and carefully removed anything that she could use to harm him or herself: razors, of course, and the rope that he used to hang laundry, scissors, all medicines, and matches. Even without these items, she could still drown herself. It was awkward. He drew her a warm bath.

She was in a robe when he let her out of her room. It was the first time that she had stepped foot in the rest of the apartment, though it was only to walk a few feet down a hallway. Her hair was up and she looked unkempt in a becoming sort of way. He paused at the open bathroom door and let her enter. She began to close the door, but he stopped it with his hand.

"You must leave the door open."

"Are you going to watch me bathe?" she said with a pout. Was it a flirt? A taunt? A challenge? Whichever, it made him uneasy.

"No. I'll sit in the hall, but I can't let you shut the door. You could hurt yourself."

She smiled. "Think I'd drown?"

Feral didn't smile. "I don't know."

She gave him an indifferent shrug, turned, and without warning shed her robe. Feral looked away quickly and moved a step down the hall so that he could not see in, his heart pounding.

"The water is perfect," she called out.

He wasn't sure how to respond, so he said, "Do you see the soap?"

"Thank you."

Feral stood silently in the hall, listening to the gentle sloshing of the water as she moved about in the tub. After a brief silence, he called out to her, "Is everything okay?"

"It's lovely," she said, sounding as if she meant it.

"There's a towel on the sink when you're done." He kept his voice level but wanted to hear her again.

"Yes, I see it. Thank you."

After a few more minutes he heard the sound of water displacement and then dripping as she got out of the tub. He heard the soft noise of towel against flesh as she dried herself. Feral stayed rooted to his spot in the hall.

She appeared in her robe, her hair wet and pulled back, her face shining. As she passed him in the hall, small beads of water dropped from her hair onto his hand. She walked directly to the door to her room, then turned to wait for him to open it with a key. They were close now, close enough that he could feel her breath on his face.

"Thank you," she whispered, and slipped through the threshold.

He closed the door behind her and found himself alone in the hallway.

Chapter Sixty-Six

Bernal arrived first.

Fog had come in off the river and penetrated Frings's trench coat, leaving him shivering in his damp clothes. Frings would not have found Bernal but for the orange glow of his cigarette intensifying with each inhalation. It was incredibly stupid for Bernal to arrive first, but Frings resisted the urge to confront him. He was probably already sufficiently on edge.

"You're early," Frings whispered.

"You're not the only one who is nervous about being watched."

Frings couldn't see Bernal's face. "Are you sure you weren't followed?"

"Are you sure?"

It was a fair enough point, so Frings got on with it. "Your guy Samuelson. He's a convicted killer but was never incarcerated. How am I doing so far?"

"Go on."

"There are others, too. Other murderers who were convicted but never sent to prison. They were shipped out to the country."

Fog had a way of dulling and diffusing sound. When a sudden noise, like a scraping and then a thud, came, Frings could not pinpoint its exact nature or direction.

"I don't like it down here," Bernal whispered. "Let's go up on the bridge."

A little-used trestle bridge ran directly above them, spanning the river. At one time it had been a railway bridge, but it had converted to an auto and pedestrian bridge when the railroad was rerouted. Frings followed Bernal by sound as he scrambled up the rise to the pitted gravel-and-dirt road and then to the bridge. For some reason, Bernal walked fifty yards or so onto the bridge before stopping and leaning with his arms on the railing. The river rushed beneath them, shrouded in fog.

"So you found out about Samuelson."

"I don't understand it. Why didn't they send those sons of bitches to prison? Why ship them out to the sticks?"

Bernal had a new cigarette in his lips and he struck a match, illuminating his face. The brief peek at Bernal's psyche showed a man close to his limits.

Bernal fished into the pocket of his trench coat and handed Frings several sheets of paper, folded together in quarters.

"What's this?"

"Two things. The first is Samuelson's address. Talk to him. He'll have answers for you. The second is financial records. They're not the originals. I copied them by hand. I didn't get everything, but you have the parts that are important. Talk to Samuelson. Look at the records. That should give you the story."

Headlights shown through the fog as a car approached. Frings and Bernal stood in silence as it crept by them on the bridge.

"You know that car?" Bernal asked.

Frings shook his head, then, realizing that Bernal might not have been able to see his response, said, "No."

Frings heard Bernal inhale hard on his cigarette and hold it for a beat before exhaling in a rush. "I'm taking a big risk doing this. A big risk."

"You're doing it so you won't sink with the ship. You're hedging your bets."

"Easy to say from where you stand, Mr. Francis Frings. Where I stand, there are no good choices. Where I stand, I'm likely to get hurt no matter what choice I make."

The time when Bernal had had real

choices was long gone. He'd made them and enjoyed the benefits for a time. The bill was now due, though, and Frings had no sympathy for the man before him, invisible in the darkness but for his cigarette. He did, though, have an interest in keeping Bernal from a complete mental collapse. "I can help you with one thing. The man who took the photos of you."

"Yes?"

"I talked to him. I convinced him that he would be better off if he sat on them."

"How did you do that?" Bernal's tone was flat. He was under too much pressure to feel much relief from this news.

"He sent them to me. I got in touch and told him you were helping me out and that his pictures would ruin the whole bit."

"I suppose I should thank you."

"No," Frings said. "I did it for selfish reasons. Thought you might want to know, though."

They shook hands.

Frings thought of something. "Who's Casper Prosnicki?"

Frings thought he heard Bernal gasp.

"You know him?" Frings pushed.

"Samuelson will explain. He will . . ." Bernal's voice trailed off.

Frings waited, but the life seemed to have

left Bernal. Frings turned and, without another word, headed back to the shore. He clenched the papers tightly against his chest and, the tension of the meeting now released, felt the true force of his fatigue. A figure brushed past him on the bridge. He stopped and turned, watching the man's silhouette recede into the fog. Frings was indecisive, and before he'd figured out what to do, he heard someone — with the fog playing tricks with the sound he could not tell if it was Bernal or someone else — shout, "Who's that?" A beat of silence was followed by a violent splash from below as something hit the river.

Frings turned and sprinted off the bridge, barely able to see where he was going. He stumbled twice, the panic getting him back on his feet and pushing the pain from his consciousness. He ran until he found himself in a residential neighborhood, unable to continue, his lungs burning for oxygen, his legs rubbery. He placed the papers on a stoop and sat on the steps with his head down, gasping for air.

He thought about what had taken place on the bridge. The man who brushed by him on the bridge now seemed familiar. A trick of hindsight? He wondered who it was and how this stranger had known about the meeting. He wondered if the stranger knew that he, Frings, had met with Bernal. Mostly, though, he wondered why Bernal hadn't cried out as he jumped — or was pushed — from the bridge into the frigid waters of the river.

Unable to get this last thought from his mind, Frings stood unsteadily, put his hands on his knees, and retched until he had nothing more to give.

CHAPTER SIXTY-SEVEN

Nora lay on top of the sheets in white satin pajamas that she found in the bureau. Her wet hair dampened the pillow, coaxing the smell of soap from its fabric. She was, if not comfortable, at least beginning to have a better understanding of her situation, and she found this energizing and could not cross over into sleep.

Years of being the focus of attention of just about any man she encountered gave her a strong sense of a man's intentions. Her captor was difficult to read. He was quiet and shy, often a good sign, though shyness was sometimes the product of intentions that a man knew were beyond societal bounds. That was why she had tested him with the bath.

She now believed that he would not harm her. He was smitten, but not in a way that would lead him to use force on her. He would not want her in any way that he did not feel was reciprocated honestly. This was her one advantage among all the disadvantages she faced; an advantage that she had already begun to use, but to what purpose she was still uncertain. She had sensed the tension as she brushed by him. The brief suggestion in his mind that she might actually fancy him as he fancied her. She could use this weapon against him. She needed to figure out how. Or maybe just having it would be enough.

CHAPTER SIXTY-EIGHT

Henry had to lift Siobhan off him to roll over to the phone. She began kneading his back, which was slick with sweat.

"What is it?" Henry's annoyance was tempered by the knowledge that it had to be significant for anyone to ring him at this hour.

"Mr. Mayor," said the doorman, "two men to see you, sir."

"Names?"

"It's your, uh . . ." There was a pause. "It's your assistant and a man named Smith."

"Send them up." Henry felt the tension in his muscles against Siobhan's strong fingers; the anticipation of bad news and the need for difficult and important decisions to be made.

He stood up and pulled the sheet from the bed, wrapping it around his waist. Siobhan, naked, lay back on the pillows and used both hands to brush the red hair from her face.

"A couple of boys are coming up," Henry said to her. "Why don't you curl up and get some sleep. I'll wake you up when they're gone." He took a blanket that had been discarded to the floor and threw it over her. It was a relief to him to have her body covered. Modesty was not her strong suit.

Henry walked out to the living room to wait, listening to the grinding of the elevator gears. He smelled, he realized, of her and of sweat. His massive chest was mottled with red from exertion. He ran a hand over his scalp, feeling the prickly hairs just starting to emerge on the sides.

The elevator opened into the living room, and Peja and Smith hesitated before stepping out, balking at the sight of the mayor, naked except for the sheet around him, sitting in his oversize leather chair.

"What the hell are you waiting for?"

The two men entered and sat. Peja looked tired and miserable. Smith just looked worried.

Henry looked back and forth between the two men. "What in God's name is going on? Why are you here?"

Smith began to speak, then thought better of it. Peja said, "Bernal's dead."

Henry turned his attention to Smith.

"True?"

Smith nodded.

"Jesus Christ. What happened?" Henry leaned forward in his chair, glaring at Smith. "Goddamn it. Tell me you didn't bump him."

Smith was avoiding eye contact by staring over Henry's shoulder. "I followed Bernal, like you said. A cab picked him up at his house a little after ten thirty and headed north. I found a cab, not so easy to do in his neighborhood, and the cabbie found Bernal's cab and tailed it. The farther north we got, the foggier it got, so it was hard to keep the other cab in sight, but easy for us to stay hidden, if you follow. So he gets out of the cab — what? — about three blocks from the river. I make my cab go past him and go right for another block before letting me off. Trying not to tip him, you know?

"I figured Bernal was going to the river, so I looped around. It was foggy as hell there. Barely see your hand in front of your face, you know? So even though I knew basically where he was, it was hard to be sure. So I found a spot just under the bridge and waited and listened. Then this other gink comes. I can hear him walking down towards the river and then stop, and then I can hear them, him and Bernal, having a

382

chat. I couldn't really make out what they were saying, so I thought about trying to get closer, and then they suddenly start coming up the hill towards me. So I kind of hid behind this pillar, even though there's really no need because the fog is so thick.

"Anyway, they go up on the bridge, and I follow as close as I can, you know, trying not to make noise. So I get up there and I can hear them talking, but again, I can't really make out what they're saying. Then, like that, they're done and someone is coming my way. So I just start walking towards them, like I'm out on a stroll. I walk past him and I realize that it's goddamn Frankie Frings."

"You're joking."

"I'm not. It was Frings. I just kept on walking until I came to Bernal. I can tell as I get close to him that he's in a panic. You know how you can kind of tell?" Smith looked at Henry for confirmation, trying to get the mayor on his side. Henry nodded.

"Anyway, I get up real close so that he can see my face, so he knows who I am. Well, he gets a look and pulls away and takes a jump. He just threw himself over the railing and was gone." Smith stopped and looked at Henry, who was rubbing the sides of his face with both hands.

"What were they talking about?"

"Like I said, I don't know."

"What would you guess?"

"Jesus, Mayor, I have no idea. It could have been anything."

"And, Peja, why are you here? Are you his insurance that I don't kill him?"

Peja laughed nervously. "No, sir. We figured you'd probably want something done."

Henry sighed. "Where's Frings now?"

Peja and Smith looked at each other. Peja said, "We're not exactly sure. I'd guess that he'd go back to Nora Aspen's flat."

"You'd guess," Henry mocked. "Listen to me. You get Feral over here first thing in the goddamn morning. I need someone who isn't going to ball everything up."

Henry stayed in his seat for a while after the two men left. Bernal's talking to Frings could only mean bad things. The question was, how bad? The Poles would sign tomorrow, if he could keep things under control until then. When that was tied up, he could focus his attention on Frings and even play a little rough with the girl if that was what it was going to take.

CHAPTER SIXTY-NINE

Cold and wet, Frings entered the apartment at the edge of exhaustion. The painkillers and marijuana magnified his fatigue.

There was still no Nora. He had been counting the steps until he could fall into bed, but Nora's absence sent his adrenaline surging as for the first time he seriously considered the possibility that something had happened to her. Was it this sudden sense that she might be in danger — or worse — that caused him to now notice the note on the table in the foyer, or had it not previously been there? It was written in block letters:

MR. FRINGS — THIS IS TO INFORM YOU THAT WE HAVE NORA ASPEN. CEASE YOUR INVESTIGATIONS OR YOU WILL GET HER BACK IN PIECES. WE WILL KNOW IF YOU DISREGARD THIS INSTRUCTION.

Frings rubbed his eyes. She'd been abducted, no conditions for her release. Meeting the demands simply kept her alive. And the demands were vague. "Cease your investigations." This could refer to any of a number of investigations that he was either actively pursuing or that were still open. But he knew that the message came, at least indirectly, from Red Henry.

He sat at the kitchen table with the note and thought about his options. The absence of a mechanism for getting her released troubled him. Was she going to be held indefinitely? She was a celebrity and would be missed not just by a small circle of friends and family, but by the public at large. What would be necessary to satisfy her captors that he had given up on his investigations? He sat with his elbows on the table and his hands supporting his head. He was exhausted and his lip burned, but his mind was clearing for the first time in a while. There was, he decided, no way of guaranteeing that following the demands in the note would lead to Nora's safe return. Quite the reverse was true, he thought. They could not afford to let her go for fear that he would begin his inquiries again once she was safe. The only way to guarantee her safety was to acquire a bargaining tool himself, and the only way to do that was to continue to pursue Bernal's leads.

This decision brought renewed urgency, and he put off sleep to examine the papers that Bernal had passed to him.

On the first sheet someone, probably Bernal, had written directions to Otto Samuelson's place. He lived in a town called Freeman's Gap, which Frings had heard of, somewhere in the hills outside the City.

The rest of the papers — twelve sheets in all — were ledgers with handwritten names and figures. This was what Bernal said he'd copied from the originals. It took a couple of minutes for Frings to figure out the layout, but then it was easy to follow. It was an accounting of money paid bimonthly by a group of individuals to four different accounts. Each sheet was titled "Navajo Project," followed by the month. The pages covered the months from November of 1932 to October of 1933. The names of the individuals paying in were familiar from Puskis's list: Samuelson, DeGraffenreid, Smithson, Acton, McAdam, and others. The money was paid to four accounts, labeled "St. Mark's," "All Souls'," "St. Agnes'," and "General Fund." The amounts that each of the men was paying every month were staggering, often between eight hundred and fifteen hundred dollars. Incredible amounts. How could they be generating that much? The bulk of the money went to the General Fund, with a smaller portion designated for All Souls', a still smaller portion for St. Mark's, and a pittance to St. Agnes'. The dispersal seemed to be based on a percentage of the total amount paid each month.

Some hints were here. He knew of St. Mark's and All Souls' — an orphanage and an asylum, respectively. The orphanage, in particular, was rumored to be squalid and neglected. These convicted killers seemed to be contributing money to these two institutions and another, St. Agnes'. But why? To what end? It was hard to imagine a label more vague than General Fund, and that most of the money was going into it made it particularly frustrating. But the amount of money was what was truly curious. How were these convicted murderers coming up with this kind of money? It was hard to figure, especially if they were out in the sticks like Freeman's Gap.

Bernal had said that these papers and a meeting with Samuelson would give him the full picture. From what he had here, it did seem that an explanation from an insider would be revealing. With this in mind he set his alarm for six and crawled into bed. It was four thirty in the morning.

CHAPTER SEVENTY

There was a new shift of minders the next morning, a tall one with a crooked nose and his partner, a human pit bull, all jaw and shoulders. Puskis went through the conversation about keeping his own per diem all over again. Crooked Nose seemed less inclined to go along with it until Puskis told him that the previous day's shift had allowed it, at which point the minder relented, his discretion lasting as long as his culpability.

Breakfast at Kostas' was considerably busier than dinner — the turnover faster, the talking louder. The two officers had an intense conversation about a boxing match they had attended the other night. It sounded as if the Pit Bull had lost a fair amount of money when a fighter named Tino Juarez had knocked out his guy.

"When did that little wetback get cojones?" he complained to his partner, who made sympathetic noises.

The conversation gave Puskis time to think. Police officers had moved desks and two machines that looked like huge typewriters into the Vaults. The officer in charge said that more machines would be added as they progressed through the files and more room became available. Today the people who would actually use the machines were to arrive, and the converting of the files to the form used by Ricks's machine would begin. The first day of the Vaults' death throes.

The officers' gabbing had slowed their eating, and their plates were still fairly full when Puskis finished.

"I'm going to pay my bill," Puskis said as he stood.

The officers nodded at this and watched as he strode to the counter.

"Good morning, Mr. Puskis," said Ferenc.

"Good morning. Are they watching us?" Puskis asked through a forced smile. His heart pounded and there was fear, but it was thrilling, not debilitating.

Ferenc smiled. "Yes."

"I am going to give you two slips. Please put them both on the spike. When we've gone, I need you to find the one I've written on and get it to Francis Frings at the *Gazette*."

Ferenc smiled and nodded. "I understand."

Puskis handed him two fives. "Please only give me a couple of bills to make the transaction look legitimate."

Ferenc kept the smile, but his eyes were concerned.

"Don't argue with me please," Puskis said. "I can't afford to have attention drawn."

Ferenc handed back the change and shoved both slips down on the spike.

Puskis had composed the note the previous night:

Dear Mr. Frings,

I am a prisoner. There are two men watching me at all times. They (I know that you know who I mean) are destroying the evidence held in the files. I write you this note so that you will know the reason for events that may follow. They can not destroy the past, but they can edit our memory.

A.P.

CHAPTER SEVENTY-ONE

Poole was back in the Hollows, wondering why the hell it kept coming back to this. A bitter wind drove a mixture of rain and sleet like darts, challenging the limits of the turnout jacket he had received from a fireman as a gift for all the money the guy had made while Poole was playing football.

He was back at the old railroad tracks, trying to remember from which warehouse he had heard Casper's name the previous day. He spent twenty minutes narrowing the choice down to three warehouses that fell within the span of two blocks. He stood outside the building on the far right, gathering his courage to enter. In the end, the sting of the freezing rain on his cheeks sent him inside for shelter, his adrenaline surging.

Inside, it was surprisingly warm. The smell of burning wood mixed with the smells of other, unidentifiable burning things. The

393

warehouse seemed to be organized around a score of fires that danced like serpents out of oil drums. Each fire was encircled by people either standing around or sitting or even sleeping, but keeping close for the warmth. It was also surprisingly quiet. What conversation occurred was kept at a low murmur, and the sum of all the voices came to Poole as a low hum.

He walked through the center of the warehouse, looking for a group of kids. The floor was strewn with glass, debris, and the bones of small animals. He drew glances from hunched figures that seemed to be parts of their huddled groups rather than individuals. But he did not receive the amount of attention that he feared he might. He completed a circuit of the warehouse without finding a group of children. Individual children were with groups of adults, probably with their parents. The composition of other groups was impossible to discern, the people huddled in blankets or in clothes that completely concealed them. A film of greasy smoke residue covered everything. The few faces that he saw up close were filthy and vacant or deranged with hunger and disease. He felt revulsion, then disgust with himself for this reaction, flashing to what Carla would think if she knew his thoughts. He wanted to leave, forget the whole thing: Casper, these people, the ASU. But he was more disgusted with cowardice and knew that retreating now would gnaw at him. It would confirm the doubts he had about his resolve, doubts that originated in part from his participation in the point-shaving. He couldn't allow the prospect of personal comfort to dissuade him from his duties. So he continued on.

He chose to approach the group closest to the door for two reasons. First, they seemed marginally better off than the other groups, and Poole thought this might explain their favorable position on the floor of the warehouse. He imagined a social order that determined various groups' locations based on some strange intuitive criteria. Second, it was the easiest point from which to escape. The urge to flee filled a space in the back of his mind like ambient noise.

He approached them with an assertiveness he did not feel, using the same strategy, he realized to his disgust, that he would with a pack of strange dogs. Approach with benign confidence. They would smell fear or hostility. He was dismayed that he regarded as less than human these people whose only deficiency was very likely ill fortune. He did not change his approach, however.

"Excuse me," he said to the group of six men and a woman standing around an oil barrel that pitched flames and noxious smoke.

Their expressions ranged from surprise to distaste, but stopped short of outright hostility. The woman, he noticed, had bruises under both eyes.

Poole tried again. "I'm looking for a boy named Casper Prosnicki."

The group continued to watch him in silence.

"Does he live here? Do any of you know who he is?"

One of the men spoke. He had long, unkempt hair and a stringy beard that fell to his chest. Poole thought he might be thirty years old, though it was hard to tell under the black filth on his face.

"You with the force?"

Poole shook his head.

"Then why you looking for him?" The man's voice sounded as though filtered through boiling water.

"His mother asked me to find him. This child is missing from his mother."

"Lots of children missing," said another man, with patches of hair growing around a spattering of burn marks on his scalp. "Lots of kids running around without kin."

Poole nodded, trying to look sympathetic. "I know. I know. But I'm just trying to find one of them. Casper Prosnicki."

"You sure you're not a blue?"

"I'm private. I'm a private dick. I'm trying to find Casper Prosnicki and bring him back to his mother. Do any of you know him? Is he here?" He was speaking slowly, enunciating carefully as if speaking to children.

The man with the beard spoke again. "Nah, we don't know him. Nobody around here knows nobody. You keep going around asking questions, people going to think you're a cop. Cops have a way of disappearing around here at the warehouses. Cops sometimes come in and somehow don't seem to get back out again. Sometimes cops come in bunches now. Watch each other's backs. Mostly cops don't come around at all."

"I'm not a cop."

"Maybe you aren't and maybe you are. You go around asking questions, people are going to think you're a cop. Then maybe you don't leave one of these warehouses next time."

The man held Poole's eyes. His body language and expression were not threatening. Poole took his words as a warning.

"Thanks for your time," Poole said, and tipped his hat. The group returned to their fire without acknowledgment.

The rain and cold outside shocked his body. He squinted against the rain and wind and marched toward the adjacent warehouse. As he approached the door, he heard voices coming from the next warehouse down the line. In the storm, it was hard to discern anything but the silhouettes of ten or twelve men. Poole began to move in their direction, but more slowly now. The men did not notice him approach, apparently involved in some commotion by the door. Poole walked still closer and could now see what was happening. Men were escorting — or was it dragging? — kids out of the building. There was yelling, unintelligible over the howl of the storm.

Poole was so transfixed by the scene in front of him that he didn't notice the two men approach until they were ten yards from him. At this distance he could see that what he had guessed was, in fact, true. These men, and the group of men at the warehouse entrance, were ASU.

CHAPTER SEVENTY-TWO

The rain had abated somewhat by the time a sober Frings found his way to Freeman's Gap, but the ruts in the road had turned to canals. He would have had no chance of finding this hardscrabble community except that Lon Kingsbury down in Advertising had grown up in Sylvan, the adjacent town to the west, and had given him precise directions. The village consisted of a couple of taverns, a country store, a gas station, three churches, and a post office. No one was on the streets. Frings continued on through and out the other side.

Outside town he encountered unmarked roads branching off at irregular intervals and, unable to figure out which might lead to Samuelson, returned to the town. He stopped at the country store, where he asked an elderly man wearing square bifocals for directions. The man paused to think for a minute, gave him directions, decided that they weren't quite right, then gave him a second set that he seemed happier with. Frings thanked him and got back on the road.

As the man had promised, a road branched off by a giant felled oak. He took this road, which quickly turned into a dirt drive that led into the forest. It was slow going on this track. Rain-fed streams crossed the narrow road at intervals, and Frings had to build up momentum to ensure that his wheels didn't get stuck. The road eventually curved to a clearing where a ramshackle cabin dominated a yard cluttered with rusted car chassis, broken bicycles, and other assorted large junk.

Frings pulled his car into an open area near the front of the house and got out, wishing for the first time in his life that he had a gun. It was the country, he thought, that had him so ill at ease. He had been with thugs and murderers hundreds of times in the City. But that was his turf. Out here in the sticks he felt vulnerable.

A porch ran the entire length of the front of the house, and Frings trotted to it through the steady rain. On the porch he wiped the water from his face and knocked on the wooden door. The windows were covered from the inside — there was no way to look in. He could see light coming from inside through the gaps in the planks of the door. The place was buttoned up. The floor inside creaked under footsteps. Frings knocked again.

"Who's that?"

Frings was surprised by how close the voice was. Possibly just on the other side of the door.

"Mr. Samuelson?"

"Who's that? I'm not asking a third time."

"My name is Frings. Roderigo Bernal sent me to talk to you."

No response.

"Mr. Samuelson? I want to talk to you about the Navajo Project."

"Stand back from the door."

"I'm going to move to my left, your right," Frings said, taking two sideways steps to his left.

"You clear?"

"Yes."

The door came open fast and hard, and Samuelson emerged with a shotgun braced against his shoulder, sighting Frings. He was a huge man, not fat but not thin either, a round Scandinavian face under his tangled blond curls. He assessed Frings with suspicion.

"You're Frank Frings?"

Frings nodded, looking at the shotgun.

"How do I know?"

"I've got my press pass in my wallet if that means anything."

Samuelson snorted. "To hell with it. Come in." He nodded toward the open door. Frings was careful not to make contact with Samuelson as he eased by.

The interior was a marked contrast to the outside. Warm-colored rugs hung on the walls and over the windows. What had seemed forbidding on the outside seemed somehow pleasant now that Frings was inside. He figured the rugs had as much to do with insulation as decoration. The sparse furniture was simple and clean and well-ordered. Samuelson might have made some of it himself. Samuelson nodded Frings to a chair and then, to Frings's relief, leaned his shotgun against the protruding stone fireplace.

"Coffee?"

Frings nodded. Samuelson stuck an iron pot into the fire and sat down opposite Frings.

"So you know about the Navajo Project."

"That's right."

"Who peached?"

"Bernal." There was no harm in saying it. Bernal was dead.

Samuelson's face was blank, but he was rubbing his calloused hands up and down the tops of his thighs. "That's right, you said that." He pondered this for a moment. "What do you want to know?"

"The details. How does it work?"

"Jesus, I've been waiting a long time for someone to find one of us. Yeah, I can tell you that. Where do I start?"

"After the trial. You were convicted."

"Yeah, that's right. I was guilty. So what they do, they lead me out of the courtroom, but they don't take me down to the holding cells. They take me to this meeting room. There's a bunch of suits there, mayor's guys. Not Henry, this is just before his time. Shit, hold on."

The coffeepot was blowing steam and Samuelson fished it out with fireplace tongs. Frings stared at the fire while Samuelson retreated to the kitchen to make the coffee in silence. He returned with two large mugs, the strong, acidic aroma spreading through the room.

"There were guys from the mayor's office," Frings prompted.

"That's right. They tell me I'm not going to the big house, and I'm half-happy and half-trying to make what the fuck's going on. They say that there's been so much killing with the gangs and all that, and there's all these widows and kids without fathers, and that between paying for the killers to be in jail and keeping these widows and kids from starving to death that it's eating away at the City's money. So they say I'm not going to prison, they're going to send me out to the fucking sticks, and I am going to have a farm and the cash I make is going to go back to the family of that gink I killed."

"Cy Leto."

"That's him. So they sent me out here, which is where I've been ever since. Farming, bo, I'm a goddamn farmer."

"That's it?"

"For a couple of years. You know how when Henry became mayor he worked the White Gang over pretty good, and as far as I know, they stopped sending people out to be farmers. What ever. One day, this guy comes out to talk to me. Cake eater, but tough. You could tell. Name of Smith. So he comes out and tells me that the money we're sending back isn't enough, that we have to be making more. I say how the fuck am I supposed to make more money. But he's got a plan for me to make a lot more."

"What's that?"

"I think you're going to need to see it for yourself."

CHAPTER SEVENTY-THREE

Excerpt from Van Vossen, *A History of Recent Crime in the City* (draft):

A word or two is appropriate on the Anti-Subversion Unit, or the A-S-U as it is more commonly known. After the election of Mayor Henry and the subsequent massacre at Lentini's restaurant that we have earlier visited, the ASU became, with the regular police force, the most consequential force for order in the City. But the story of the ASU begins not with Mayor Henry, but more than a decade earlier, during the Great War.

The United States of America's entry into the War led to an accompanying concern for the security of certain valuable resources. Many port cities and industrial plants were given protection by the Army or Federal Government. The City received no such allocation, but was nonetheless an important supplier of steel, tungsten, and other strategic materials. The threat posed to the strategic materials by Anarchists, Communists, and Criminal Gangs was met with the creation, by one-term mayor Clement Lassiter, of the ASU. The ASU was drawn from the ranks of the police force and served mainly as guards at the plants, railroad, and river ports in the City. Other ASU "squadrons" were more aggressive in their pursuit of Subversive Elements, using both undercover schemes and surprise raids to aid in suppression of Subversive Elements.

The terminus of the War ended the need for the ASU and it was dissolved, though the law authorizing the unit was left on the City's books. It was this law to which Mayor Henry turned after the so-called Birthday Party Massacre.

The ASU was reestablished and was made answerable directly to the mayor. It comprised, as had the original incarnation of the ASU, the most aggressive and successful officers from the regular force, but now also untrained street thugs whom Mayor Henry had counted on as allies during his days running the neighborhood known as Blue Hill.

The ASU, distinguished by their light

gray uniforms, began a particularly brutal assault upon the White Gang at all levels from the block bosses to Tommy McFadden himself.

Though purportedly charged with the eradication of the gangs, rumor, whether founded or not, struck fear in the common citizenry. Even the reckless kept out of the way when the Grey Uniforms arrived.

CHAPTER SEVENTY-FOUR

Poole ran.

The officers gave chase but were losing ground. Poole thought frantically as he ran. Could he get to his car? Was his car even a safe destination if the ASU were searching for him? Were other cops in the area? Headlights cut through the rain, a couple of hundred yards down the street. Desperately, Poole veered left, heading for the warehouse that he had just visited.

He made the door twenty yards ahead of his pursuers, closing it hard behind him. His eyes needed time to adjust to the light. All he could make out were the glows of isolated fires. Unable to wait, he sprinted toward the back of the building, where he had seen a staircase during his earlier visit.

As he ran, he yelled, "Cops coming. Cops coming."

The murmuring that he'd noticed on his first visit had stopped. A figure appeared in front of him, too close to avoid, and Poole ran him down, the man hitting the floor hard. Poole kept going. He reached the staircase and turned back to face the front of the building, holding on to the banister and struggling for breath. The front door was still closed. Poole guessed that the officers were waiting for reinforcements before entering the warehouse. He would have.

Seconds passed and the muted conversations began again. Poole climbed three stairs, continuing to watch the door. It opened, nearly a dozen ASU officers spilling in, staying in tight formation.

"Police! Police!" Poole yelled, then took the stairs three at a time.

At the top of the stairs he paused. The second floor was much like the first — groups huddled around scattered fires in oil drums. Gray light filtered through tall, narrow windows. There was silence downstairs, Poole picturing the officers moving slowly forward, scanning the indigent crowd for him. He had hoped that the antipathy toward the police voiced by the men he had talked to would translate into action once the police entered. This didn't seem to be happening, and Poole wondered if it hadn't been bluster after all.

Then a clanging noise came from below

and a yell and all hell broke loose. Up from the ground floor came the sound of yelling and large things crashing against the floor and walls. The building shook.

Poole hurried to a group gathered around an oil-drum fire near one of the windows. He pushed two men out of the way, grabbed the lip of the drum in his left hand, and felt the hot metal sear his flesh. He flung the drum one-handed through a window. Shattering glass and the subsequent impact of the drum on the ground added to the cacophony from downstairs and, Poole hoped, would draw the attention of the officers that were surely posted outside.

Two indigent men angrily grabbed at Poole's soaking jacket, shouting at him incoherently. Poole threw them both to the ground with little effort and raced across to the far wall. The commotion from below was working the second floor into a frenzy, and the volume rose as people began to bang on the walls with sticks or cans or their fists. People yelled unintelligibly, and projectiles of all sizes flew through the air.

Poole's hand throbbed with pain. He moved with his head down in an effort to avoid flying objects. The sheer volume of the noise made it difficult to think. He found a scrap of two-by-four and used it to break a window and clear the glass shards from the sill. He looked down, the rain slapping him in the face, to find that no one was below. Hopefully, they had run to the other side.

He could hear people ascending the stairs now, so he sat down on the windowsill and swung his legs outside. The drop was twenty-five feet, and Poole took two deep breaths before pushing off. The ground came up fast, and he rolled with the impact, careful to keep his hand from hitting the ground. He stood and sprinted past the rear of the warehouse, then left down an intersecting street. Halfway down that block, he heard the pop of a pistol. He turned and saw a half dozen officers running at him, a hundred yards behind.

He covered the rest of the block at full speed, then turned onto a block of abandoned row houses, each fronted by a cracked concrete stoop under which was an entrance to a basement apartment. Poole ran to the fifth stoop and ducked behind it, chest heaving. A group of rats, picking at some spoiled meat, scattered at his arrival.

The police knew he was somewhere on this block, but it was to his advantage for them not to know exactly where. It was also to his advantage that they did not know that he was unarmed. They would be hesitant to enter the street if they thought he would be able pick them off one by one.

He heard the officers assemble at the corner, but couldn't make out their conversation over the sound of the rain. Time was crucial. Once adequate reinforcements arrived, they could seal the entire area and take their time ferreting out Poole. Poole had to be quick, but not rash. It was better to take a brief pause to think than to make an irrevocably wrong decision and get caught. Poole leaned back on the concrete and considered his options.

CHAPTER SEVENTY-FIVE

Frings followed Samuelson into the forest, the rain coming down in heavy sheets through the trees. Frings wore a borrowed poncho, and the water ran in streams off both men. Frings would not have been able to find the path himself, but following Samuelson, it seemed quite clear. They walked a half mile in silence until Frings caught sight of a clearing up ahead and picked up a familiar scent, even through the rain. Not the smell of the pines or the wet leaves, but a sweet, moist odor.

The trail came to an end between two ancient hemlocks, their foliage so thick that the ground beneath them was nearly dry in the downpour. Samuelson stopped and gestured for Frings to step into the clearing. When he did, the amount of money accounted for in the ledger suddenly made sense.

"Jesus," Frings whispered. Before him, like

a meadow, were acres of marijuana plants. *Acres.* And around the field, deep forest.

"Welcome," Samuelson said, holding his arms out to the field, his mouth contorted into a rueful smirk, "to my humble farm."

"This was Red Henry's idea?"

"I didn't say that. Got the word from the cake eater. But, yeah, if it was that guy who came out, then the mayor's behind it."

"You're farming reefer."

"That's right. It's not really farming, though. More like just harvesting. It's a fucking weed. Throw the seeds into the ground and let them do their own growing. Certain dates, you know they're coming to make a pickup and you harvest so it's ready to go."

"Who comes?" Frings was still stunned by the sheer volume of plants. He imagined being alone here, if only for a moment, and stuffing his pockets full.

"Started off, it was different guys, some white, some colored. Come out on the scheduled day, bring a girl with them, too. You could spend some of your cut on the girl, if that's your way. Things changed when Vampire took a runner. Waited for a day when they made a pickup, took the cash, and left in his truck. Next day Smith shows up and can't fucking find him. Comes around to all the rest of us, says where the fuck's Vampire? Nobody knows, we just guess he screwed, and everyone in their own mind starts thinking that's maybe not such a bad idea, you know?

"Well, they shipped out some private guards to keep the rest of us in line for a couple of weeks until they found him. You see, what they decided to do was promote a few of the guys, make them responsible for the rest of us. This was when Henry was all close with the Bristols and he made of few of those ginks his men.

"So, of course, Whiskers ended up as leader. Don't know if they planned it or he just took it over or what. They sent him out after ol' Vampire, and he got him all right. Cut him up, from what we heard. Used to come around with Vampire's balls in a mason jar right on the passenger seat of that truck they gave him. Showed them to all of us. No one thought too much about running away after that.

"Some ginks keep making the dope runs and bringing the girls, but Whiskers runs the show the rest of the time. No one crosses him much. Things kind of settled down once he sorted out who was in charge."

They were walking back. "Why did they

decide you had to start making more money?"

"You know, they said it was getting more expensive to take care of Leto's wife and kid. And Vampire got bumped, and Whiskers and his boys started running herd on us instead of tending their land, so we had to pitch in for their share."

"That's queer."

"How's that?"

"I'm pretty sure the wives are shut up in some run-down asylum and the kids are in an orphanage, though a bunch of them are running around the streets tossing bombs all over the place." Frings saw the big man's eyes narrow. He'd said too much.

"The Letos don't have a house like regular fucking people?"

"I'm pretty sure they're more or less locked up."

Samuelson stopped walking. "That's not the way it started. That's not what they tell us. What the fuck happens to all that money?"

Frings shrugged.

Samuelson's eyes went blank. "You know, there are some hombres out here. Some of these ginks, they should have put them in prison. That's where these fucking lunatics belong. Like when I found out Whiskers was

416

part of the project. I couldn't fucking believe it. He's a goddamn psychopath. That guy should have been given the fucking chair or sent up for good. But he's out here, like Johnny fucking Appleseed, and now he's running the fucking place. But I tell you what, he's not getting rich.

"He's not going to be too happy to hear about this. Not at all."

They weren't far from the house when Samuelson came to an abrupt stop in the trail. Frings, lost in thought, continued on a couple of steps before realizing that Samuelson was no longer with him, bringing him back to the here and now. He turned first to Samuelson, then followed Samuelson's gaze up ahead where the trail jogged to the left between two venerable oaks and then over a brook, across which Samuelson had laid two weathered railroad planks as a bridge. Three men were crossing that bridge. They were soaked in their wool coats and dungarees and carried shotguns that they held easily, with familiarity. Frings didn't recognize the other two, but the one in the lead was Whiskers McAdam.

There was no point in running. He took a quick look over at Samuelson, who was showing Whiskers his palms. No weapons.

Ignoring Samuelson, Whiskers, with his head cocked to the right and an expression of mild regret on his face, took in Frings.

"Who's the gink?" Whiskers asked Samuelson without taking his eyes off Frings.

"Francis Frings."

Whiskers' eyebrows climbed. "No shit?" Whiskers took a step closer to Frings, making a show of looking him over, Frings smelling the foul alcohol coming off Whiskers like heat from embers. This close, Frings could see the strength in the man's shoulders, the size of his hands, the instinctive fighter's stance. His face, squeezed between the famous sideburns, was near handsome — a long, flattish nose, wide mouth, and neat teeth. But the hollow, greedy eyes rendered all the rest of it moot. He could inspire nothing but disgust and fear.

"I've been waiting for you," Whiskers said, his face now inches from Frings's. Frings leaned away reflexively and Whiskers smirked. "I've been waiting years for you to come."

Frings began, "I'm not sure —"

"Of course you're not fucking sure," Whiskers yelled. Samuelson moved over to stand with the other two men. Whiskers took a couple of steps away from Frings, maybe getting his thoughts together, then turned. "We've been out here years, Brother Frings. Years. Not once did one of you come poking round. Where d'you think we were? You think they killed us, dumped us in the river?"

Frings wasn't sure if Whiskers wanted an answer to this, but there was a pause and Frings felt compelled to say something. "Everyone thought you were in prison. All of you." He nodded toward Samuelson and the other two.

Whiskers spit off to the side. "The fuck you doing here now?" He had his chin raised slightly, accentuating the height difference between the two men.

Frings's mind raced, trying to suss out the right answer. Whiskers glared at him, then grew impatient. "Well?" he roared, back in Frings's face.

"Bernal sent me."

Whiskers stared at him. Frings found the courage to meet his eyes.

"Bernal? Bernal sent you to do what?"

"Talk to Otto."

Whiskers paused, chewing thoughtfully on his lower lip. He turned and walked toward Otto, who had gone white, getting right up to his chest. He was inches shorter and maybe fifty pounds lighter than Otto, but there was no mistaking that he terrified the bigger man.

"Why the fuck'd Bernal send this fucking gink to see you?"

Otto stared back at Whiskers. "I don't fucking know. I don't."

Whiskers made a feint with his shoulders and Otto flinched.

" 'I don't fucking know,' " Whiskers mocked. "But you took him to the field."

Otto nodded. Whiskers nodded his head thoughtfully and stepped away from Otto. Frings saw Otto begin to tremble with panic.

"Jesus, Whiskers," Otto said, then looked to Frings. "Tell him what you told me."

Whiskers stopped and glared at Frings. "Say again, Brother Otto?"

"He told me something. Something you want to hear."

Whiskers' lip curled up in a sneer. He nodded and walked back to Frings, staring hard. He brought the shotgun barrel up to Frings's face and began to trace his lips with its cold end.

"What'd you tell Brother Otto, friend?"

The barrel found the stitches on Frings's mouth, and Whiskers applied pressure until Frings could feel the mineral taste of blood in his mouth. Whiskers pulled the barrel away.

Frings wanted to spit, but didn't dare. "The families that are supposed to be getting your money; they aren't getting it. It's getting skimmed. Almost all."

Whiskers pulled his head back, surprised. "You being straight?"

"You've been making money for the mayor. Maybe his friends, too."

Whiskers closed his eyes, his mind elsewhere. Though the rain continued to fall, the sun had emerged high and to the east, and the drops that clung to the underside of the leaves looked to Frings like little hanging diamonds.

Whiskers reached into his coat pocket and came out with a tin flask. He unscrewed the top and took a long pull, put the flask back, and walked over to the three men.

"You heard that, I expect," he said with chilling calm. "Fucking Red Henry, that fucking goatfucker." He laughed and shook his head. Frings felt the fear ratchet up, his chest constricting.

Whiskers spoke louder now. "You know, I'm done with those little boys and their firecrackers. That was for fun. That . . . was for fucking fun. This is different. That fucking . . . You know, I am in the mood to do some killing. I think that's about right." He looked to the three men. "Does that sound right to you?"

They stared mutely back at him.

Whiskers took three quick steps and had Frings's jaw tight in the grip of his left hand.

Frings winced. "Shit."

Whiskers said, "Johnny, bring me your fucking blade."

"Wait," Frings gasped.

Whiskers dropped his shotgun and held his right hand out, waiting for the knife.

"I can help you," Frings said.

An ugly smile crept over Whiskers' face. "They all say that. Ain't never true." He had the knife in his hand now.

"You're going to kill Henry."

"I expect so."

"You need my help."

Whiskers snorted a quick laugh. "I need your help? How you figure that?" He let go of Frings's jaw, but didn't give him any space. "Go ahead, Brother Frings, save your life."

Frings took a breath. "You're going to need to get out of the City. You know, after you kill him." Frings struggled for a rationale, talking without a plan. "I can help you. You'll need confusion. You'll need the cops distracted." Frings paused.

"That's all? You think that's going to save you?"

"I write the story about the fields. About you and the fields. They'll come out here looking for you. Either here or in the City. It's a distraction, you see? That's how you walk away. Kill Henry and leave. Go anywhere but here. The City is going to be in turmoil. You can get away."

Whiskers frowned thoughtfully, nodding. He turned from Frings and walked to the three men.

"You heard the reporter man. What do you think?"

None of them spoke, scared to give the wrong answer.

Whiskers turned back to Frings. "Okay. You'll live today. You go back to your newspaper and you write your story. You write it real quick, like."

Frings nodded.

Whiskers came up close again. "And let me tell you something, brother. You get back to the City, don't be thinking that maybe you can go back on your word to Brother Whiskers. Don't you do it. 'Cause I got something to tell you. Something might give you pause. I know you got that little singer woman. That story don't run, I'm going to take a trip into town and find her, hear? She most likely provide some real entertainment for me. Real entertainment. That sound about right to you?"

Frings stared back at him.

Whiskers picked up his shotgun and shook his head. "I still got that killing feeling. Still do."

The three men seemed to shrink at these words.

Whiskers walked over to a tree, holding his shotgun by the barrel, then assaulted the trunk with the stock, swinging again and again with savage force into the tree until the stock broke off and he was left holding the barrel. He turned to Frings, mouth open, chest heaving, eyes wide, steam rising from his head into the rain. He threw the shotgun barrel into the low bushes.

Whiskers walked over to Frings and stuck his index finger hard under Frings's chin. He got his face so close that their noses nearly touched. He whispered, "You write that story, or I swear to God that I will find your girl and she will never be the same."

CHAPTER SEVENTY-SIX

The Vaults were different now, no longer Puskis's sanctuary, but an active office. His two minders were present along with the typists and the police officers who showed up periodically to take the used files away. It was, Puskis thought, like returning home after a war and finding someone living in your house. He had always been comfortable in this place, but this was no longer possible.

He spent all of his time retrieving files as he was now responding to both Headquarters and the typists. One of his minders took responsibility for the logbooks. Puskis had taken great pains to explain how the logbooks worked, but the man did not give Puskis the impression that he understood in even the most rudimentary sense. Puskis would normally have agonized over this type of thing, though in the current context it seemed an almost insignificant detail. He shunted that bit of anxiety to a far corner of his mind.

Of greater concern was the fate of the files once the typists were done with them. Where did the officers take the files when they left the Vaults? Puskis had asked his minders about this and they had pleaded ignorance, but Puskis felt sure that they *did* know. One of the uniforms had been more forthcoming.

"We take them to the incinerator down in the Hollows."

Puskis's chest had contracted at the news that they were burning the old files. There would be no record except for what the typists were entering onto those odd sheets. The uniform, barely more than a boy, had sensed Puskis's unease and tried to make friendly conversation.

"You must be excited about this new machine, Mr. Puskis. It will make your life much easier."

Puskis had managed a neutral grunt, aware of the boy's meaning even if he had been too distracted to catch the exact words. How could he explain the impact of this machine on him? Could this boy understand the plight of the newspaper artist who is replaced by the photographer? That this loss takes one layer of humanity away from the information that people receive? That a photograph does not convey an essence that can be shown in illustrations? And even if the boy understood this, would he be able to make the leap from there to Puskis's own case? Would he be able to understand that through a combination of logic and intuition Archivists had, purely through organization, transformed an impossibly large trove of facts into a system that was, in and of itself, information? How many people understood this? How many would understand if Puskis tried to explain it?

In these beginning stages of the process, the typists were busy with the files from the years 1926 to 1931, or from the first of the PN files through the brutal dismantling of the White Gang after the Birthday Party Massacre. This was particularly troubling because Puskis knew that the source material for at least some of the files, which was supposedly being typed in verbatim, was faked. Therefore, the fake information would now become the official file in that wretched machine, and the file with the faked papers would be burned, the evidence of the senses now gone. There was no longer any way to detect the subterfuge. Puskis could not call attention to the obvious freshness of paper supposedly nearly a decade old; could not point out that the handwriting on the papers did not match that of any of the transcribers during that period. The machine would have the "official" facts and there would be no way to refute them.

Puskis wondered about the other files. Were the files that were not already faked being changed in any way during the typing? It wasn't possible to read what was being typed. Only one line of words was visible at a time, the rest hidden within the typing machine. The question was of vital importance to Puskis. He spent the morning planning a way to find out.

Before lunch, he paused out of view of his minders and read the file on a White gangster named Lezner. He then took the file, along with the others he had collected, and gave them to the typists.

At noon, he told his minders that he was not interested in eating lunch and that he just wanted to rest, as the day had already been more physically taxing than an entire normal day. The minders didn't seem to care, and they sent a guard from the lobby to fetch them lunch to eat in the Vaults. Puskis collapsed in a chair at the desk in the Stable — where the reference tomes were kept — with a blank white piece of paper and a pencil. On the sheet he drew a diagram of a typewriter keyboard. Then, with his fingers on the paper, he determined what movement was made by which finger in order to type a particular letter. Right index finger up is a *u.* Right index finger up and left is a *y.* Right index finger down is an *m.* And so on.

Puskis sat back in his chair with his eyes closed in complete concentration. From afar he must have looked asleep. In his mind he spelled out words in finger movements. Left index finger right; right index finger up; right index finger down and to the left. That spelled *gun.* Right pinkie up; right ring finger up; right ring finger; right middle finger up; left middle finger down; left middle finger up. *Police.* He made the words more complicated and began to formulate sentences. When he felt comfortable with this, he sped it up, his goal to process fifty words in a minute. It took him twenty minutes of intense mental effort before he could do this consistently.

The challenge, he knew, would be in trying to interpret what someone else was typing.

He used the fatigue excuse again to take a break for a cup of tea. It was not much of a stretch. He was both mentally and physically exhausted, and the prospect of the brief but intense mental challenge ahead seemed to sap him even more. He leaned against the wall behind the two typists and watched as the Lezner file rose to the top of the pile.

The typist on the left took it and opened it on a stand. For the first few seconds Puskis merely watched her type, getting used to the cadence of her fingers. The key, he determined, was to watch the space bar. That indicated a change of words. When it came time to actually "read" her fingers, he found that she moved too fast for him to identify both the letters and the order in which they were typed. Instead, he was getting anagrams. He would remember these and decipher them later.

He wanted to memorize three paragraphs in the first section of the report, potentially the most damaging section to someone in City government. The case involved a construction company that had been giving favorable rates to some of Red Henry's cronies, then receiving no-bid contracts with the City.

He watched and memorized the three paragraphs' worth of anagrams. One sentence was committed to memory like this:

The ssucpet was bsorvde meetngi with two kownn rbitslo ssaocaties and xehcaginng tsaclehs in a amnner sgguesitgn secrecy. Finished, he left his cup at the front desk and retreated into the aisles to where he had left himself paper and a pen. He wrote quickly. When he had all the acronyms down, he found that he could read the paragraphs without spending time to decipher the words on paper.

It was as he had feared. These new files were being altered. This one had subtly shifted the language so that the construction company was involved with the White Gang instead of the City government.

CHAPTER SEVENTY-SEVEN

Sirens in the distance stirred Poole from his moment of thought. He didn't like his options. Knowing that police reinforcements would shortly arrive, he had to get off this block. But making a run for the far end was suicidal.

Behind him, concrete steps led down to the door of a basement apartment. He tried the knob. Locked. He pulled off his jacket and pressed it against the pane of the door window. He made a quick movement with his elbow, shattering the glass. The noise was not as loud as he had feared. Certainly not loud enough to be heard down the street over the sound of the wind. He reached through and opened the door from inside.

This accomplished, he walked back up to see what was happening on the street. The eight ASU officers marched tentatively up the street in a fan formation with their guns drawn. He descended the stairs again, slipped through the door, then quietly closed it behind him.

Inside it was pitch-dark and smelled of animal feces and decomposing garbage. He gagged. Spitting, he crept through the apartment, keeping his hands out to avoid walking into a wall and lifting his feet high as he stepped, so as not to trip. The sounds of rats scuttling away preceded him as he walked. He met a wall and moved along it to his left, hit another wall, and crept sideways to his right until he found a doorway.

He heard the scrape of feet outside. Not in the well by the basement entrance, but up on the street level. He froze and listened. The steps moved on.

If he were conducting the search, he would walk the street first. If that came up empty, he'd search the houses one by one until there was success. He wasn't surprised that they weren't checking the houses now, but he knew they would be back. His hope lay in there being a second exit opening onto a parallel street. He walked through the doorway and into another room, mostly pitch-black. But light filtered in from a doorway to the right, and Poole hurried to it. Through this door was a small foyer leading to a door with a barred window.

He unlatched the security chain. This door opened onto street level. He cracked it and looked out onto an empty street. He couldn't hear sirens anymore and wasn't sure if that was because the cars had already arrived or because they had been heading elsewhere.

Poole took off his shoes, opened the door, and sprinted across the street and then to his left, away from the warehouses. He ran silently and shoeless for five blocks, his feet aching, becoming soaked and frozen, as they pounded on the concrete. Finally, he determined that he was at a safe distance and stepped into an alley to catch his breath. He was wet, his hand throbbed from the burn, and the bottoms of his feet were bruised. He leaned back against the brick wall and closed his eyes, making his mind blank for a few seconds. Then he pulled his shoes back on and struggled to his feet for the journey home.

Two cabs ignored him before a jitney picked him up, despite Poole's drenched clothes and the way he held his injured hand. The cabbie was ancient, wearing a golf hat. He used to be tough, Poole thought. Something about his voice and the way he held his now frail shoulders. He was certainly entertained by Poole's story.

"You running from those cops?"

Poole nodded to the man's eyes in the rearview mirror.

"What you do?"

"Nothing."

The cabbie gave an unattractive laugh. "Yeah, nobody does nothing."

Poole sighed. "I was looking for somebody and they were looking for the same person. I think they figured that they had issues with me because of that."

"So you ran even though you didn't do nothing." Skeptical.

"What'd you have done in your day if a dozen cops came running at you?"

"I would have given them a good one-two." Even from behind, Poole could tell the cabbie was smiling.

"Of course you would have."

"You know what?" the hack said after a while. "I been looking at you in my mirror here, and I'm thinking I must know you, but you know what? You're Ethan Poole from the U."

Poole nodded.

"It's a pleasure to have you in my humble flivver."

Poole nodded again. "It's right up here."

They were on Poole's block, but something didn't seem right. Two men stood in front of Poole's building, looking casual, doing nothing. Something was wrong with the street's rhythm. Too few people. Too many of them doing nothing. Waiting.

"Here?" the hack asked.

"Keep driving."

"What's that?"

"Keep driving," Poole said louder, and slid back in his seat.

The cabbie eased past Poole's building and continued on to the next block.

"Something wrong?"

"Yeah, something."

"Where we going now?"

"Keep driving. I've got to think."

The cabbie shrugged and continued on into Capitol Heights. People were out on the street, hurrying to get to this place or that. The contrast with the abandoned Hollows was striking.

"You know Little Lisbon, uptown?"

"Of course."

"Okay. Head up there."

"You got an address?"

"Just get me up there."

Enrique Dotel would be known in Little Lisbon. Poole prayed that Carla was with Enrique. If not, he feared she was in custody, and that brought with it a whole different set of problems that would be difficult to negotiate.

CHAPTER SEVENTY-EIGHT

The Palace did not open until five, so Frings and Floyd sat at the mahogany bar while the early shift set tables and swept and prepped for the evening. It seemed like a different place with the house lights turned up and the air free of smoke. With the essential elements of atmosphere missing, the club lost its glamour and instead looked merely like a big room.

Floyd drank whiskey on the rocks while Frings choked down a cup of muddy black coffee.

"Cuban," Floyd said.

"It's pretty goddamn strong."

"You need it, bo."

Frings wasn't going to argue that point. "You know how you said you were lousy with reefer these days?"

"You're out already?"

"No. That's not it. When you say 'these days,' you mean that it used to be harder?"

"Yeah, that's pretty much it. I could usually get what I needed, because of the club and all. But there was less to go around. Wasn't just there for the asking. You had to plan a little and there were times when most people couldn't get anything at all. Dry times."

"But not anymore."

"Not for a while, Frankie. It's just not an issue. You get what you want when you want it. No problems."

"When did this embarrassment of riches begin?"

Floyd squinted his eyes a little in concentration and took a long sip of the whiskey. "You know, maybe five years ago. Something like that."

"Five years ago. You sure?"

"Yeah," Floyd said, nodding slowly. "Yeah, I think that's about right."

"So about a year or so after Henry became mayor."

"Sounds good. What are you trying to get at here, Frank?"

"Floyd, who do you buy from? I need to talk to him."

Floyd winced. "Where are you going with this?"

"Look, trust me. I'm not trying to take anybody down here." Frings corrected himself. "That's not true. I am trying to take someone down, but you know it's not you and it's not the guy who sells you your dope."

"You're going to have to give me more than that."

"Okay. You heard of a guy named Otto Samuelson?"

"Bad gee, right? Sent up the river a while back?"

"Yeah, well, that's the thing. It's not the river you're probably thinking of."

"Don't get all inscrutable with me, Frank."

"I'm saying I just got back from visiting him out in a place called Freeman's Gap."

"He's already out?"

"Never went in."

"Shit," Floyd said. "Why the hell not?"

"That's what I'm trying to figure."

"You think talking to my guy is going to help you out?"

"That's right."

"Connect the dots for me, Frank. I don't follow."

"When I was out there with Otto Samuelson, we went for a little walk in the woods, and you'll never believe what's growing back there."

"No," Floyd said, eyes widening.

"More than you can imagine."

"So instead of going to jail, he moves out to the sticks and grows reefer?"

"That's exactly right. And he's not the only one. You know that story you told me about Whiskers?"

Floyd nodded slowly. "I see what you're saying."

"So I want to find out from your guy who he gets his reefer from. I'll bet it's from a guy named Smith who has it brought into the City by some other ginks from a decade back or so. Maybe even Whiskers."

"Jesus, Frank, you sure you want to go here?"

Frings nodded and sipped his coffee.

Floyd sighed. "I'll be back." He walked off, shaking his head a little.

"Where you going?"

"I can't just bring you to my guy. You can imagine that he'd be a little nervous talking to the famous Frankie Frings. I've got to get him used to the idea and hopefully drag him back here to talk to you."

"I hate to say this, with you doing me a favor and all, but I don't have a lot of time."

"I know, Frank. I'll be as quick as I can."

Floyd's well-earned reputation for discretion paid off and Frings was only kept waiting for the better part of an hour. Floyd's man was dressed in expensive silk slacks — black with light blue pinstripes — suspenders, and a white undershirt. His arms were strong and scarred, his hair matted together into little nubs. Underneath his beard, his obsidian face was hard, his eyes yellow around the pupils and red around the edges.

"This is him," Floyd said to Frings.

Frings extended his hand, but the man didn't even look at it, instead zeroing in on Frings's eyes.

"Floyd tell you why I want to talk to you?" Frings asked.

The man nodded.

"Who do you get your supply from?"

The man gave Frings a hard look. Frings wondered how Floyd had persuaded him to come.

"I don't see that it makes sense for me to tell you." His voice was thick and carried some kind of accent. African?

"Why's that? I guarantee that none of this comes back to you. Floyd'll vouch for me."

The man shook his head in disgust. "Why would I turn in this man? If he's gone, how do I make my money? Where do I get the mesca?"

Frings had anticipated this. "I know where they grow it. If they go down, I'll show you where the fields are and then you can cut out the middle man. It'll be more for you. You'll control the whole process."

The man stared at Frings. Without moving his eyes, he asked Floyd, "He on the level?"

Floyd said he was.

"Better be," the man said. "Better be."

"So?" Frings prompted.

"Ofay. Big. Calls himself Mr. Green. Not his real name. Don't see him much. Usually sends some hard men with the pounds. But Mr. Green is the man in charge."

Frings described Smith.

"That's him." The man spoke as if half-asleep or drugged. His eyes still held Frings's.

"How does it work?"

"His boys come with a shipment once every two weeks. I pay them for the last shipment and then I spread the supply around to the people who sell it."

"Like Floyd."

The man nodded.

"Does he deliver to anyone else?"

"Sure. Plenty of others down here."

"East Side?"

"Yeah."

"What about other parts of the City?"

"Just here."

"Not in the white parts of the City?"

"No.

"How do you know?"

"You buy mesca in Ofaytown?"

"I . . ."

"No. That's why you come here to buy. Because there isn't any mesca in Ofaytown. Mr. Green told me that I was not to distribute to Ofaytown. I told him maybe someone I give it to decides to take it there themselves. Mr. Green says he'll take care of that. I should just worry about where I sell."

"So you stay on the East Side?"

"No angle in crossing Mr. Green," the man said with a sad shake of his head.

CHAPTER SEVENTY-NINE

Pesotto, Red Henry's tailor, was on his knees, marking with chalk where the hem of the mayor's tuxedo pants should be let out. This was the usual ritual before any black-tie event in the City, and tonight's celebration of the Poles' decision to locate their factory in the City was to be a black-tie affair. Henry was obsessive about how he looked at such occasions and had his tux altered the day of, so that it would fit perfectly. Often, Pesotto merely went through the motions, the tux fitting perfectly as it was. The important thing was for Henry to feel for his satisfaction and confidence that some minute adjustment had been made.

As was the case at all these fittings, Pesotto had followed instructions and Berlioz flowed tinnily from the Victrola. Henry stood with his eyes closed, seemingly lost in the music as the stooped tailor made chalk marks on his pants.

Henry's rapture was broken by the arrival of Peja, along with Smith and Feral. Henry opened his eyes slowly, keeping the rest of his body motionless. Pesotto ignored the interlopers and continued with his work.

"We need to talk," Peja said.

Henry nodded.

Peja said, "In private."

Henry grunted. "Pesotto is discreet. Aren't you?"

Pesotto did not answer because he was deaf.

"You see?"

Peja looked uncomfortably at Feral and Smith, both of whom ignored him, then said, "First, we got some of the kids and we were right, they *are* the bombers."

"Some?"

"Some got away. It was chaos, apparently."

"Chaos?"

"I'll get to that."

"Did you at least find out why they're bombing the houses of the most important goddamn people in this City?"

"Yes, they —"

Smith interrupted, "One of the boys broke down in the wagon on the way to the station. It was a little hard to get exactly what he was saying because he . . . well, he doesn't seem to know a whole lot of words. But we have the basic story. He says that several months ago — that's our guess, he couldn't be more specific than not a long time and not a short time — anyway, someone went to the orphanage to visit the boys. He said it was a man who had red and gray hair and big wide chops." Smith scratched his cheeks to make the point.

"Christ almighty," Henry said. "Whiskers?"

"We're pretty sure. I'll get to that in a minute. So this gink — probably Whiskers — visits the kids and lays out the whole Navajo Project to them, if you can believe it. The whole bit. You can guess how this goes over with a pack of boys, and they get all belligerent. Then this gink tells them he has a present for them, and, according to this kid, he has a trunk with him that turns out to be filled with dynamite and everything else they need to make those bombs. He shows these kids how to make them, you know, wrap them in rope, tie a long fuse. Then he takes one of them, the leader I guess, on a trip around the City. Shows him all the points of interest."

"Block's house. Altabelli's, Bernal's, mine." Henry still hadn't moved.

"Those and some others. That's how you

get at these people who have ruined your lives, he says. You bomb their fucking houses. So when this kid gets back to his buddies, they decide to screw the orphanage, and they head out to the warehouse village with their trunk and start putting the bombs together."

Pesotto straightened and Henry obligingly stepped out of his pants. He now stood in only his boxers, socks, and a sleeveless undershirt. Pesotto took the pants and, with a nod to Henry and the others, shuffled into a back room.

"Where's Whiskers?" Henry asked.

"Well, that's another thing," Smith said. "Once we heard this, I got in touch with Kragen out at Freeman's Gap and he went by Whiskers' and says he's not there. I said to go check Otto's place, and Otto isn't there either. He's checking on the others right now."

Henry was reddening. "What else?"

"You remember Poole?" Smith asked.

"The Red dick?"

"That's him. I worked him over a little a few days back. Told him to lay off the Prosnickis."

"I remember."

"Well, funny thing, he turns up at the warehouses as we're taking the kids out."

"The hell's he doing there?" Henry's shoulders were becoming mottled with red patches as his blood pressure rose.

"Didn't I tell you? The leader of those little shit kids is Casper Prosnicki. He was there looking for Casper, just like I told him not to."

Henry sighed with impatience. "So you have Poole."

Now Smith looked nervous. "No. We went after him, but he got away."

"You've got the Prosnicki kid?"

Smith stared at the floor.

"You don't have the goddamn Prosnicki kid?" Henry roared.

Smith kept his gaze on the floor.

Henry calmed himself a little. "How the hell did you let that happen?"

Smith shrugged, knowing that nothing he could say would do him any good.

"You've got people looking for Poole?" Henry asked quietly, a deliberate attempt to keep his temper in check.

"Everybody. ASU, police, the whole bit. We have his place staked out and people on the street."

Henry rubbed his bald scalp thoughtfully. "That it?"

Peja answered this time, getting it out quickly. "We think Frings might have gone to see Otto."

Henry didn't answer. His body tensed, producing visible fear in Smith and Peja. Feral continued to stand silent and relaxed.

"He was seen coming back on the road to Freeman's Gap and then straight to the Palace."

"And Whiskers and Otto are missing."

"That's right," Peja said.

"Where is Frings now?"

"He's at the *Gazette.*"

Henry looked at Feral. "Hurt the girl. Send Frings a piece of her. He doesn't take us seriously, but we can change that in a hurry."

With his eyes, Feral acknowledged that he had heard, a display of unresponsiveness that would have infuriated Henry if it had come from Peja or Smith. But from Feral it just confirmed Henry's impression of efficiency and ruthlessness; and it helped him relax somewhat.

Henry looked at Smith and Peja. "Take care of these things now. I do not want anything going wrong at the signing or the party tonight. Understand?"

The Berlioz had ended and the needle skipped, filling the silence with its rhythmic banging against the center of the record.

CHAPTER EIGHTY

In Little Lisbon, merchants were setting out their wares as blue sky emerged from the clouds and the remnants of the deluge washed into the storm drains. The streets were so congested with pedestrians, merchants, and delivery trucks that the hack let Poole out at the fringes.

Poole waded through the crowd, holding his hand gingerly against his body. His wet, disheveled appearance drew occasional glances. There was, he knew, a café in the neighborhood that was a headquarters of sorts for the Portuguese communists. If Enrique was not there, they would at least know where he could be found.

The crowds made the maze of narrow streets even more disorienting, and he had to ask directions several times. The smell of fish and unfamiliar spices assailed him. At last he found the place, no sign above the door and no windows, but three tables on the sidewalk outside.

He drew instant attention from the five men, small and lean and hard, who sat inside drinking pungent tea. Poole walked to the counter where an old man with a white beard that hung to his waist said something to him in Portuguese.

"I'm looking for Enrique."

"Don't know him," the old man wheezed.

"I don't have time for this. I'm Ethan Poole. Carla Hallestrom is my girl."

The man stared at him impassively.

"I was at the strike."

A man at one of the tables got up and walked over to Poole. His breath stank of garlic. "I saw him there. The police cracked his head with their nightsticks."

The old man looked at the man with the garlic breath and then at Poole. "Upstairs." He motioned with his hand for Poole to go back to the street, then around to the left.

She must have heard his footsteps on the stairs because when he reached the landing, the door was open and Carla was waiting for him. They embraced, Poole lifting her off the floor so that her feet dangled around his shins.

"I was so worried," she said, letting go of his neck, as he lowered her to the floor.

"How did you . . . oh my God." She noticed his hand.

"They were at the warehouses, arresting kids."

"Casper?"

Poole shrugged. "Could be."

"And you?"

"They chased me. I got away, but they got a good look at me. They know I was there."

Enrique was in the doorway. "Come in. We'll clean your wounds."

Later, his hand cleaned and wrapped in gauze, Poole sat on Enrique's ancient couch with Carla. Enrique was in the kitchen with his wife, and the smells wafting from there had Poole's stomach grumbling.

"Tranghese from the apartment above us met me on the street and warned me," Carla explained. "He said they came asking questions about us."

"How long before they look here, do you think?"

"I don't know, but we shouldn't stay long. I don't want to put Enrique's wife in harm's way."

"Okay. Maybe we eat and go. Did you have your meeting?"

"Yes," she said, smiling. "It had the effect we wanted."

Chapter Eighty-One

Frings watched Ed, the assistant, struggle through the newsroom to catch him before he reached Panos's office. Frings sped up a little, making Ed practically break into a run.

"You got something for me?" Frings asked.

Ed was clearly annoyed. "You asked me to run those names by Lonergan, see if there was anything in the papers about them in the past five years."

The names from Puskis's list. "That's right. Anything come up?"

Ed shook his head, a little smile creasing his face at the thought of Frings coming up empty.

Frings nodded. "That's what I thought."

Ed shook his head and walked away to other business, muttering.

Panos was talking to a young reporter whose

name Frings couldn't remember. He looked up as Frings walked in unannounced, his face turning from annoyance to pleasure.

"Frank. Good to see you this afternoon. I'm briefing Caskin here about the big gala tonight to which I am sending him."

"That's what I want to talk to you about, Panos."

"What? You want to go to the big party and drink some champagne and eat those beautiful little treats that they always have? Is that why you want to talk to me about this thing?"

"I, you know, I apologize, buddy," Frings said to Caskin, "but I really need to talk to Panos privately."

Caskin got up from his chair. Frings carried a lot of clout in the newsroom, especially among the new reporters, who were still intimidated by his reputation.

Panos said, "Go get some coffee, Caskin. I'll talk to you again when I am done with Frank here."

When Caskin was gone, Frings closed the door and Panos sat forward in his chair with his forearms on the desk.

"What is this, Frank?"

"It's the big one, Panos. I've got the big one. Red Henry could go down within the week."

Panos's eyes widened. "What is this you are talking of?"

"Panos, I'm going to tell you. But you've got to let me play it my way. Can I trust you on that? There are other factors."

Panos gave a look of exaggerated hurt. "You know you can trust me, Frank. You get the story, you tell me when it can run. I just make sure that it is okay. Good?"

"Okay."

Panos opened his desk drawer and tossed a flask to Frings. "Dip the bill, Frank. You look terrible."

Frings unscrewed the lid and took a pull. It tasted like gasoline and felt like molten lead in his stomach.

"Christ, Panos. What is this?"

Panos took the flask from Frings and had a drink himself, making a funny face and then smiling. "This man who lives in the alley by my house makes this in a still."

"This is from a hobo's still?"

Panos shrugged. "With what goes into your body, Frank . . ."

Frings shuddered a little from the lingering effects of the moonshine. "Okay. Have you ever heard of the Navajo Project?"

Panos frowned.

"Go back seven or eight years to the last couple of years of the war between the

Whites and the Bristols. This is before Henry's time. The mayor wanted to do something dramatic to stop all the gang hits. The prisons were filling up with cons on murder raps. The City had to take care of more and more widows and fatherless kids. The situation couldn't last. So they instituted a secret program called the Navajo Project. What this was, was a system where certain people convicted of gang murders weren't sent to prison. Instead, they were sent to these farms out of the City where they grow crops to support themselves — and here's the real point of the program — to support the widows and orphans of the men they had murdered."

Panos was nodding his head slowly, his eyes closed, concentrating on what Frings was saying.

"Go forward a couple of years to the Birthday Party Massacre. Red Henry has just become mayor. Some Whites think they find a way around the whole program. They just kill the entire family. No one to support, so if there's a conviction, the killer goes to prison, which the Bristols and Whites pretty much run anyway. But they didn't understand Red Henry, and you know the shit that he rained down on them. So that ends any new Navajo Project cases.

But there's still the people they've already farmed out.

"So about five years ago, maybe a little bit less, Henry gets this idea that the Navajo Project could work a little more to his advantage. He can make it more profitable by getting more money out of the convicts and spending less on the families of the deceased. So he does two things. One, he puts the widows in a sanitarium and the kids in orphanages. Two, he gets the convicts to grow a crop that will bring in more cash — marijuana."

Frings expected a crack from Panos about reefer, but didn't get one.

Frings continued, "Henry has his guy Smith run the program. Apparently Smith put some of the Navajo Project cons in charge of running the day-to-day and keeping the other ginks in line. Some of Smith's boys go out to the sticks, make a pickup, and bring the reefer to the East Side for sale to the colored folks and whatever whites venture in there to buy."

"Such as yourself," Panos suggested.

"Of course. So now, with all this cash flooding in, they can use some of it to bankroll the sanitarium and orphanage and spread the rest out amongst themselves."

"Who else besides Henry?"

"Who do you think? The usual: Block, Altabelli, Bernal."

"This has something to do with the bombings, too, doesn't it?"

"Yes, though here I'm guessing. The kid I met who is sort of the leader of these kids with the bombs is named Casper Prosnicki. His father was killed by Reif DeGraffenreid, who was a Navajo Project convict until he was murdered a few days back, out on his dope farm. I've got it on good authority that someone told those kids about the project and they think this is how they can get their story out and also get some payback."

"You have proof? You know I can't run this without a lot of proof. A lot."

"I've got proof. But I'll have more than that."

Panos smiled. "Oh, shit, Frank. What are you thinking in that brain of yours?"

"I told you there were extenuating circumstances."

Panos nodded and leaned back in his chair. Sweat stains had blossomed under his arms.

"They've got my girl."

"Not the beautiful Nora Aspen?" Panos said, shocked.

Frings nodded. "They left a note. Said to

459

drop this investigation or they'd hurt her."

"But you continue."

"Where would it end, Panos? If I cave, when do they let her go? When are they ever satisfied that I won't just pick up and begin again once I get her back?"

Panos nodded. "That's a tough one, Frank. That's shit tough."

"That's why I need to go. I need a bargaining chip. I tell Henry what I've got. I tell him to let Nora go and I'll let it pass. She gets hurt, he goes down."

"So you come to me with this story and now we won't be able to use it?"

"Come on, Panos. Of course we'll use it. After I get Nora, we print the whole thing."

"That is not so honest."

"They kidnapped my girl. I'm supposed to be a goddamn saint? You joking?"

Panos let out a grim laugh. "I see, Frank. And it is my humble guess that you want to confront our esteemed mayor at his big fancy gala party tonight?"

"That's right. I want to get him tonight, in a public place, where he doesn't have time to think. I don't want Nora being held any longer than necessary."

"Just so. Okay, Frank, you go to the big fun party tonight. You just be careful, okay? For you and your lovely Nora."

■ ■ ■ ■

On his way out, Frings saw a note written on a restaurant check at the top of a stack of papers on his desk.

Dear Mr. Frings,

I am a prisoner. There are two men watching me at all times. They (I know that you know who I mean) are destroying the evidence held in the files. I write you this note so that you will know the reason for events that may follow. They can not destroy the past, but they can edit our memory.

A.P.

Frings frowned. If they were destroying the evidence in the files, then only one other thing could expose the Navajo Project and that would be the convicts themselves. Red Henry would send his thugs after them, then all the loose ends would be tied up. No more evidence. He thought back to his time with Otto Samuelson and his meeting with Whiskers and wondered if they hadn't already come to that same realization.

CHAPTER EIGHTY-TWO

They knew Feral at the morgue and regarded him with the same combination of curiosity and fear that most City employees who knew him did. It wasn't clear exactly who he was or what type of authority he held, but he had the backing of the mayor, and they knew to accede to his requests.

The morgue was a bright, sanitary place. Shining white-tiled walls provided a weird, near heavenly environment for the corpses spending their brief time there. None of the three steel autopsy tables were currently in use, and a large metal door led back to the refrigerated corpse room. The chief examiner was a small, portly man named Pulyatkin. He had huge hands and a face that took up a surprising amount of his head.

"Nice to see you today, sir," Pulyatkin said to Feral.

"And you, Mr. Pulyatkin." Feral had his hands in his pockets, and his right hand played with the handle of a short knife.

"What brings you here?"

"I'm looking for a missing woman."

"Oh?"

"That's right. White woman. On the younger side, late twenties, early thirties."

"Is that it? Is that all you have?"

"Last three or four days."

"Come." Pulyatkin led Feral into the corpse room. The room was kept at a constant thirty-five degrees, and Feral pulled his collar up around his neck. The corpses — perhaps forty in all — were laid out under sheets on bunks stacked four high.

"Over here is where we have the John and Jane Does," Pulyatkin said, leading Feral to the far left corner. "I think we have two women. Let's see." He drew back the corner of the sheet from a corpse and found the mostly missing head of a man. "Not that one," he said, laughing nervously.

He found the two unidentified women and left the sheets pulled back to reveal their faces. "Is one of these the one you are looking for?"

"I will have to make a closer examination to be sure."

Pulyatkin frowned and gestured for Feral to inspect.

"I need a minute to myself," Feral said.

Pulyatkin had heard this request from Feral before, and as in the past, he acquiesced with a small nod and retreated back to the examination room. Feral looked at the two faces and picked the one that looked most like Nora, though it was not a close resemblance. The face would have been gaunt even in life. Pulling the sheet away so that he could get to her right hand, he fished the knife from his pocket and used it as a saw on the corpse's right pinkie. The bone provided some resistance, but he soon had it off. He wrapped it in a handkerchief, tucked it into his coat pocket along with the knife, and pulled the sheet up over the corpse.

It was a toss-up whether Pulyatkin would notice that the finger had not been missing before. If he did notice, it seemed unlikely that he would do anything about it. In the past when Feral had been alone with the corpses, it had been to alter them in some way to protect someone from the evidence that might be found on or in the body. The two men had an unspoken agreement that these incidents would not be reported. If Pulyatkin did notice the missing finger, he would assume that it pointed to someone whom the mayor didn't want identified.

Pulyatkin was at a sink, scrubbing scalpels, when Feral returned.

"You find your lady?"

"No," Feral said.

"That's good news. She might yet be alive."

Feral nodded. "I wasn't here of course."

Pulyatkin laughed. "You never are."

CHAPTER EIGHTY-THREE

Puskis had his mostly full cart in the farthest corner of the Vaults, a section that he had rarely visited in all his years as Archivist. It held records dating back nearly three-quarters of a century. Some of the crimes described by the files were not even crimes anymore, the people in them either dead or long past the point of causing any mayhem.

Puskis pulled a box of matches from the interior pocket of his jacket and contemplated it in his hand. He had thought a lot about this moment in the previous twenty-four hours; about the implications of what he was about to do. Was no memory better than a false memory? For that was what the Vaults were — the City's official memory. Puskis had based half of his life on the notion that this memory was of vital importance to the City's proper functioning. Now that this memory was being tampered with, now that the information was no longer pure, was its destruction the only moral choice?

He lit the first match and held it to a file. It didn't catch immediately, instead smoking until the match burned down too far and Puskis dropped it onto the floor. The second match did ignite the folder and Puskis held the file so that the flame crept up the folder and grew. He replaced the folder on the shelf and watched as the flame spread to adjacent files. The smell of the smoke imbued Puskis with a sense of urgency, and he hastened down the aisle to ignite another folder. This accomplished, he moved back to the original fire to find that it had spread to three shelves now and would not easily be extinguished.

He walked ten aisles forward and lit another fire. Another ten aisles and another fire. Puskis was perfectly calm, even serene, looking back to see smoke billowing and flames licking at the ceiling. It was like a dream — more real than waking life. All this paper would go up quickly. He walked to the front of the Vaults, finding his two minders leaning against the wall chatting while the typists worked their keyboards.

Puskis pushed the elevator call button.

"Look here," said one of his minders, "where are you going?"

467

"The men's room, if that is permissible." No nerves. Weightless.

The cop shrugged. Puskis entered the elevator and turned to look out as the operator pulled the gate closed.

The two minders were back in conversation; the typists were absorbed in their work, fingers manic. In the distance, tendrils of smoke slowly snaked forward, emerging from rows of files as though encircling the main center aisle.

The elevator operator pulled a face, sniffed, and asked, "Is that smoke?" Then rattled home the door.

Puskis felt no need to reply.

In the lobby, everything seemed oddly normal. People were oblivious of what Puskis had just done. *The Vaults were burning!*

Puskis imagined the scene that would surely unfold in mere minutes; the panic that sets in when you introduce fire to a confined space crowded with people. He headed for the door.

"Can I help you, Mr. Puskis?" asked a cop stationed at the front entrance.

"Yes. If it is not too much trouble, could you send the elevator man back down to the Vaults? I suspect there may be people down there who are eager to come up."

The cop gave a good-natured shrug. "Of course, Mr. Puskis," he said, and wandered off to the bank of elevators.

Puskis, his face inscrutable, watched the guard's progress for a moment, then slipped out the front door and headed toward the house of Joos Van Vossen.

CHAPTER EIGHTY-FOUR

In Red Henry's office, a cherrywood liquor cabinet was stocked with expensive liquor but rarely opened. Henry did not often allow himself to lose even the slightest amount of self-control. He frequently drank beer, but at his size he rarely got at all drunk. He was now sitting with a tall glass of Four Roses Whiskey over ice, sipping aggressively. Three hours until the party began, and he didn't like the way the day was progressing. The Poles were beginning to worry him. He had ASU guards discretely posted around the hotel where the contingent were staying. Nobody was getting to them at this late hour.

He grabbed a handful of cigars from a box on his desk and laid them out in front of him. He would bring five with him tonight. One for Rinus, or whatever the fuck his name was, and four for himself. He rolled the thick Cubans around on the table absently, letting his unconscious do the selecting while his mind wandered to Bernal. Henry did not have close emotional ties to people. Had he ever? He couldn't remember any. But some people he liked to be around, people who amused and interested him. Bernal, like Block and Altabelli, had been one of those people.

He found himself equally disturbed by Bernal's death — he would leave a void in Henry's small social circle — and his apparent betrayal. Why would Bernal turn on him? What did he have to gain or, as might be the case, what was he trying to avoid losing? It didn't make sense, which troubled Henry more than anything else.

Then there was that goddamn Frings, who for some reason was so pathologically single-minded in his pursuit of Henry that he was willing to sacrifice his girlfriend — and not just any girlfriend, but Nora Aspen — rather than give in on even a single point. How the hell had Frings found Otto Samuelson? It must have been Bernal. But again, why? Possibilities ran through Henry's mind, but they always led to one thing — the Navajo Project. That could be a catastrophic problem. As he began to ponder the consequences of having Smith kill Frings, Henry realized his glass was empty. With pewter tongs he snared more ice from the bucket and poured the whiskey slowly, watching it cascade over the cubes.

The Four Roses had him feeling warm, but rather than mellowing, his mind raced more frantically. Where was Otto Samuelson? More important, where was Whiskers? What the hell was going on out in the sticks? Trevor Reid, the Vampire, had made a run, and Henry thought that the number that Whiskers had done on him would have cowed the others into staying put. Samuelson and the others, they were hard men, but like most hard men they recognized when they were had. Whiskers, on the other hand, was not adequately described as hard. He was on an entirely different fucking planet. It was odd, Henry thought, that the person who seemed most like Whiskers to him in this respect was Feral. Not that the two had anything else in common. Feral was controlled and literate and seemed to have some kind of moral sense, screwed up though it was. Whiskers was a homicidal maniac. But they shared a quality of other-worldliness. You couldn't outhard them because they weren't being hard. They were something entirely different. And that was why they alone worried Red Henry, the hardest of the hard.

CHAPTER EIGHTY-FIVE

Red light flickered across Van Vossen's face, reflections of the flames dancing in the brick fireplace. Puskis sat in a cavernous upholstered chair across from Van Vossen, who lounged in its twin. No tin was in his lap this time. A Bach violin concerto whispered from the Victrola's horn. The place smelled of Van Vossen's pipe tobacco.

"You burned the Vaults?" His tone was dull and his eyes without expression, but a sudden tensing of his body had alerted Puskis to his alarm.

"They were corrupting it. They were changing the information." Puskis felt shaky from excitement; the finality of the act.

Van Vossen nodded. "Better no files than a record of lies."

He understood, as Puskis had known he would. "It would have been a collective dementia."

Van Vossen sucked on his pipe, avoiding

Puskis's eyes by looking into the fire.

They were silent for a while, then Van Vossen poured them both brandies from a crystal decanter. Puskis did not enjoy alcohol, but sipped it to be polite.

"Your book is the only record left. It is now the most complete story of the workings of justice in the City."

Van Vossen thought about this, staring into his glass as he swirled the dark liquid in circles. Puskis had wondered what the reaction would be. Would the gravity of this responsibility intimidate, or would Van Vossen find pride, even exhilaration, in this duty?

"I'm having a difficult time organizing the book," he said.

"How do you mean?"

"I mean, how do you organize a work like this? What is the organizing principle? Surely not time."

This surprised Puskis. "In the Vaults, we organized by —"

"In the Vaults," Van Vossen said peevishly, "you organized by whim."

Puskis felt his temper rising. "By whim? The system of organization in the Vaults is a complex, organic system. It is the closest reflection of the very nature of crime."

Van Vossen gave a disgusted laugh. "Is that

what it is, Mr. Puskis? Are you sure that you don't force events into categories that bear only certain of the essential characteristics? Are crimes really that similar?"

Puskis's reflexive answer was yes, but he stifled it. The question was not adequately answered with a single word. Yet, if he was unable to answer the question affirmatively, what had been the point of the Vaults or his three decades of work therein?

"How well did you know Abramowitz?" Van Vossen asked, seeming to change tack.

"He was my mentor."

"Did you know him before his decline?"

"Well, I didn't have anything to compare it to, but I imagine that he was already, um, troubled, by the time I worked with him."

"Do you know why he went insane?"

Puskis didn't respond. He had pondered the question for almost twenty years. He had no idea.

"He went insane because he was looking for a pattern. He was looking for a pattern or a theory or some kind of organizing principle to explain the crime and evil that passed through his hands every day and every week and every year. He tried to find a design, you see, and it drove him insane because in the end there was no design. He looked for God in the deeds of man, and he discovered that all there was were the independent acts of thousands of people. No pattern, no design, no sense. So, as I said, I am having a difficult time organizing my book."

Chapter Eighty-Six

The signing gala was being held at the former armory, which had been converted to a cavernous ballroom. Red Henry leaned against the temporary bar and watched the workers as they made preparations for the evening. Already, giant American and Polish flags alternated along the walls. Tables were appointed in red and white, and red, white, and blue. Caterers scurried back and forth, carrying crates of glasses, putting out place settings, and carting food to the kitchen. Henry glowered at the lot of them and was rewarded with their nervousness and, in some cases, fear.

A polka band was setting up on the stage at the far end of the room, the musicians tuning their instruments and playing brief phrases that Henry vaguely recognized. The music added to the cacophony of clanking dishes and slamming doors and chatter in a half dozen languages. Henry took a long draft off a pint of beer. He was getting drunk and comfortably aggressive.

He heard the maintenance door slam and footsteps approach. He turned to find Peja striding reluctantly toward him. Henry scratched his head with his free hand, knowing he was about to get some news he didn't want to hear. He could tell by Peja's eyes.

"Out with it," he growled by way of greeting.

Peja avoided his eyes. "Okay, sir. The Poles, well, the Poles aren't coming."

Henry stared at a spot twenty feet behind Peja, focusing on maintaining his temper. "The Poles aren't coming?" he said, carefully enunciating each word.

"My understanding is that they're backing out of the deal. They don't want to sign the contract."

Henry considered this for a moment, finished his beer, and threw the empty glass down hard on the floor, where it shattered into tiny shards. Peja flinched, then gathered himself.

"Is this just your understanding or is this a fact?"

"It's a fact, sir. I heard it from Rinus himself."

Henry spoke with chilling calm. "Why, in your opinion, have they changed their minds

478

at this late date?"

"I checked into that. The officers who had surveillance at the Poles' hotel said that the woman from the strike at Bernal's had been to the hotel. Presumably she met with Rinus."

" 'Presumably she met with Rinus,' " Henry mocked. "We're talking about the woman Carla Hallestrom?"

"I'm fairly sure it's her."

"They just let her walk in? That goddamn labor chippie waltzes right into a hotel where a very important group of businessmen is staying on the afternoon of a crucial deal and they just let her walk in?" Henry's voice was rising in volume, and the workers cast worried glances in his direction.

"I addressed that very point with them, and they said that they had not been given any directive for that situation."

"Can't they fucking think, for Christ's sake?"

"They pride themselves on their discipline, as you know, sir. They held off and monitored the situation, as they put it."

Henry knew that he had insisted upon this unstinting discipline. "So this Carla meets with Rinus and he decides — what? — he's not going to move his factory here after all?"

"That's not exactly what he said. He said

he wanted to look at some options before committing to us."

"It's the same goddamn thing. If he leaves here without signing the contract, he won't return." Henry sighed. "What did she say to them? Did she threaten them? Bribe them? Did she whore herself for their compliance?"

Peja shrugged. "Rinus was not forthcoming."

"Bring me a beer," Henry yelled to nobody in particular. He wanted to go over to that hotel and grab Rinus by his fucking collar and drag him down here to sign the fucking contract and drink this shitty Polish beer and fulfill his goddamn responsibility. But experience had shown Henry that waiting would be more effective. Let them sleep on whatever it was that the little commie bitch had told them. He would speak to them in the morning, bring the entirety of his overpowering personality to bear on the Poles, and they would see sense. His powers of persuasion were rarely resisted.

He still had this evening to get through. He gave Peja a wolf's grin.

"Don't tell anyone that this deal has gone south. This is still a celebration. The story is the Poles have come down with food poisoning. Understand? This goes on as usual."

Peja smiled. "You'll go and talk to them?"

"Tomorrow."

"You'll use all your charm?" Peja said, and winked, feeling cocky again.

A young Mexican arrived with a beer that Henry took without comment. He took half of it down and refocused on Peja.

"There's going to be a lot of goddamn charm for everyone," Henry said, then drank the other half. He beckoned Peja closer so that they would not be overheard. "I need you to do something. I will not be crossed by any pissant union communist subversives. I want you to get in touch with Martens at the ASU. All resources are to be focused on finding Dotel and the girl. By morning, they need to be dead. Tell Martens his career is in the balance."

Peja nodded, happy that someone else was now in the crosshairs.

CHAPTER EIGHTY-SEVEN

When her abductor came in, Nora was reading a copy of *Othello* she had found in the bookcase in her room. She'd seen the play years ago and could picture the performance as she read. She glanced up, no longer startled by his abrupt entrances.

Something about him had changed. The nature of the change was not entirely clear, nor what it signified, but it was there nonetheless. Was it a slight slump in his posture? A subtle line of stress in his usually placid features? And what accounted for it? The sexual tension that she had carefully fostered between them? Or something else? Was it a prelude to action? Was he gathering himself to do something to her? This thought scared her and also gave her hope. This was another crack in the dike, another possibility where there had once been none. She needed to figure out how to exploit it.

CHAPTER EIGHTY-EIGHT

The setting sun had turned the sky a dark purple, spotted with magenta cirrus clouds. Poole kept to side streets and alleys as he made his way back toward the Hollows. His left hand was immobilized in a bandage. As he walked, he periodically felt in his right pocket for the reassuring grip of Enrique's pistol. He'd never shot anyone. Showing a gun was usually enough to discourage; a shot over the shoulder was always more than enough. People were in no hurry to die.

This, however, was a different situation. Previously, a gun had given him control over a situation, given him confidence. Now he was scared and knew that he would shoot to kill if confronted by the ASU. Preferring to avoid them at all costs, he kept to the shadows as he made his way toward St. Mark's, where he hoped to find Casper Prosnicki.

Carla had been reluctant to let him leave.

"We've hurt him," she said. "The Poles won't be signing. Henry will be mad as a hornet."

How had she accomplished that? She knew how to talk to them, she said. She knew what they would fear most in America, and she'd played to those fears. *Organized crime.* She'd told them that soon after they opened the plant, they would start to experience vandalism and theft. They would get a visit from one of Henry's hatchet men — she'd described Smith, specifically — and the payments for police protection would start. *Labor.* She told them that she, personally, would organize the workers they brought over. If the workers initially resisted being organized, she had the muscle to intimidate them into compliance.

Rinus had looked at her, she said, with relief in his eyes. Something about Henry bothered the Poles. They weren't coming to America to be pushed around, Rinus said. The pressure Henry was putting on them to sign the contract had given them pause. Carla's visit merely reinforced their misgivings and gave them a reason to back out.

"So there's no need to find the boy," Carla pleaded, knowing that this was no longer about subverting the mayor. It had become something else.

Poole was wary when he got to St. Mark's Square, keeping to the shadows and watching for a full five minutes without seeing anything that concerned him. He finally broke from cover, moving swiftly — not running, but almost. He took the steps three at a time and came to the door. Locked. How could a door this decrepit be locked? He pushed again, harder this time, and it gave a little. Not locked. Barricaded.

He took a step back, got low, and exploded into the door with his full weight. Somehow the impact registered in his damaged hand, and he shook it in a vain attempt to ease the pain. He'd moved the door enough to slip through. Movement came from the darkness, barely audible noises, a subtle shifting in the air.

"It's Poole," he said in a stage whisper. "I was here the other day. You brought me upstairs to see the Brother."

Hearing no response, Poole pulled his flashlight from his pocket and shone the light on his face. A stirring came from in front of him, by the stairs.

A prepubescent voice said, "You come to see Casper?"

"That's right. Is he here?"

485

The boy didn't reply, and Poole heard footsteps running up the stairs, though whether in retreat or to fetch Casper, he wasn't sure.

At least three sets of footsteps returned, and when they reached the landing above the ground floor, Poole could tell that one of them was carrying a lantern. The footsteps stopped before entering the lobby. The boy carrying the lantern must have been second in line because an elongated shadow was cast onto the illuminated patch of floor. A boy spoke, the movement of the shadow telling Poole that it was the boy in front.

"Who're you?" The voice was in that funny place between boy and teen. It was not, however, scared.

"What's that?"

"Who're you? Name?"

"Ethan Poole. Call me Ethan. Are you Casper Prosnicki?"

There was murmuring on the staircase, the shadow contorting with the boy's movements. The boy spoke again. "What you want?"

"What do I want?" Poole wasn't sure whether he was not hearing clearly or whether it was the boy's speech.

The boy grunted in the affirmative.

"Casper, your mother asked me to find you. I'm here because of your mother." No answer. "Her name is Lena."

"You lie," the boy said.

"Casper, listen. Why are you using those bombs?"

Again there was a consultation on the stairs. The shadow shrank as the boy squatted.

"It's not me."

"Casper, I know it's you. I'm not here to punish you or take you in. I just need to know why. I need to know why you're using the bombs. I need to know why your mother asked me to find you. I need to know why they killed your mother, Casper. You know they killed her, don't you?"

There was another silence, and this time Poole let it hang there in the darkness.

Finally the boy spoke. "The man came. The man with red hair on his face. He came and told us who killed our mums and dads. He told us." Then the boy said the names with great ferocity: "Red Henry, Ian Block, Roderigo Bernal, Altabelli. We know their names."

It was Whiskers. Poole had known him before Whiskers had finally been sent away. He cringed at the thought of Whiskers around children. What had he been doing?

"Did he want you to hurt those men?"

The boy made that affirmative grunt again. "He brings the bombs. He showed us how to make them work."

"He brought you the stuff for the bombs and showed you how to make them and told you who to use them on?"

Whiskers was using children to get his revenge on Red Henry and the whole cabal. Poole took off his hat, rubbed his bandaged left hand through his hair, and replaced the hat at the angle he liked.

"Are the rest of the bombs at the warehouse?"

"Nah."

"They're not?"

"The man came by today and took them. He came today."

Jesus Christ. Whiskers had come by to retrieve his bombs, which meant that he had either given up on the kids or was in some kind of hurry. To do what? The obvious answer raised a number of troubling questions — first among them, should Poole do anything about it? Let actions take their course and it could be a great favor to Carla.

He was still digesting this information when he heard the scrape of footsteps on the granite steps outside.

CHAPTER EIGHTY-NINE

Frings headed straight to the bar. He'd timed his arrival pretty well, he thought. The armory was humming with the City's elite and beautiful. He'd managed to arrive during the interval between the first wave of the punctual and the second wave of the fashionably late. In an hour the place would be teeming. Now it was merely crowded.

He got a scotch on the rocks and worked his way to some breathing room at the edge of the crowd. His relative anonymity without Nora was almost nostalgic. With Nora, Frings would have been making small talk with wives and friends and hangers-on while Nora went through her act of harmless flirtation with the men and girl-to-girl intimacy with the women. He was grateful for the lack of attention at the moment, though it made him think of Nora and how crucial his upcoming confrontation with Red Henry would be.

Tannen, with the *News,* appeared out of the crowd with two pints of beer. A small man in an oversize suit, he'd carefully trimmed his mustache so that it was merely a line tracing his upper lip.

"Howdy, Frank," he said, proffering one of the beers.

Frings placed his empty whiskey glass on a ledge and accepted the beer, nodding in thanks.

"Congrats on finding the bombers," Tannen said. "You scooped us on that one."

The *Gazette* scooped the *News* on just about everything, Frings thought. That was the price the *News* paid for being the unofficial official newspaper of Red Henry. Lots of access, little news.

"Good fortune," Frings said.

"Don't be so modest, Frank. We make our good fortune, you know that as well as I do. And you, Frank, make the best fortune of anybody. I always tell people, 'I don't know how he does it.' But you do it, Frank. Again and again you do it. What's the secret?"

Frings scanned the crowd as Tannen talked, hoping that he would take the hint and leave. "There's no secret. You just plug away and sometimes something turns up."

Tannen laughed. "That's right. Plug away. Something turns up. From what I hear, sometimes you don't even have to plug away before something turns up. Sometimes you walk into your office and someone has sent you a letter and promises to let you in on all the secrets. How does one make that kind of luck, Frank? Surely it just doesn't happen."

Frings returned his attention to Tannen. "Sometimes, people make decisions based on what they've seen of you. Sometimes, if you work hard to establish a reputation, people trust you and want you to tell their story. Is that what you're asking me?"

"I see," Tannen said, and Frings suddenly realized the extent of the little man's intoxication. "But that couldn't happen with me, I suppose. That couldn't happen with Erroll Tannen at the *News* because I've got the mayor's cock in my hand and I'm giving it the back-and-forth. Nobody's going to trust that kind of story to me."

Frings shrugged. "You do things your way, I do things mine. I'm not making any judgments."

"Like hell you're not," Tannen said loudly, attracting some attention now. "People are getting pretty sick of this self-righteous crap you're throwing around, Frank. Your time in the limelight is nearing its end."

"Thanks for the beer," Frings said, and

took a step to walk past Tannen.

Tannen moved sideways to block his way. "Not yet, Frank. I've got more to say."

A crowd had gathered around them, and Frings, realizing he had to tread carefully, leaned forward so that his mouth was close enough to Tannen's ear that he did not have to yell to be heard over the din in the big room.

"If you want to talk about this, Erroll, I would be happy to. But not here." Frings straightened up and began to walk toward the middle of the room where couples briskly polkaed.

"That's right, Frank. Walk away. What're you afraid of, Frank? Why don't you want to talk?"

The crowd parted to let Frings through. He felt their eyes upon him, and it was like being there with Nora, though instead of the adoration she received, he was the object of confusion and even distaste.

Frings let the crowd find something else to take their attention and went to the men's room. Returning to the floor, he surveyed the crowd to locate Henry. It was amazing that a throng of this size would turn out at an event that had so hastily been arranged. But, then again, what did these people have to do otherwise? The idle rich of the City were in this room. Most of them likely didn't know what the affair was about.

The band was playing some sort of tuba oompah music. Frings spotted Henry leaning against a brick wall surrounded by maybe a dozen men in a far corner of the room. Oddly, Frings could not identify anyone from the Polish contingent. There was a story there, he thought, but not for him.

Frings was feeling the alcohol a little and went to the bar for a shot of whiskey. For courage. The next few minutes would be crucial. He waded through the crowd, occasionally jarring someone's drink or brushing an arm. Recognizing him from the incident with Tannen, people exchanged knowing looks with friends. Frings ignored them.

He was within five yards of Henry's group when the mayor spotted him. Frings nudged his way past the outer ring of the group until he was right in front of Henry, who was staring at him in an unfocused kind of way.

"Get these people the hell out of here," Frings said. "We need to talk."

CHAPTER NINETY

Nora lay on the bed in her odd cell, reading Saki. Feral, whose name she still did not know, sat in a chair by the door, silently watching her. He had been there for over an hour. She had initially been self-conscious and had moved around the room, keeping physically active trying to draw him into conversation. But Feral just sat, dressed in slacks and suspenders and a sleeveless undershirt, following her with his eyes, but not his head. Eventually, she realized she had no reason to be self-conscious. This was, in fact, a sign that she had seized the power in their relationship. She was no longer scared and he was — what? Smitten? Infatuated? Obsessed? Whichever most accurately described his mental state, he had no control over it, and while she was his captive physically, emotionally he was hers. In different circumstances, she would have worried about being raped. But this odd little man wanted her on her terms, and his silent, brooding watchfulness was an acknowledgment that if under no terms would she be with him, then he would not have her. Instead, he would watch and brood.

The troubling thought was, how did this end? Did she walk away and continue life as if this had never happened? Were promises made? Or did something worse happen? Was it necessary, in his eyes, for this to end with her death?

CHAPTER NINETY-ONE

Van Vossen produced two heavy crystal goblets and poured from a decanter until both were three-quarters full. When Van Vossen walked, Puskis could see just how weak he was, barely able to lift his feet from the ground. Van Vossen lifted his cup to Puskis, who returned the gesture. They drank. It tasted of mint and dandelion and herbs that Puskis could not identify; burned a trail down his throat and sat in his stomach in a concise pool.

"What is this?" he asked.

Van Vossen smiled. "I don't know if it has a name. It goes back to medieval monks in Hungary. I've heard that there was a small war fought over the recipe back in the eleventh century."

"What are you trying to find in your encyclopedia of criminal activity? Are you searching for a principle?"

Van Vossen shook his head slowly. "There

is none. I can tell you that. If Abramowitz could not find it, then I am quite certain there is none. What was — is — my purpose? Am I a chronicler? There is an understanding that can be arrived at without a single guiding theorem. Does that make sense? There doesn't need to be a grand organizing principle for things to make sense. There are, for instance, patterns."

"You have identified patterns?"

Van Vossen laughed scornfully. "Patterns? Of course. I've found patterns. There are so many goddamn patterns that interlock and overlie each other and contain others. Everywhere you cast your eye there are patterns. But when this is the case, are they truly patterns or does the mind construct an artificial organizing feature? If you cannot even be definitive about patterns, how can you identify a single, overarching, perfect principle?"

"Which is why Abramowitz went mad?"

"Listen, Abramowitz went mad because he found out that there is no design. This world, this life, is just the product of independent decisions made by millions and millions of people each day. You add to that random chance and you see that it is all just chaos. Predicting events is an impossibility."

"Why does that matter? Why did

Abramowitz want to predict events?"

"Why in God's name do we even have the Vaults?" Van Vossen's words were coming louder and quicker. "Why do you compile and store that information if you are not hoping to glean the future from it? If you are not trying to use the past to inform the decisions made in the present?"

"But why did it drive him to insanity? Many people believe in free will. Many people accept that there is no order in the universe."

Van Vossen laughed and smiled. "These words that you use, *accept, believe.* You and other people accept or believe in free will because it seems to make sense or it fits in with your basic view of the world. But you don't know. You suspect because it seems more likely to be that way than some other way. The difference is that Abramowitz knew. He proved it. To himself, at least. He was never able to explain it coherently, because by then he was a lunatic. It is one thing to believe, Mr. Puskis, it is another thing entirely to know. Abramowitz proved that God did not exist, and the knowledge drove him mad."

CHAPTER NINETY-TWO

The footsteps on the stairs outside sent the boys in a panic. Poole, thinking about Whiskers and the fear that he must have inspired in these kids, talked calmly, trying to calm them, give them a plan. "Go upstairs, quickly. Don't come back down until you're sure that I've left and whoever is about to come in has left. Don't come down if there are any adults inside. Understand? Go."

Feet, either bare or wearing soles worn to softness, padded the stairs, ascending. The footsteps from outside paused at the front door. Holding his gun by the barrel, Poole opened the door.

The three ASU officers were caught off guard by his sudden appearance and went straight for their guns.

"Hold it, hold it," Poole said with genuine fear. He dropped his gun at the officers' feet and showed them both his palms, one wrapped in bandages.

"Who're you?" asked the reedy one with sergeant's stripes.

"I'm Ethan Poole. You're looking for me, well, probably not you exactly, but the ASU, and here I am. I need to see the mayor immediately. His life is in danger." This was going to be his play.

This torrent of words did not have any noticeable effect on the sergeant. One of the men behind him leaned forward and mumbled something into his ear.

"Jesus," the sergeant breathed, and then, from out of nowhere, delivered a professional punch to Poole's kidney. Poole's knees sagged, but he stayed on his feet. The sergeant grabbed Poole's right biceps and tried to turn him to face the wall, but Poole didn't budge. From behind the sergeant, one of the officers tried to hit Poole in the shoulder with the butt of his gun, but Poole saw it coming and shifted out of its path. He grabbed the hand holding his biceps and wrenched it around, bringing the sergeant to his knees, then wrapped his arm around the man's neck. The pain in his hand made him wince.

The two officers had their guns out, but pointed them at the ground.

Poole used the sergeant as a shield. "I'm

going to let you go. I'll even let you cuff me. But don't hit me again. You need to take me to the mayor. There is someone in the City right now who is out to bump him and will do it if something is not done quickly. Savvy?"

The sergeant croaked a "Yes" with what little air he could squeeze out and Poole let him go. The sergeant staggered forward, trying to keep his composure while gasping for air. The other two officers advanced on Poole, who put out his arms to accept handcuffs. They cuffed his hands behind his back and marched him to a police car parked in front of the orphanage. At the car, the sergeant called to Poole. Poole turned and the sergeant hit him again, this time in the stomach. Poole was ready and tensing himself, so the blow hurt but did not knock the wind out of him.

"Never touch a goddamn cop," the sergeant said, and forced Poole into the back of the car.

CHAPTER NINETY-THREE

Red Henry glowered at Frings, flexing and unflexing his fists.

"We can talk about it here," Frings said. "I don't think you'd like it too much, though."

All eyes were on the mayor, and while he was used to giving orders, he was not used to being drunk and under such immediate pressure. He hesitated for an instant before calculating that he had less to lose by talking to Frings in private.

"Go," he said dully to his companions. They were uncertain, looking at him. Henry glared back. They dispersed. Some instinct from his street-fighting days had Henry focusing on Smith as he strode off. The posture and speed and tension of his gait were signs that Henry reflexively associated with violence. He stared as Smith worked his way to the door, bumping people indiscriminately as he pressed through the crowd. This, too, Henry knew — a big man marshaling his confidence by using his size to intimidate. At another time, Henry might have worried about Smith's intentions. He trusted Smith to cause pain, not to make in de pen dent decisions. With too many other things to worry about, though, Henry didn't imagine that Smith could make anything worse.

Henry shifted his gaze back to Frings, who was waiting patiently for his attention. "What do you have to say to me?" Henry asked.

"I know about the Navajo Project."

A boxer learns how to maintain a front of indifference while enduring pain. Until this moment, exposure of the Navajo Project, while a real possibility, was just the worst of a number of potential scenarios. Now it was out there. When Henry spoke, it lacked conviction. "You going to let me know what the fuck you're talking about?"

Frings actually let out a brief, scoffing laugh. "Don't bullshit me, Mayor. You want me to walk you through it?"

Henry shrugged. It would be useful to at least know what Frings knew.

"All right, the way I see it, it went like this. You take the mayor's office without any idea that the Navajo Project exists. As you're getting adjusted to your new position, you, or probably someone else, comes to you with something that doesn't seem quite right. I'm guessing it was probably a budget item. Anyway, it seems that the government is distributing money to the families of certain murder victims. That's queer. Where does this money come from? you wonder. You, or one of your accountants, traces this money back to payments made by some farmers. Odd, you think. What's going on here? You — and I keep saying *you*, but I mean your people — do a little digging around, probably head out to the sticks and have a little look-see. There you find, to your great surprise, a bunch of professional killers are working farms to make money that they pay to the City. This ring a bell so far? I can give you names if that helps you out. DeGraffenreid. McAdam. Samuelson. That's just three. I've got more if you need to hear them. You with me?"

Henry glared. Frings had it pretty much nailed, but the sheer temerity of the man was infuriating.

"I'll take that as a yes." Frings went on, "You don't need to be a genius at this point to crab what was going on. These murderers have been shipped out to the country to make money to support the families of their victims. In short, the Navajo Project. So you, having an eye for opportunity, realize that this is an area where you can chisel some cash for yourself. So you take these surviving families from their homes and you stick them in institutions — asylums and orphanages. You can essentially let these go to seed and pocket most of the cash coming out of the Navajo Project farms. I'm doing pretty well so far, right?"

"You're bluffing" was all Henry could think to say. He focused on his breathing in an effort to keep his temper in check. Things were slipping away at an alarming rate. The fire in the Vaults. The Poles. Bernal. Now this. His mouth was dry. From the stage, the polka band played on, the sound ridiculous. People danced, enjoying themselves.

"Really? Tell you what, why don't you just speak up when I get something wrong. Does that work? Call my bluff."

Cheeky son of a bitch. Henry resisted the instinct to hit Frings. Probably kill him with a good punch.

Frings continued, "So after a while, maybe a year or so, you start to get a little dissatisfied. You're not actually getting all that much money flowing in. Must be something more you can squeeze out of them. So you,

or maybe it was Block or Bernal or someone, gets the idea that there are more profitable cash crops that could be grown. Specifically, you can make a hell of a lot more
money if they start growing reefer."

This was the crucial detail that Henry had
been waiting for. The other aspects were
troublesome, but survivable; a mea culpa
and pinning it mostly on the previous
mayor. A minor scandal at worst. The dope
changed this picture. This was now a major
problem, and the consequences for him
were no longer just disgrace and resigna-
tion. He flashed on a vision of himself in
prison garb.

Frings kept talking. "Your boy Smith runs
the operation, using some handpicked ginks
to make the deliveries, keep people in line.
I'm not exactly sure why you only deliver it
to the East Side. Why only the Negroes?
Because they don't vote for you? Is reefer
only suited for the Negroes — you want to
keep it away from us ofays? It doesn't really
matter, to be honest. Smith's boys bring it
into the City and it gets distributed through
a network in the Negro community."

Henry cut him off. "What the fuck are you
after, Frings?"

Frings, Henry thought, was like a dog that
senses fear, or maybe a shark with blood in

the water. Pick your goddamn analogy. His posture became more aggressive.

"This story's been written. It's sitting on my editor's desk. Unless I call by an hour before deadline, it will be run in the morning paper. I think we both understand what this will mean for you."

"The fuck are you after?" Henry repeated, loud enough that the people closest to them gave quick glances before seeing Henry's anger and looking away again.

"I want Nora back. If I get her back before deadline, and she's unhurt, I'll kill the story. If not, you go down. You want a minute to think about it?"

CHAPTER NINETY-FOUR

Out in the crisp night air, Smith sobered up. Frings had completely disregarded the warnings about what would happen to that little girlfriend of his. Now Smith was going to get to do what he did best: inflict pain in a way that would encourage Frings to pay better attention. The mayor had been clear: If Frings did not stop investigating, Smith could go off the rails on the girl.

A line of partygoers were waiting for the incoming taxis, so Smith hoofed it down the street, past a line of idling limos whose drivers carried on muted conversations in groups of two or three. It felt good to work off some of the adrenaline. Smith passed the mayor's Phaeton and saw the driver — couldn't remember the name — talking to a man with his hat pulled so low that Smith wondered how he could see out from under it. Another man leaned against the back of the car with his back to Smith. Something about him was familiar. But then again, anyone friendly with the mayor's chauffeur was probably around quite a bit. Smith walked on, though unable to shake the feeling of something about those two men . . .

He flagged down a cab on Buchanan Avenue and had him drive to Feral's apartment in the Theater District. He had the hack drop him a block from the building and gave him a five, suggesting that he forget about the fare. The cabbie nodded in silent agreement and drove off.

Sidewalk traffic was sparse; the usual theatergoers were at the armory or watching the shows, which were under way. The streets, he noted with disgust, were littered with garbage. He kicked an empty can at a stray cat and watched it jump and then cower, hissing, in a doorway.

Smith strolled to the door of Feral's apartment building, found the right key on his crowded key chain, and eased his way in. The mayor made sure that all of his triggermen had access to each other's flats or houses, thinking that this lack of security would encourage obedience. This was true to a certain extent in Smith's case. He certainly didn't relish the thought of that little freak Feral creeping around his place. On the other hand, Smith was confident

that he could take care of himself, no matter the circumstance.

He took the stairs to Feral's floor and
listened at his door, trying to ascertain what
was going on inside. Hearing nothing, he
unlocked the door and slipped into Feral's
flat.

CHAPTER NINETY-FIVE

The ASU station was in turmoil that had Poole's escorts glancing nervously at the sergeant. Gray-suited officers were leaving the building in pairs and fours, while others bustled around the station, faces grim. The two officers led Poole through this confusion, one on each arm with the sergeant walking point.

The sergeant stopped a young officer and asked, "Where's Martens?"

"Don't know, sir. But I bet he's either on the street or headed that way." Poole watched drops of sweat roll down the kid's temples.

The sergeant asked, "What's the rumble?"

"You don't know? Word came down straight from the mayor. We need to bring in that union gink Dotel and that woman. The mayor wants them tonight. However we can get them. Everyone's on it," the kid said, eyes wide. "Everyone."

Poole felt the blood drain from his face. He sagged a little and his escorts tightened their grips to hold him up. He fought back a torrent of panicked thoughts, trying to focus, think clearly. He needed to address this step-by-step. The first thing was to get out of the station as fast as possible. Without thinking, he pulled against his handcuffs. But they were too strong, of course.

The sergeant motioned for his officers to follow him as he walked farther into the station. He asked a couple of other officers about Martens before someone pointed toward an open door off the squad room. The sergeant led Poole through the door into an interrogation room, where three men sat around a metal table in a haze of cigarette smoke. One, a small man with a receding forehead and a weak chin, was doing the talking. He stopped as Poole followed the sergeant into the suddenly cramped room. The small man turned, glaring, to face the two newcomers. Poole noticed the military mustache.

"What the hell is this?" the small man said with undisguised annoyance. The two officers stayed outside. The room was too crowded as it was.

"Ethan Poole," the sergeant said significantly.

"Why is he here?"

"He claims that someone is out to assassinate the mayor tonight."

The little man, who Poole assumed was Martens, looked thoughtful for a moment. "Poole, yes. The name . . . we were looking for you . . ." His voice trailed off, then he found himself again with a start. He barked, "There's not time for this tonight." He ground the lit end of his cigarette into the table.

"The mayor . . . ," the sergeant said.

Martens turned to Poole. "What is this? Someone is trying to kill the mayor tonight? Who? Who's trying to kill him? For God's sake, how do you know?"

Poole had been thinking about which answer to this question would be most likely to get him back on the street as fast as possible. Nothing better than the truth had presented itself. "Whiskers McAdam."

Martens coughed out a laugh. "Whiskers McAdam? He won't see the outside of a cell for another twenty years. My God. What do you take us for?"

Poole shrugged. He had to play this out a little further; make it look as if he were really trying to convince them. "It's what I've heard. People say they've seen him on the street."

Martens regarded Poole as he might have a dumb and intransigent child. "I don't know what your angle is on this, Poole, but it's a bunch of horse shit." Martens turned to the sergeant, waiting.

"I should lock him up?" the sergeant suggested.

"Christ." Martens was reddening. "Are you suggesting that you spend tonight at your desk typing up a report that you brought Poole in because he claimed that Whiskers McAdam was going to kill the mayor tonight? Is that it? While the rest of the goddamn unit is out complying with a direct order from the mayor? Is that what you're suggesting? Whiskers McAdam?"

The sergeant looked back miserably.

"Let him go," Martens growled. "Let him go."

CHAPTER NINETY-SIX

Frings watched the big man run through the possibilities in his mind. He knew that Red Henry was smart and that self-preservation would be his first priority. But Henry was drunk, and Frings knew that this was unusual. It added an unpredictability that Frings had not anticipated coming into the confrontation. As the options were laid out, the rational thing for Henry to do was to give up Nora and save his own skin. But this would only be true based on some assumptions that Frings was not at all certain Henry would make. The first was that Frings would, indeed, not run the article if Nora was released. Henry had good reason not to trust him, since Frings fully intended to run the article regardless. The second critical assumption was that Frings would be able to substantiate his allegations in the face of Henry's denials. This, in Frings's mind, would be a close one. But people were willing to think the worst of their leaders, and Henry would most likely not be given the benefit of the doubt. But would Henry make the same calculation?

Another critical assumption that Frings was making as well was that he knew all the cards that Henry had to play.

Henry looked at Frings with furious, drunken eyes. Frings maintained his air of self-assurance, trying to intimidate Henry with his attitude because there was no hope for it physically. Henry's next action had him wondering if he had miscalculated. The big man picked Frings off the ground by the lapels of his suit, Frings sinking so that the coat bunched up around his neck. Henry turned him and propped him against a wall, holding him up with one hand by the chin. Frings stared at Henry with bulging eyes. Half the room turned to them and the band stopped. Frings felt helpless and humiliated. Henry leaned forward and put his lips next to Frings's ear.

"I will let your quiff go. But if you publish that article, I promise you that you will be killed soon, and you will be killed painfully. And then the same will happen to your girl. Don't doubt that I can make that happen."

Henry let go of Frings's jaw, and Frings fell gasping to the ground. Henry turned to the onlooking crowd and smiled a terrifying smile. "Please return to your goddamn drinks," he bellowed. "The Poles are not coming tonight. They're leaving town tomorrow and they're not coming back. Through treachery and dealing in bad faith, they have whetted our appetites for their presence and then withdrawn it at the last hour. It is my greatest wish that they leave the City safely because I know that there will be great anger among our citizens."

Frings watched from the floor, recovering. Henry was absolutely in the bag. Henry swayed slightly as he ranted. The guests looked on nervously. Frings noticed men at the fringes of the crowd who seemed amused but kept their mirth quiet. No one wanted to be the target of the mayor's wrath.

Peja materialized from the crowd and spoke into Henry's ear. Henry pushed him aside, then turned back to loom over Frings, who was still sitting on the floor.

"Don't forget what I said. Kill that goddamn story," Henry slurred. "You can find Nora Aspen at Draffert's Pub in an hour."

Henry lumbered toward the entrance, Frings watching as the crowd parted in front of him. The attention of the whole room was on the big man. The band had begun to play again, this time at a dirgelike pace that might just have been mocking Henry's slow progress.

Frings stood up and pushed through the crowd after Henry.

CHAPTER NINETY-SEVEN

Nora was still reading when she felt the room's atmosphere change, turning electric. The small, dark man was listening intently, his head cocked to something she could not hear. She began to speak but was hushed by a wave of the man's hand. He was up, moving silently across the room. He turned the knob of the door with two fingers, inching it open. From her bed, Nora could not see the hall, but the man's demeanor did not indicate any trouble. Then, without seeming to move, he was gone and the door was shut.

Odd, she thought, returning to her book. She heard sounds from the hall and put her book down. Voices. Too muffled to be understood. This was the first time since her incarceration that she had known of another person in the apartment except her captor.

There was a thud and the floor shook, the motion magnified by the springs in the mattress she reclined on. She sat up on the side of the bed with her feet planted on the floor, her heart racing. She prayed for it to be the police. The alternative scared the hell out of her.

Footsteps approached in the hall. Not the little man, who did not make any noise when he walked. Nora fought back nausea. The door swung open hard, the knob banging against the wall and the door rebounding back. Through it came a big man, his face a mask of determination under his fedora as he advanced on her. He held a pistol by the barrel, brandishing it like a club. She had seen plenty of actors simulate a pistol-whip on the screen. She lay back, bracing herself for the real thing; pulling her knees up to her chest and putting her arms out to protect her face. He was standing over her now, trying with his free hand to knock her hands out of the way so he could get in a clean strike with the pistol.

She didn't scream, but flailed with her arms and kicked out with her feet, trying to fend him off. He was patient, working to clear himself for the first, solid blow that would enable him to inflict the rest without resistance. Behind him, his grace belying the brutality of his intentions, the little man struck. He came into the room with speed, his arms crossed at the elbows and a thin rope dangling from his hands. He flipped the rope around her assailant's neck, then pulled his hands apart so that they uncrossed, pulling the cord tight around the bigger man's throat.

The big man's eyes went wide and he staggered backward, turning slightly. From this angle, Nora could see her captor with his knee in the big man's back, giving him leverage to pull the cord tighter. The big man clawed at the rope around his neck with increasing desperation. With his free leg, the little man kicked hard into the back of the big man's knee, and he went down on his face, the gun slipping from his grasp. The little man now was on top. The effort he was putting forth did not show on his face, but the banded muscles of his arms were fully tensed.

Nora slid from the bed and picked the gun off the floor. She knew how to use one, a requisite part of growing up in the sticks. She stepped around the two men. The fight was gone from the bigger one, and her captor continued to pull on the rope, dropping his ear to the man's back, listening for his heart to stop beating. When at last the little man judged his job finished, he straightened up, and for the first time saw Nora, holding the gun confidently, the barrel aimed at his chest. The head, she had been told, was too easy to miss.

The little, dark man who had been her captor for nearly two days; who had kept a vigil, watching her as she read, for God's sake; who had reminded her of Tino, the gentle man who practiced the savage art; the little dark man sat, deflated, on the bed. His mahogany eyes showed not fear but hurt. Had he really thought that he'd been courting her?

"I'm going to walk out of here, and if you follow me, I'll kill you. I'm a good shot."

The man nodded. "I believe you. I will not attempt to keep you here."

If he thought his acquiescence was going to lower her guard, he was mistaken. She took a last look at the room that had briefly been her prison. It was not, from her perspective now, an imperfect model of her room, but a parody. All the details were right, but the whole was wrong.

"What's your name?"

The man did not answer. He had retreated within himself.

She leveled the gun at him. "What's your name?" she asked louder. Something about this detail was important. She didn't want to live the rest of her life without even knowing his name.

He looked up at her with sleepy eyes, considered for a moment, and said, "Feral."

Minutes later she was on the street, hailing a cab, the hack's jaw dropping when he realized who she was. She hadn't experienced the adulation — Feral's spooky attentions were not the same — for almost two days, and she realized that for all the lines she gave the magazines about intrusion into her private life, she loved it.

CHAPTER NINETY-EIGHT

Red Henry, the mayor of the goddamn City, lumbered unsteadily out into the night air, pausing at the top of the steps to survey the lines of cars, looking for the black Packard Phaeton that came with his office. The guests queuing for taxis looked up as he emerged, and he realized that he was cursing aloud. He smiled at the queue, reminding himself that they were voters, and finally located his car. The driver was chatting with two men, their hats hiding their faces. The drivers tended to socialize with each other while they waited, but the men his driver was talking to clearly weren't fellow drivers. Something about the way they held themselves. And their fedoras. Henry wondered who the hell they were. He took the steps slowly, careful not to reveal the extent of his inebriation with a stagger or hesitation.

He needed to get back to his office. He needed to get Feral to take that singing bitch to Draffert's. He needed to find out exactly what the fuck had happened to the Poles and decide whether he wanted to give them the scare of their lives before they left the City. He had a reputation to maintain. He needed to hear about the fire in the goddamn Vaults, though as he thought about it, it might not be the worst thing that had ever happened. But it infuriated him because it had not been part of his plans. Someone would have to be held accountable.

He needed to figure out a new strategy for Frings. He'd always assumed that it would be counterproductive to have him bumped, but now he wasn't so sure that Frings was more trouble dead than alive. He was too drunk to assess it clearly.

He needed to get Smith out into the country to find out where those Navajo Project psychopaths had disappeared to. Come to think of it, where the hell was Smith? He hadn't seen Smith as he left the gala. Smith was usually the type to be right there, ready to cause whatever mayhem Henry would allow. Then he remembered Smith's leaving the hall with a sense of purpose about him, and he wondered if he shouldn't have his driver take him directly to Feral's place.

A panhandler came up to him and rattled

the coins in his cup. Henry stopped and glared at him. The panhandler backed away, mumbling slurred, semicoherent curses.

His driver was no longer talking to the men from before and had the door open for him. Henry remembered that he had a question to ask him but could not, for the life of him, recall what it was. Fucking alcohol.

"Feral's. Quickly."

"Feral's, sir?"

"That's what I said." Was it a complicated request?

"Of course."

Henry rested his head on the leather seat back and let his lids drop, willing himself to sober up. Willing himself to consider his problems one at a time rather than deal with the flood of anxiety that was threatening to overwhelm him.

There was a crash, maybe a foot away from his head, and he opened his eyes to see glass shards littering the seat, reflecting the streetlights like tiny stars. Hands appeared from outside, tossed a package on the seat next to him, then disappeared. He heard the sound of footsteps running away.

CHAPTER NINETY-NINE

Poole hailed a cab and, after wading through a snarl in traffic caused by the mass deployment of ASU squad cars, headed toward Little Lisbon. He stared out the window, exhausted and concentrating. He needed to continue to take things in order, just as he had done in the ASU station. The primary thing now was to find Carla — and Enrique. He was going to Enrique's apartment first because that was where Carla was headed when Poole went to St. Mark's. He was not confident she would still be there, but it was a place to start.

He forced himself to put off thinking about the next step. It seemed too dependent on the circumstances when he finally found her.

He had expected it, but was still dismayed to find a dozen or so ASU officers on the sidewalk as the cab pulled up to Enrique's building. The officers were conferring, not in a hurry, getting their plan straight before heading in. Poole walked past them, head down, and through the front door. He took the stairs three at a time up to Enrique's floor, heart racing. His mind was getting ahead of him, thinking about where they could lose themselves in this neighborhood. The obvious places were out, since that was where the ASU would look first.

He pounded on Enrique's door with his elbow. No one answered at first and he yelled, "It's Poole." Footsteps sounded in the apartment, and the door opened to Enrique, wearing slacks, a white shirt, and an anxious look.

"Enrique, is Carla here?"

Enrique nodded.

"Where?" Poole nearly shouted.

Carla emerged from a back room looking unkempt, her hair askew, her face flushed. "Ethan?"

Poole closed his eyes briefly in relief. He looked to Enrique. "Where's your wife?"

"She's at her mother's," he said carefully.

Poole nodded, understanding. He closed his eyes for a moment, pinching the bridge of his nose. "Listen, the ASU are here for you. Orders direct from the mayor. A group of them's down on the street. We need to get out of here."

Enrique and Carla exchanged a glance. Some of the tension seemed to drain from Enrique as his shoulders relaxed.

"It wouldn't be the first time I've been brought in."

"It's different this time. Any means possible."

Carla spoke. "What does that mean, Ethan?"

Ethan shrugged impatiently. There wasn't time for this conversation. "Dead or alive."

Enrique looked at Poole. "You still have my gun?"

"No. I was picked up by the ASU. They kept it."

Enrique nodded. Poole was impressed with the man's nerve.

Enrique said, "There are three ways out. The front door."

"Too many men out there."

"Fire escape."

"Too visible. They'd be waiting for us before we got down."

"Then the service entrance out back."

"Let's go."

Carla said, "You don't think they'll have that covered?"

"Of course they will," Poole said. "But there's nothing else."

■ ■ ■ ■

They took the back stairs, Poole in front and Enrique last. At the ground floor they found the service entrance and Poole put his ear to it. He couldn't hear anything, but that wasn't surprising. He looked back at the other two. "You ready?"

Carla and Enrique nodded. Poole grabbed Carla's hand and gave it a squeeze. He pushed open the door to a landing three concrete steps above an alley. Dirty light shone in from the street. Two ASU men, hands on their holstered guns, leaned against the far wall. Poole thought about turning back into the building, but this alley remained their best hope. The three of them walked down the stairs as the ASU officers walked toward them, guns out.

One, a tall, thin kid, walked up to Enrique. "You Dotel?"

Poole watched, wondering how Enrique would play it; looking for an opening.

Enrique nodded. "I'm Dotel."

The officer lowered his voice. "My brother, Victor, is in the union. We need to get you out of here. I don't think you'll make it back to the station alive."

Enrique looked over at the other officer.

"Kevin's okay," the kid said. "He owes me."

"How does this work?" Poole asked the kid, but watched the other officer. Something wasn't right.

"Just go. Quickly. Down that alley and then right. Get lost. They'll do a search, find nothing, go to the next place. You just need to get out of here now, before they send more men."

Poole shifted his gaze to the kid, calm while pulling off this bit of subterfuge. Enrique was already walking down the alley. Why wasn't the other officer watching for ASU reinforcements? Surely they'd be —

Carla tugged at Poole's sleeve. "Come on." Poole allowed Carla to pull him down the alley, but kept his eyes on the officers, who exchanged glances. This wasn't going down right. He wrenched his arm free from Carla's grasp. "Keep going," he whispered.

"What?" She looked at him, startled.

"Go," he said louder, and pushed her down the alley. Enrique was thirty feet or so farther along. Poole turned back toward the officers. They had their guns drawn, aiming down the alley.

Over the top of the trench. Poole had less than a dozen yards to cover to reach the officers. He moved fast, but their guns were ready. He took a shot in the shoulder and one in the groin and stumbled, the pain overwhelming him. Thoughts started to become hazy but he focused on one thing: *Keep them busy for a couple seconds more.* Let Carla and Enrique get around the corner.

He pushed with his hands and feet toward where he saw the two officers' legs. Behind their legs he could see trash cans and empty beer bottles and the bricks in the opposite wall. He felt it was important to look up, to see the men's faces, but somehow he couldn't. His arms and legs seemed only partially under his control. He couldn't bring to mind what he was trying to do. There was just the imperative — move forward. Another searing bolt of pain — hard to tell where — and a brief moment, less than a second, when Poole realized, at some level, that it was all over.

CHAPTER ONE HUNDRED

People didn't clear out of Frings's path the way they did for Red Henry. Frings pushed through the throngs, who eyed him curiously. He'd made quite a spectacle of himself. People talked. Why had the mayor assaulted the newshawk Frings? Where was his jazz-singer girlfriend? People spilled drinks on him as he jarred them in his haste to get to the door. He muttered insincere apologies.

Two ASU men intercepted him twenty feet or so from the door, one on each arm.

"Get your mitts off."

"Sorry, bo, the mayor needs his space."

Frings couldn't shake them off.

"What, are you just going to hold me for the rest of the night?"

He followed their eyes as they looked to Altabelli, arms crossed defensively, his face pale and oily. They stood as they were for two full minutes, Frings furious, before Altabelli finally signaled the men to release him. Frings pushed away and ran for the door.

He was at the top of the armory steps when the two men crossed the street to Henry's car. Even from that distance Frings recognized the gait of one of the men. He had spent the morning walking behind him, and the slight bow of the legs and the angles of his feet were as easy to identify as a mug shot. The other man was familiar from the morning as well, his menace somehow undiminished over this distance. *Otto and Whiskers.*

Frings watched, knowing the men's intent, but not sure how it would play out. Samuelson got to the car first and smashed the rear driver's-side window with what looked like a brick. Whiskers followed, pulling a parcel from his coat and tossing it through the open window. Both men turned and ran, and Frings ducked below the low granite walls.

The explosion made a short, loud thud, followed by the rain of glass and steel shrapnel tinkling on the sidewalk and street. Frings stood up and saw the twisted mass of metal that had once been the mayor's car. He thought he could see inside the flames a mass that might have been the mayor in black silhouette, burning and lifeless. But the smoke became too dense and he put it down to a trick of the eye.

On the street, the cars nearest to the mayor's burned. Drivers, injured by their proximity to the blast or from shrapnel, lay in the street and on the sidewalks. The line of socialites had been far enough away to escape injury, but Frings heard traumatized sobs from some of the women, and a few had fainted and were held by their stunned escorts.

A cop came bounding out into the night, panicked. "Oh, dear Lord." He looked around, found Frings. "Did you see what happened?"

"Two men, one smashed the window, the other dropped the bomb in the backseat."

The cop looked over Frings's shoulder at the commotion beyond. Frings could see in his face the struggle to take in what had just happened.

"Do you know who they were?"

"Yeah," Frings said, "I think I do."

CHAPTER
ONE HUNDRED AND ONE

Van Vossen had gone mad. The realization did not come to Puskis as a sudden insight. Rather, it was a product of the accumulation of the thoughts Van Vossen had expressed in their conversation over the past several hours. The Vaults had got him, too. Van Vossen could claim to be indifferent to any conclusions he had reached from the information he gathered and pored over and ruminated about, but he had eventually been overwhelmed by it. Puskis was in no doubt.

Van Vossen put another log on the fire and sat down again. His eyelids drooped over bloodshot eyes, his energy waned. He looked like the children Puskis occasionally saw as he walked home from the Vaults at night, struggling against fatigue to control their thoughts and actions.

"What will you do now that the Vaults are gone?" Van Vossen asked in a rasping whisper. Puskis felt that he could see Van Vossen's life escaping with each breath.

"I don't know," Puskis replied truthfully. He hadn't even thought about it. It had seemed too abstract until now.

Van Vossen leaned forward, his crimson smoking jacket gapping to reveal his sweat-drenched shirt. "You have the most complete knowledge of anyone living. The files. Not even I know as much as you."

Puskis nodded, feeling weary.

Van Vossen went on. "There is value to what we know, you and I. There is. Information does not need to conform to patterns or rules or formulae to be of vital importance."

Was this true? Puskis nodded again, mostly to placate Van Vossen.

"It is crucial that this information not be lost. If it is lost, what was the point of my life or yours?"

And this was the crux of Van Vossen's madness, Puskis realized. What was the point of his life?

Puskis stared into the fire. Van Vossen stood up from his chair mumbling something about returning shortly and wandered out of the room.

Hours later, Puskis watched the last embers

of the fire slowly extinguish. Van Vossen had not returned, as Puskis had felt sure he would not. Puskis felt too weary to move. And where would he go? Eventually, the fire exhausted its fuel and Puskis sat alone. In the dark.

CHAPTER
ONE HUNDRED AND TWO

Black smoke plumed from the burning cars, adding to the confusion on the street. An area had been cordoned off around the mayor's car. Frings stood off to the side with the Chief and the officer from the steps, who held a handkerchief over his face to filter the air.

The Chief was grim, but calm. He took off his hat and rubbed his hand through his thinning hair.

"O'Donnell here tells me you know who it was."

"That's right, Chief. One of them was definitely Otto Samuelson." Frings dragged off a Lucky.

The Chief raised an eyebrow with interest. "Otto Samuelson? Surely he's in the pen."

Frings smiled despite himself. The Chief was a lot of things, Frings knew, but he was not a clever bullshitter. He was clearly not in the know about the Navajo Project.

Frings said, "He's not. You'll find out more about that. You'll be surprised by the other name I'm going to give you, too. Blood Whiskers McAdam."

"Whiskers?" The Chief shook his head. "He's out, too?"

"Never was in, actually. But they were the two. I'm sure about Samuelson and almost about McAdam. You need to put out a search for them."

"I guess I'd best. You going to fill me in, Frank? Or would it ruin your story?"

"Chief, I'd be happy to give you the rumble." They made plans to meet at Headquarters at midnight, giving the Chief time to settle things at the site and begin the search for Samuelson and McAdam. But he would still hear from Frings before the early addition of the *Gazette* alerted the rest of the City.

The Chief offered Frings his hand and they shook. "Thanks, Frank. I owe you one." The look in the Chief's eyes, Frings thought, was telling. There was resolve, knowing the work ahead of him in tracking down the mayor's killers; but mostly a sense of incredible relief.

As Frings walked past the confusion and smoke and flame, he wondered if he was

540

too cynical for fearing what would fill the void that Henry left.

■ ■ ■ ■

EPILOGUE

■ ■ ■ ■

CHAPTER
ONE HUNDRED AND THREE

Frings sat in the back of a cab, watching out the window as the hack navigated through Capitol Heights, avoiding Buchanan Avenue, where he had heard there was an accident. It was the thirteenth day since the death of Red Henry, and the City still seemed in shock. Not from grief, necessarily, but from the sudden demise of a personality who had seemed almost superhuman to many. Red Henry's absence had never been contemplated, and now, suddenly, it was a reality.

Frings watched as people shuffled home from work or hurried to make a night shift. It was a little past eight in the evening, the City harsh under the streetlamps. Frings hoped this wouldn't take long. Nora was at the Provençal Restaurant across from the opera house, with her trumpet soloist, Arthur Hall, and his wife, Lillian. Pilar Rossi was singing Verdi that night and he wanted to be back for the opening curtain at nine. Nora and Pilar had met in Paris several years ago and had formed a bond as prima donnas of their separate genres. Tonight Nora and Frings had box seats. It meant a lot to Nora, and it meant a lot to him because it meant a lot to her.

This was not the feeling he would have had even a month ago. But her kidnapping had changed things — for the better. He knew that the dynamics of her escape were largely responsible, somehow settling their roles in her mind. She, after all, had effected her own escape, getting the drop on her abductor when he was attacked by Smith. But this opportunity would not have presented itself without Frings's pressure on Henry. She had been able to take matters into her own hands because of his actions. This seemed to give her confidence in their relationship, and that confidence had, in turn, rekindled his attraction to her. So now, he wondered, why the hell am I riding in a cab away from her on this big night? Because the Chief owed him a favor and payback did not necessarily come at the most opportune time.

The apartment building was technically in the Hollows — it was one block north of

Bolivar Street — but in an area that was slowly being annexed into the working-class blocks of Capitol Heights. Cops in blue uniforms guarded the front door, though no one was on the streets.

"I'm —"

One of the cops interrupted that they knew who he was and gestured him through the door.

"Third floor," the cop called after Frings as he started up the stairs.

The building had partly been reclaimed from its abandonment. About half of the apartments had functioning front doors, which Frings took to mean that they were occupied. He didn't hear any noise coming from the apartments. In this type of place it made sense not to call attention to yourself.

More cops were on the third floor, standing in the hallway, smoking and talking in low tones. One of them beckoned Frings down the hall.

"He's in this one," a muscular officer said, and nodded through the open door. "Back in the bedroom."

The police had set up bright lights in all of the rooms in this small apartment, and the effect was a stage set of abject squalor. Refuse, broken glass, empty liquor bottles, a broken couch, yellowing newspapers.

In the bedroom, a uniform watched as two men in suits knelt over something by a stained bare mattress, a ragged blanket bunched at the foot.

"Mr. Frings," the cop said, and the two kneeling men turned and stood. Frings recognized them as Detectives Olshanski and Korda. They shook hands, and Frings saw that the man lying on the floor, his head in a pool of blood, was Otto Samuelson.

Frings and Korda sat on the stoop outside the building, smoking.

"We talked to the other residents on the hall. They say Samuelson and another guy — they all mention his red hair — were squatting here for the last week or so. People on the hall weren't happy about it either. A woman told Olshanski that she told her kid to come back in the apartment if he ever saw either of them. Anyway, it's likely that the second man was Whiskers McAdam."

An ambulance pulled to the curb, and Korda sent the crew up to Samuelson's squat.

Korda continued, "Our best guess is this: They have an argument — the neighbors heard shouting, but that isn't so unusual in this building according to them — probably over money. You figure that's why they're still in the City if they know that they're the main suspects in the mayor's assassination. Anyway, they have some kind of argument and for some reason Samuelson turns his back to McAdam, and McAdam hits him in the back of the head with a baseball bat or a club or some other blunt instrument. Samuelson bounces face-first off the mattress and ends up on his back on the floor next to the bed. It all seems pretty clear from the physical evidence."

"You say you figure it was over money," Frings said.

"That's conjecture," Korda conceded. "The force was crawling the City looking for these guys, so there must have been a damn good reason for them to stick around. Maybe they had some money stashed somewhere. Maybe they were grifting. Who knows? But we're working on the theory that they got the money they wanted, McAdam got greedy, killed Samuelson, and blew town."

"You think he's gone?" Frings asked, though it made perfect sense to him.

"I would be."

"So would I," Frings agreed.

An hour later he eased himself into the box and took a seat in the shadows behind Nora.

Pilar Rossi was singing an aria, and Nora did not notice Frings until he brushed her arm. She turned to him, startled, and gave an inquiring look. Frings winked and smiled, and Nora grabbed his hand and they settled back to enjoy the night.

CHAPTER
ONE HUNDRED AND FOUR

Fog crept into the Hollows, encircling buildings and obscuring roads and alleys. Standing in the square across from St. Mark's, Carla watched as the boys were led out of the crumbling building by groups of adults. The City at least had the sense to send nurses along with the police. The boys seemed so small as they traversed the short distance to the wagons waiting to take them across town to City Hospital.

She smoked a cigarette and thought about Poole and the way he had died. She felt vaguely uncomfortable that she had not grieved more. Losing him was hard on her, but as a fellow soldier lost in a war, not a lover. She wondered why this was and couldn't quite find the answer in herself.

She had, of course, arranged this rescue. Her greatest weapon was always her ability to spot weakness and opportunity, and she had put this insight to work at City government, reeling after the mayor's death. The deputy mayor, whom Henry had successfully marginalized during his reign, floundered to take control of the government. Carla had sent word that she wanted a meeting, or the press might start wondering why the ASU had killed an unarmed private citizen while botching an assassination attempt on a couple of union organizers.

When the meeting was granted, she explained that through some error of omission or commission, the boys of St. Mark's had been separated from their mothers, who were being kept at All Souls'. A perfunctory investigation followed. The orphaned girls were found in a shabby nunnery attached to a lunatic asylum in the Hollows. The administration of drugs to the women was to be stopped, and plans were made to move them out of All Souls' and into ordinary life. First, though, they would be reunited with their children. To prepare the women, City health officials gradually reduced their drug dosages, until they were deemed capable of normal interaction. Then the officials went to bring the children in.

In the end, this was Poole's legacy, Carla thought. These kids were going back to what remained of their families because Poole had sacrificed his life for her and Enrique.

This brought tears to her eyes, and she dropped her cigarette and ground it into the sidewalk with her shoe.

CHAPTER
ONE HUNDRED AND FIVE

Puskis sat amidst piles of paper in Van Vossen's study. Shafts of morning sun lit particles of floating dust in the air. Puskis drank tea and read. Van Vossen's manuscript was part factual representation of material that had been in the Vaults' files, part credulous reporting of rumor and innuendo, part partially developed analysis, and part conjecture and speculation. Puskis read, fascinated, with a pen in hand, annotating the pages with additional information he knew or connecting related incidents. He began an organizational system. Not a filing system. A system to organize these pages into a linear book.

It was a new kind of challenge. In the Vaults, he had been saddled with the decisions and quirks and even contradictions of his predecessors. He did not have to navigate the treacherous waters of rape files, for instance, that Abramowitz considered a crime of violence and that *his* predecessor, Decatur, had considered a sex crime. Puskis was liberated to make his own decisions from the outset, creativity that energized him such that he had only slept for three or four hours at a time since beginning this task several weeks ago.

The room was littered with short piles of paper, arranged in the synthesis of subject and chronology that was Puskis's organizing system. He finished a section on the mad Turk Belioglu and walked to the kitchen, made a fresh pot of tea, and closed his eyes, letting the smell of mint and orange and cinnamon drift up to his face and past. He walked back to the study and looked out a window onto the narrow, enclosed garden that constituted Van Vossen's backyard. The killing frost had come two weeks ago, and the garden soil was littered with the remains of dead flowers. In the middle of the garden was a barely perceptible mound, roughly six feet in length and perhaps three feet wide. Unconsciously, Puskis rotated his shoulders, remembering the physical strain of digging the grave for Van Vossen and how that strain had been exacerbated by extracting the needle from Van Vossen's lifeless arm, dragging his corpse out to the garden, and replacing the rich garden soil.

The first week had been nerve-racking. Puskis stayed alert for the dreaded sound of the doorbell, or a hard knock, or a footfall in the entranceway. But it never came. No one seemed to miss Van Vossen, and Frings wondered who the man ever saw other than the clerk at the grocer's.

Puskis was now thoroughly assimilated into the house and into his new routine. He worked on Van Vossen's manuscript because Van Vossen had known that Puskis would, and that was why Van Vossen had finally allowed himself the peace of death. Puskis worked on Van Vossen's manuscript because, having destroyed the Vaults, he was now recreating the vital knowledge that the Vaults held. Puskis worked on the manuscript because, in the end, he couldn't not work on the manuscript.

Puskis turned from the window and resettled himself in the chair at the table. He picked up the chapter on the counterfeiter Pericles Nickopolidis and began to write in the margin with Van Vossen's green ink.

The employees of Thorndike Press hope you have enjoyed this Large Print book. All our Thorndike, Wheeler, and Kennebec Large Print titles are designed for easy reading, and all our books are made to last. Other Thorndike Press Large Print books are available at your library, through selected bookstores, or directly from us.

For information about titles, please call:
  (800) 223-1244

or visit our Web site at:
  http://gale.cengage.com/thorndike

To share your comments, please write:
  Publisher
  Thorndike Press
  295 Kennedy Memorial Drive
  Waterville, ME 04901